SAFE AT LAST

Golden in the window's glow, Caley was the personification of vulnerability. Martin saw it in the curve of her shoulders, the slight bend of one knee, the delicate uptilt of a profiled breast. The sun drew fire from her hair; she appeared encased in slow flames. Turned entirely inward, his eyes spanned the gap between them; everything was forgotten. She was his alone.

Martin slowly put down the pencil and moved through the fire to stand gazing at the flawless length of her spine. She turned, having sensed rather than heard his approach. *Don't pity me,* she begged silently . . .

"It's all right," he said, his arms encircling her, clasping her to his chest. "It's all right."

He held her, his cheek resting against her hair and she subsided, steadying as if, for a very long time, she'd been racing, beating her way past limitless obstacles, headlong into a gale that had blown past.

Berkley books by
Charlotte Vale Allen

DADDY'S GIRL
DESTINIES
MEET ME IN TIME
MEMORIES
PIECES OF DREAMS
PROMISES

Pieces of Dreams

Charlotte Vale Allen

BERKLEY BOOKS, NEW YORK

PIECES OF DREAMS

A Berkley Book / published by arrangement with
the author

PRINTING HISTORY
Berkley edition / February 1985

ISBN: 0-425-07582-6

ACKNOWLEDGMENTS

I am indebted to Dr. Jeremy Freeman and Dr. Robert Newton for their generous assistance with the information on facial reconstructive surgery I have used in this novel. I am, as well, in perpetual debt to Kathryn Conway-Marmo for her insights and understanding. I am greatful to Roger Cooper, Rena Wolner, and Meg Blackstone for the sideline cheering; and to Linda McKnight, Uncle Jack McC., and Tanya Long. To my friend Carolynn Meinhardt, my fond gratitude for the introduction to her incredible Cadillac; the streets of Manhattan will never be quite the same for me. Finally, I must say thank you to Walt and Kimmie for tiptoeing around and allowing me to rearrange completely all our lives during the final stages of work on this book.

For Lorrie

PART ONE

Chapter 1

SHE WAS SEARCHING inside her handbag for her cigarettes when she heard Ron hiss, "Jesus Christ!" and glanced over to see his face reflected, twisted and unnaturally white in the glare of oncoming headlights. His hands were a blur, spinning the wheel. The brakes screamed. Everything that happened, each motion, was distinctly encapsulated in its own fragment of time. She turned her head to see what was happening out there, ahead of them on the road, her hands motionless now within the confines of her bag. David Gates was singing "If." His voice emerged with a surprising clarity from the stereo speakers, pure and positive behind the steady shrieking of the brakes. Her body was lifting. Instinctively, she sought to free her hands as the windshield seemed to move inexorably toward her.

She soared through the glass as if executing a perfect dive: neatly, with no hesitation, nothing to interrupt her body's flow as it broke through the barrier. She flew, aware of a crescendo of conflicting sounds. Her body a tumbler's precision instrument gone out of control, she somersaulted off the hood of the car, bounced very high, it felt, into the air, then collided with metal before bouncing again—a stone skipped across high-breaking waves—and then landed.

She could see the pebbly surface of the paved highway, and could feel what might have been many small, jagged rocks beneath her. She heard the unmistakable sounds of fragments of metal falling all about her and, incredibly, David Gates

singing how you and I would finally fly away, the music wafting into the stratosphere. Shouts and cries and the sounds of
feet pounding—their reverberations jarred in her skull. She
thought, inconsequentially, randomly, of Indians placing their
ears to the ground to detect the sound of oncoming hoofbeats,
of people putting their ears to railroad tracks in order to feel
the vibration of oncoming trains. It was almost funny, and she
thought she might be smiling. She felt ridiculous and decided
she'd better get up. She would make some joke about her
hitherto unknown acrobatic skills as she sauntered back to the
car, and to Ron.

She closed her eyes for a moment, concentrating, and then
tried to move. She couldn't. The effort of her attempt caused
pain to flare throughout her body. It was all at once terribly
important that she get up, and again she shut her eyes briefly
before making a second, failing attempt to rise. She rested,
hearing voices and the continuing burr beneath her ear of cars
passing on the far side of the highway and feet moving very
near to her. Someone was murmuring, "Jesus, Jesus!" over
and over again. Someone else was moaning close by. There
was too much noise. It interfered with her concentration. She
wanted to think about the problem of her inability to move,
but the voices and, now, the far-off whine of sirens, got in the
way. She knew absolutely that if the noise could just be made
to let up, if she could be free to concentrate, she'd be able to
relocate her mobility. The idea that she was lying, probably in
the middle of the road, was both peculiarly satisfying and horribly embarrassing.

Summoning all her strength, she managed to turn slightly,
but at once hands stayed her and a voice ordered, "Don't
move! Just stay still!" Something—a coat or a blanket—was
draped over her and she gave up, shut her eyes, and let them
stay closed. She'd been freed by that command from the
responsibility of movement. She could remain as she was,
mentally trying to sort out her possible injuries.

It seemed a very long time before people came and hands
shifted her. She was turned over, at last. As she was carried on
a stretcher toward a waiting ambulance, she could see the
scene of the accident. There were so many cars! She wasn't
sure what she'd assumed, but it in no way involved what ap-

peared to be the remains of four or five cars. And where was Ron? She strained, twisting her head in an effort to locate him.

"Just relax!" a voice said from behind her head. "Take it easy now."

"Where's Ron?" she tried to ask, perplexed by her lack of control of her facial muscles. It was much the same sensation as the aftermath of a dose of Novocaine: thickness through which it was difficult to speak. She repeated her question slowly, striving for distinctness.

Voices conferred behind her, then someone responded, "He was in the first ambulance."

Ron had been injured. What if he died? She wouldn't think about that. He couldn't possibly die. He'd been perfectly all right. She could see him clearly, spinning the wheel, cursing under his breath as he fought for control. He was bound to have established it. He was always in control—of situations, of people, of stereo equipment, and automobiles. It was, in large part, what had attracted her to him initially: his easy authority, his aura of capability. No piece of machinery, no automobile could deprive Ron of his control. The possibility that he might have been critically injured, might even have died, was too upsetting to contemplate. She gazed steadily at the roof of the ambulance as one of the attendants checked her heart and blood pressure, then looked searchingly into her eyes.

The man's expression revealed nothing, as if he'd worked years to attain total mastery of his features. She found this reassuring. It was confirmation of something, perhaps that she was not seriously injured. If she had sustained serious injuries, she reasoned, she'd be unconscious. There was pain, though, more and more of it as the ambulance raced toward the hospital. And she felt very cold, so cold she began to shiver. The shivering seemed to accentuate the pain, heightening it, perhaps even causing it to spread, because it was beginning to seem as if every area of her body was now afflicted, most especially her face. She longed to free her hands and explore her features, once more recalling her astonishing flight through the windshield. If she closed her eyes, she was again in flight, breaking effortlessly through the glass.

• • •

Awareness returned to her in the emergency examining room, and she looked up into the face of someone she knew. She thought she must be in Fairhaven, if Barbara was here.

"Barbara?" It had become even more difficult to speak.

"This is a hell of a way to get to see me, Caley," Barbara said with a soft laugh. "Other people make dates to meet for lunch or dinner or something."

"I went through the windshield," she articulated carefully, somewhat wonderingly.

"I know." Barbara's voice remained hushed as, with a pair of surgical scissors, she sliced away Caley's shredded clothes.

"How is it?" Caley asked, exhausted now by her efforts to communicate.

Barbara finished cutting one of the sleeves before answering. She dredged up a smile and patted Caley lightly on the shoulder. "You're going to be fine. Rest now. They'll be in to see you in a minute."

"I'm cold."

"We'll get you warmed up," Barbara promised, then silently escaped.

Outside, the scissors still in her hand, Barbara sagged against the wall, one arm wrapped around herself. In her eight years as an O.R. nurse she'd seen her fair share of accident victims, but never anything quite like the destruction of her friend's face. She didn't want to go back inside and assist in the preliminary examination of Caley Burrell. She didn't want to be the one to reveal to Caley the extent of her injuries, and she was bound to give it all away if she had to spend one more minute in there.

She went to the desk and swapped with Karen Moore.

"She's a friend of mine and I can't take it. Do me a favor and let me take your patient."

"That bad?" Karen asked, willing to make the change.

Barbara simply nodded.

Before she received the anesthetic, it occurred to her that she'd been afraid, and was even more afraid now. It was fear, she thought, that had held her internally immobilized, in a transfixed state, as her body had been sent rocketing from the car.

Why hadn't Barbara come back? she wondered. Did her failure to return mean something?

Trussed, as if she were a package of meat on display in a market, she was agonized, anguished at her inability to move. She screamed silently in protest and struggled upward from sleep, determined to rid herself of the effects of the anesthetic. She wanted to be fully conscious, to be able to tell someone that she had to be freed, had to have some degree of mobility restored to her limbs. The anesthetic, though, like powerful lips sucked her back into damp darkness, into amnesia. Four times, five, she fought to open her eyes and, at last, succeeded, only to discover that her eyes refused to focus. It intensified her anguish. She told herself she would not again succumb to the temptation of that enticing darkness, and fixed her eyes on the ceiling light, striving to bring it into definition.

If she could be repositioned, her head elevated, she'd be better able to survey the landscape of her immediate self and determine the possible extent of any attainable freedom. Her tongue floundered inside her parched mouth, seeking to create the moisture that would enable speech. Swallowing, she was aware of the stripped sensation at the back of her throat. It was as if someone had forced her to swallow razor blades.

Sensing a presence, she shifted her eyes, trying to catch sight of whoever was there. The person came within her viewing range. It was a woman. "It's about time you started coming around," she said. "You've been out for seven hours." A pause, and then she said, "I'll get you some water. It's anesthetic dehydration."

A glass straw was insinuated between her lips and Caley tried to draw water up the length of the straw. The effort aroused so much pain that tears flooded her eyes. The straw was withdrawn and a moment later a wet cloth replaced it. Her tongue touched gratefully against the moisture. The water tasted metallic, rusty.

"Dr. Morgan's on his way in to see you. He'll be here in a minute or two."

"Am I tied down?" Caley tried to ask, distressed by her inability now to maintain her eyes' focus.

It took a few seconds, and then the woman seemed to understand. "Restrained," she corrected gently. "Now that you're awake I think we can get rid of these." She proceeded to release a series of straps, and at once Caley's anguish diminished.

"Sit up?" Caley begged, distraught at the hybrid sounds issuing from her so unintelligibly.

"Try to stay calm."

It was a needless admonition. Her brief effort at speech had drained her. It was as if she'd been silent for years and the attempt to speak for the first time was unfamiliar and infuriatingly difficult, her mouth, her entire face protesting. She returned her eyes to the ceiling globe and swallowed experimentally, only to confirm that the rawness was still there.

When next she opened her eyes it was to see a man standing beside her bed. Beneath his white coat, which he wore with undeniable panache, his puffy chest was covered by a white shirt with thin red stripes. Knotted to Windsor perfection around his neck was a burgundy silk tie, and framing both the tie and the somewhat tight-looking collar of his shirt was a stethoscope. A subtle white-on-black tag on his coat lapel identified him as Dr. M. Morgan. He was looking down at her with slightly narrowed eyes, as if debating whether she was worthy of his time.

"I'm Dr. Morgan," he announced abruptly, seeing that he had her attention. "They called me in last evening to attend to you." He paused, and she felt she should say something, but didn't, couldn't. He appeared to be a man of more than usual impatience, and she had no desire to irritate him. He exuded a quiet anger that might be prompted to flare by less than meticulously chosen words.

"Dawson called me in for a con-sult," he went on, breaking the final word into two distinctly separate syllables. He was addressing her as if she were on parole, or possibly on a suspended sentence. Even before he continued speaking, she'd decided she didn't like him: didn't like his Rolex watch, or the Gucci belt with the telltale back-to-back *G*'s; she disliked his gold tie tack and the rigidly starched cuffs peeking from beneath the sleeves of his white coat. Everything about him shouted of vanity and an insistence that all matters in which he might be involved should be directed solely to his satisfaction. Yet despite her immediate dislike, she was momentarily intimidated by his authority. He was, after all, a doctor.

Behind him, in the background, she could see the woman who'd spoken to her earlier, the one who'd released her from the restraints. Her presence now gave Caley a measure of confidence. Both women waited as Morgan prepared to speak again, reading now from a clipboard he held to one side with his left hand and to which it was obvious he intended to refer.

"Has Dawson been in to speak to her yet?" He addressed the other woman, as if Caley were incapable of answering even the simplest of questions.

"Not yet," the woman answered, and Caley could see that she, too, was negatively affected by this rather florid-faced, angry man. "He's due."

He returned his attention to the clipboard and, only incidentally, to Caley. "There are," he declared momentously, "fractures to the clavicle, the left femur and left tibia, and a pelvic fracture. The facial damage is of a more serious nature: a displaced fracture of the malar bone, comminuted compound fracture of the nasal bones with avulsion of the nasal skin. We have, of course, addressed the various fractures. In particular, I have created a temporary nasal skeleton with side-to-side wires holding bone fragments in place; external lead plates either side of the reconstructed nasal bridge, and a split skin graft from the hip for resurfacing." Again he stopped and looked meaningfully at Caley, as if expecting some enthusiastic response. When she once more failed to speak, he tucked the clipboard under his arm and leaned slightly closer to her. "I'm a head-and-neck man, cosmetic surgery, reconstructions."

He was presenting himself like a used-car salesman, she thought.

"I did your facial work," he declared proudly.

He was insane, she decided, trying to turn her head to avoid the minty smell of his breath. The other woman took several steps, then stopped, closely watching Caley. "Perhaps we should wait for Dr. Dawson," she began tentatively.

"Get out!" Caley mouthed.

Morgan whirled around at the sound of her words, his mouth ready to emit more technical jargon.

"Get out!" Caley managed to utter the words distinctly.

"You won't touch me again!" Each word provoked a new and different sensation of pain. "Go . . . away!"

He gaped at her, a flush overtaking his too-small features. "The woman's clearly confused," he told the other woman.

"She doesn't seem to want you here."

"This is absurd!" He turned and stomped to the door, where he collided with Dawson coming in. "Get yourself another man!" Morgan bellowed. "I disassociate myself from this case."

Dawson watched Morgan storm off down the corridor, then turned and entered the room, asking the woman, "What's going on, Hannah?"

"He was his usual diplomatic self," Dr. Hannah Lincoln told him. "Just marched in with a list of fractures and a recitation of the details of his procedure. Another minute and he'd have dragged out a mirror so she could more fully appreciate his skills. The whole thing sounded like Anatomy 404." She smiled and shrugged.

"I understand Dr. Morgan upset you," Dawson said, approaching Caley. "He has an unfortunate manner, but he really is a good man."

"I don't care," Caley whispered, trying to get a grasp of some sort on the implications of reconstructive surgery. "Tell me in English," she said, at ease again. Dawson had been her physician for more than six years.

"What he did was partially temporary and partially, we hope, permanent. Basically, he rebuilt your nose." Apologetically, he went on to explain, in readily comprehensible terms, how her flight through the windshield had had the effect of reducing her nose to pulp. Along with the other facial fractures, a fair amount of skin had been sheared away. "It's not an uncommon procedure, Caley, but in this case he apparently didn't have a lot to work with. We're keeping our fingers crossed that we'll avoid any infection."

It meant nothing to her. Words came from his mouth and bounced off her consciousness like Ping-Pong balls. Yes, her face hurt. But she could not relate the ongoing pain to the descriptions he offered. She was concerned, suddenly, with Ron's whereabouts, and interrupted him to ask, "Where's Ron?"

"He was discharged a few hours ago. He'll probably be in to see you this evening. He was lucky. A few cuts and bruises, a badly sprained shoulder, and that's about it."

"He did come by before he left," Dr. Lincoln added. "But you hadn't come around yet."

There were more words, but Caley didn't listen, and finally the two doctors left.

Late that afternoon, she asked for and received, from one of the nurses, the Stamford *Advocate*. She read the account of what had happened and then studied the photograph of the accident scene for quite some time. It didn't seem real or possible that she had been involved, especially when she now knew that the driver and passenger of the other car—the one whose headlights she'd seen coming at them—had died. Their car had gone out of control, crossed the median, and struck them. In swerving to avoid the oncoming car, Ron had sideswiped another car, and a fourth vehicle had rear-ended both these cars. "Caley Burrell of Stamford, a passenger, is listed as in serious but stable condition at Fairhaven Hospital suffering from multiple fractures and facial injuries." Ron was credited with fast action which resulted in his sustaining only minor injuries.

She allowed the newspaper to slide from her hands. Her eyes drifted over the ceiling. She'd decide how she felt, what her reactions to all this were, when she saw Ron. Until he came, everything was held in suspension. Her eyes closed and the words "reconstructive surgery" shunted relentlessly through her head until she slid deeper, and slept.

Chapter 2

HE STALKED THE EASEL, approaching it sidelong, then stalled, wavering, and squinted at the canvas. Something was to happen today, but he couldn't remember what. He reached for the fantail brush. Needed a bit more ocher right in that corner. There. "Bloody beautiful!" he muttered, setting aside the brush.

With a last look at the canvas, niggled by this thing he was supposed to remember, he gulped the remaining half-inch of rye and plonked the glass down on the cluttered old kitchen table that held the paints and turps and mayonnaise bottles of brushes. He wiped his hands on a Varsol-soaked rag, then pulled on his old cardigan.

The air outside was a cold shock. His hands thrust deep into the pockets of his sagging sweater, he trudged, head down, up the driveway toward the front of the house. As he rounded the bend in the gravel drive, he saw the moving van and remembered what was happening today. He wished he'd taken a final, hefty drink. He was far too sober. Another ounce or two of the rye would have insulated him, so that the departure would have no effect. Somehow, he'd have to hold himself together.

Marian was in the foyer overseeing the withdrawal from the house of the last of the boxes. The coveralled workmen were loading them directly into enormous wooden containers which would be sealed and then delivered from the truck into the hold of the ship. Marian was monstrously organized, always had been. At the other end, once home again and held close to the familiar British breast of a Cotswold hill, she would witness the off-loading of these same boxes.

"I thought you'd stay in your studio till we'd gone," she said now, her eyes taking him in. He waited for her to comment on the cardigan. "We'll be on our way within the half-hour," she informed him.

He took several steps and peered into the living room, wondering what she'd done with the children. He couldn't remember if they'd already exchanged their goodbyes. The two wing chairs remained either side of the fireplace, but the brass-trimmed screen and all the tools were gone, as were most of the books from the shelves flanking the fireplace. Discolored wall areas indicated where certain of the paintings had hung. The hated puce curtains remained, and he vowed that the moment the door closed behind her he'd tear the bloody things from their moorings. Marian, for all her good taste in other areas, had no goddamned sense of color.

Watching him lurking inside the living room, Marian tensed, praying there wouldn't be a confrontation. All she wanted was to see the last of their things loaded into the van, then get the children and leave. She didn't want to have to defend herself, either physically or verbally; she didn't want to have to spend one extra minute in this house with this still-handsome ruin of a man.

"Where are the children?" He had turned and was looking at her.

It was amazing, she thought, the effect of his eyes upon her. After all these years, all the turmoil, his eyes still caused her insides to shrink in anticipation of pleasure.

"They're up having a last look round," she said in a softened tone he at once picked up on. "They'll be down in a moment or two." He was all but sober. His sobriety was hazardously misleading, almost as much as the oddly lyrical remarks he was capable of uttering when profoundly drunk. It hadn't been safe for a very long time to trust him in any state. Their departure today, hers and the children's, should have occurred years before, but it had taken all that time for her to

accept that the situation was never going to change, that *he*
would never change. She had entered into the marriage believing she possessed the power to inspire him to reroute his
energies. She'd been mistaken. It had taken her twelve years to
learn how thoroughly wrong she'd been.

Martin Andrew Maddox was a drunk. She no longer considered it possible that he might give up his romance with
alcohol. For twelve years she had traveled on an ever-narrow-
ing road of optimism, arriving at last at the inescapable exit
marked "Reality." Nothing, not love for her or for his children, not fear or threats or personal injuries, not blackouts, or
a waning of his once-indisputable talent, nothing could per-
suade him that this one-sided love affair between man and
bottle would, in the end, destroy him. Since she was unwilling
to stand by as a hapless, albeit helpless, witness to the destruction of someone she still cared for deeply, she was exercising
her last remaining alternative: she was taking the children and
returning home to England, where she hoped to live out the remainder of her life in a blessed evenness of days. She'd had
enough drama, enough giddying adrenal surges to satisfy permanently whatever brief longing she might once have had for
excitement. Now she wished simply for a predictable procession of days, and the attractive tedium of a routine and
unspectacular life.

"Well . . ." Martin sighed, shrugged his shoulders, and
ambled down the hall toward the kitchen. He should have
stayed in the studio until all this was over and done with; but
he'd forgotten today was the day. Much as he wanted to tell
himself it didn't matter, he couldn't quite accept that. His wife
and kids were leaving, and he was going to miss them.

He stood in the doorway looking in at the kitchen, head to
one side as he studied the fall of light through the far window,
light that placed itself in geometric chunks. There was ordinary light, that diffuse amorphousness that enriched or
deprived an object, or model, of color. But this other, this
particular form of illumination might have been delivered in
blocks, like hundredweights of ice from the back of an old
truck. He'd tried several dozen times to effect on canvas the
placement of these cubes, these squares and oblongs and rec-

tangles of light, but he'd yet to succeed to his satisfaction. Perhaps it wasn't possible. It occurred to him after each failed attempt, with the added perspective of several clarifying ounces of rye or whiskey, that he might be angling after what was nothing more than some illusive configuration visible only to him, and therefore impossible to render visible to others.

But all vision should be transposable! he'd argued, both silently and aloud, on countless occasions. It had to be possible to find some way to redefine that mathematics, that all but palpable mass of light. He could feel himself responding now to the challenge, and debated for a moment the wisdom of continuing on his way out through the kitchen door and back around the drive to his studio atop the garage. From where he stood he could see the studio windows. He was tempted. But no. Best to stay, wave off the wife and kiddies. There'd be plenty of time later to work, all the time he'd ever need.

It was going to be so bloody quiet, though. Even now there were intimations of an awesome, depthless silence that would take hold of these rooms with their carefully intricate Victorian moldings and majestic proportions. The twelve-foot ceilings that had been nothing more than an ineffectual, percolating lid on the raucous sounds of his children, and on his and Marian's fulminating disagreements, would now impose an entirely new weight upon his consciousness.

He liked to drink. There were times when he liked to drink until the world and the people around him took on an entirely new look. A fish-eye distortion, a compelling grotesqueness, altered everything, and through the wavering, miasmic boundaries of his drunken state he gazed entranced, riven by the simple subtlety of change. Despite repeated and prolonged attempts to explain this, and many other things, to Marian, she remained unconvinced. She saw his drinking as self-indulgent and destructive, and as the years of their marriage had accumulated, she'd become ever less tolerant until finally, now, they had arrived at the end.

No more fun. No more whispered plots with the kiddies, no more the elaborately conceived and haphazardly executed surprises prepared by Dad and the boys for Mother's Day, for Christmas, for birthdays, or Halloween. No more seeing two small rib cages working to contain a turmoil of laughter as two grimacing faces fought against allowing convoluted whorls of giddyness to escape small, beautifully delineated lips.

"Bugger it!" he whispered to the defeating geometry of kitchen light and the heedless hum of the refrigerator.

The coveralled moving men were closing the last of the crates. The twins, mumbling angrily, fastened themselves into natty little topcoats of their mother's choosing. Martin looked at them and felt sorrow blossom in his chest like the first glorious swallow of the finest Scotch whiskey. The poor little sods, with scarves draped round their slender throats, and those foppish Chesterfield coats. All that was missing was a pair of bowlers and a couple of black, tightly furled umbrellas and the two of them could go briskly into the sober-suited business traffic without creating the slightest ripple; the stream would simply expand to surround them.

"It's too hot for all that gear," Martin protested to the boys' mother.

"Don't start a scene," Marian entreated. The expression in her eyes told what a difficult time she'd had getting the boys into these outfits.

The damage was already done, though. Harry was pulling at his scarf, saying, "Dad's right. It's way too hot." And Ian, after a moment, nodded his agreement and tugged off his scarf to shove it into the velvet-trimmed pocket of his topcoat.

"Say goodbye to your father." Marian sighed, barely able to contain her well-earned exasperation.

"Say goodbye to the old sod!" Martin laughed, gathering the two boys into his arms. "Say goodbye to the loutish old bugger! Give your old dad a kiss!" He laughed, and the boys laughed. They exchanged kisses and hugs and then stood separate. Their parents eyed each other, volumes of history filling the space between them. Yet for all that, for the dozens of humiliating incidents she could have recited without undue effort, and for the equal number of exclusively logical explanations he could offer for those incidents, this moment contained all the caring and sadness, all the hilarity and disappointment and optimism they'd shared for twelve years.

The boys exchanged a bemused look as their parents embraced for a long moment, then stood apart. Marian appeared flushed and odd, a smile distorting her mouth. Martin simply looked old, his eyes unusually clear, although the flesh around them had a decidedly yellowish tinge.

A taxi pulled up outside. Marian and the twins waved, and then they were gone. Martin gazed out at the road for quite a while before finally closing the front door. It was time to inspect the house and see what he'd been left with.

Sentiment aside, there was no question that this arrangement would benefit everyone involved. He'd be free to paint, to come and go when he wished. Marian and the boys would be able to settle into an existence devoid of unnecessary trauma. The boys would lose their edge, though, that lovely susceptibility to mischief, and that would be a great pity.

It wasn't as if he never drew a sober breath, he thought, suddenly angry. He wasn't one of those pathetic dipsos who wandered in and out of the hostels down on Jarvis Street. He had, one afternoon a few years earlier, pulled into a gas station opposite a hostel to fill up the car. The attendant had been busy, so Martin had waited, captivated by the manic actions of a fairly well-dressed middle-aged man who'd patrolled the sidewalk in front of the innocuous building across the way. The man had marched back and forth with a kind of military-bred frenzy, from time to time erupting into parade-ground shouts at the passing motor traffic that had startled more than one unheeding matron on her way home from the St. Lawrence market with a trunkful of steaks-on-special and New Zealand lamb.

Back and forth, the man had paced out the perimeters of his territory, guarding access to the hostel—or so it appeared—with bewildering dedication. Martin had, of course, assumed that the man was an alcoholic. It came to him now that his assumption might have been completely misguided. The man might very well have been a totally legitimate nutcase, in which event alcohol was an innocent victim, condemned solely by association.

Whatever! The fact was that Martin was someone who,

upon occasion, liked to have a bit of a tipple. And if the worst he could be accused of—by Marian, for example—was dallying every so often with a bottle, it wasn't likely he'd be condemned to spend eternity in perdition as a result. He'd never harmed anyone—at least not knowingly—and he'd always made it a point never even to entertain the notion of driving the car while drinking. He was, all things considered, a gentlemanly drinker, and it was unreasonable and somewhat hysterical of Marian to deprive him of his boys and of the comforts of a well-maintained home just because he refused to succumb to her hysteria and forswear the old demon booze.

"Bugger it, bugger it!" he declaimed, daunted by the feckless-sounding echo of his discontent off those twelve-foot ceilings. Maybe he'd just sell this bloody mausoleum and be done with it. But who'd want it? Who was in the market for eight bedrooms, five bathrooms, sundry sitting and living rooms, not to mention a conservatory, all of which cost a bomb to heat in winter?

He climbed the stairs to the second floor and roved through the rooms. Perhaps he'd get a crowbar and some sacks of plaster and knock all the bloody walls down. He could readily envision the wonderfully curious arches and retaining columns that would enhance the otherwise unsullied expanse. Marvelous. He could feel his energy collecting itself. How splendid it would be to take a good run, a twenty- or thirty-pound mallet in hand, and fell those walls, one after another! He'd do it, too, by God, he decided, going almost at a run now from room to room. Hundreds of square feet of space just begging to see the clear afternoon light.

The house had been Marian's choice, not his. He'd gone along because of the usable space over the garage, and had spent more time in his studio than he ever had in the house. The plan, of course, had been to fill this place with a half-dozen kids.

He stopped on the threshold and stared in at the halfway stripped old whore of a room he'd shared with his wife. For the daughter of a lord—granted old Hugh had only had lifetime use of the title—Marian had decidedly peculiar notions. One of her rather more idiosyncratic ideas was that men enjoyed frolicking in a bedroom done up like an adolescent's wet dream—all pastels and slick, slippery fabrics over rounded, padded surfaces.

He saw, mercifully, that she'd taken her kidney-shaped dressing table with its flounces and frills, as well as the matching bedspread and draperies. The room, he thought, looked worthy now of containing the dream machinery of wearied humans. It looked so appealing, in fact, that he thought he might stretch out for a few minutes and absorb the full impact of his new independence.

Chapter 3

Something was wrong. Ron was behaving like someone meeting her for the first time, an abashed candy-striper perhaps, or one of the crew of older women who filled their empty hours with good intentions by wheeling trolleys of flowers, or paperbacks, or handicraft items the patients might have some use for.

"The car's a write-off." He spoke, but his eyes shied away from her. "They're going to cover it, and they're going after damages for you," he went on, referring to his insurance carrier. "In the meantime, I've got a loaner. It's not bad." He drew a ragged breath. "How are you feeling?" He searched to find something recognizable about her. Only her mouth and eyes were visible; the bandages covered the rest.

"Do you know something I don't?" she asked, suspicious. It was possible Dr. Dawson had confided to Ron details of her condition he'd felt she was in no shape to be told.

"About what?" Ron's eyebrows arched.

"About anything," she whispered wearily. She was growing fatigued by his presence, by this prolonged effort to talk, and by something else that was happening. It was as if the bandages served as a wall between them, so that from her vantage point behind them she was literally unseeable. She could gaze out through the ramparts with a substantial degree of impunity. He couldn't see in, despite his efforts, and she was captivated by how distanced from him she felt. There was a

frightening element to all this: here was a man she loved, with
whom she'd lived for three years. Why did she feel so wary of
him? It had to do with the small talk, idle chitchat he affected
in order to stay away from the obvious matter of her injuries.
It had to do with his visible discomfiture and the manner in
which he sat, his body angled toward the door.

"You're still in shock," he stated, addled. "I know exactly
what you know. Period. D'you really think Dawson would say
anything to me he wouldn't say directly to you? I mean, Jesus,
Caley! He's your doctor, not mine."

"I know." She backed down. "I know that." She reached
for his hand and held onto it, her flesh absorbing information,
recording it. Another shock: it might have been the first time
she'd made contact with this man. It was as if she were holding
a taut package of bones, not anything as recognizable as a
hand that had its own intimate knowledge of her body. What
was going on? She squeezed this hand-object, searching for
familiarity. It didn't want to come. Ron's resistance was real,
undeniable. She didn't know how to reestablish contact. Then
she reminded herself that she did know this man, after all.
He'd never been able to cope with illness. Even a cold was
alarming to him, especially when he contracted one himself.
Then it seemed as if intimations of his mortality shrouded his
logic, and he became unreasonably fearful. He could scarcely
be expected to cope now when what ailed her was considerably
more than a cold. Once she was recovered, out of the hospital,
he'd be at ease again, with himself and with her.

"I'm still so shaky," she said in apology. "This plastic
surgeon came to see me yesterday, the creepiest guy. Awful."
She gave a slight shake of her heavily bandaged head to em-
phasize her words.

"You're going to have plastic surgery?" His features
creased with . . . what? Confusion? Concern?

"Already had it." She laughed, hoping he'd respond
positively to it, but his expression remained unchanged, and
she saw he hadn't interpreted her noise as laughter. Possibly a
suppressed sob? "I hurt everywhere," she complained, at
once regretting it. "But I'm not dead," she concluded, striving for a lighter note.

"It's a goddamned miracle you're not!" he declared
staunchly. "The way you went through that windshield . . ."
He freed his damp hand from hers and tugged a handkerchief
from his pocket, spending quite some time drying his palms.
"I've been up for two nights, seeing it all happening over and
over again. I never . . ." He stopped and chewed on the inside
of his cheek. "I'm just glad you're all right," he wound down
lamely.

What was he talking about? She wasn't all right. She'd just
told him she'd had plastic surgery. That could hardly be construed as all right. Was he hearing her? Was she making
herself form words comprehensibly? The kindest thing she
could do, perhaps, for both their sakes, would be to let him
off the hook, encourage him to go home and try to catch up
on his lost sleep. They could think kind thoughts of one
another from a safe distance.

"You're worn out," she said, her face taking up its theme
of pain. "Go home, try to sleep. We'll talk tomorrow."

She watched gratitude steal across his features and return
a degree of warmth to his brown eyes. He had a nice face,
unthreatening and likely more revealing than he'd ever realized. She'd been able to read him from the day they'd first met
at the office. In large part, her ability to transcribe his
moods—like the ability to read someone else's shorthand—
had accounted for much of the security she'd found in their
relationship.

At once he accepted this suggestion, gave her hand a
reassuring pat, and fled. She was both disappointed and
relieved to have him go. She allowed her head to fall back
against the pillows and let her eyes close behind the helmet of
bandages. It was all distortion. How could she expect things to
be as usual when they might never again be as they'd once
been? Plastic surgery. The words created for her an image of
silicone-engorged breasts, of faces pulled smooth as freshly
made beds, of eyes lacking the creases generated by years of
laughter and expressiveness. The words spoke of vanity, of
self-indulgent women striving for physical perfection. They
had nothing to do with her.

• • •

"I'm just going off duty," Barbara said. "Thought I'd stop in and see how you're getting along."

"Okay. I'm tired, and there's still a lot of pain."

Barbara stood by the side of the bed. She looked crisp and efficient in her uniform. "You must've wondered what happened to me the other night. It was busy in the O.R.," she lied, "and one of the girls didn't show."

Caley nodded.

"Shit!" Barbara looked over at the curtained windows. "I just couldn't handle it. First time that's ever happened. I . . . uh . . . wanted to let you know I'm sorry about running out on you. It's rough, seeing a friend get wheeled in. There's only been one other time, and I couldn't hack that one, either."

"It's okay."

"It sucks!" Barbara said disgustedly. "I'm sorry."

"It's okay," Caley said again.

"I'll check in on you. Take it easy, huh?"

Caley nodded once more.

"Well, I guess that's it. I'm on nights this month, but I'll try to drop in on my day off." She backed away, then turned and left.

Mystified, Caley sank back into sleep.

Dawson said, "I've got a new man to replace Morgan. I think you'll find O'Connor more easygoing. He'll oversee your progress."

It made no difference to her. She'd become inured to the parade of hospital personnel that traveled through her room. Conspicuous only by his absence was Ron. The gaps between his visits grew steadily wider. She sympathized with his inability to deal with the situation, but most of her energy had been used up, and what small amount remained was being put to use maintaining her sense of self. It was, she'd discovered, quite easy to surrender to illness. She could have fallen effortlessly into line with the routines of each day, but it seemed more important to keep a firm hold on her independence, and on her need to be freed, and soon, from her imprisonment here in order to salvage her previously happy life. She wanted to go home. If that meant allowing yet another doctor to examine her, she would acquiesce with as much grace as she could muster. It wasn't easy. These examinations were painful emotionally as well as physically. Each time another small portion of her facial bandages was stripped away, it seemed some hitherto unsuspected flaw was revealed. She felt humorless, weak, and incomplete. She remained in unrelieved pain, and couldn't understand why. She longed to have all this ended, but putting an end to this experience seemed to hinge on her acknowledging the extent of her injuries, and she hadn't yet arrived at a point of confidence where she'd be able to confront what a mirror might reveal to her. Once she and a mirror were set in close conjunction, something in her, of her, would be lost. So she merely tolerated the hospital staff, awaiting some declaration of her fitness.

After almost two weeks it still hadn't come and her resolve was beginning to weaken. There seemed some direct correlation between her loss of resolve and the augmented pain in her face. Today might present that moment of inevitable confrontation, and she was filling irrevocably with fear. She didn't wish to see what had been, until now, only a series of referential points: nose, cheeks, chin. As long as she didn't look, she could remain, to herself, as she'd always been.

The bulk of the bandages was less, and they came away readily enough. O'Connor was the antithesis of Morgan. He was calm, soft-spoken, almost hesitant. His face close to hers, his breath freshly sweet, his hands worked adeptly to bare her face to his scrutiny. A nurse stood at his side to receive the discarded wrappings in an enamel basin. Her eyes remained on Caley's face as if something extraordinary were about to be revealed to her. Both the nurse and O'Connor exhaled audibly as the air wrapped itself around Caley's denuded face. Caley studied the woman's features, seeking telltale signs, but the woman remained impassive, attentive only to O'Connor's needs.

"There's been increasing pain, you say?" he addressed Caley.

"Yes."

He leaned away from her and extended his hand to the nurse, who at once placed a clipboard in it. He made notes, pausing occasionally to refer to Caley's face. He might have been an artist, and she the model. Several minutes passed in this way, and then he spoke.

"It would appear that infection's set in. We're going to start you on a course of antibiotics and hope that this kills off the infection. It's only fair to warn you that if the antibiotics aren't successful, there's a strong possibility we'll have to go back for additional surgery."

He waited, and she didn't know what to do. Was she supposed to encourage him? Or was it up to her to state some argument? The only way she could possibly formulate any response at all was by taking stock, finally, of the damage. She had to have some idea what was actually being said here.

"Why?" she managed to ask.

"Let me explain." He perched on the side of the bed, facing her. "If we're unable to control the infection, there's a chance, putting it bluntly, that the entire reconstruction will collapse. In that event, we'd have to do a cleanup operation to remove the dead bone and the wires. It's called a debridement. Afterwards, there'd be the application of a series of wet saline dressings. The area would have to be allowed to heal completely before we could go back in for another procedure. At that time, we'd put on a graft over the granulation tissue, then send you home for a couple of months' more healing. You'd have the option, at this point, of a prosthesis. Eventually, we'd do a Converse rhinoplasty, a forehead flap. But I'm getting way ahead of myself. For the moment, we'll get going on the antibiotics and hope they do the trick."

What the hell was he talking about? Infection, prosthesis. It was no good. The only way she could possibly determine the correct response was by taking stock, finally, of the damage. The time had come: she was going to have to examine a mirror replication of her image. Only in that way would she be able to apply logic and meaning to what, for the moment, sounded like medical mumbo-jumbo.

O'Connor and the nurse tactfully volunteered to step outside, and she waited until they'd gone, her hand fastened to the rim of the mirror the nurse had given her. She wished she could find humor in the situation: here she was, trussed in

gauze and plaster and tape like some outsized pupa, unable to
mine the courage to look at herself. She swallowed several
times, feeling overheated and a little desperate. She wished
Ron were there; his presence would help. But she was alone,
and the doctor was waiting outside for confirmation of her
understanding of the situation.

She closed her eyes, lifted the mirror and held it at arm's
length, then opened her eyes.

She gawped at the mirror image, a child in a side show at the
circus. What lay revealed before her on the silvered surface
bore no connection to any form of her personal reality. This
was science fiction, a horror story, the worst possible night-
time terror. It had nothing to do with the uncatalogued memories, thoughts, and ideas she contained—the living repository
for all that had pertained, until this time, to the existence of
Caley Elizabeth Burrell. That person, that woman, lived, intact, within her own concept of herself. This "thing" in the
mirror was the pulsing distortion, the fear-inspiring, crippled
monster of some Grimm tale. Not her.

God knows, she'd never been beautiful. But she'd known
about makeup, and how to do her hair. In the course of her
adulthood she'd managed to attract the people she'd cared to;
she'd felt relatively satisfied with the degree of prettiness she'd
been able to conjure up with creams and colors, and rinses to
highlight the auburn aspects of her long hair. It could no
longer matter now what she did to her hair, or how skillful
she'd managed to become with Merle Norman cosmetics. If
truth were this mirror, she was a freak. Shame deluged her, accompanied by a crawling depression, and by fear.

With a jolt, she considered Ron. He was bound to turn
away from her. Anyone would. She herself was utterly repelled, mortified by what she'd become.

"Go ahead," she told O'Connor when he returned to the
room. "Do whatever you can."

"We'll start the antibiotics right away, and keep our fingers
crossed." His hands again lightly grazed her face. "In time,
we'll want to replace these areas with full-skin grafts." He
looked mildly angry, viewing another surgeon's efforts. Did
that mean, she wondered, that the demented Morgan had

screwed up? She thought of asking O'Connor outright, but knew that professional discretion would forbid his commenting. "First and foremost," he was saying, "I want to see the antibiotics take hold. Then we'll know where we're going. Eventually, I'd like to take some grafts from . . ."

"Take whatever you need from wherever you want," she said urgently. "Just don't describe it all to me in advance. If I have to lie here and think about it, I'll lose my mind."

He understood, and went off promising to return twice daily to check on her progress. The nurse lingered to administer the first of the antibiotics and to ask if Caley wanted her painkillers early. Caley said nothing, her hands still fastened to the mirror.

"Why don't you let me take that?" the nurse suggested, and Caley looked down at her lap for a moment, then surrendered the mirror. "It's only temporary," the nurse attempted consolation. "O'Connor's a good man. He'll do his best for you."

Caley nodded, wishing they'd replaced all the bandages. O'Connor had explained the necessity of letting the air assist in the healing process, but all she could think of was the moment that evening when Ron would come through the door and see her for the first time without her concealing gauze. Her entire body shriveled with apprehension and her hands trembled. As the nurse was going out the door, Caley called to her.

"Could I have my handbag?" she asked. "Is it here?"

"I think it's in the locker there." The nurse opened the compartment and found the bag.

"Thank you," Caley whispered.

"Anything else I can get you?"

"No, thank you."

Caley fumbled the bag open, found her cigarettes, got one lit, and drew the stale, dizzying smoke gladly into her lungs. A drink would have been good, too. A gallon of drinks.

She held her hands over her face, unwilling to have Ron see her. Fear was a bitter fluid in the bowl of her mouth; she couldn't speak. He sat in the chair beside the bed, his hands busy with the magazines and newspapers and small amount of mail he'd brought for her. It was more than a minute before he raised his head, smiling, to look at her.

"Hey! They took off the bandages."

She inclined her head, hands still shielding her face from his view.

"Come on," he coaxed, as if this were a game. "Let's see, Cale."

She shook her head, her heartbeat chaotic. She wanted him to go home and return in a week or two, when the medication had done its job and she was out of danger. Why hadn't she called him at the office and told him not to come tonight? Because she hadn't known whether or not he'd be coming. His visits now were unannounced, usually brief, and always distressing.

She sat behind her hands, more aware by the second of the enormity of what had happened to her. Initially, she'd considered only how people might respond to the sight of her. She'd failed to recognize that people would undoubtedly be reluctant to go beyond the sight of her, that their repulsion would be sufficient to turn them away entirely; they'd never bother to try to find out if the interior woman lived up to her radically altered externals. Ron knew her though, she thought, experiencing a thin hope. He knew and claimed to love her. He'd know that it was only her face that was changed, not the person inside.

"Come on." He tugged lightly at her wrist, his legible face like a child's first efforts at cursive script.

A silent tussle ensued. He cajoled, she resisted. At last, he withdrew and sat back in the visitor's chair.

"You're being silly," he said flatly. "What d'you think I'm going to do, anyway?"

In a spasm of courage and defiance, she uncovered her face and turned stiffly toward him, her hands braced either side of her on the bed as she gauged his reactions.

His mouth opened, then closed. What might have been a smile hung dangling on his face like peeling wallpaper. "Jesus!" he whispered, unable to look away. "I, uh . . ." His voice tapered off and he could only gape at her, in much the same way she'd stared at her mirror image earlier.

Defiance won out and she stared him down, willing him to assert that he still loved her. He squirmed miserably under the weight of her gaze, moistened his lips, tried to speak, and failed. His eyes filled and he shook his head, the boy he'd once been suddenly clear behind the older man's dismay.

"I'm sorry," he managed to get out. "I had no idea. . . ."

Pity for him overwhelmed her. "It's all right. Eventually, they're going to redo the grafts. Right now, they're trying to kill the infection lurking under all this metal and wire." She'd tried for humor; what she'd managed was a kind of graphic grimness.

He wanted to ask how they could possibly restore her face, re-create what she'd been. It didn't seem possible. He wanted to look away, but was unable. He was wondering how he'd deal, in future, with the sight of her. They'd been planning to get married, had talked about children, and about buying a house. Of course, he reminded himself, any children they might have wouldn't be disfigured. There'd been an accident, and her present condition was as a result of that. She wasn't carrying the genes of monstrosity that could be passed along to an infant she might conceive. But how could he make love to her? The thought of touching her made his insides lurch menacingly. His immediate concern was how he'd get through what remained of this visit. He doubted he'd be able to stay in his chair and simply talk.

"It's all right," she said again, sensing the direction of his thoughts. "I know it's a shock. I felt the same way."

"I'll say," he agreed. "You say they're going to redo the grafts?"

"Eventually. If the medication doesn't work, though, I'll probably have to have four or five more operations."

"Four or five?" He was horrified.

"I don't know." She turned away to study the yellow curtains gathered at the head of the bed. They ran on a track and could be drawn all the way around the bed. Since it was a private room, this touch of delicacy seemed needless. Yellow had likely been selected as a heartening color, less intentionally institutional than medium green. "I have no choice," she said, trapped in place by the various casts weighting down her limbs. "What else can I do?" she asked pleadingly, seeking his reassurance.

He might have said something, but she missed it. She was thinking suddenly of dreams of flying, dreams she'd had since childhood, of a fine, freeing talent that allowed her to soar above the children in the playground, over teachers who raised their voices. She could fly in dreams, although it was sometimes difficult gaining sufficient momentum for takeoff. She required enough distance to get her speed up, running, before the air allowed her to lift. She relished that moment when her body rose and she could smile down into the upturned, astonished faces of those below. Her ability to fly was venerable, even to her, and she cherished that time when she spiraled, cushioned by air, shifting her shoulders to alter direction.

Why wasn't this a dream? she thought sadly. Why was she unable to accomplish waking any of the multitude of wonderful things she could do in sleep? She could ice-skate brilliantly; she could sit down at a piano and her fingers would produce the most glorious sounds; she could dance; she could sing; she could fly. But this wasn't a dream, and she could do nothing more than rely upon the skills of strangers, hoping that the polysyllabic technical terms they were so fond of spouting were tied to very real talent.

"I want to sleep now," she spoke into the pillow.

He got to his feet and stood over her, his hand on her arm. "I'm really sorry, Cale. It's just that there was . . . I wasn't ready. I mean, Dawson told me, but it didn't really register."

He waited for a reply, but she lay silent.

"I'll run along, come back tomorrow night. It doesn't change anything, Caley. Anybody would've reacted the way I did. I mean, I just couldn't help . . . Hell! I'm only making it worse. Listen, don't worry about anything. Okay? I'll call you tomorrow, come by after work. D'you want me to bring you anything?"

"No."

He bent, his fingers gingerly touching her cheek. "I love you," he said almost inaudibly, then kissed her forehead at the hairline.

Outside in the corridor, he had to lean against the wall and take several deep breaths before heading for the elevator. He had no idea how he was going to get through this, and had to keep telling himself she wasn't always going to look this way. They'd patch her up. Maybe there'd be some scars, but she'd look all right in the end.

She listened to his receding footsteps, consumed by the idea that the worst was still to come. No matter how she yearned to believe otherwise, the ongoing pain was telling her the surgery was a failure. The nightmare had only just begun.

Chapter 4

THERE WAS A TERRIBLE strangeness to the house now that Marian and the twins had gone. For the first few weeks after their departure, Martin prowled through the rooms at random hours of the day or night, distracted, depending upon the extent of his alcohol consumption, by the reenactment in memory of scenes that had taken place in the kitchen, or the living room, or the conservatory.

The conservatory, he noted now and then, was in trouble. The plants, once so luscious due to Marian's slavish attendance upon them, grew progressively paler and more limp. Many had died. He told himself repeatedly to fetch a watering can and restore the dozens of plants to a state of well-being, but somehow, as soon as he left the immediate vicinity, he forgot the many small deaths occurring in that overly hot room.

He wished he could so readily erase from his mind the way things had been before his family life had come to so abrupt a close. He loathed being alone, and this surprised him. He had thought the return of his freedom would be momentous, that he'd work with renewed vigor and produce paintings that accurately reflected his disencumberment. If anything, the reverse was true. He'd go to the studio over the garage, prepared for a productive session with a fresh canvas, only to find himself caught anew by those distracting little films of family life that insisted upon playing themselves out for him.

He sat in the studio, in the old, tattered armchair Marian

had long since disowned, claiming it was fit only for the trash, and gazed into the dusty air, watching entranced as the dust motes collected, gathering themselves together to form images. His two sons, clad in cast-off shirts of his, the cuffs rolled back and the tail ends dragging on the paint-splattered floor, stood before two small easels, each with newsprint pads in place, and eagerly spread colors upon the paper with the ease and brilliance only small children seemed to have. Their paintings—of houses and flowers and huge, grinningly benevolent suns—had been rich with energy and vibrantly alive in a way Martin's own paintings no longer were.

It alarmed him to think that those boys and Marian's ceaseless work at establishing some sort of family routine might have been attached in some way to his creativity and that, without them, his ability to work, let alone work well, might be gone. It was unthinkable, especially since his desire to work remained intact. Daily he went to the studio filled with the intention of committing himself to canvas. And daily he failed to accomplish anything. All he'd done was to clean his brushes, mindlessly rubbing the turps from the bristles with an old tea towel. The place had never been so tidy. Everything was at the ready, yet he couldn't begin.

After an hour or two, he'd leave the studio and return to the house, where he'd study the walls and doorways, engaged in the mental reconstruction of the house. Glass in hand, he'd progress from room to room, as if that wall-less expanse of uncluttered space was already a reality. Sooner or later, though, the ghosts got in the way.

He spent twenty minutes in the foyer recalling how he and Marian had reacted when coming through the front door for the first time; how he'd chased Harry and Ian up that grand staircase at bedtime, their short legs lifting to span the risers, their reckless laughter swirling behind them. He was shocked to discover how very involved he'd actually been, not only with his children, but with their mother.

Late at night, he'd lie on top of the bed he'd shared with Marian and wait for her to emerge from the bathroom or the dressing room. Her failure to arrive was a repeated injury. He'd drink himself to sleep and awaken late in the morning, swearing this would be the day he'd get himself together.

Several times he actually went so far as to ring up the airlines with a view to booking a ticket. He'd fly over, hire a car, and drive up to the Midlands, where he'd shoo Marian and the boys into the hire-car, drive directly back to Heathrow, and return all of them to their rightful places. There was no sense to any of this. The boys belonged with their father; he wanted his wife back. He hadn't yet managed to get to the point of booking a ticket. Each time he put an end to the call, saying he'd ring back when his plans had solidified.

After a month of this wavering, he decided he'd capitulated long enough to indolence. It was time to get to work, and if he was going to continue to be plagued by memories of his family, he'd use those memories to get himself going again. He spent two hours restoring the kitchen to order, rinsing soiled dishes prior to loading them into the dishwasher, wiping down the counters and tabletop, and giving the floor a good sweep. With a pot of coffee, he went out the kitchen door and along to the studio, set the pot on the warmer, poured himself an initial cup of the smoky French roast he preferred, and started roughing in with charcoal on an outsized canvas.

He planned to do, if necessary, an entire series based on those scenes lodged in his brain. The first would be a telescoped view of the boys and himself going up the stairs, and he would use those wonderful primary colors his sons had always favored.

It came easily, and he toiled steadily, stopping only to refill his cup, until the pot was empty and the images were there on the canvas, ready for his brushes and the oils. The daylight was used up; he was hungry. He switched off the warmer and stood holding the empty coffeepot, studying with pleasure the roughed-in canvas.

That evening he went out to pick up some food from the Chinese take-away up on Mount Pleasant near Eglinton, brought it home, and ate off the coffee table in the living room while he watched the local, and then the American, network news programs. He'd been incommunicado for over a month and he needed to find out what was going on in the world.

What was going on was the same old rape, murder, plundering, and pillage. The Russians were all frightfully naughty boys, and the indignant Americans were offering the usual strong threats. The kindly Polish pope was traveling abroad, a sole voice of sanity and reason, attempting to make himself heard and understood. Mr. Trudeau and Mr. Clark heaped thinly veiled invective upon one another, and there were rumblings among the Tories about calling an election.

Meanwhile, the prime rate went up and down, and the Dow-Jones industrial index kept pace with the prime: graphs of zigzagging red or blue or green lines someone like that shocker, Andy Warhol, might autograph and sell, given the least opportunity.

On the local scene, people were robbing Toronto banks with a frenzy. It was due, one commentator suggested, to the troubled economy and the high jobless rate. A rape-murderer was on the loose in the Beaches; the area's population lived in fear.

He ate hugely, then went down to the workroom in the basement to find a crowbar and a small sledgehammer. He'd knock out the wall between the living and dining rooms first. In preparation, he covered the few remaining pieces of furniture and the television set with dropcloths. Then he picked up the crowbar and approached the doorway, running his hand over the fine old oak moldings. It would be a pity to ruin this good wood.

With care, he began to pry the strip moldings away from the wall. The outside, quarter-round trim, came away easily enough and he laid the strips down carefully before tackling the wide, inner trim.

By three in the morning, the long oak pieces lay in a tidy pile on the floor behind him. The doorway was ready to be brought down. He planned to take the wall up to within a foot of the ceiling and right back to the main, exterior wall. What he couldn't decide was whether or not to extend the doorway to the interior hallway wall or to demolish this interior wall altogether. If he took it down, upon entering there would no longer be a foyer, but simply an area that would reach all the way back to the kitchen.

Setting aside the crowbar, he went up to ready himself for bed, considering the appeal of a living area that would be about thirty-five feet wide by seventy-five feet long. The concept was almost as satisfying as his return to active work had

been, and he dreamed that night of opening his front door to
see this new, vast space where his planned series of family
paintings hung with importance. In the dream, he moved from
one canvas to the next, ingesting the images with intense gratification. Around him the air flowed serenely, sweetly, and he
breathed with deep contentment as he contemplated this extraordinary sequence of paintings.

The first letter from Marian came as a surprise. His mind
had been so filled with her and the boys that he'd managed to
forget they'd gone. The letter made the wound of their departure freshly raw, and even more painful. She told of their
passage home, and of the boys' ready adjustment to their new
life. She hoped he was well and that he'd keep in touch, if not
with her—which she'd certainly understand in the circumstances—at least with the boys. Enclosed was a page with mes-
sages from Harry and Ian, in their best script, and signed with
the nicknames their father had long ago given them, Marks
and Spencer.

He was more touched by their recalling this silliness than by
the actual content of their notes, which, after all, consisted of
nothing more profound than: I am fine. How are you? It's
cold and rainy. That they should send their personal signals,
with Harry signing as Marks, and Ian as Spencer, caused
renewed grief to surge into his throat. He had to have a drink
and reread the contents of the envelope.

This done, he had to go at once to the studio to examine
again his portrait of the boys, to see if he'd succeeded in cap-
turing what he loved in them. Eyes slitted, head to one side, he
inspected the tidy half-turned heads and the open-mouthed expressions of hilarity. It was all there, too much there. He sat
heavily in the old armchair, his eyes on the newly commenced
painting, and wondered how he could possibly get through
another twenty-four hours without the real-life sight of old
Marks and Spencer.

He laughed aloud, then wept briefly. "Bugger it!" he announced, his voice overloud and startling to his own ears.
He'd go out to the bloody airport and get himself a seat on the
next flight to London. Now that he had an actual address,
he'd go visit his boys and try to talk some sense into Marian.

He ought to have done that in the first place, instead of simply accepting her decision to go, without making room for a discussion of the matter. The thing of it was he just hadn't understood what it would mean to have them leave. And he'd stayed dry for more than a week now. A week was readily stretched to two, and then three. He'd have the occasional tipple, prove to her he could stay off the drink.

In a hurry, he closed up the studio and returned to the house to push a few things into a suitcase. A quick shower and shave, into some comfortable clothes for the flight, and he was ready. A taxi came in under five minutes, and he settled in for the ride to the airport, edgy with renewed purpose. He'd bring the family home, return them all to a familiar life-style. Marian had undoubtedly been waiting to be asked. Fool that he was, he'd failed to see it. He'd called her bluff, allowed her to take the boys and go. Suddenly, he could see so clearly the mistakes he'd made; he only wished it were possible to be instantly transported to England instead of having to waste additional hours sitting about in an airport lounge, and then on a plane. Well, it would be the last of any wasted time. He'd hire a car at Heathrow and drive directly up to the Cotswolds. If he slept for a few hours on the plane, he'd be in good enough shape to make the drive. Once he got there and had stated his case, he'd worry about catching up on sleep.

There was a first-class seat available on a British Airways flight that was already boarding. He shoved a credit card across the counter to the ticketing agent, signed the chit, then raced along what seemed to be miles of corridors, to the gate. It took him close to half an hour, once in his assigned seat, to catch his breath. He huffed so tremendously that the flight attendant came by several times to ask if he was all right.

"Just had a hell of a run," he wheezed, his chest an inefficient bellows. Undoubtedly she thought he was about to keel over with cardiac arrest. "A brandy would go down beautifully," he told her.

"As soon as we're airborne, sir." She presented him with a glossy, professional smile, convinced no doubt he was merely another ill-conditioned drunk and not the potential stretcher case he thought he might be. She glided sedately through the first-class cabin, taking drink orders, and Martin watched her with mixed admiration and annoyance. He disliked people, no matter in what position, who felt they held some degree of power over others. Crews on airlines often enjoyed flexing their power muscles on their transient victims, and he sensed that this young woman—Helene, according to her nametag —was about to play a bit of a power game with him. She'd pegged him as a drunk and she'd be late with his drink, if she brought it at all. In the course of the flight, she'd natter with her cohorts behind the partition up front about the boozer she'd been lumbered with in seat 5A.

Under ordinary circumstances, he'd have worked himself into a state to suit the situation, but he wasn't up to it tonight. He detested flying. Always, when taking off, he had the arbitrary notion that were he to take his eyes from the runway, the plane would crash. His concentration was tied directly to the pilot's, and without his active assistance the pilot would be unequal to the task of getting this bloody great beast of a jumbo off the ground.

He stared steadfastly downward until the lights below were lost and a discreet chime indicated that the No Smoking sign had been turned off. The crew were up and moving behind their partition, fixing the drinks orders and hotting up hors d'oeuvres to offer the half-dozen occupants of the section. He realized he was hungry, and sniffed the air appreciatively, ready to gulp down a batch of those little unidentifiable doughy things airlines invariably doled out in lieu of real food.

While he waited, he withdrew Marian's letter from his pocket and read it again, then sat looking out at the blackness beyond the window, thinking of his boys.

If she had her way, the lads would be rigged out in short gray pants and pullovers of whatever color the school dictated—navy and burgundy were popular. They'd have neckties and stiff-collared shirts to get into every morning and silly little peaked caps to round off the gear. In wool knee socks and oxfords, their skinny knees bared to the miserable British elements, they'd come hurrying home at day's end with their hands and legs red-raw. Their nice nasal Canadian twang would quickly vanish as good-old-boy accents took over. "Bloody hell!" he muttered, growing heated at the prospect of the boys' hasty assimilation into the establishment system.

It was bad enough both he and Marian had had to suffer through all that public school rubbish. He couldn't believe she'd managed to forget it to the extent that she'd be willing to see it all inflicted on their kids. Maybe she'd relent and let them toddle along to the local grammar, where they'd learn to hold their ground and gain some basic comprehension of the world they'd eventually have to live in.

What the hell good had Roedean done Marian? Aside from that unbearably ripe accent the years in Canada had thankfully managed to tone down, she herself was the first to confess that she'd done nothing more than put in her time, learning not a lot more than the rudiments of maths and grammar. His own education had been a dead loss until he'd succeeded in gaining entry to the art college. Only then had he begun to acquire knowledge pertinent in any viable way to his interests.

Of course Marian had always insisted he'd been spoiled because he had a private income and didn't have to "work" for money. Painting, to her mind, contained no element of genuine labor. She was a damned fanciful woman if she still thought all those hours on one's feet didn't constitute work. His success, she'd long maintained, was due in no small part to the fact that their friends—first in England and later in Canada—insisted on attending his showings and snapping up his paintings almost before they were dry. Pissed him right off the way she denigrated what it had taken him the better part of his life to accomplish. Perspective, tone, texture, color, none of it had value in her eyes. The paintings were just "clever," and he was just lucky. How she could think it lucky to have one's parents die and to be raised by that wretched old harridan, his grandmother, was beyond him. He laughed aloud, recalling Lady Barnes, with her lifetime's use of her husband's title and the temporary use of her grandson's inheritance. She'd gone to her grave accusing Martin of growing up simply in order to deprive her of *her* money.

Marian's family were a better lot altogether. Old Grace had been a great beauty—still was, for that matter—with a fine, even ribald, sense of humor. She'd needed it, though, to live with liverish Hugh for some thirty years before he'd finally turned purple in the face one afternoon over tea and died of a

coronary occlusion with his mouth full of cream tart. Old
Grace would be on his side, he thought, considering it. She'd
advise Marian to stop being such a ninny and take the boys
and herself home where they belonged. He could count on
Grace's support.

Damn it! Marian had to be made to see; he had to convince
her that everything that had gone before was of no conse-
quence now. Different rules applied, because she'd altered the
course of play.

"Your brandy, sir." The attendant held a tray bearing a
snifter.

"Ah! Thank you." He immediately revised his opinion of
the attractive Helene and granted her a grateful smile before
helping himself to some of the seafood offerings on the platter she extended. She was not going to play at power broking
after all, but was someone who would ease his passage. With
several large shrimp and a delectable slice of smoked salmon
sprinkled with capers on the tray table before him, he looked
up to give the young woman another smile. She had spectacular hair, long and thickly golden. It was hair that invited one's
hand to plunge into its cool, silken depths. He was briefly
tempted to ask if he might touch it, but thought better of it,
thanked her again, and sat back to eat his seafood tidbits and
drink the Remy-Martin VSOP. Another eight or nine hours
and he'd be driving up to the door of the cottage Marian had
rented, to see the delight, and hear the laughter of his boys.

Chapter 5

CALEY LAY IN A state of semi-wakefulness imagining her family. It was something she hadn't done in recent years, and even in her not-quite-waking state, she remarked to herself on the oddness of starting at this point in time to speculate again on who her mother and father might have been.

She viewed her unknown mother, as she always had, as too young and lethally vulnerable. Only someone utterly threatened by the situation in which she found herself could have abandoned a newborn infant, wrapped in newspapers, outside the emergency entrance to a Manhattan hospital. The infant had been found by a police officer escorting a stab-wound victim to the emergency room, and had subsequently been named in honor of Officer Caley. The Elizabeth had come from her adoptive parents, who had, on Caley's sixteenth birthday, presented her with the truth of her origins in the form of a manila file folder containing the press cuttings her abandonment had generated.

She still had the clippings. They were preserved now in laminated plastic, and kept in a locked metal box that housed her important papers, along with a photograph album kept by the Burrells over the years, the two wedding bands—thinned to the breaking point with age and wear—that had been her parents'. There wasn't all that much more in the box: her birth certificate listing parents as unknown, her high school diploma and one from Katharine Gibbs secretarial college, and an insurance policy on her life in the amount of ten thousand dollars.

Periodically, she sat down with the box and reviewed its contents, finding them a fairly meager commentary on thirty-four years of a life. The clippings, though, still intrigued her, recounting as they did her discovery, and then the search for her missing mother. The woman never had come forward, although the cuttings included outraged letters to the editors of the New York newspapers, and offers by a startling number of people willing to adopt the days-old infant.

Her daydreams of her real family had commenced soon after her parents had confessed to her the truth of her origins. She had first fabricated an image of the girl/woman and then, bit by bit, like a paint-by-numbers kit, added in dots of color here and snippets of information there until she'd contrived an appropriately melodramatic scenario of her conception, her natural mother's panic at the young man's refusal to accept responsibility for her plight, and, finally, the furtive placement of the newborn, newsprint-swaddled baby outside the hospital doors. The young woman had then gone on to live her life. Most likely she'd married and given birth to other children, and out there somewhere were men and women who had, unbeknownst to them, a sister alive in the world.

Throughout most of her adult life, Caley had mused about chance encounters with some man or woman who would turn out to be blood-related. These fantasized revelations were never tainted by unpleasantness or rejection, but always incorporated joyously tearful reunions. She drew tremulous comfort from these scenarios; they were as narcotically peace-inducing as the infrequent joints she'd smoked during her sojourn at Katharine Gibbs, illicit yet pleasurable.

Now, groping upward from her anesthetic-induced stupor, she was impatient with her ceaseless speculations. She had, through misadventure and the unstated but strongly suspected incompetence of an inept surgeon, lost her nose. She wanted to be fully conscious in order to study this new, ruthless reality. She floundered, a wearied swimmer, toward the higher levels of consciousness, aware that someone was nearby.

As she surfaced, her throat parched from drugs, she experienced an explosive panic at the idea that she might spend months on end, even years, hospitalized. Her medical insurance would run out, there'd be no funds left to subsidize her return to physical normalcy, and she'd be thrust out onto the streets permanently disfigured. These procedures—the one just undergone and the one promised—had to be successful. She would rather die than be someone who drew the choleric stares of strangers.

O'Connor was speaking to her. "This part of it's gone very well. You're going to experience a residue of pain, but only for a few days. Caley?"

She managed to locate, and fix him, in her vision. Gradually, he came into focus, and she tried to work her mouth into mobility.

"Try not to exert your facial muscles," he cautioned. "You're bound to be very tender for a while. We'll start with the saline dressings this afternoon, and if everything goes according to plan, we'll try for the graft in a couple of weeks. All being well, there's no reason why you shouldn't be home in a month or so."

She sucked water through a bent glass straw into the desert bed of her mouth, eased enormously by this simple act. She was learning to seek simple gratification in order not to have to think about the time that was passing or the fact that her future might consist of endless surgery.

The day nurse lowered the sides of the bed, then drew the yellow curtain along its track before folding back the bedclothes. Prompting Caley's assistance by nudges and pats, she reached up and deftly removed the catheter tubing. At once Caley felt the internal irritation.

"A little sore, huh?" the nurse observed. "I'll leave the buzzer right here in case you need anything." She placed the cylindrical call mechanism in Caley's free left hand. The other was still anchored to a Styrofoam form with an intravenous needle taped in place. She was receiving glucose and something else. She didn't care. "Want some juice?"

Caley blinked, and the nurse smiled. "Back in a flash."

Later, after the chilled apple juice was a cooling reference point in her stomach, Caley rested, aware of the various parts of her body as they hummed with differing degrees of discomfort. Her mending leg and pelvic bones itched and ached. Her face, fortunately, was still under the influence of the anesthetic. But it, too, would sing with pain once the drugs were out of her system. Trying to ignore her many discordant melodies of pain, she wondered how drugs knew which part of the body to go to. It was something that had always baffled her. How did a chemist go about drawing this vitamin or that protein from its source and then pack those numbers and letters into a small multivitamin capsule? How did a painkiller know how to locate the pain? What if it went to the wrong area and worked its magic mistakenly? What did a vitamin look like? What did skin grafts actually look like? Would she someday emerge from this place with expanses of raw meat on her person?

For someone who had never had to deal with anything more serious than a bout of flu and a hairline wrist fracture as a kid, she felt almost incapable of coming to terms with this lengthening stay in the hospital. It was like imprisonment, and all her thoughts fused on the idea of getting out of there. Once the bones had mended, once the next procedure had been completed, she'd be free to leave, to resume her life.

Her boss had sent flowers and so had several of the secretaries. Ron had spoken to her boss and had relayed back the message that her job would be waiting for her. But for how long? She'd already been in this room for a month and, by O'Connor's count, she'd remain for another. There'd been no mention yet of recuperation time at home. That could be an additional two or three months.

There were endless hours to get through, and smoking was presently strictly forbidden. She'd never been a fan of soap operas or game shows, and she was unable to lose herself in reading any of the books and magazines Ron seemed reluctant to arrive without, as if tangible physical offerings were the toll he paid for passage to this room. The periodicals and paperbacks sat stacked on the bedside table, slowly mounting with each visit.

Since the evening he'd first viewed her without benefit of bandages, Ron seemed different. The change was so slight it might have been unnoticeable had she not been alert to any sign. In acknowledgment of the changes in him, she had begun to accept that their relationship would come to an end sometime soon. It was better, she reasoned, to accustom herself to that reality in advance of the fact. That way, when the hurt came, it would be diminished. It was no longer about Ron that she dreamed; she projected herself into the future alone. She saw herself as a shapeless, moving mass of rags, scuttling along the pavement as passers-by hustled themselves out of her path. The image was so laden with self-pity it made her want to laugh, yet even when in that semi-sleeping state in which she spent much of her time here, she couldn't deny the elements of truth contained in the image. She was going to be badly scarred, and to most people that was the visible equivalent of leprosy. She'd read and seen enough to know that.

When she'd met Ron, one of the most attractive things about him had been his aspect of honor. He was someone who sought always to do the right thing, not necessarily what was acceptable, but *right*. This instinct, he claimed and she supported, was directly responsible for his failure to rise quite as he should have in his career. There were other men in the company so intent upon success that treachery was a part of their daily fare, like martinis at lunch and undercooked steaks. Ron couldn't sacrifice any portion of his integrity in order to garner corporate success; nor would he stoop to using his associates as they so frequently used him.

"When I get there," he was fond of saying, "it'll be under my own steam and on my terms. There'll be no dead bodies in my wake, no one bleeding. The only person I'm in control of is me, and I intend to keep it that way."

She liked him for it, but wondered about the wisdom of a philosophy that had seen him passed over for promotion three times in as many years. Working for the same company allowed her to hear the gossip that wafted between desks like germs. Despite the fact that she was an administrative assistant in the marketing department, and Ron was one of the intermediate executives in the research and development area, news of promotions, of hirings and firings, was carried on the air, in the elevators, up and down the stairwells, from one floor of the corporate headquarters in Greenwich to another.

In the six years she'd worked for General Brands she'd seen men go up and down the corporate slide like bemused children engaged in some barely comprehensible game. She had started out in the secretarial pool and had worked her way up, first to personal secretary to the assistant marketing director, then to personal assistant to the marketing director, and finally to administrative assistant to the associate vice-president of regional marketing. With it all, she remained fairly much what she'd been to begin with: a secretary. But promotions meant more money, better benefits, and profit-sharing; so she'd put in the overtime hours without pay and ignored the comments from the women in the secretarial pool who spread the rumor that she was sleeping her way up through the company. She'd become adept at smiling away the stories that found their way back to her. The only difference between the men and the women on the climb was that the women seemed more openly resentful of anyone of their ranks who succeeded in breaking past the management barrier. She'd been determined, prior to the accident, to work her way into management. She'd even been taking night courses in business and economics at U. Conn. All that concentrated effort might come to nothing now. She probably wouldn't have a job when all this was ended. They wouldn't be willing to keep her job on hold indefinitely. God! She was going to have to go out looking for a new position.

And Ron, with his damnable honor and integrity, would try to do the "right" thing by her, so she wasn't going to know where she really stood with him.

She was getting panicky again and, recognizing the symptoms, tried to bring herself back under control. There wasn't a damned thing she could do about anything, so getting worked up was a waste of energy. Behind her gauze helmet, she closed her eyes and tried to conjure up dreams of flying. Every other territory seemed fraught with imminent peril.

"It looks like a deboned chicken," she said of the temporary graft over the granulation tissue. Flesh seemed to have been melted into place over her facial skeleton. "I look like I've been parboiled."

"The color will go down," O'Connor assured her, "and the scars will fade. At least now you've got full-thickness grafts in these areas." He touched her cheeks. "There's still the option of the prosthesis, if you'd be more comfortable with that.''

Plastic was a wholly accurate word to describe the present texture of her face. She looked like an assembly-line concoction that had gone wrong. Overall, though, her appearance was improved, in spite of the absence of a nose. It was no less than amazing to her that she'd come to a point where she could contemplate this radically distorted image and actually see improvement. The use of a forehead flap to form what would, ultimately, be her nose was next on the agenda, and the procedure would be started once all healing beneath the temporary graft was complete.

She had, wisely, she thought, refused to look at the results until now, when, with the aid of crutches, she was ready to go home and wait out the weeks. Two months at the outside, and she'd return for the second-to-last round of the reconstruction. By then, she'd have something like acceptable features. People wouldn't be sickened by the sight of her. Even Ron commented that evening, when he came, on the success of the grafts.

''What a difference!'' he said, attempting to fill his briefcase with some of the books and magazines she hadn't read. ''I'll have to get the rest of these tomorrow when I come back for you.''

''I can't wait to get out of here,'' she said happily, feeling human for the first time since the accident.

''How is it, getting around on those things?'' He indicated the crutches propped against the bedside locker.

''I'm getting pretty good at them, especially now that I've got the walking cast. I can't go very far, but it beats hell out of lying here.''

She did feel so much better. She was filled with the anticipated pleasure of simple things like watering the plants and sitting with Uncle Sam, their elderly gray Persian, on her lap. She wanted to cook a meal, to sleep in her own bed with Ron beside her; she wanted to wear clothes again instead of hospital gowns; she wanted to go back to being an ordinary woman living her life.

''Have you heard any rumbles at the office?'' she asked. ''Anybody been saying anything about hiring someone to replace me?''

"Far as I know, Art's still waiting for you to come back. They've given him a girl . . ."

"Woman," she interjected.

"Woman from the pool."

"Who?"

"Jesus, Caley! I don't know. Someone from the pool. It's going to be months before you're ready even to think about going back to work."

"I know that, but I'd like to think that when I *am* ready, my job's going to be there."

"Will you relax?" He smiled at her. "Let's worry about getting you out of here first."

"Bring me something to wear when you come tomorrow, will you? I don't have any clothes."

"Oh, right," he said, remembering. The dress she'd been wearing that night had long since been consigned to the trash.

On impulse, happily, she reached for his hand, but was halted in her intent by the sight of her wrist and forearm, which looked wasted and frail. It was a great way to lose weight, she thought wryly, being stuck in a hospital for a couple of months. Ron's hand had reached to close around hers, and she looked at their linked hands wondering if he was acting out of integrity, putting on a good face, or if he still genuinely cared for her. She wanted their caring to have survived whole, but couldn't help wondering if the accident and her injuries had affected his feelings for her as they'd affected her trust in him. God! she thought anxiously. Please let it be the way it was before! All she'd ever wanted was a family of her own, the knowledge that there were lives adjoined to hers. It wasn't a lot to ask.

Chapter 6

MARTIN CAME TO in aching stages. His eyes and mouth, both withered with exsiccation, opened first. His hands, benumbed knots, lay trapped beneath him, and through a titanic effort of will, he managed to get them free. The rush of blood back into these temporarily paralyzed extremities was accompanied by a buzzing pain, as if the blood were being drawn the length of his veins by microscopic beasts of burden too large for the channels along which they struggled.

As he waited for sensation to return to his outstretched hands, he attempted to generate some moisture in his mouth and gingerly swiveled his head to take in the details of the place in which he found himself. It was a hotel room, and not a bad one. But where? His head, a pavilion where a drum corps played, felt enormous, echoey with the resounding tattoo of the drums; his tongue, a swollen sea creature, labored to raise itself from the arid bed where it had been beached by the flood of cognac he only dimly recalled consuming.

At last he was able to get to a sitting position on the side of the bed. He looked again at the room, involuntarily squinting at the daggers of sunlight piercing the edges of the curtains. He couldn't recall if he'd set his wristwatch ahead. If he had, and the time reflected was accurate, it was four in the afternoon. If he hadn't, it was eleven in the morning. He prayed it was still morning because it was going to take him at least an hour to assemble himself sufficiently to clean up, find a good amount of hot coffee, hire a car, and be on his way up to the Midlands.

There was, of course, the possibility that he already was in the Midlands. But, braving the glare, one look out the window confirmed he was in the environs of Heathrow. Below, a steady stream of traffic rolled, on the one side toward London, and on the other toward the various terminals. During those moments while he stood taking stock, his cumbrous head threatening to tumble from the fragile stem of his neck and his eyes shooting in and out of focus in protest against the hostile daylight, he suffered through several realizations: he'd managed to get pissed as a newt, he'd lost any number of precious hours to alcohol-induced amnesia, and he was in no fit condition to go claim the wife and kiddies. He only hoped he hadn't done anything aboard the aircraft which would result in his being barred, ever again, from flying British Airways. Air Canada had, several years ago, sent him a very harsh letter suggesting he refrain from imbibing if he cared to continue availing himself of their services. He'd had to switch over to American Airlines for a time when it was necessary for him to visit his New York agent. Bloody inconvenient it had been, too, when he'd finally managed to acquaint himself with all the loos in Terminal Two to have to switch to Terminal One.

The curtain back in place and the room cast once again into gloomy definition, he groped his way to the bathroom. A few seconds' experimentation with the bathroom light was ample illustration that the wisest course would be to shower in the dark. The compounded throb in his skull created both by his time at the window and the study of his wildly disheveled image in the mirror would be soothed only by a half-dozen aspirin, several cups of strong coffee, and some hair of the old dog.

Having shakily shed his clothes, he looked about for his suitcase, with relief spotted it standing to one side of the door, and made his way to it. Its bulk was too much for him. He sank to his knees on the low-pile carpet, maneuvered the case onto its back, and got it open. He had, thank God, remembered to pack his shaving kit, had even remembered to toss in a tin of aspirin tablets. He only wished he'd had the foresight to tuck a pint of something or other into the side pocket. Never mind. Sponge bag in hand, he returned to the bathroom, got the shower going, and lifted his heavy legs over the rim of the tub.

Ninety minutes later, wearing dark glasses, his valise having all but wrenched his shoulder from its socket, he was in a courtesy van driven by a young man whose aspirations plainly lay in the direction of Le Mans, toward the car he'd hired. The short ride left Martin nauseated, so that he had to sit behind the wheel of the hire-car for close to ten minutes before being able to turn the ignition key.

He ran a check of the interior workings of the machine: lights, turn indicators, windscreen wipers, petrol tank; he ran through the gears and then, having received directions out of the lot from the young man, shifted into first and made his way onto the access road.

The route came to him automatically. He left the M1 at the A422 and drove along the pleasant secondary road, stopping on impulse at a pub just outside Banbury, thinking to have a pint of bitters and something to eat. It was, however, off hours, and the pub was closed. He had to settle for a tearoom a little farther along the road, where he wolfed down several rounds of cheese and chutney, downed three cups of tea, left an enormous tip by British standards but only a fair-sized one by Canadian, and climbed back into the car.

Past Banbury he switched onto the A361 and drove at a more leisurely pace, awed by the lavish green of the rolling countryside. There was no green on earth like this: a green of such depth and liquidity that the foliage seemed to reach its tendrils right inside you; a green so intense it heightened the tones of everything else. Each of the golden Cotswold stone houses, and frequent small churches and outbuildings, seemed worthy of an individual portrait. For all his time spent away, every return trip to England renewed this shock of gratification, and he wondered again how he could bear to live anywhere else. Then, practicality overtaking the artist, he considered the taxes and knew why he continued to live in Canada.

At Chipping Norton he connected with the A44. Bourton-on-the-Hill was only a few miles distant. There was a small inn in Moreton-in-Marsh, and he booked in for a week. Being off season, the place was otherwise empty and he had his choice of rooms. He opted for a large corner one at the rear of the first floor, had a quick look round, left his suitcase just inside the door, and went back to the car.

He stood with his hand on the bonnet, the engine warmth transmitting itself to him through the metal, debating the wisdom of scouting out an off-license. If he did purchase a bottle, he'd be bound to take a drink, and he didn't want to arrive with any evidence on him of his continuing addiction. No, he'd wait until he'd seen Marian and the boys. Perhaps he'd take them to dinner at the hotel in Broadway; they'd celebrate their reunion.

Harry and Ian were at play in the garden at the side of the house. Martin parked on the verge and remained behind the wheel, content to watch the elaborate unwinding of their game. The interior warmth of the car was quickly dissipated by the drop in temperature as the late autumn sun was lost behind a Turneresque sky. The boys, red-cheeked and sturdy, had grown visibly taller and fuller in only a couple of months. They seemed less his own, suddenly, and he had an alarming intimation of the true impersonality of fathering children. It was possible that the time of their dependency on him was already past. If their self-involved play was anything to go by, the two of them needed only each other. And he marveled anew at the mystery of twins, two separate beings spawned from a single seed. The astonishment of Marian's fecundity had been immensely heightened for him when, in the delivery room, where he'd gained access by sheer stubbornness, the first miracle of birth had been followed by a second. No one had suggested that Marian might give birth to two infants, and so everyone present was elated when Marian's labor continued on after the delivery of a good-sized infant boy. Martin re-called the obstetrician's bemused expression as the man had stood between Marian's bedraped, blood-splattered thighs, announcing, "There's another one coming!" Martin recalled too how his presence, initially met with frowning disapproval, had melded into a memorable oneness as he and the doctor and the two nurses had assisted his wife through the second delivery.

Never in his life had he loved anyone more than he'd loved Marian at that time. He'd cradled her damp head to his chest, their hands tightly tangled, and the two of them had laughed together, and wept. Now, as he watched Harry and Ian play in the chaotic garden of a rented cottage in the south Midlands, he knew that whatever happened that time, at least, was his. He wondered whether Marian also cherished that memory.

Brimming with rekindled fondness and the need to have his family reunited, he got out of the car and walked across the road, led by his conviction that people who loved one another should not live separated by an ocean, and by an almost dizzying desire to do absolutely anything necessary to make this conviction generally understood.

The boys reacted to the sight of their father by standing stock-still for several seconds before breaking into ecstatic shouts as they flung themselves into his outstretched arms. The impact of their weight and substance on his body was the solid pleasure he'd imagined throughout the miles he'd traveled to get here. He held them, breathing in the grassy scent of their hair, as the front door opened and Marian, attracted by the boys' shouts, stepped outside.

In spite of herself, the sight of Martin with his arms spread to contain the boys, brought a wide smile to her mouth. Everything in her lifted on an interior gust of hope, and she sailed down the path to present herself into their midst, offering her mouth to his.

"Come home with me," he entreated her as they sat around the table in the cottage, the remains of their meal still on the table. "It's no good this way."

She studied his bloodshot eyes and the telltale yellowish pouches under his eyes and knew he hadn't yet found their bisected lives enough of an inducement to give up his drinking.

"It's time to get ready for bed," she told the boys. "You've got school in the morning."

Grumbling, the boys went off to do her bidding. She rose and began to clear the table. Martin followed her into the kitchen, carrying with him several of the serving dishes.

"You haven't given me an answer," he persisted, watching as she started hot water running in the sink, then added a squirt of Fairy Liquid—a product he'd always publicly denounced as being responsible for turning housewives sterile or producing from them children of doubtful sexual persuasion.

"I can't. Nothing's changed."

"Of course things have changed. The three of you are here, and I'm stuck alone in that bloody great Victorian relic. That's a change!"

"You're still drinking," she accused, turning. "You're sweating whiskey. No, I lie. It's brandy."

"Good God!" Abashed, he stood aside as she went back to the dining room for the rest of the dishes. The bloody woman had a nose like a bloodhound.

"All right, I had a few on the flight over," he admitted. "You know I can't board one of those beasts without help."

"More than a few," she observed coolly. "Your eyes . . . they look like roadmaps."

"You should see them from the inside," he quipped with a bark of laughter.

She laughed. The washing-up cloth in her hand, she rested against the sink for support and laughed until tears spilled from her eyes. "You bloody fool!" she gasped. "You absolute bloody fool!"

They made love with more heat and energy than they had in years. Sated, Marian fell into a deep sleep. Martin crept about the small bedroom collecting his clothes. In the chilly lounge he dressed, then located some paper and a Biro by the telephone and penned a hasty note saying he was returning to the hotel in Moreton-in-Marsh and would come back to the cottage later in the morning with his gear. Moving as quietly as possible, he left the note on the dining table where she was sure to find it, then let himself out. Dazed by the night cold, he dashed over the road to the car and put the shift into neutral, allowing the Cortina to roll down a slight incline away from the cottage. A hundred or so yards along, he got the engine started and headed back to his rented room.

Before he slept, he imagined Marian giving birth to another

child. The idea was captivating. "Go forth and multiply!" he intoned into the darkness, then chuckled contentedly to himself. In a few hours' time, he'd repack his bag and move into the cottage. They'd make plans for the return to Toronto. He saw a newly pregnant Marian and himself, the boys in tow, boarding a plane at Heathrow. She'd be ill with it, as she'd been with old Marks and Spencer, and he'd stroke the length of her spine as she suffered through the initial nausea. He'd brew cups of tea and take them in to her as she rested in the afternoons. And he'd work better than he ever had.

Suddenly, jarringly, there came to his mind a view of the partially demolished interior walls of the house, and he promised himself he'd make arrangements well in advance of their return home for the repair of the damage. He did very much like the idea of creating a gallerylike environment of the lower floor, but doubted Marian would endorse his plans. It was important to consider her feelings from now on; no more arbitrary or unilateral acts without due consultation.

He stood in the doorway of the cottage with an armload of flowers and his suitcase by his feet, and once again she fell victim to his charm. When he cared to make the effort, no detail was exempt from his personal attack on her defenses. She'd risen several hours earlier to get the boys fed and off to school, and once they'd gone, had suffered through varying aspects of guilt, anxiety, and indecision. It was all too obvious Martin intended they should return to Canada with him, and he was launching himself at her weak points with an unerring instinct for how best to win her over.

After tidying the bedrooms and clearing away the breakfast dishes, she had sat at the kitchen table with a fresh pot of tea, and for the better part of an hour had redefined for herself the pros and cons of the situation. On the one hand, she did love him, and there was no question that he reciprocated her feelings. He was a wonderful parent, his interest in the boys the most consistent thing about him. He was liberal with his income, offhandedly generous with surprise gifts and spontaneous outings. He was undeniably handsome, despite the fact that the drink was causing him to age far faster than he should, with a Nordic regularity to his features, gray eyes that were sometimes blue or green, and dark blond hair. He was sexually attentive and had the ability to make her feel good about her body. He had yet to come to terms with his alcoholism, however. Written down on paper, perhaps, in columns of debits and credits, that one debit might not appear significant in view of so many credits. That one debit, though, had been the cause of more upheaval in the last twelve years than anyone could have imagined. All she had to do was think back to dinner parties she'd arranged at which he'd failed to make an appearance, to theater outings he'd been too drunk to attend. She could recall, with a shiver of distaste, the besotted bedtime kisses he'd wetly planted on the faces of Harry and Ian, and she knew positively she was unwilling to pack up and return to that life.

She worked through all her reasons, found them entirely unchanged, and geared herself up for the inevitable confrontation. But when she opened the door to see him standing there, his arms laden with flowers and his face adorned with affection, her resolve simply evaporated. As she accepted the anemones, the freesias, and cornflowers, she knew she would probably go to her grave in love with this man, but she was determined not to resurrect their marriage.

"You're welcome to stay as long as you like," she informed him, "but the boys and I will not go back with you, Martin."

"You'll change your mind," he said confidently, measuring the circumference of her breast with his hand. "We'll knit ourselves up another infant, and that'll put paid to all these petty arguments."

"What makes you think I'm in the least interested in having another child?" she asked, forever fascinated by his sometimes childish logic.

"Well," he said with a smile, stroking the milk-white mound of her belly, "if we keep on at this, we're bound to, aren't we?"

"Surely to God you're not that simple-minded." She smiled back at him.

"What do you mean, simple-minded?"

"I've got a diaphragm, Martin. I've had it for years."

"You mean to tell me you're so premeditated that that little trip to the loo last night was so you could push a bit of rubber inside you?''

"If you call protecting oneself premeditation, then yes."

"Protecting one's 'self' against what?"

"I don't care to have any more children. I'm thirty-four years old. We've got two energetic, young boys. I'm not about to go back to changing nappies after all this time."

"I'm not averse," he said, his eyes glinting, "to reaching in and taking the damned thing out."

"Well, I certainly am!"

"All right." Seeing defeat in this area, he quickly retrenched. "Never mind, then. It makes no difference. I'm planning to stay on until you change your mind about coming back with me."

"It won't happen," she said softly. "Stop that for a moment and pay attention to what I'm trying to tell you." She captured his hands and held onto them. "I love you, and you know that. But the only way the boys and I will ever leave this place is if you stay sober for good. Not just a few days or weeks, Martin, but for months, years. I can't trust you anymore. You're all too capable of staying away from the drink just long enough to convince me, and then, the moment I've capitulated, you'll go straight back to it. It's happened too many times before."

"And precisely how am I supposed to prove myself to you if you're not there to see it?"

"I don't know. I honestly don't know. I'm simply no longer willing to gamble on your good intentions. Perhaps if you got some sort of professional help with—"

"Bugger that!" he snapped impatiently. "I'm perfectly capable of sorting myself out."

"You're *not!*" she declared in that same soft tone. "All these years later, there's only one thing I know as a certainty, and that's that you're categorically incapable of sorting it out yourself. If you were, you'd have come to grips with it long before now."

"That's torn it! Now I bloody well *will* prove it to you. I'll stop here for as long as it takes."

He gazed hard into her eyes, daring her to argue. She didn't.

"What about the house?" she asked at last.

"I'll make arrangements to see it's looked after. Well?"

She turned, presenting him with her splendidly defined profile, and gazed straight ahead for a long while. After a good five minutes, still staring ahead, she sighed and said, "I'm a fool, but all right." She turned back, revealing a hardened expression. "If you so much as set one foot in a pub, I'll turn you out."

"It won't happen," he promised. "It bloody well won't happen."

Chapter 7

THERE WAS ONLY one area where Caley's emotions held
steady: the ongoing grief she experienced each time she came
up against the visible truth that she no longer looked as she
once had. Every other arena of feelings was open to change at
any moment. She subjected Ron to an impossible scrutiny; his
every act, word, gesture, and facial expression underwent pro-
cessing. What did he *really* mean when his hand fell briefly on
her shoulder? Was he pitying her, or did his touch indicate a
continuation of his caring? When he said, "Things are going
nuts at the office," was he trying covertly to warn her that her
job was about to be given to someone else? Did his opting to
sleep on the sofa bed for the time being signify that he found
the sight of her repulsive?

It was impossible to maintain a stable grip on her emotions.
During the day, while Ron was at the office, she constructed
elaborate dreams around him. She listed mentally all his fine
qualities, and studied the deference he displayed toward her as
if she were a jeweler examining a gemstone through a loupe.
The facets of his goodness shifted, reflecting a light that
threatened to blind her with its illusion of warmth. By the end
of each day she'd managed to work herself into something approximating a fit of loving; she was in a state of complete
agitation until he came through the apartment door.

Once he was home, however, she recommenced her silent
examination of him. He was preoccupied, his thoughts still on
the business of the day; he was interested in a drink and in

what they were going to eat for dinner. His awareness of her seemed to float, drifting near, then away from her. She was debilitated. She wanted to pin down his love, fix it in place so that it was on permanent, accessible display. He didn't seem to recognize this need.

"I don't know what you want me to do," he lamented after five weeks of her surveillance. "Tell me what you want!"

She wasn't sure she could. If she risked putting words to her fear, he might act upon them. If she failed to communicate her doubts, he might act anyway, out of his inability to comprehend her terror of abandonment.

"There's something I want to show you," she told him, limping off to the bedroom. "I'll be right back."

Hands trembling, she opened the metal box and lifted out the file. Back in the living room she presented it into his hands. He looked up at her in confusion.

"What's this, Caley?"

"It's self-explanatory."

She watched for a few seconds as he lifted the cover of the file, then she hobbled away to the window where she stood looking down at the traffic on Strawberry Hill. The view from their eighth-floor apartment was a good one. She could see much of downtown Stamford and, in the distance, the waters of the Sound. She'd always thought that when she and Ron married they'd try to buy a small house near the water, in Riverside, or Old Greenwich, or even Stamford, although Stamford lacked the charm of the smaller towns. It was in the process of what the *Advocate* termed "urban renewal" with old buildings being demolished to make way for high-rise office towers. Many of the streets at the bottom end of town were being widened. The train station had had a face-lift, and work was going on improving the access ramps to the turnpike. When she'd first moved into the apartment with Ron, she'd enjoyed the novelty of so much space, and during that first summer they'd often sat out on the balcony in the dark to gaze down at the city, their words muted and all but lost in the heavy air. They hadn't used the balcony the previous summer. The furniture outside had rusted over the winter, and leaves now rustled against the metal panels enclosing the area. An ambulance approached up Bedford Street and she tracked its progress, guessing it was on its way to St. Joseph's Hospital a quarter-mile or so farther up Strawberry Hill.

Behind her she could hear Ron setting aside the pages of the file, one by one. She tried to ignore the sounds. Perhaps she'd come to regret having revealed any of this to him. He might find her worthy only of more pity, or even of ridicule. Dear God! She despised herself, and longed to be free of the crop of doubts and misgivings that seemed to ripen almost hourly. She no longer had any idea of how to live inside herself. She wanted a miracle, wanted to go to sleep and awaken in the morning with her face, and her life, intact. It appalled her to think of how much she'd taken for granted: simple things like a complete face with decent skin, and a body that functioned effectively, without pain. The pelvic fracture had entirely mended, according to the doctors, yet standing in place for just minutes created an ache in her lower body, and her shoulders felt disaligned, unbalanced as a result of the fractured clavicle. Altogether, she considered herself like a doll someone had smashed and then reassembled haphazardly.

"Cale?" Ron's hand came to rest on her shoulder. She remained motionless, tensely waiting, her breathing shallow. "Why didn't you tell me about this?"

"I've never told anyone."

"Did you really think it'd make any difference to me?"

"I don't know. It made a lot of difference to me, when I found out."

"Why? You're not an abandoned infant anymore. Could we sit down? It feels kind of peculiar just standing here."

She allowed him to direct her to the sofa where she sank into the cushions, sighing involuntarily at the relief. He sat in the armchair opposite, the coffee table between them, and leaned forward, his arms folded across his knees.

"Look, I'm sorry. About that"—he indicated the file on the table—"and about the accident. Has it occurred to you that maybe I feel a little guilty about what happened? I mean, maybe if I hadn't been in the passing lane, or if I'd insisted you put on your seatbelt . . . I don't know. I just don't want you to think I've put the whole thing out of my mind and forgotten I had a part in it. It really wasn't my fault."

"I know that." Her mouth was dry. "I don't blame you."

"You blame me for something, though. I wish to hell I knew what. You go around here glaring at me, as if you're waiting for me to do or say something that'll give me away. I know it's been really rough on you, and I've given it a lot of thought. A lot." He reached for his cigarettes. After lighting one, he said, "Maybe it'd help you to talk to someone—professionally."

"I'm not crazy! I haven't gone out of my mind!" She was horribly offended.

"Slow down! Nobody's saying you're crazy. It could be we both need to talk to someone. We're not doing all that well trying to talk to each other. I keep having this feeling you're waiting for me to slip up and prove what a bastard I really am. I'm trying my best."

"Then why're you still sleeping on the sofa bed?" she burst out.

"Because I thought you wanted it that way. I was trying to be considerate. If that's what's bothering you, no problem. I can move back into the bedroom any time."

Uncle Sam appeared in the kitchen doorway and posed with his back arched before padding across the room to the sofa. He struck now a thoughtful, considering pose and, after a moment, leaped up onto the far end of the sofa and strolled nonchalantly over the pillows to Caley. With a brief look at her, he decided permission was implicit, and he walked into her lap, tucked his tail under his haunches, and settled in. Instinctively, her hand began to stroke his deep gray fur. She could feel his contented vibrations against her belly. Ron observed their communion, wishing he could, with as little effort as Uncle Sam, reassure her with his presence.

"I'll move back into the bedroom tonight," he informed her, drawing hard on his cigarette.

"I hate sleeping alone," she confessed. "We don't have to make love. . . ."

"Isn't it still a little soon?"

All at once she was able to read his fear. So far, he'd done a masterful job of concealing it, but this conversational tangent gave him away. Instead of arousing her sympathy, or anger, he simply made her sad. The sadness was partnered by a sudden, frightening insight: he really was trying his best, but she was going to drive him away. Their life together was going to end because it wasn't primary to him, and it was to her. The two of them had priorities that weren't entirely dissimilar, but their orders of significance were diametrically opposed. For her, the emotional climate of existence had paramount importance, and a job was just something most people had to have in order to survive. For Ron, his career was the central focus, and his emotional life placed second, or even third, on the list. She couldn't see how they'd ever reconcile this.

"We don't have to make love," she said again. "I'm not suggesting it. I'd only like to know you're there, beside me." Her eyes fell on Uncle Sam, now heavily asleep in her lap. Her hand continued its stroking of his luxurious pelt. "You know," she said huskily, "I wish they'd never told me. I mean, as far as I was concerned, they were my parents. I had a good childhood. It wasn't until I was in my teens that I noticed how old they were. But I rationalized it. I was one of those 'late in life' babies people have by accident, that sort of thing. They gave me that file, and all of a sudden I wasn't who I thought I was anymore."

"I can imagine."

"Maybe you can. I still haven't managed to get over it. Once in a while I'll look at those newspaper clippings and try to get back the sense I had of belonging, of having a rightful place. They gave me the file on my sixteenth birthday, and it was as if everything just stopped. There was a terrible silence. I'll never forget it. They sat and watched me read all the stuff, and the silence was like a howling in my ears. 'We thought you should know,' my mother told me. 'But I guess it was a mistake, after all.' They gave me a home, and a name, and then they took it all away again. I sound like an angry child," she said, her voice distorted.

"I'd be angry, too, Cale. Anybody would. The thing is, though, I'm having a little trouble putting all that past history together with what's going on here right now. I could use some help."

"I thought showing you the file would help. It's probably only made things worse."

"Come on. You're feeling kind of sorry for yourself. It hasn't made a bit of difference to me."

"I shouldn't feel sorry for myself, should I? I should be like one of those wonderfully inspirational articles in *Family Circle* or *Woman's Day*, one of those first-person stories about how I've survived and triumphed against the unbelievable odds. A tidy, wholesome article wedged between the latest diet and helpful hints on what to do with empty coffee cans. I don't happen to feel that way. I'm scared to take the garbage down the hall to the chute in case another one of the neighbors happens to see me. It's happened twice now, and you should see! They don't know whether to laugh or go crazy. I can just see them rushing back to their apartments to say, 'My God, Harry! I just saw a woman in the incinerator room, and she didn't have a *nose!*' "

Ron laughed.

"That strikes you funny?"

"It *is* funny," he said almost entreatingly.

"Well, maybe if we had your nose amputated by that lunatic Morgan, we'd be on equal footing here."

"Maybe, if it'd do any good." His unexpected agreement effectively silenced her. He put his cigarette out and then, straightening, said, "Listen. I'm over the first shock of it.To me, you're the same as you ever were. I think it's pretty encouraging that your sense of humor's coming back." He got up from the chair and came around the coffee table to sit beside her. "Scram, Sam!" He shooed the cat from her lap, then took hold of her hand. "There's a lot about all kinds of things I don't understand. I'm just a small-town boy from Norwalk, Cale. My dad was an insurance broker and my mom just looked after me and my brothers. They thought Mantovani was pretty high-brow music, for Pete's sake. All the guys I went to grade school and high school with have been married for years. Hell, most of them're on their second and third marriages. They've all got kids, and they listen to Mantovani. Do you follow what I'm saying? I never said I was a whiz at appreciating subtleties. I'll admit it was a hell of a shock seeing you when they first took off the bandages. But it's a lot better now, and it'll be better still when the rest of the surgery's finished. I mean, you're not going to look the way you do now for the rest of your life."

"I'd kill myself if I did."

"Don't talk that way! I'll tell you one thing. I'd get rid of that"—he again indicated the folder—"stop thinking about it. It doesn't do you any good that I can see. It's like keeping a dead body in the bedroom, stinking things up."

"I want to stop feeling this way." She left her head rest against his shoulder. "I want to stop feeling like a freak. It's only since the accident that the clippings have begun to bother me again. I'd actually forgotten all about them. Then, lying in that damned bed, I started thinking about it again."

"Then toss them out."

"I can't, not yet."

"Okay. It's up to you. But you've got to give things a chance. Sure, some people're going to be bothered. That's kind of inevitable, I suppose. But there're going to be lots of people who won't be bothered. You'll see. It depends on you, too, you know. I mean, if you go around thinking of yourself as a freak, and acting as if you think it, then people're going to react to that. So, what you've got to do is try to act as if you're aware of what's going down, but you're still the same person. Does that make sense? I think it makes sense."

"I'm tired," she backed away. "I spent too much time on my feet today."

"Let's get you to bed, then."

He gave her a hand up from the sofa, saying, "I've got some work to do before I hit the sack. Maybe an hour's worth."

"Okay. I think I'll try sitting in the tub for a while. Will you come give me some help when it's time to get out?"

"Sure."

She sat in the tub with her cast-enclosed left leg suspended on the rim, the chest-high hot water drawing the ache from her body. Ron spoke of keeping a grip on her sense of humor. It certainly struck her as funny each time she slid, bum first, into the hot water in order to keep her cast dry. She examined, for at least the fiftieth time, the areas of her hips from which the grafts had been taken. The new skin looked paler and thinner than the surrounding flesh, and the areas were clearly demarcated by a perimeter of faintly raised scar tissue. Her upper left thigh had a withered look to it, and the skin there was only just regaining some appearance of normalcy. When the cast had been removed, her skin was revealed to be in shreds. The daily and nightly applications of moisturizing lotion had restored the tone, but the previous fullness was still missing.

"Shit!" she whispered, sickened by the sight of her body. What was she thinking of, talking about making love with Ron? If she could scarcely bear the sight of herself, how was he supposed to deal with it? She would have to stop pressuring him. Objectively, he appeared to be making more progress coming to terms with the situation than she was. But his thought processes were unimpeded by anguish. Could her mind have been depicted diagrammatically, it would have appeared as a deeply rutted roadway where travel was, at best, inauspicious.

He helped her from the tub, saw her into bed, then returned to the living room, where he sat with his open briefcase on the coffee table, telling himself to get to work. He couldn't begin. Guilt and self-dislike held him suspended. He was saying things he knew she wanted to hear, demonstrating an affection he didn't quite feel. Why didn't he have the courage to tell her how the sight of her distressed him, made him wince internally? He was trying to prove what a good guy he was, how adept he could be at rising to the moment. It was all deceit.

The contents of her file had aroused in him a strain of contempt for her. She had actively sought his sympathy, and he'd responded only with negative reactions he'd felt forced to conceal behind a barrage of philosophical platitudes. He was saying and doing things in order to assuage the guilt, but rather than alleviating the grubbiness he felt, his words and deeds compounded it. He was becoming entangled in a net devised of untruths, and wished he could cut free. Instead of admitting to an understanding he didn't possess, he wished he'd had the guts to say, "Look! I don't know how to handle this. I don't even know if I *want* to handle it." Instead, with a kind of distorted etiquette, he was showing his party manners. As a result he had a rapidly growing case of malaise. All his hopes for a resolution were pinned on her next rounds of surgery, from which he was certain she'd emerge restored. Then his somewhat fraudulent efforts would have been to the good, and he'd be able to continue on into the future with her, justified in having made these repeated dishonest attempts to console and bolster her. But what if something went wrong? What if she came out looking much as she did now, or worse? There was no way he could commit himself to her under those circumstances. He couldn't, just then, conceive of spending the rest of his life with a woman so disfigured that everywhere they went people would speculate on the nature of the accident she'd had. They'd look at him and wonder if he wasn't with her out of guilt for having caused the accident, and how was he supposed to enjoy life with everyone believing him guilty of something he hadn't done?

He gazed blankly at the paperwork awaiting his attention, searching for something that would validate the terrible, continuing dishonesty of almost every word he uttered to this woman he'd loved above all others until only weeks ago. He came back again and again to her future operations. If her face could be restored, he'd be able to live with her. Her body was all right, or would be, once the last of the fractures had fully mended. He wasn't bothered by the areas on her hips where the grafts had been taken, or by the shrunken look of her left leg. No, it was her face. He knew, and hated himself for it, that he was one of the people who, had he not known her, would stare, horrified, before turning away with relief. The realization shamed him utterly. He should have been big enough, his caring should have been such, that he was grateful she was alive. Maybe he just didn't love her as much as he'd thought all along that he did, and because of this, he'd go on and on holding these scummy little pep rallies, working to build her ego to the point where she was strong enough to withstand the truth when it came.

Christ! He hated himself. She was going through hell, and all he could think about was himself. It wasn't right. He was going to have to dig deeper, look more closely at his feelings.

He wiped his damp hands down the sides of his trousers, lit a fresh cigarette, and reached for the paperwork waiting in the bed of his briefcase. He was having trouble paying attention to his work. All he needed was to screw up on the job because of all this, then they'd both be in big trouble. Why the hell hadn't he told her to fasten her seatbelt? Usually, it was an automatic instruction, but they'd been having a minor argument that night. He couldn't even remember now what it had been about.

She woke up for a few minutes around three A.M. and opened her eyes to see Ron asleep on his side of the bed. He slept, as he always had, almost without moving. She smiled in the darkness, touching her hand lightly to his shoulder as if to prove that he was, indeed, there. Then, heartened, she eased back into sleep.

Chapter 8

MARTIN SAT ON the far side of the road and sketched the boys as they played. He worked rapidly, his hand and eyes linked in dynamic concert. The absence of alcohol was having a strange effect upon him. He felt oddly light-headed and receptive, as if his prior consumption of drink had been blocking the thrust of his skills. With that block gone, his efforts were amended to the good, his visions translating into sketches that revealed themselves with such an incredible confluence of motion and roundness that he wanted to spend his every waking moment witnessing the process. He was feverish with creativity and ready, after seven weeks, to begin transferring some of the sketches to canvas.

He drove up to Stratford, where he was certain there'd be an artists' supply outlet. The car, an old Rover he'd bought through an advertisement in the local newspaper, was a spectacular ruin. On the weekends he and Marian and the boys had taken to driving around the countryside, investigating nearby towns and villages. He'd also bought a camera with a full complement of lenses, and took dozens of rolls of film, thinking to capture forever what he saw as the genesis of his life. All that had gone before had been merely preliminary to this, his actual beginning, and he meant to keep a record of it. He was discovering he not only enjoyed the rather arcane mechanics of the camera but also that this was an intriguing way to broaden his scope. He'd dabbled with cameras briefly while at art college, but had always dismissed photography as a craft for those who couldn't paint. He saw now that photography itself could be a viable art form. He disassembled the camera in order to study its inner workings, infatuated with and mystified by the entrapment of reality on a slim strand of celluloid.

Leaving the Rover in a car park, he strolled into the center of town, stopping to look in the windows of the Midlands Educational Centre. There were artists' supplies on display inside, and he pushed into the shop to see if what he needed might be available here.

He emerged with a parcel of Reeves watercolors and newsprint blocks for the boys, and directions to another shop where he'd be able to purchase canvas and stretchers and the tubes of oils and the brushes he was after.

He spent the morning sauntering through town, his purchases safely stored in the boot of the Rover, then stopped for something to eat at the Cobweb. He climbed the steep, irregular flight of steps from the ground floor up to the restaurant. The place was bloody ancient and chockablock with tourist goodies, but he liked its grotty quaintness, and positioned himself at a small rickety table by the casement windows, where he could watch people passing on the street below and in the restaurant itself.

The coffee was the best he'd so far had, served with heavy cream, and the Welsh rarebit had a nice mustardy bite to it. With a second cup of coffee, he sat back to look at the other patrons, listening with amusement to three American girls with backpacks natter about Coventry Cathedral, which was evidently where they were headed. He liked the look of them, robust and ripe. Their faces still had the softness of childhood, but the bones were beginning to shift closer to the surface so that one could readily see the definition of the women they'd soon be. American kids always looked so bloody healthy, as if they'd been fed special diets to grow that long, glossy hair and those big white teeth. It was the food, of course. Undoubtedly the Kellogg's company put steroids or somesuch in the corn flakes. And all that disgusting squidgy Wonder Bread they consumed. Chemicals ingested with their Twinkies.

It had started to rain and he drove with care back to Bourton-on-the-Hill. Marian clung to her wariness, doubtful of his tenacity, and he worked daily to prove to her that he intended to keep off the booze for good. They'd established a routine quite unlike the one they'd had in Toronto, where, because of all sorts of pressures both personal and professional, their time had been much in demand. Here, the routine revolved around the boys' departure for school in the morning and their return home in the afternoon. Marian busied herself with marketing, with keeping up her correspondence with friends, and with cleaning and cooking and laundry. She seemed to thrive on the ordinary, Martin observed; she'd never looked better or been more at ease. She left him free to paint or practice photography, and had offered no argument when he'd commandeered the shed for a darkroom.

He set up his newly bought easel by the windows in the lounge, then spent the remainder of the afternoon stretching and priming a number of canvases.

"I take it you've decided to set up shop in the lounge," Marian said at tea.

"If you object . . ."

She laughed. "I don't object," she cut him off, still unused to his new determination to accommodate her. She was already thinking of things they'd do once they returned to Canada, of plans she had to redecorate the boys' rooms. It was becoming daily clearer that Martin intended to make good his promise, and this realization left her free to enjoy him. She did wonder, each time he went off in the battered Rover, if he wouldn't come back red-eyed with drink. When he continued to return as sober as he'd gone off, her guard gradually lowered. "Are you planning to paint the boys?" she asked.

"The entire family." He grinned at her. "Get you in there too, my girl. Maybe push the old sod himself somewhere into the background. Right, Marks? Right, Spencer?"

The boys chortled, titivated always by Martin's swearing. His use of words strictly forbidden to them made him seem fabulously wicked, daring. Their tales of his exploits took their classmates' breath away, and some of the boys had started offering small bribes—a Kit-Kat, half a pack of Opal Fruits, a comic—in order to garner an invitation to the cottage to meet Harry and Ian's famous dad.

•   •   •

Marian astonished him by agreeing to pose.

"I don't mind," she said with studied offhandedness.

He didn't dare ask what had changed her mind after all these years; he didn't want to give her an opportunity to change it back again.

"Get those clothes off, then," he told her, "and be sharp about it. The light's good just now."

Her shyness was touching as she sat in the Queen Anne chair he'd set before the window. She couldn't seem to look directly at him, as if the contact of their eyes might shatter this fragile newly formed alliance of purpose. He sketched in charcoal directly onto one of the freshly prepared, larger canvases, making notes in pencil on the side about the quality and tone of the light; reminders to suggest to him later on that ocher and a dash of burnt umber would go well with the flesh tones. She sat, her lovely profile highlighted by the wet glow from the window, her knees turned to one side, one shapely arm resting on the windowsill.

He kept falling in love with her. On this particular morning, he adored the wheat shades of the hair that fell in a slippery line over her shoulder; the plumpness of her breasts and belly were perfectly offset by the long lines of her torso and legs. Her composition was an invitation and a challenge. If he could, in this profoundly receptive new state of being, capture all her beauty as well as his immense caring for her, he would at last succeed in forging a permanent and ongoing communication between eye and heart and hand. This painting and the one he'd started of the boys would, along with the nearly completed one in the Toronto studio, be the basis of his family series. He intended to document what he had come to value most: the unity of his family, and its currency of loving.

Marian viewed the morning sun lifting by degrees until it rode the crest of the sky, her initial embarrassment forgotten. She watched the dew evaporate from the bushes and flowers in the front garden, tracked the progress of an inquisitive squirrel as it darted, then paused, then darted on. As she immersed herself in the details of the countless small activities taking place immediately beyond the window, serenity saturated her. She felt enclosed, almost impenetrably, by the weightless certainty of well-being.

At the very point when she'd resigned herself to a life alone with her sons, believing Martin to be well beyond redemption, he'd come in pursuit, eager to prove her wrong. To be proved wrong suited her perfectly; being loved by a man in full control of his faculties was all she'd ever really needed or wanted. His love lay like silk upon her skin; she felt cloaked in it, secure. This time he really was going to keep his promise; she knew it. The knowledge aroused in her a protectiveness toward him, as well as the sense of her own secureness. Love, like armor, could shield them, could create an effective wall around them, chinkless, seamless. It was only the fear of losing that love that had created rifts through which other realities could penetrate. With that fear all but erased, it was possible for them to coexist peacefully. The minor irritations inherent in any situation where very different types of people tried to live together were acceptable because they truly didn't matter. So what if Martin simply abandoned his clothes at day's end, leaving them wherever they happened to fall? So what if life with three males meant having always to check that the seat on the loo was down? Martin had become engaged, finally, had become an integral part of *them*. It made her happy.

He completed the roughing in within three hours, just when the light became too sharply hot. He lowered his hand, setting aside what remained of the charcoal stick, and stood, for a final moment, examining his vision. Marian had remained motionless, contained, for hours. That, in itself, was extraordinary. Even more extraordinary was the sense he'd had throughout this time of their acting in concert, of a tacit unity of purpose. In the absence of alcoholic stimulation he'd located within himself a more potent source of energy: his undiluted emotions. With it came a recognition of the need to move prudently; too-loud celebration might shatter their transparent containment.

She turned as he approached. He knelt on the worn floor before her and laid his head in the yielding warmth of her lap. Her hand came to rest on his hair as she turned once more to witness the passage of time across the garden, noticing how the undersides of the leaves now reflected the transient light.

• • •

The paintings consumed him. He drew constantly, filling notebooks one after another; references for future works. He'd set aside his knife and fork during a meal to pick up pencil and paper, caught by the line of Harry's neck as he bent to his food. His hand flew across the page, working frenetically to capture the image of his wife and children feeding morsels of carrot to the hesitant deer at Charlcote Park.

He sat on the bathroom floor with his back against the wall and a pad propped against his knees, sketching Marian in the tub, her hair escaping in damp tendrils from the hasty knot atop her head, her arms and shoulders glistening. Heady from the oily perfume rising from the bathwater, he set aside the drawing in order to gather the moistly scented, slippery wealth of the woman into his arms. He held her amused face in his hands, smiling down at her.

"Ah, the hell with it!" he said and climbed, fully dressed, into the tub.

"You're mad!" she laughed, going without argument into his beckoning arms. "You're absolutely mad!"

"No fear," he countered. "My watch is waterproof."

She sat away from him after a time, thoughtfully turning the soap in her hands. He watched, hourly more taken by everything about her: the length of her fingers, the suppleness of her arms, the glossy shifting of her breasts as she breathed.

"It's good for you here, Martin. You're starting to look more your age." Her eyes rested comfortably upon him.

"You mean I no longer look like a dissipated old codger?"

"I mean you're looking thirty-six instead of fifty. You've lost those frightful pouches under your eyes."

"Good, clean living, regular baths." He splashed the water lightly with the flat of his hand, chuckling at his own foolishness.

"You're enjoying it here," she persisted. "In a way, I wish we didn't have to go back."

She'd made up her mind that they'd return to Canada together. He had to stifle his sudden jubilant impulse to crow.

"We've got to go back," he said. "It's a matter of taxes. You know that."

"I know. It's just that things are so much simpler here."

"Tell you what. We'll buy a place in the area, come back for the summers."

"I'd adore it!" She smiled radiantly. "It'd be good for the boys, too."

"I'll ring up old Shipley and find out what he'll allow us to spend. You look rather fetching yourself, you know."

"Do you think about it constantly? Do you keep finding yourself wanting a drink?"

He nodded, serious for the moment. "Seventy or eighty times a day."

"I know how difficult it is for you."

"There are worse things," he said, playing it down. "It gets easier as the days pass. I might become one of those sanctimonious types, all puffed up with self-righteousness, who go about lecturing others on the evils of drink."

"I expect you'll become a superb bartender, one of the types who's forever refilling the glasses, taking a somewhat malicious pleasure in seeing everyone else get pissed while you stay sober."

"That's possible, highly possible."

"You might as well take off those clothes. I'll leave them to soak overnight."

"I'm quite happy." He smiled again at her. "I could just lather up the lot, give them a rinse, and get on with it. Give an entirely new meaning to wash and wear."

She laughed softly, enjoying the echoey quality the ornately tiled walls and low ceiling gave their words.

"I love you," he said, aware under his hands of the cool porcelain tub rim.

"I've always loved you, Martin. I don't think I could ever care for anyone else as I do you. No one else makes me laugh."

"No one else better bloody try."

"Are you going to take off those clothes?"

"Oh, someday. One never knows."

"You seem busy, but are you honestly finding enough to keep you occupied?"

"More than enough. Don't worry," he said quietly. "I'm not going to go back on my promise."

"I know that. I'm simply afraid you'll get bored."

"Not possible. The only time in my entire life I've ever been bored was when you and the boys left."

"Good." She returned the soap to the dish positioned between the faucets. "I'm starting to get chilled. I do miss the central heating."

"I could arrange for some personalized central heating, if you're at all interested."

"I'll consider it." She rose and reached for a towel.

"I think these things are shrinking," he said, plucking at his trousers. "I recall seeing an American film once upon a time that showed a number of delectable nymphets in blue jeans sitting in bathtubs filled with hot water to make the jeans shrink. I don't suppose it'll have the desired effect on corduroy."

"I don't suppose it will," she agreed, toweling dry. "But you're welcome to stay in there and find out. Mother rang this afternoon while you were out."

"How is the old beauty?" he asked with affection.

"A bit under the weather. She rang to ask if we'd care to come down at the weekend. I said I'd speak to you."

"We'll go Friday. I wouldn't mind including her in the family album."

"What does that mean?"

"I'll do some drawings."

"Good God, Martin! You'll drive her round the twist. Not everyone's in favor of having her every move documented by a mad artist."

"She'll love it. I'm willing to wager there's a nude portrait of your mum hanging on some old duke's bedroom wall."

"Martin! You're talking about my *mother*."

"You tend to think that mothers don't get up to that sort of thing. How d'you suppose she had you? I've always wondered about that. I've never for a moment believed that cantankerous old ferret could've fathered you. I'll wager anything you care to name old Grace has a few secrets tucked up her knickers."

"You're vile!" She draped the towel on the rail to dry.

"Part of my charm."

Her nightgown over her arm, she started toward the door. "If you don't hurry, I'll be asleep."

"Well, why didn't you say so?" At once he pulled the plug and began shedding his sodden clothes.

In the dry attic paintings began to accumulate. They leaned together against the inclining stone walls, ranked according to size. Several times a week, Martin climbed the rickety ladder and pushed up through the trapdoor into the low-ceilinged area, able to stand fully erect only at the roof's peak. In a crouch, he arranged the paintings face outward to study them in the dusty light offered by the single grimy window set in the northern face of the roof.

The boys tumbled about in the garden, their shouts and whispers clearly audible. Directly below, Marian moved about in the kitchen. Martin sat on his haunches seeking flaws. All it took were the sounds being generated below to fix indelibly in his mind the true look and feel, the actual sound and scent of his boys, his wife. Those sounds might have issued from the portraits themselves, so successful were they.

The paintings one by one returned to their places against the wall, he remained a moment longer, breathing slowly, deeply. He could readily imagine the excitement his agent would display upon sight of this work. The question that nettled him was whether or not he'd ever be able to part with any one of these images. It was possible that he might live out the remainder of his life unable to be separated from them.

"Come walk with me, Martin." Grace stood by the French windows, the afternoon light behind her going gray with impending rain.

At once he set aside the copy of *Queen* he'd been holding. Marian and the boys had gone upstairs to nap after the heavy midday meal, and he'd been sitting for at least ten minutes, gazing at the cover of the magazine, the threat of sleep overtaking him. He much preferred the idea of a walk with his mother-in-law. Afternoon naps usually meant being up half the night, unable to sleep while the rest of the household lay locked in nocturnal communication with their subconscious stirrings.

Grace stepped out onto the terrace and he followed, stopping a moment to secure the doors before falling in at Grace's side, impressed as ever by the innate elegance of her carriage.

"You're looking well, Grace," he said, and watched her raise her hand as if to deflect the compliment.

"Marian looks better than I've ever seen her," she said, stooping to pluck several dead blooms from a bush. Martin couldn't identify the flowers. He was useless when it came to gardens. Grace spent hours each day on hers, examining the profuse, meticulously planned beds. "I knew you'd come for her," she went on, dropping the deadheads into a bushel basket to one side of the path. This garden, the focal point of so many of her days, was over two hundred years old. From family to family, it had been passed as a living legacy. Each resident family had dutifully clipped and pruned and dead-headed, according to custom. The very thought of it made Martin yawn.

"You did, did you?" he asked with a smile.

"Yes, I did," she replied, choosing not to respond to his smile. "If you hadn't, I'd have been most surprised."

"Really? Why?"

"Because I've never thought you capable of a callous act. And because I do believe the two of you love each other, despite your sometime differences."

"*My* sometime difference," he said, "has to do with drink."

"Oh, I know that, Martin." She bestowed upon him a delayed but approving smile. "It's rather disconcerting to see you go a day and a night without so much as a thimbleful of sherry." She slid her arm through his as they continued along the path. The rising wind played at her hair, attempting to free it from the cautious twist she'd worn as long as he'd known her. "Let's walk to the bench." She pointed ahead to where the path circled back. At the apex of the circle was a curved stone bench, flanked by stolid urns filled with Michaelmas daisies.

The bench was still warm from the sun that had, only in the last half-hour, been superseded by rain-filled clouds. They sat side by side, Martin with his legs extended and crossed at the ankles. Grace, her knees touching and turned slightly toward him, leaned back on her hands, her expression reflective.

"Do you think you'll be able to see it through?" she asked.

"Oh, I think so," he answered airily. "I may end up crazed, rooting in the dirt with my nose like some pig searching out truffles, but I think so."

"Everything isn't a joke." She pushed the silver-streaked, still-blond hair back from her forehead. "Over the years, I've noticed that you tell the most jokes when the situation is the most serious. Is it intentional? Are you aware of it?"

He nodded, finding himself becoming entrapped in her mood. She was a woman of formidable intelligence. He'd never been able to fool her.

"It's the way I am," he said, knowing she wouldn't accept this as suitable justification.

"That's too simple," she said at once. "The way you are is infinitely more complex than you would have one believe. Do you honestly think you'll stay off the drink?"

"I have to. Would you consider sitting for me for an hour or so?"

"I expect so, but don't change the subject. *Will* you stay the course?"

"It's already been sixty-seven days," he said, caught by the Pampas grass bowing to the wind.

"Counting days." She sighed and shook her head. "I hope for everyone's sake you manage to see it through."

"Don't you mind rattling round this superannuated pile of rubble all on your own?"

"Not at all. If the truth be known, I've never enjoyed the house more. Hugh and I didn't get on all that well. He had such a frightful temper. Luckily, Marian doesn't seem to have been affected by it. If he hadn't died, I'd have left him. It had gone well past the point where keeping the family together for Marian's sake was a reasonable excuse."

"Then why did you stick with him?"

"Habit," she said simply. "Just like your drinking." She smiled again, and he could see Marian in her mother, the distillation of this woman. Both had magnificently aristocratic profiles, strong chins, well-placed eyes. In her late fifties, Grace had the appearance of a much younger woman, but the set of her shoulders and the erectness of her chin indicated the tremendous discipline she'd exercised throughout much of her life, the practices circumspection and incisiveness that had allowed her to survive her marriage relatively intact. "I loathed him," she admitted, traces of color riding her cheeks as if an interior flame had suddenly been lit. "He represented everything I dislike: arrogance, self-absorption, unreasoning anger. He was a dismal husband and a worse father. It's why I set such store in your and Marian's marriage," she explained. "Because it was evident from the outset that yours was a love match. I sound like one of those tiresome old women"—she laughed—"who spend their dotages cooing over the romances of the young. It isn't at all what I mean. Over the years, I've watched the way you look at Marian, how your eyes follow her so admiringly."

"She's a bloody beautiful woman."

"No. It's more than that. There you go again, making light. You watch her as if you're afraid she might go into a room where you couldn't follow."

The image distressed him; she'd managed to put his precise feelings into words. "You're a canny old thing, aren't you?" He patted her knee. "Don't miss a bloody thing, do you?"

"It's the people like me, Martin, who really do know about love. We've spent our entire lives studying it from a distance. We know precisely the look and feel of it. The difficulty is we've never been fortunate enough to have it for ourselves." She spoke without a trace of self-pity, as a teacher might to a recalcitrant student. "We'd best start back to the house now. The rain's due at any moment."

As they neared the terrace, she stopped him, her hand on his arm. "I care very much for you. You're as much my child as Marian, so I feel it's my right to play mother to you, from time to time. You're stronger than you realize, Martin. The truly weak people, like Hugh, for example, simply give in. If it gets difficult, you're always welcome here."

"Thank you." He held open the French doors and allowed her to precede him inside. He gazed at her, captivated by her contrasts: all tweeds, matched pearls and sensible shoes, she looked as if the most serious notion she'd ever entertained might be what to serve the bridge group for tea. In fact, she was one of the most intensely serious-minded, passionate people he'd ever known. "Grace," he called, halting her progress. "How would tonight after dinner be? For an hour or so?"

"What's it in aid of?" Her smile now was girlish.

"I'm doing portraits of the lot of you, myself included."

"I would be"—she paused significantly—"honored to sit for you."

"Ah," he said, going instantly Highland, "you're a lovely auld girl."

"You"—she waved a heavily beringed hand, the spoils of marriage glinting on her fingers—"are a charming scoundrel. I'll see you at dinner." She continued on her way out through the drawing room.

He stood and watched the rain overtake the garden. It came with gusting winds that thrashed through the Pampas grass and forced the flowering bushes almost to the ground.

Chapter 9

IN THE FEW SECONDS between the administering of the anesthetic into her arm and its effect, her attention was drawn to the surgeon, covered from head to toe in pale blue surgical garb. Something was wrong. It wasn't O'Connor. Fear rocketed through her system. She wanted to protest, to halt the procedure, but already her head was dropping heavily back onto the table; her mouth filled with the bitter taste of the drug, and she was under.

"Morgan was able to step in at the last moment," Dawson was explaining the next day. "O'Connor had a personal emergency. Look, there's nothing to worry about. It was a straightforward procedure, one Morgan's done hundreds of times. I can't say I'm personally crazy about his bedside manner, but as surgeons go in this field, he's one of the best. You should see some of the work he's done on facial cancers."

"He dislikes me." She could hear the strains of paranoia in her voice. "And you didn't think the work he did the first time was all that great."

"I never said that! I might have disagreed with his choice of procedures, but as far as what he did goes, everything was strictly by the book. Look, Caley, be reasonable. Think for a minute about what you're saying. No professional's going to let his personal feelings—allowing for the moment that he even *has* any about you—interfere with his work."

"We'll find out soon enough," she said, unable to keep the anxious edge off her voice.

"Take it easy. The procedure was a success."

"According to Morgan."

"That's right. I can appreciate how upsetting all of this has been for you, but you have to understand that no surgical procedure's guaranteed foolproof. Things go wrong all the time, for no reason anyone can pin down. In ten days, once the blood flow has been established from the flap, it'll be cut, and you'll be more than halfway there. A quick trip back into the O.R. after that, and all this will be finished. Rest now and I'll see you tomorrow."

He left and she moved to get up. At least she wasn't confined to bed. As she limped along the linoleum corridor the elevator doors opened and a group of people emerged. The hospital staff paid her no attention, but of those who had come to visit patients more than half glanced at her, undoubtedly speculating on what was hidden beneath the scarf she'd draped over her face to conceal her features. The scarf was vital; it prompted only speculation. She had refused to look at herself, and wouldn't until the operation had been declared a success and she was free to go home and wait out the days until the last trip to this place would come due.

It no longer bothered her to have people see her in her dressing gown and slippers. Being in the hospital validated every aspect of her appearance. Relieved to find the solarium deserted, she sat in one of the modern armchairs by the window and looked at the thriving plants positioned in clusters around the open-ended area. The heat of the room was not unpleasant, and she relaxed, wishing she had something to drink. Her mouth was constantly dry, due to the necessity of breathing open-mouthed. It was amazing, really, how much people took for granted about their own anatomies. Until you didn't have a nose, you didn't give much consideration to all it did for you.

Ron had promised to stop by on his lunch hour, and she waited, trying to rid herself of the ominous thought that Morgan's involvement in her surgery would have disastrous results. But Jesus, the guy was a nutcase. Anybody could see it. How could they let someone like that mess with people's lives? And why hadn't they just postponed the operation when they'd learned O'Connor wasn't going to be able to be there?

Ron came rushing in, almost at a run. "Hi. Hey, I just talked to the guy at the insurance company who's handling our claim." He spoke eagerly, unbuttoning his coat as he perched on the edge of an adjacent chair. "He says they're pretty sure they can get you a good out-of-court settlement. The other company isn't going to want to go to court because it's bound to cost them a hell of a lot more."

"Why hasn't anybody talked to me about this?" she asked, the scarf hampering her vision. "Maybe I'd like to go to court."

"You wouldn't want to do that, Cale. A court case could go on for *years*."

"I'm not going anywhere."

"Well, no. But hell! If they're inclined to settle, what's the point of waiting for years when you could have money in your hands in a matter of months, or even weeks?"

"Maybe I'm stupid, but how can anyone do a thing without me?" She lifted the edge of the scarf slightly to see him more clearly.

"They've got all the medical records so far." He was beginning to look uncomfortable, even angry. "They've read up on the injuries you sustained. Morrison, he's the guy I talked to, he says they'll go after compensation for the hospital bills, and for a lump-sum settlement. I told him to go ahead."

"How could you do that without even discussing it with me?" She was staggered by the fact that he'd usurp her prerogatives in this way.

"I'm trying to look after your best interests. I mean, you're hardly in a position to do it for yourself right now."

"I see."

"It's not as if I'm getting anything out of this," he went on. "I honestly thought you'd be glad to know I'm not just sitting around on my duff letting things happen." He stopped and pulled out a piece of memo paper—it read *From the desk of Ronald Briggs*. "Morrison's asking for a hundred thousand."

For a few seconds she thought of all that a hundred thousand dollars would buy. It was a lot, but not enough to buy a house outright, unless it was a very small house. She could live for six or seven years on that much money. But what would she do when it was gone? Wryly, she thought that it was just about the right amount to purchase a Rolls-Royce. She could walk into the dealership in Greenwich, pick out a Rolls she liked, write a check, then climb into the car and drive it into the nearest wall.

"He's asking for extra to cover your hospital expenses," Ron added significantly.

"You told him to go ahead?"

"Well, sure I did." He was on the defensive now.

"Which means that if I don't happen to agree with this, there's a problem."

"You 'don't happen to agree' with me? You mean you don't *want* a settlement?"

"I don't know what's fair, Ron. I mean, how much d'you think a face is worth? I wish you'd talked to me before you told this Morrison guy to go ahead."

"I can't do the right thing, can I?" He got up and walked over to the window. "No matter what I say or do, I'm wrong."

"It's not that at all. It's just that you're treating me as if, because of this goddamned accident, I can't *think* anymore. I know you mean well, but you're making decisions for me, as if my mind's been damaged."

"I thought you'd be glad that I cared enough to take the time to look after things for you."

"I appreciate that. I do. You just should've talked to me about all this before you gave the go-ahead."

Aggrieved, he said, "Well, I'm sorry. Next time I'll know better."

She sighed, taxed by the stalemated aspects of the conversation. "Forget it," she said, reluctant to pursue the matter further. There seemed no possible resolution. "It doesn't matter."

"I've got to get back to the office." He came away from the window so that the sun was no longer behind him and she could once more transcribe his features.

"Ron, I know you meant well." Suddenly, she didn't want him to leave annoyed with her.

"Yeah. Look, I've really got to go. I'll talk to you later." He approached and looked quizzically at her scarf-shrouded head. The most he could bring himself to do was place the flat of his hand lightly on her shoulder. "Take it easy, Cale."

Once the sound of his footsteps had ebbed, she sank back into the unyielding armchair and gazed, unblinking, at the sun patterns on the floor. For the first time she had a sense of complete hopelessness. She had lost control of her life. Ron was making decisions unilaterally. A surgeon she feared and distrusted had performed upon her an operation that was crucial to her return to something like normalcy. No one from the office had called to confirm that her job was still waiting. Where was there to go from here? If she sought legal help with the claim, Ron would interpret that as a personal insult, a sign of her lack of faith in him. If she called the office, she might learn something she didn't want to know. And the success of the surgery would be an unknown for perhaps two weeks.

This was no good. She needed some sort of contingency plan, because if Ron's attitude was anything to go by, people in general were only going to be tolerant of her to a degree. After that, impatience would set in, the way it had when her adoptive parents had died and her friends had grown tired of her prolonged grieving. "It's time you got over it," they'd told her. "They lived their lives. Now you've got to live yours." She'd had to bury her grief, submerge it beneath the momentum of her day-to-day life in order not to bore her friends.

It had been terribly difficult, and she still had no clear idea how one could successfully reconcile years of conversations, of memories and images, with the absence of those very people who'd been responsible for the creation of all that. It sometimes scarcely seemed possible to her that deaths could occur with such horrendous finality. One day, someone you deeply loved was there, smiling and chatting, and the next day, there was only a hazy silhouette remaining. Added to that now was the engulfing sense of loss she felt for the face that had been hers, the appearance that had constituted her identity. Everything was changed, and she hadn't yet managed to stop thinking the way she used to. It was all so entangled and bewildering. The only clearly identifiable emotions she had were anger, fear, and confusion. What she needed, she suddenly saw, was to talk to someone with professional detachment who'd be able to review all this objectively. Ron had been right about that. And really, there was no shame inherent in a dialogue.

She'd thought Dawson would send a woman. She'd geared herself up to the idea of sharing her thoughts with another female. The sight of this slight, bearded man seated opposite dried her out like alum. She wet her lips, trying to get past her embarrassment. Her fingers nervously twitched the scarf into place so that only her left eye was visible.

"There's no need to be nervous." He smiled at her. "I'm not here to pass judgment."

"I had the idea," she confessed, "that you'd be a woman."

"And that would've been easier?"

"I thought so."

"It's a possibility," he agreed. "Why don't we see how it goes? You might like me. I'm not a bad guy."

"Are you a psychologist or a psychiatrist?"

"Psychologist."

"What's the difference?"

He laughed and folded his arms across his chest. "I don't have an M.D. But if it's any consolation to you, the guys with the M.D.'s don't have the long-term practical training we nonmedical types do. We spend a whole lot more time actively working on our specialty. There's some interesting friction between the Ph.D.'s and the M.D.'s."

"Why?"

"A question of who's more qualified."

"Oh? Who is?"

"We are, of course." He laughed again.

"I don't know how to start." She wet her lips.

"Jump in anywhere." He unfolded his arms and made a sweeping gesture with his hands.

"When Ron—he's the man I live with—when he first suggested I talk to somebody, I was so offended. As if he was telling me I was crazy and I was the only person who didn't know it.''

''Maybe we're *all* crazy and don't know it.''

''What's your name again?''

''Stanley. Call me Stan.''

''Do you work for the hospital?''

''I'm on staff, but I've got a private practice too.''

She gave a slight shake of her head as if to clear it. ''I, uh, feel really odd, shaky kind of.''

''Because of me, or because of the accident?''

''Both, I guess. I don't know who I am anymore.''

''That's understandable.''

''Is it?''

''Sure. We rely pretty heavily on our externals for purposes of identification. Change those externals and all sorts of crises occur.''

''You know other people this has happened to?''

''One or two. Everybody's different.''

His easy manner was gradually having a conciliatory effect.

''This accident,'' she began, ''is changing everything. Ron's doing things, taking charge, as if I got brain-damaged in the crash. And I feel so angry . . . with him, and with myself too. I have this feeling that he thinks once I stop wearing this thing over my face I'll be exactly the way I was before.''

''And you don't think so.''

''No. I think things're going to get worse.''

''What if you're wrong?'' he asked interestedly.

''I'm not wrong. I couldn't tell you why, but I know I'm not. I feel as if I should make plans, but if I make plans . . .'' she shrugged.

''If you make plans you might inadvertently reshape events. That's an old superstition. I don't believe that's how things work necessarily.''

''I thought I was going to have to do all the talking, that you'd just nod now and then, and say uh-huh.''

He laughed again. ''You've been watching too many old movies on TV. I don't operate that way. Maybe I'm just naturally gabby, but I've always disliked one-sided conversations. What's your plan?''

"I don't have one yet."

"But you've got a few ideas," he prompted, crossing his denim-covered legs. He wore a well-cut sports jacket over a starched white shirt and carefully knotted tie, so that from the waist up he looked like an executive. His Levis, faded and thinned at the knee, told a conflicting story about him. He wore blue socks and scuffed penny loafers, minus the pennies.

"I'll sound crazy," she said tentatively.

"When you get to the really nutty stuff, I'll let you know."

She smiled, her dry lips splitting so that a tiny bead of blood appeared on her lower lip. "I think they'll come to check on how this thing's going, and they'll start hemming and hawing, trying to find some way to tell me that it's all screwed up and they're going to have to do it again. The doctor who did this . . . he didn't like me. I didn't like him. I thought he was creepy. He wasn't the one who was supposed to do it. He operated on me right after the accident, and he screwed up. I'm afraid this one'll go wrong too, and the thing is, I'm running out of . . . There's only so much skin they can use. I mean . . ."

"You think he intentionally screwed up?"

"Not exactly. I think he wouldn't do the best possible job because he didn't care about me. And because he wouldn't think about who I was, or even if I *was* anybody. He'd give me forehead flap number seventy-two, without considering all of me. It's like, so-and-so would get chin number twelve, and somebody else would get ear number forty-one. You know? Like he's got these set things he does, and if you don't like it, tough."

"For the sake of argument, let's say he did a terrific job. What'll happen to your theory then?"

"Naturally, I'll feel a whole lot better," she acknowledged. "But I still think everything else is shot. And if that's the way it turns out to be, I don't know what I'll do. The thing is, all I've ever wanted is an ordinary life, just being married, having a home of my own, and kids. Ron won't even touch me now. He says it's because I'm still recuperating, but I know the truth is he can't stand the sight of me. I can't blame him for that. *I* can't stand the sight of me. And they're not going to keep my job on hold forever. Who's going to hire me, looking like a freak? Who's going to want me? How am I going to *live*?''

"Let's back up a little. I'm interested in knowing why you're so convinced the surgery isn't going to take.''

"It's a *feeling*, just a feeling. Don't you ever have those?''

"Sure I do. It's called good old intuition. We've all got some. Tell me why you've got this particular intuition.''

"Who knows?'' She shrugged. "Maybe I'm just someone who happened to be in the wrong place at the wrong time. I'm trying hard not to feel sorry for myself, but when I tell myself not to feel that way, what I feel instead is anger. I'm angry about every damned thing that's ever happened. I'm angry that somebody wrapped me in newspaper like a package of fish and chips and left me outside a hospital door. I'm angry that my parents told me about it instead of letting me go on being happy with my life. I want Ron to keep on loving me, and I just know it's over. Who wants to be with someone who doesn't want you? I don't. Maybe I wouldn't want to be with him if he got all smashed up in an accident, but I think I'd still be able to see him as the person he was.

"What really scares me is that I don't have anywhere to go. Ron's talking about this settlement the insurance company's going to make, maybe a hundred thousand dollars, and half of me thinks it's not enough to pay for what's happened to me. The other half of me thinks, Who am I anyway to expect to be rewarded for what happened?

"If I were a man,'' she said abruptly, "I don't think things would be shaping up the way they are. I mean, if Ron were me, I wouldn't start trying to do his thinking for him.''

"Well, I'll say one thing.'' Stan again smiled at her. "You're definitely angry, and your focus is a little off to one side. What I'd like to know is why you assume everything hinges on this procedure. If this round's a failure, there's always the next one.''

"I don't want any more! Have you any idea what it's like, getting prepped, being put under, then the sickness, waking up? I've had five sessions already. I can't do it again. It's like being born over and over again. You die; they put you down; and then you come back. Birth, death, over and over.''

"Okay," he said calmly. "You could always wait awhile before having another go."

"It's supposed to be that way," she said agitatedly. "This thing"—she held her hands in front of her face—"is supposed to come out just so. Then, they'll wheel me back in for this little quickie procedure, and that's that. *They say*. I've already told you: I just know in my bones it's not going to be that way. So what I'm telling you is, I can't handle another one of these big operations. Someday, maybe. Someday, way, way off. *Maybe*. Right now, I'd rather die than get wheeled back in there one more time. God! I think I needed to have somebody to say that to. You're not supposed to want to die. People are supposed to hang on, by their fingernails if they have to. I don't see why," she said bitterly. "I don't want to hang on so they can find a last little bit of usable skin from here, and one little bit from there, and try to make a patchwork quilt out of my goddamned face. I feel really strange." Her tone became more confiding. "*Really* strange. It's like there's this thing—I don't know how to describe it—some kind of covering or wrapping around me, and it's starting to come loose. I'm here, behind it, or in it, and I know that if this thing does come loose, I'm going to be crazy for real. It's like a pot, sort of. Like I'm inside the pot, maybe, and the lid's being taken off. Inside the pot, I'm bubbling and cooking."

"Does the idea of that lid coming off scare you?"

"That's the really weird thing," she said softly. "It doesn't scare me at all. It feels as if it'd be a huge relief. When I think about it, I get the sensation of taking an enormously deep breath. I could be anything, a goddamned bag lady or maybe just one of those fruitcakes you see talking to themselves. But the idea of it, the thought of it, is kind of good."

"And that's what scares you. Right?"

"Right. It scares the hell out of me. Why is that?"

"Could be you're talking about stepping outside a lifetime of conformity; maybe you're discovering you like the idea of being different."

She thought about that for a long moment, a quiet excitement simmering beneath her skin. "If I have to be a freak," she said slowly, thinking it through aloud, "then why shouldn't I live up to it? The only way I could live with this is by not caring. The way I am now, I can't *help* but care. I'm going to have to be different so I won't care, at least not as much as I do; maybe get to where nothing will matter.''

''Where nothing will hurt,'' he amended. ''That's a tough one. We're none of us exempt from pain, Caley. And what about those things you've always wanted: the house, the kids, the husband? What'll you do with the hole left by those dreams?''

''I don't *know*. That's why I need to have some kind of plan.''

''Well.'' He took a deep breath. ''From what you've said so far, it sounds as if your present contingency plan is a calculated move into being a banana.''

''Is that what I said?'' she asked wonderingly.

''It sounds like that from here.''

''Maybe I *am* crazy.''

''You're trying to anticipate all the eventualities,'' he explained, ''covering all the bases, just in case. That could tend to make a person a little nuts. I think we'd better try to deal with things one step at a time.''

''I've got to find someplace to put my feelings, Stan. I mean, I can't go out there''—she pointed at the window—''feeling the way I do this minute.''

''That's what we'll talk about, then. And we'll talk about your 'fish and chip' anger, and your fears about Ron. How about if we talk again after you've seen the results of the surgery?''

''Would you do me a favor?'' she asked.

''Sure, if I can.''

''Could you be here when they come to tell me if it's a hit or a miss?''

''Oh, sure. No problem. Dawson'll let me know when that's going to be.''

''I like you, Stanley.'' She met his eyes, for a moment wondering if he'd react differently to her once he saw her without the concealing scarf.

''I like you, too.'' He smiled and stood up. ''Until we talk again, why don't you give some thought to your alternatives?''

"What alternatives?"

"The ones you're going to consider as possibilities. They're always there, you know. Sometimes it takes a little extra effort to see them, but they're there."

Even before he was out the door, she was turning inward, scanning the interior horizon for some signpost to her options.

Chapter 10

"AND SO THE POOR, innocent little sod was sent off to live with Lady Bee, his wicked grandmother. Now, old Lady Bee was a true dragon, cleverly disguised to look like a proper grandmother. She had lovely blue hair and crafty little grandmother frocks, but underneath, *underneath*, she sported dragon knickers."

Harry and Ian shrieked on cue. The mention of knickers would always guarantee the titillated laughter of small boys. In the kitchen, Marian laughed briefly.

"Now," Martin continued, "you may wonder what sort of knickers dragons have been known to wear, and so I'll tell you. But you must give me your most solemn vow never to repeat to a living soul what I'm about to reveal to you. Have I your word on that?"

"We'll never tell, Dad," Harry promised, with Ian underscoring the word *never*. "Honest."

"All right, then." He lowered his voice dramatically. "Dragon knickers, my old darlings, are a cunning form of torture and disguise devised by those fiendish creatures to hide their true identity from the world while reminding them at every turn of their secret powers. Dragon knickers"—he paused a moment—"are made of *white scales*. Imagine that! Imagine having to go about with white scales all over your privates! Only a true dragon could do it."

"But how did the little sod *know* Lady Bee had dragon

knickers?'' Ian asked earnestly. "Did he ever see them?"

"Just once,'' Martin said in hushed tones. "It was an extraordinary occasion, one the little sod was to remember throughout his life. Lady Bee and our poor little chap were out on the grounds for their postprandial constitutional when a sudden gust of wind lifted Lady Bee's frock, thereby revealing to the little sod's horror the infamous knickers. He knew at once what they were. Perhaps he'd heard tales, or perhaps it was simply instinct, but he knew. Of course, the dreaded Lady Bee went on as if nothing had happened, but he knew. And from that evening on, he began to plot his escape from Scunthorpe Manor."

"You said it was called Pisslethwaite Hall,'' Harry interjected.

"The little sod had many names for the ancestral home,'' Martin said smoothly. "The longer he spent there, the more names it had: Cessbane Hall, Fartsworth Grange, Crappermore Castle. Many, many names."

Marian laughed again in the kitchen, her laughter accompanied this time by the threatening clatter of crockery.

"Hold it down in there!" Martin admonished her. "The staff are not supposed to eavesdrop on the master of the house."

A derisive snort was Marian's response.

"Well!" Martin cleared his throat. "We'll have to see a new scullery maid, I do believe. What say you, Lords Marks and Spencer?"

"I think not, sir,'' Ian jumped in judiciously. "The last three have left without stopping to collect their wages."

"He's right, sir,'' Harry agreed. "This one's stopped the longest. We'll never get another. All the girls in the village fear coming to the Hall."

"I suppose you have a point, gentlemen. But I'll have to have a word, put a stop to this unforgivable snooping. Now, where was I?"

"The little sod began to plot his escape from Scunthorpe Manor,'' recited Ian.

"Precisely! Now, as you well know, the grisly Lady Bee nightly locked our little hero into a small round turret room with no window but only a narrow slit in the brickwork, well above his reach. Lady Bee carried the key to this room on a long chain she wore around her raddled neck."

"What's raddled?" Harry asked.

"Like this." Martin illustrated, pushing the flesh at his throat with both hands so that it appeared a crepey mass of wrinkles.

"That's horrid!" Harry's brows drew together. "I'd have hated her, too."

"So would I!" Ian agreed fervently.

"As I was saying, she carried this key on a chain, and the only time she took off the chain was when she bathed."

"Do dragons bathe, sir?" Ian asked.

"Oh, they must, young Marks, else their scaly knickers dry out."

"I'm Spencer," Ian corrected him.

"The two of you concocted these cunning faces simply to devil me!"

"That's right!" Harry laughed. "And we've done jolly well, haven't we, Marks?"

"Jolly well, Spencer," chorused Ian.

"Enough of these pettifogging interruptions!" Martin declared.

"Coffee?" Marian called from the kitchen.

"Coffee, *sir*!" he amended, then whispered to the boys, "Despite your fondness for the wench, she really will have to go. She fails repeatedly to accord me the honor of proper address."

"We'll have a word with her, sir," Harry promised.

"She won't do it again, sir!" Ian concurred.

"See to it, then! These ceaseless interruptions put me off the track."

"The only time she had the chain off was when she bathed," Ian, of the prodigious memory, prompted again.

"Quite so." Martin patted the boy on the head. "This meant that somehow the little sod would have to sneak into the bathroom while the old dragon was having her fortnightly splash, and lay hands on the key. But how? Since she always took great pains to lock him in before she went off to perform her ablutions, he would have to devise some scheme so that she'd believe she'd locked him in when, in fact, she hadn't. Or, he'd have to create a diversion, thereby causing her to forget the locking-in procedure.

"During the mornings while on his hands and knees, in all weather, weeding the endless acres of flower beds, he thought and thought, discarding one idea after another. During the afternoons as he swept the long, gravel drive—a fruitless pursuit if ever there was one—he sifted through more and more ideas. In the evenings, after his nightly meal of cold toast and tepid, milkless tea, he sat with the horrid old crone in the drawing room—always at a goodly distance from the fire because the heartless dragon claimed the mere sight of the poor little sod gave her ceaseless acid indigestion. As he sat, he studied the chain that hung about her neck, wondering if he might just run up behind her, wrench the blasted thing from her neck, and then scarper. But what good would that do? She'd simply summon the servants and have them unleash the bloodhounds, who'd come after in hot pursuit, catch him, and tear him to pieces. No. He had to have a plan; he had to find some way to dupe the old tart into believing she'd locked him into the turret room. But wait!" Martin cried with a wild tremor in his voice, startling both boys. "There was something he'd forgotten!"

"What?" both boys cried in concert.

"He'd forgotten the locks on all the other doors. He'd *never* escape. He'd be forced to spend the rest of his life scrubbing the scullery floors, sweeping the gravel drive, and weeding those interminable miles of flowering beds. He sat in the farthest corner of the drawing room, shivering with the cold, and felt a great and terrible despair.

"Why had his darling mother and his knightly father had to die and leave him in the clutches of this misanthropic old harridan, this wretched dragon? Things looked bleak indeed. And then, one night, something quite extraordinary occurred. As the little sod lay on his rough pallet in the turret room, gazing at the pale light that came in through the slit high up on the wall, a vision came to him. Oh, it was simply marvelous, this vision! His darling mother appeared before him in long, flowing white robes. She smiled, and whispered into his ear."

"What did she say, Dad? Sir?" Harry asked eagerly.

"She said, 'My dear little sod, my darling boy!' " Martin's voice rose to a squeaky falsetto. " 'Try to be brave, my one and only boy. There is a way to escape, if you'll just be very still and think with great care.' Well, you can just imagine the effect this visit had upon the unlucky little creature! He was filled with renewed hope, and spent his hours mindlessly tending to his chores while, inside, he tried hard as he could to be very, very still, and to think carefully.

"And then, one gray afternoon as he waxed the oaken floor of the great hall, it came to him. He looked around quickly to be sure no one was watching, then dropped his polishing cloth and darted over to the ancient dragon's writing desk. Quick as a flash, he snatched up some pencils and half a dozen sheets of writing paper and tucked them inside his ragged trousers. Then, breathing hard, he dashed back to retrieve the polishing cloth. Back on his hands and knees, he rubbed at the golden oak of the floor. He knew now what he must do."

"The coffee's made," Marian announced from the doorway.

"Just another minute, *please*?" the boys begged. "We're almost to the end."

"It'll go cold," Marian warned.

"Just another minute," Martin promised.

Marian carried the tray with the coffee things into the room, set the tray on the table by the settee, then sat down, curious to hear the end of Martin's tale.

"Where was I?" Martin asked, maintaining the ritual.

"He knew now what he must do," Ian reminded him.

"Indeed! That night, after the scaly-knickered old ferret had locked him into his cold, stone room, the little sod set to work. With a bit of flour and water he'd nicked from the pantry, he made a thick paste. Making sure the edges of each page fit, one to the other, he pasted them neatly to the wall, so that when he was done he had a good-sized square. Then, with pencil in hand, he set to work drawing a window and, beyond that, a path leading away from Grotty Groves. It was important, you see, that the details be accurate, because this was the little sod's escape route. The window, of course, was open, and merely a few feet above the path. When the drawing was complete, he turned and took a long, last look at the damp stone walls and the thin, rough pallet upon which he'd been forced to sleep. He drew a deep breath and let it out slowly, then turned once more toward the window he'd created. He could hear his mother's voice whispering, 'My darling boy, my dear little sod, be free.' He took a step, and another, and then climbed through the window and out. He was free. Off he went along the path he'd drawn, off into the future."

"But it wasn't a real window," Harry, the pragmatist, argued.

"Of course not," Martin agreed. "He'd *created* it. It was a magic window."

"How did he live?" Ian asked. "Where did the path go?"

"We'll cover that in tomorrow's chapter. Go get ready for bed now."

The boys climbed down from his lap and went off, immediately deep in discussion of how it was possible to draw a window and then, magically, have it become real.

"It's a bloody *allegory*!" Martin called after them. "It's *not meant* to be *literal*."

"Where's the dictionary?" Harry was asking as they went into the bathroom.

Marian poured the coffee and handed Martin a cup. "Quite the story that was," she observed with a smile.

"Rather a good one, I thought."

"Was she so dreadful, Lady Barnes?"

"Well, she didn't have me sweeping the gravel drive, if that's what you mean. But yes, she was every bit as dreadful as I've said."

"And you painted your way out. I've never thought of it in those terms. I don't think I've ever really understood that aspect of it."

"What? That I drafted up a bit of never-never land and went off to live there in my head? Perhaps I did, to a degree."

"Tell me something. Is it magic?"

"Equal parts magic and bloody hard work." He got up, carrying his cup, and moved to sit beside her on the settee. "Those little sods are getting too heavy. The old legs're about dead from the weight of them." He positioned his cup on the table and rubbed the heels of his hands into his thighs. "Cut off my circulation," he complained.

"It frightens me a little," she said. "Perhaps it's why I've never been able to take your work quite as seriously as I should have."

"You mean you're taking it seriously now?"

"I've been watching you these past few months, seeing how much of an obsession—no, that's not at all the right word. It's more than an obsession. It's really a compulsion, isn't it?"

"If you like," he said offhandedly.

"No. Be serious a moment. I'm not talented. I've never had any sort of urge to be creative, so I suppose it's rather prejudiced me against you."

He turned more toward her, intrigued.

"I think that's the truth," she went on. "I don't mean to say that it's the natural course, or anything like that. I mean, one needn't automatically be prejudiced against those driven by compulsion. But I do suspect that those of us who don't feel the urge simply see those who do as frivolous. I believe I am guilty of that. It makes me feel quite dreadful, truly. I've always thought your paintings were clever, but this is the first time I've been able to witness the entire process, and it's a good deal more than mere cleverness. You seem to be on another plane, somehow unconnected with everyday matters. I've watched you, seen your eyes grow abstracted; I've seen how long it takes you to return from wherever it is you go. And you know such a lot about color, about light and shadow and how to make those things appear on paper, or canvas."

"Too bloody true."

"Please don't be flip, Martin. I'm trying to apologize."

"Bugger it! Don't do that!"

"You so dislike putting words to thoughts and events. That's something else I've come to recognize. Things are to be 'understood.' It's so damnably British, and you're wrong to perpetuate it, or to set up an impression in the boys' minds that it's the right, or good, way to be. Such a lot gets taken for granted when one leaves things to be 'understood.' I think we should put a stop to it. Living in such close quarters has been highly revealing. Do you realize this is the first time we've ever spent so much time together, and in such a small space?''

"I realize it well enough," he grumbled. "Half the time we're falling over one another."

"You love it!" She pointed a finger at him. "I think it's why you spend all your time at home in the studio over the garage. Because it's compact enough to suit you."

"Don't point! One of Lady Barnes's best rules: Never point, young man! It's shockingly bad manners."

She jabbed at his shoulder. "Pisslethwaite Manor!" She laughed. "Sweeping the gravel drive! Honestly! You put Dickens to shame."

"He didn't know the half of it."

In their robes and pajamas, the boys came running in to wedge themselves between their parents.

"Have you washed?" Marian asked suspiciously. "You weren't gone long enough to wash properly."

"We did!" Harry insisted. "The flannels are wet and everything."

Martin turned each of the boy's faces toward him, narrowing his eyes in inspection. "The old wet-flannel ruse! Look at these hands!" He caught two small pairs of hands and held them aloft for a moment before bending their heads forward to peer behind their ears. "Good God!" he groaned. "You could grow potatoes in this dirt! Go have a proper wash or I'll be forced to flog you with the old dragon's knickers."

"Oh, no!" Ian squealed. "Not the old dragon's knickers! Hurry, Harry! He's going to fetch the dreaded dragon's knickers!"

The boys hurled themselves out of the room, Harry losing a slipper on the way. He came dashing back to fish it onto his foot, threw a gap-toothed grin at his parents and whispered, "Get Ian first. It was his idea to wet the flannels."

"Tales out of school!" Martin thundered, pretending to rise from the settee. "We don't tolerate that sort of thing here, and well you know it!"

Still trying to get his foot back into the slipper, Harry hobbled out.

"You're lovely with them," Marian said quietly.

"I have a ten-year-old brain," he said. "I know exactly

what they're thinking. I fooled the old tart for years with the wet-flannel gambit.''

While Marian was getting into her nightgown, he tiptoed in to look at the boys. The nightlight cast a gentle glow on the uneven, whitewashed walls. He straightened the bedclothes around Harry, who slept with splayed limbs, his head hanging over the side of the bed. Ian, true to his nature, lay like an arrow, the blankets neatly folded across his chest. Martin stood between the beds looking first at one boy and then the other, noting the lines and shadows, studying the soft curve of sleep-flushed cheeks. He pressed his lips to the sleeping warmth, the grassy scent of their hair in his nostrils.

At the door, soundlessly, he said, "God bless," then pushed the door closed on their active dreaming.

Marian was already in bed, reading. "Everything all right?"

"Harry, as ever, is thrashing his way through rest and reward. And the resident encyclopedia of all acts, trivial and otherwise, is hard at work cataloguing the day's pursuits. In a word, yes."

"Good." She returned her attention to the book.

"It's been one hundred and twenty-two days." He sat on the edge of the bed to remove his shoes.

"Is it *that* long?"

"As if you didn't know," he scoffed. "That's the new world's record."

"It's wonderful, Martin. Honestly. I wouldn't have be-lieved you could do it."

"Little faith," he chided, "oh ye of."

"Oh me of a lot of experience." She marked her place in the book and set it aside.

"True," he allowed. "But of little faith nonetheless."

"No," she said judiciously. "Of great faith, actually. Are you planning on coming to bed?"

"No. I'd thought I might go for a nude stroll down the lane."

"In that case." She reached for the book.

"You've become a veritable wanton," he said, stopping her.

"It's just that I fancy the sober you. It's quite exhilarating knowing in the morning you'll actually remember what the two of us said and did the night before." As she said the words, she felt again the anguish she'd experienced through the years at discovering that the sometimes profound exchanges offered at the peak of passion fell into lost darkened regions of his mind. Too many times she'd been deceived by the rational-sounding sincerity of his tone, by the paradoxically Quixotic lure of his promises. Again and again, she'd arrived at morning with newly rekindled optimism, only to learn that it hadn't been the conscious Martin who'd uttered the words that had so tempted her to hope.

Now, by tremulous degrees, her trust in him was reestablishing itself, and so the appeal of the man himself grew accordingly. The more she knew of this nondrinking Martin, the more desirable he became.

"I fancy you," she said. "If that makes me a wanton, so be it."

"I was probably a good deal more fun drunk."

"Only for everyone else."

"Aaaarrgh!" He pressed his clenched fist to his heart and rolled over onto his side. "A mortal wound!"

"Happily for you," she said placidly, unimpressed by this display, "had you failed as a painter, you'd have had an undoubtedly meteoric career in the theater."

He straightened and leaned on his elbows gazing at her. "You," he said, "were probably a good deal more fun."

"Not possibly," she quipped. "I know with absolute certainty that my capacities as a 'good fun' type could never rival yours, drunk or sober. Also, happily for you, I've never felt compelled to try to compete with you, sober or not. I did a thoroughly good job playing the role of long-suffering spouse, and don't for a moment think I didn't know it. It was, in my defense, the role you cast me in. And since I've never been especially assertive, at least not where my assigned roles are concerned, I went along and played it out with you. *Are* you coming to bed?"

"I don't know that I like being a sex object. I don't recall your ever being quite so frank and outspoken."

"I wasn't. And you adore being a sex object."

"You're right. I do." He lifted one strap of her nightgown and craned forward, peering down the front of her gown. "I think," he said, letting the strap fall back into place, "I'll just come along to bed now."

"God!" She rolled her eyes, her lips tilting upward at the corners.

"Got your rubber whatsis in, then?" he asked, hurriedly undressing.

She reached out to turn off the light on the bedside table. "Wake me when the monologue's done, there's a love." She turned on her side away from him, smiling to herself as his weight on the bed bore her toward him.

For just an instant, before the contact was made, she vividly recalled a drunken Martin weeping into her breasts as he whimpered out a declaration of love for her that, had he been sober, would have enslaved her for a lifetime. He might never again, sober, offer up quite so poetically rending a declaration, but his occasional I-love-you's, uttered almost casually, had a more durable impact.

Chapter 11

THE ONLY TRUE reaction she had was one of distorted justification. There was no disappointment, no sadness, nothing but this justification to compound her sense of loss. It was all as she'd guessed it would be; her instinct had been right. Stanley held her hand, maintaining the contact throughout O'Connor's explanation of why her nose collapsed inward as the packing was withdrawn.

"It'll be corrected," he told Caley. "These are always iffy procedures. The surgery was well done."

"The operation was a success," Caley said with a laugh, "but the patient died."

The pressure of Stan's hand increased sympathetically; he was an anchor preventing her from drifting off into space.

"Not quite." O'Connor was visibly rattled by her humor. "There's never a guarantee with this kind of work. It *can* be corrected."

"I'm not going through any more of this," she said flatly in a tone that suggested she was no longer subject to persuasion. "At least it's a nose."

"Let's talk about this again later," O'Connor said, "when you've had a chance to think it over."

"I've already thought it over, and right now I'm not having any more surgery."

"Look," O'Connor said patiently. "No one's saying it has to be right away. There's time. In a month or two, we can get you in again and do something—"

"No!" She was adamant.

"Just *think* about it," O'Connor gave one final try. "I'll see you tomorrow."

"When can I go home?"

"Three more days, probably. I want to see some more healing before I let you go."

"Fine." She freed her hand from the psychologist's and waited for O'Connor and the nurse to leave. She thought perhaps Stan might go, too, but he didn't. He drew the visitor's chair over closer to the bed and sat down. "Is it going to fall off if I smoke?" she asked O'Connor as he was going out the door.

"You may smoke," he said morosely, then went on his way shaking his head.

"You gave him a pretty rough time," Stan said, watching her light a cigarette. "Does it make you feel any better?"

"No." She watched the smoke spread in the air. The acrid odor of the spent match filled her nostrils. With the packing gone, her sense of smell had returned. No doubt the meal they'd bring her that evening would taste bad. She'd eaten the bland food disguised by cream sauces, unable to tell the difference between apples and potatoes. Only textures had given her any hint of the identity of what she thought of as platefuls of "white food." She was perpetually disgusted by the meals in this place, and viewed the arrival of the next tray with displeasure. She'd lost a great deal of weight in the previous months, and her few weeks at home hadn't added enough back to return her to her former roundness. Under the pale blue hospital gown her flesh felt slack upon her bones; altogether she felt puny, a bantamweight battling a bruiser.

"This smacks of self-punishment," Stanley commented.

"What does?" She turned to look at him.

"Well," he said, "ultimately, who d'you think's going to suffer from your refusing to have the additional surgery?"

"You don't know what you're talking about!" she flared. "Have you ever had an operation?"

"Nope. That doesn't disqualify me from discussing this situation with you, though."

"As far as I'm concerned, it does."

"I see. You want to get a shrink in here who's had a fair

share of surgical bouts so you'll feel there's some measure of equality in the dialogue. Doesn't that strike you as a little unreasonable?''

"I have no interest in being reasonable. Being reasonable only means that I behave like a good girl and let them practice their techniques some more on me."

"I detect loud sounds of self-pity."

"It's my privilege."

"It's nonproductive."

"Oh, spare me," she said tiredly. "Talk like an ordinary person for a change. Okay? Stop being a shrink for a few minutes."

"It's what I am, Caley. Can you try thinking clearly for a few minutes?"

"I'm thinking very clearly. I told you how this was going to turn out."

"Things go wrong all the time. D'you think you've been singled out?"

"I don't think that at all. I'm not paranoid. I just knew this was going to happen."

"So it happened. Now you're justified as hell. You can go out into the world as an honest-to-God martyr. What'll it get you?"

"Don't tell me how I feel! I'm no goddamned martyr. I'm just a freak, and you can't sit there and tell me I'm not."

"I've seen worse," he said, refusing to rise to her baiting. "I can show you worse, if you're interested. I can take you downstairs to the kids' wards and show you birth defects that make you look damned good by comparison. I can take you into rooms right on this floor and show you faces that'll make you glad to go out of here with the one you've got."

"Oh, shit!" she said softly, deflated. "Shit!"

"You don't have enough history as a hard case to maintain that pose," he said gently. "You need years of experience toughing it out, and you don't have that. I'll say it again: You're only punishing yourself by refusing to let them do more work. You go out of here the way you are now, you're saying loud and clear, 'Look what happened to me! Don't you feel sorry for me?' The only snag is, it won't work. You know from your experiences with the other tenants in your building

that people aren't going to take the time to feel sorry for you.
Everybody's got things to worry about. The net result of the
position you're taking is self-abusive. You had an accident. It
wasn't your fault, but you're going to make yourself pay for
it. That's really not smart, Caley.''

"I never said I was smart," she argued lamely, sensing she'd
already lost this argument.

"As a rationale, that sucks hard," he said with a smile. "At
least if we're going to have an argument, let's see you drag out
your front-line defenses."

"You're going to talk me into letting them operate again,"
she said fearfully. "I don't want to let you do that."

"Why not?"

"Because no matter what they do, I won't be the same as I
was before."

"You mean inside or outside?"

"I don't know. Both, maybe. I don't know." She put out
her cigarette and sat back finally against the pillows. Up to
this point she'd kept her back straight; sinking into the pillows
felt like a defeat, but she lacked the energy to stiffen her spine
again. "I want a mask," she said weakly. "I want a hood."

"Back to playing the elephant woman again, like you did
with the scarf." He laughed. "That only draws attention to
you."

"I'm afraid," she admitted, meeting his eyes. "Have you
ever thought that every time I let them stick that needle in my
vein, it might be the last thing I ever do? Every single time I
watch the anesthetist aim that needle at me, I'm terrified
because I'm going to go to sleep and I might not wake up. I've
got to trust someone I don't even know; I have to trust him to
bring me back when it's all over. What if I don't come back?
What if next time there's a mistake made?"

"You wouldn't know about it, would you?"

"Jesus Christ!" she exclaimed. "Is that supposed to reassure me?"

"Nope. It's just the truth. We all have to trust that these
people know their jobs, that the anesthetist is going to make
sure you come around the way you're supposed to, just the
way you trust your mechanic to put your car back together
properly."

"I don't have a car."

"Hell! You know what I mean."

"I know. But look at me and give me one good reason why I should trust them to fix me up."

"I can't do that, Caley. It's a matter of faith."

"Faith? In what? In whom?"

"In O'Connor, for one. He doesn't want you to suffer. He told you it could be corrected. D'you think he's lying?"

"No. But how do I know he won't have another emergency and get that lunatic Morgan in again?"

"You don't. You're just going to have to trust that that doesn't happen."

"You don't want much, do you, Stan? You just want me to submit again and hope that this time they get it right."

"Got any other options?"

"Maybe I do," she said defiantly.

"Name them."

"I can stay the way I am."

"You consider that an option?"

"Of course it is."

"Okay. We'll allow that for the moment. Name your other options."

She couldn't. Every idea she had hinged on her either remaining as she was or undergoing further surgery.

"You can't think of any, can you?" he said.

"I don't want to do it again," she lamented, "and you're telling me I don't have any choice."

"Listen, Caley." He put his hand on her arm. "I'm not here to force you into anything. I'm only trying to point out that you've got nothing to gain from refusing to let them correct the problem. What's the point to punishing yourself? At least give it your best shot."

"I hate expressions like that," she said bitterly. "What the hell does it mean, my best shot? It has nothing to do with me. I just lie there and they do whatever it is they do. And what if they screw it up even worse than it already is? What do I do then?"

"That won't happen."

"How do you know that? You can't guarantee me that."

"I can't guarantee you diddly. I just think you owe it to

yourself to give them the benefit of the doubt, on the chance that they'll improve your appearance."

"My dad was a salesman, you know, Stan. He used to like to say he was so good he could sell iceboxes to Eskimos. You're right up there, in his league."

"Is that a compliment?" he asked, smiling again.

"It's a comment on your powers of persuasion. I'm tired."

"Sure," he said, at once getting to his feet. "We'll talk again tomorrow, same time. For what it's worth, I don't know what you looked like before and I'm not even sure that's really relevant, but the job they've done isn't all that bad. I know you're deeply disappointed, and I probably would be too. If it were me, though, I'd take the chance. I know what you're going to say." He held up his hand. "I'm not you, and I haven't been on the table half a dozen times, so I don't know how it feels. You're not a freak, though, and I meant what I said. If you want to go down to the kids' wards, I'll take you."

"I don't need a comparison test. Maybe it's easier, somehow, if that's the way you've always been. I mean, that's the face that's always been there for you in the mirror. It's not the same thing, Stan. I feel so ashamed, as if it *is* my fault somehow."

"All the more reason to have another try."

"Maybe," she said wearily.

"Take it easy," he said, and slipped away.

She listened to the traffic passing her doorway, the clatter of trolleys being pushed along the corridor, the rubbery squeak of the nurses' shoes on the linoleum, the tinny twang of announcements over the P.A. system. All the fear she should perhaps have felt at the time of the crash, she felt now. It pulsed along her veins and arteries, made itself tangible in the moisture under her arms, at the back of her neck, on her palms. She was hot with fear, her insides molten with it. Her dread had weight and taste, even a smell, as she reached for the mirror on the bedside table.

With detached pity, she examined the prizefighter's face, the flattened nose, the fading tracery of scars, the flesh still shiny with newness. It was funny, she thought, touching a fingertip to the rubbery structure with its twin vents. The intent was evident: they'd planned that this small flesh construction should point proudly, with dignity. Intent, though, had been superseded by effect. Soldered into place sat what looked like a wad of pink bubblegum, something a child might have created out of Silly Putty. She laughed and let the mirror fall to her lap. "Son of a bitch," she thought. "How the hell can I be laughing?" Maybe she was cracking up. All that interior warfare was taking its toll on her sanity. They would come in to dose her with pills and find her chortling away to herself. What else was there to do, though? To shed tears would be too much of an admission of self-pity; she refused to give in to that. Someday, sequestered well away from anyone's view, she might just cry herself into a state of complete exhaustion, but not now. Spitting out angry words, playing at defiance, that was one thing. But succumbing to tears was proof of weakness. She would not weep over this, not yet; her sorrow repositioned itself in humor.

Stan. That was something, too. She'd wanted to kill Ron for daring to suggest she seek professional help. Now she hoarded her ideas for Stan's inspection. She'd become a prospector of introspective mining, sifting ceaselessly through thoughts to find those worthy of discussion with her therapist.

"It's not perfect, but it sure looks a whole lot better," Ron said that evening, placing the seedless grapes and Toblerone chocolate he'd brought on the locker top.

"A little Silly Putty goes a long way," she said, still caught up in finding things funny. "They want to try one more time, see if they can't get it to stand up." This struck her as enormously funny, and she laughed loudly.

"They give you something?" he asked, half-smiling as if fearful of committing himself to a wholehearted reaction. He mistrusted her mirth. "You seem a little . . . spaced out."

"Didn't give me a thing," she said. "I just had a look this afternoon and decided maybe I'd misjudged poor old Morgan. I didn't credit him with having such a well-developed sense of humor. I mean, you've got to admit it's pretty funny if he calls this a successful reconstruction."

"He didn't, did he?"

"Oh, definitely not. I thought O'Connor would have apoplexy when he started to pull out the seven or eight hundred miles of packing and my lovely new nose just fell flat. He assures me they can fix it, however."

"You're going to let them?"

She sighed, her chest suddenly achy—from either too much laughter or too many repressed emotions. She had no idea which. "I don't know. Everybody's trying to talk me back onto the table."

"Well, if they can fix it, don't you think you ought to let them?" he asked, draping his topcoat over the back of the chair before sitting down.

"That'd be number six. And if it still wasn't right, they'd want to go for number seven, and then number eight. I could be in this goddamned place for the rest of my fucking life."

"When were they talking about doing it?"

"Any old time I like. O'Connor gave me his layman's version of what needs to be done. Some jazz about hip grafts— bone, that is—and then raising the whole thing like a little circus tent."

"It doesn't sound all that complicated."

"Everything around here's complicated," she disagreed. "Every time they put you under, it's complicated. I'm scared to imagine the size of the bill so far."

"Oh, listen! I'm glad you reminded me. I've got some papers from the insurance company. They're ready to make a settlement." He lifted his briefcase onto his lap, snapped it open, and brought out a legal-sized buff envelope. "They'll cover any related hospital claims for up to three years. And they're offering fifty-eight thousand dollars as a cash settlement."

"Fifty-eight? What happened to the hundred thousand?"

"It might have been that much, but the hospital tab is already up over twenty-seven thousand. If you have another operation, that'll be a few thousand more. It seems pretty fair to me."

"Why are you so anxious for me to accept this?" she asked. "You know damned well it isn't fair!"

"Caley, add fifty-eight and twenty-seven. You know what that comes to? It's eighty-five thousand dollars. If you let this drag on, you'll have to find some way to pay the hospital while you wait out a court hearing that might take years."

"But I've got the group insurance. . . ."

"You're already into the major medical, and that's going fast. Your coverage won't last forever."

"How do you know that?"

"Because I went downstairs today and talked to Chuck Hennessy, who handles the group medical plan. He called the accounting department here to get the latest total, then he ran through the figures, and that's what he came up with."

"Oh, God!"

"There's more, Caley. You might as well hear it all."

"What more?"

"You've exceeded the sick-leave time limit allowable under company policy. They're keeping you on the payroll only until the end of the month."

"But you told me Art said they'd hold my job."

"Nobody thought you were going to be laid up for five months. I'm sorry. Jesus! I really am."

The fear came back in a rush, making her stomach seize briefly before starting to lurch about. "What about you?" she asked, holding her damp hands tightly together in her lap. "Do I still have a place to live, or has the allowable time limit on that run out, too?"

"Don't be ridiculous!" he said indignantly. "What d'you think I am, anyway, Caley?"

"I'm sorry. You didn't deserve that. Oh, my God!" She'd been too quick to find humor where none existed. Nothing was funny.

"It'll be all right," he said, trying to calm her. She was trembling visibly. "The money'll tide you over until you get out of here and back on your feet again."

"How can you *say* that?" she near-shouted. "Look at me, for chrissake! Who the hell would want me sitting outside his office door? Or bringing in coffee for the clients?"

"All the more reason," he said, determined not to lose his temper, "to have this last operation. Once that's out of the way . . . well, you'll be able to start sending out résumés, trying for another job.''

As if she hadn't heard him, she began to speak. "Give me the papers. I'll sign them."

"No, wait a minute. If you really don't want to, maybe you shouldn't. Maybe you're right, and this is an insulting offer. I don't want you coming back at me later, blaming me for forcing you into this."

"I won't blame you," she said coldly, holding out her hand for the envelope. "Lend me a pen, will you?"

He clung to the envelope stubbornly. "Caley, this is so hard. I mean . . . Jesus! What do I mean?" He looked about, trying to assemble his thoughts into some kind of reasonable order. "Maybe you won't believe this," he said, "but I don't think I've ever been sorrier about anything in my whole life than I am that this happened to you. In a way, I understand why you're fighting so hard. I mean, I really think I do. But you scare the hell out of me because I feel in my gut that you blame me. You're so goddamned angry with me. I feel it every time I walk in here. I'm doing the best I can," he said sadly. "I'm trying so hard I think I'm getting an ulcer. Don't sign the stinking papers if it's going to be one more reason for hating me. Do me a favor, because I don't think *I* can take any more. I know you want to believe that it doesn't bother me that you got all smashed up, but it bothers me all right. I *dream* about it. I'll probably dream about it for the rest of my life. I'm trying so goddamned hard. I don't know what else to do. I'm doing my job, and I come here every night, and then I go home, and go to bed, and in my dreams, that fucking drunk crosses the median again, we crash, and you go flying through the windshield. I get my work done somehow, and I'm eating TV dinners, waiting for you to come home. What more am I supposed to do? Is there something more?"

"No," she said dolefully. "Just give me the papers and lend me a pen. Okay?"

Resigned, he surrendered the documents and gave her his pen. "I just want you to know that I do care. I've got the nightmares to prove it."

"I believe you," she said softly, signing her name to all the copies. "I do believe you."

• • •

While she waited for the medication to take effect so that she could sleep, she stared at the ceiling, hearing Ron's urgent, unhappy declaration of caring. He did care; she did believe him. What hounded her was the thought that she no longer cared about him. Somehow, somewhere, along the terrain of the previous five months, she'd misplaced her feelings for him, and couldn't seem to find them. He was eager to have her come home, eager to make every possible attempt to preserve what they had together. It was the truth; there wasn't a line on his face that contradicted his words. He'd succeeded in keeping his love for her intact, but she could no longer identify what it was about him she'd found so lovable.

Chapter 12

"IF I STAY ONE day over the six months, I'll be subject to taxation here," Martin explained.

"Will you go back to Toronto?" Marian asked, the roast lamb suddenly inedible.

"I don't want to go that far away from the three of you." He looked around the table. The boys sat poised before an abyss of tears. "I was thinking of Paris," he said. "It's near enough for weekend visits, and then when school breaks up, we could spend the summer there, rent a villa."

The boys looked at their mother, trying to gauge her response.

"What would you do alone in Paris for six months?" she asked.

"Work. The other alternative would be to pack it in here, book seats, and go home."

"That would mean taking the boys out of school in the middle of the school year," Marian said doubtfully.

"We wouldn't mind," Harry offered.

"We wouldn't, honestly," Ian confirmed.

"I could go on ahead," Martin went with the idea, "set the house to rights and get everything organized, and the three of you could stay on until school breaks up in July."

"It doesn't seem entirely sensible for you to go to Paris," she said. "I just hadn't thought we'd be going quite so soon."

"We're not doing a thing unless we're all in complete agreement,'' Martin said firmly. "And there's no need to disrupt old Marks's and Spencer's schooling. I can either go to Paris for six months, or I can go back to Toronto. I'd prefer not to have to go anywhere, but I'm not all that keen on endowing the bloody Inland Revenue with a sizable chunk of my income. We've got two weeks to think about it.''

"Would you really like to go back?'' Marian asked the boys.

"Oh, yes, please!'' Harry sang eagerly. "It's way nicer there.''

"I miss my room,'' Ian added.

Marian looked disappointed, even betrayed, as if these remarks came as evidence of mutiny.

"Did you think they'd want to stay?'' Martin asked, nonplussed. "This isn't their home, love.''

"Not that. I'm simply a little surprised. I thought''—she addressed her sons—"you liked it here.''

"We do.'' Ian sought to console his mother. "We do, honestly. It's just so—different. And the school's way better at home. No uniforms, and we get to come home for lunch.'' Already the effects of their seven months in England were disappearing from their intonation and phraseology.

"Perhaps it's best if you finish out the school year,'' Martin said, then looked over at his wife.

"Perhaps,'' she said, "the three of *us* don't care to be that far away from *you*.''

"I can't stay,'' he said helplessly. "Paris *is* nearby.''

The boys' heads turned, closely following this exchange, sensing this was an issue that would ultimately be decided regardless of their opinions.

"I shouldn't be this upset.'' Marian made an effort to smile. "It's just that things have gone so well here. . . .''

"You're fearful we'll jinx it with any sudden movements.''

"I'm not superstitious,'' she protested. "And I do miss the convenience of so many things. I only wish we'd had more warning.''

"I clean forgot,'' Martin apologized. "All these asinine bloody restrictions.''

"Well.'' She gazed at the food congealing on her plate.

"We do know you can't stay. And the furniture's still in crates in storage. I expect the simplest thing would be for you to go back and get the house ready, and we'll follow when school breaks up."

The boys remained silent, understanding that this wasn't an appropriate time for celebratory cheering.

"Dad?" Ian asked. "What would happen if you went away and came back again?"

"They'd slap me with a tax bill for the entire year. I'd be doubly taxed."

"Would it be a lot of money?" Ian continued.

"More than I'd be willing to part with."

"Oh!"

"Eat up," Marian told the boys. "I don't want you coming to me in an hour complaining you're hungry."

Obediently, both boys applied themselves to their food.

Marian sat in the armchair by the window silently weeping.

"What is it?" Martin asked. He knelt by the side of the chair, his hands folded on the side of its overstuffed arm. "Are you afraid once I'm on my own again I'll start drinking?"

"Oh, no, not at all," she answered quickly. "That hasn't anything to do with it."

"What is it, then?" Her tears distressed him. Marian wasn't someone given frequently to weeping.

"I truly don't know. We've been so happy here."

"And you think that'll change once we leave?"

"I think it might," she allowed, reading the consternation creasing his features. "I do trust you," she assured him. "I can't explain this, but I promise you it hasn't anything to do with my fearing you'll start back on the drink. I don't think you will." She slipped out of the chair and onto her knees to embrace him. "I'm frightened and I don't know what of. I wish you didn't have to leave, but it wouldn't be fair to ask you to move back and forth; it wouldn't be fair to the boys, either."

"You must have known you wouldn't be staying on, otherwise, surely, you'd have arranged delivery of the furniture."

"I hoped we might eventually resolve our problems, but I

hadn't expected to feel as I do. I *can't* explain." She shook her head impatiently. "What about the paintings, all your work? What will you do with them?"

"I'll get them crated up and take them back with me, have them all framed and hung by the time you and the kids come home. I'll have the house repainted while I'm about it."

"Plain white," she said.

"Plain white," he repeated. "Whatever madam wishes. Look," he said, smoothing her hair. "It's only until July. I'll ring every night if you like."

"I don't think that'll be necessary." She smiled as he mopped her face with his handkerchief. "Oh, Martin!" she whispered, tightening her arms around him with sudden ferocity. "I do love you. I keep turning my life upside-down for you."

"But it's worth it," he teased, "isn't it?"

"To see you this way, yes. I don't know how I'll get through the next months alone."

"Old Marks and Spencer'll keep you on your toes."

"Harry and Ian," she said, sitting back on her heels, "don't climb into the tub with me, or sleep in my bed."

"Ah!" He grinned contentedly. "All these years you've lied about the torture of my nocturnal band saw."

"You don't snore all the time," she defended herself. "You only used to do it, really, when you'd had too much to drink."

"You don't snore at all. You're bloody perfect." His hands shaped her shoulders. "You're a wonder, my girl. How about a quick sketch before bed?"

"Where now?" she asked. "You've had me sit in every corner of this place."

"Right here," he said, reaching for the sketch pad on the table. "Just the way you are."

"Fifteen minutes. I'll be crippled if I sit any longer than that in this position."

He was already at work, his eyes on her yet not with her, his hand moving the soft-leaded pencil over the page. It fascinated her ceaselessly that he could instantly distance himself in work, while at the same time involving himself utterly in her. Rather than feeling segmented, as she'd once feared she might, posing repeatedly for him seemed to pull her into ever closer union with herself. The time they spent as artist and model expanded the dimensions of their life together. She offered herself up to his vision without self-consciousness, every part of her his. Being drawn or painted by him somehow rendered her flawless. She reviewed the likenesses he produced of her, each time more surprised by all he said in his work that he rarely put into words.

Time evaporated in this intense communion. She was his perfect work, the ideal realization of his skills. He thought there could never be another face or body he'd know so well; every detail was perennially familiar yet constantly new. Completing the sketch, he all at once understood her fear. It bled through the air, an impediment to his momentum, so that he had to throw aside the book and pencil and clutch the reality, pressing his lips into the satin hollow of her throat, his eyes tightly closed.

One of the boys coughed, and the two of them went still instantly, listening.

"It's all right," Marian said after a moment. "Harry's got a cold coming on."

Martin gazed down at her, halted by her magnificent disarray, by the sight of her bared breasts framed by the hastily pushed aside halves of her blouse and cardigan. With tender greed he molded his hands to her breasts. "Come to bed," he crooned, anxious to heat her with his hands and mouth, to surrender himself to the slippery mystery of her flesh.

"I haven't bathed," she said, sitting up.

"I'll bathe you," he declared, holding out his hand to her. "I'll bathe you like an infant, from head to toe."

For a week, the cottage rang with Martin's hammering as he retrieved the completed canvases from the attic and crated them. At the end of that week, he climbed up to sit breathing in the dusty emptiness, feeling as if he'd ravaged a tomb. Despite the proof of his work which sat below awaiting removal by van to the airport, he couldn't rid himself of his sense of loss, nor could he comprehend it. The crates were scheduled to go air freight; he'd be free to claim them from the airport in Toronto the moment he landed and cleared customs and immigration. No, it wasn't the removal of the paintings that bothered him. It was the feeling he had, despite the mitigating circumstances of his departure, of guilt at leaving his wife and sons.

Daily, nightly, almost hourly, he hurried to find Marian, feverish with the need to reconfirm her existence. While she appeared resigned to his leaving, he'd become the beneficiary of her fears and was unable to shake free of them.

"You're like a puppy," she said, laughing, as they drove home from marketing in the decrepit Rover. "Can't let me out of your sight for a moment."

"I'm not going to see you for months," he lamented. "I'll leave here Sunday week and stop alone for months on bloody end. Only two months nearly did me in. I shudder to think what I'll be like at the end of this run."

"You'll be fine. You'll be so busy badgering that poor chap who does your framing, you won't even have time to think about us."

"Hah! Little you know."

"Are you going to have a showing of the new ones?" she asked. "Have you decided?"

"Not yet. I told you, I've a good mind to turn the house into a bloody gallery."

"We do have to live there," she reminded him. "I don't know that I'd care to face endless family portraits day in and day out, not to mention various parts of my anatomy flung to the four winds for all and sundry who'd care to look. Please don't do anything drastic. It was terribly personal, Martin. I gave no thought, when I posed for you, of strangers gaping at me."

"I'll bet the Maja didn't nag old Goya this way."

"She had ridiculous, impossible breasts. The man was plainly creating from fantasy. You, on the other hand, go after a rather terrifying form of realism."

"Not to worry," he said. "I'll proceed cautiously. Pity we can't ship this old beauty back." He rubbed the steering wheel with an appreciative hand. "You don't suppose old Grace would consider getting shot of that thinly disguised mortuary and coming over to us?"

"I think not. When we spoke yesterday, she suggested the boys and I might like to join her in Tenerife for a week or so at the end of April."

"The two of you've been cooking up a little plot, haven't you?"

"I thought you might fly over and meet us there. It would break things up a bit. I know the boys would adore it, and so would I. It's been years since we last were there."

"I might just manage to survive that long. Listen! You're to promise me you won't sell this old beauty to just anyone. Imagine an opportunity to see your mum rigged out in a bathing costume!"

"Go gently on my mother! We'll be lucky to sell this thing at all," she scoffed. "They saw you coming from miles off when you bought this wreck."

He brought the car to a halt on the paved strip beside the house and turned off the ignition. "Women have no feeling for motors," he declared. "This machine is a classic. They'll never make anything better than the Rover. A fifties Daimler might come a close second."

"Do forgive me," she said, reaching for her basket of purchases. "I wouldn't dream of disputing your judgment."

"I detect a strong note of sarcasm lurking in those old Roedean tones. Watch your step, madam. You're treading in sensitive territory. Women should know better than to dare, ever, to risk coming between a man and his love for mechanical perfection."

"I'll see it gets a good home," she said, carrying the basket to the cottage door. "Damn!" she said, looking skyward. "I'd better get the wash in. It's going to rain." She stood poised on the threshold for only a moment, yet he was enthralled by her expression as she searched the sky. He wanted to say, Stop there! Just stay without moving! But even as he thought it, she vanished into the interior of the cottage. He remained by the Rover, that ineffable fear layering upon itself with each contraction of his heart. He wouldn't go, he thought. He'd ring up the solicitors and tell them he'd take his chances with the Inland Revenue. He'd stay on with Marian and the boys.

The rain commenced without warning. It came accompanied by a gusting wind that whipped the trees, lashing the shrubberies. He ran to the rear of the cottage, where Marian was fighting to rescue the already saturated laundry.

"There's no point!" he shouted over the wind, pulling her back toward the cottage. "Leave it!"

"Hell!" she cried, hurrying with him. "Bloody hell!"

"I'll go fetch the boys," he volunteered, already on his way back to the car. "Looks like we're in for a good blow."

The entire class leaped to its feet as Martin opened the classroom door. With his dripping clothes and wildly blown hair and his attitude of urgency, he presented a fairly frightening picture as he expressed his apologies to the master before hustling Harry and Ian out of there.

"What's the matter, Dad?" Ian huffed as they ran through the downpour to the car.

"Nothing. Just didn't want the two of you getting washed away by the flood."

"Is there a flood?" Harry asked.

"One never knows," Martin intoned solemnly, closing the boys into the Rover, Ian in front, Harry in the rear.

"It's exciting," Ian decided. "I hate maths anyway."

"I was right in the middle of a problem." Harry wrinkled his nose. "I *like* maths."

"You're a toady," Ian muttered.

"I am *not*!" Harry was thoroughly indignant.

"You are! You only say you like maths because you want Mr. Andrews to like you, because when Mr. Andrews likes someone he lets them have special privileges, and you want to be his pet. You want to clean the blackboards and give out the copybooks."

"You're a *fart*!" Harry shrieked. "You're a big, stinking fart!"

Ian threw himself over into the back seat, fists flailing.

"Stop that, the two of you!" Martin ordered, trying to see past the rain washing down the windscreen.

"I'll murder you," Ian whispered vehemently.

"Stinking fart!" Harry snarled.

"Toady!"

"Fart!"

"Belt up!" Martin raised his voice. "You're both toady farts."

There was a stunned silence in the rear of the car as both boys gaped at the back of their father's head.

"Can't see a bloody thing," Martin groused.

"We're *not* toady farts," Ian ventured, hurt.

"All right, you're not. Just wait until we get back to the cottage before you start having another go at each other. Bad enough trying to navigate in this pissing torrent without having to listen to the two of you."

Silence again, and then, in a small voice, Ian asked, "You mad at us, Dad?"

"I'm not mad at you. Sorry if I shouted."

That night, as Martin tucked the boys in, Ian's small hand fastened to Martin's sleeve. "Why were you mad at us, Dad?" he asked.

Martin sighed and sat down on the side of the bed, leaning close to kiss Ian's polished forehead. "Sometimes," he said, looking over to include Harry, "it's hard caring about people. You know that. You've seen how your mother and I have had to work to set things right. It's like those times when you boys want to do something and your mother and I say it's not on. The two of you go off grousing and plotting how you'll murder the two of us in our beds." The boys laughed. "Well, sometimes," he continued, "when you hear the people you care about being filthy to each other, you want to make them stop because it's so painful to listen to."

"You mean like when you and Mom used to fight when you were drunk," Harry said.

"Something like that," Martin agreed somberly, ashamed to have been responsible for the implantation of memories like that in his sons' minds. "The thing of it is, I'm leaving in a few days and I don't want to go off thinking of the two of you fighting when I know you're really fast friends. I also know there are times when it's hard not to fight. People never do get along all the time. But you're brothers, not enemies. When you get pissed off with each other and start having a go, I suppose it surprises me a little. Maybe it's because I've always romanced the idea of having brothers and sisters. Just go easy, and be sure to give your mother a hand while I'm gone. Okay?''

"We will, Dad," Ian promised.

"All right. Now, give us a kiss and then get to sleep."

He hung out the train window, waving long after the station was left behind. At last, he retired to his empty first-class compartment and sat gazing sightlessly out the window as the countryside hurtled past. He had never experienced anything like the pain that gripped him now. His throat dry and swollen, he remained unmoving all the way to London, where, with detached efficiency, he oversaw the transfer of his luggage to a taxi.

Throughout the wait for his flight to be called, and all the way over the Atlantic, he saw Marian and Harry and Ian on the platform, calling goodbye. A drink would have helped break up the clot in his throat, but he refused all offers and pretended to sleep, a thin British Airways blanket drawn over his head.

Ironically, he'd had the same feeling years before when, as a small boy, he'd been sent to live with his grandmother. The idea of his susceptibility to such welling emotion mortified him, yet he couldn't dismiss it. He reminded himself constantly of the work awaiting him on the house, and in the studio over the garage. He had to prepare the place for his family's return. One hundred and seventy-nine days sober. It was hard to believe, when the impulse to throw off the blanket and summon the flight attendant was overwhelming. It didn't seem possible he'd be able to survive the coming months alone, and sober. He heard again Ian asking, "You mad at us, Dad?" and frowned at the lame, ineffectual explanation he'd given his sons. No, I'm not mad at you, he intoned voicelessly. I bloody *love* you.

Chapter 13

THE TWO OF THEM were trying desperately to re-create the peaceable atmosphere they'd lived in before the accident. Their efforts were so strenuous they seemed tainted by the faint odor of perspiration. ·

She had come home from the hospital to find the apartment spotless—Ron had hired a cleaning service to erase the grime and tidy the disarray of his brief bachelorhood—and festooned with pots and vases of flowers. He'd stood to one side of the door wearing an expression of optimistic expectation and, dutifully, she'd applauded his thoughtfulness. He'd even stocked the kitchen with more food than they could possibly eat and had, having risen early that morning, pre-prepared a meal for them to have that evening. She'd been touched, and a little chagrined, by this display of his renewed interest in her. She'd found it fairly incomprehensible in view of her present inability to reciprocate.

He'd carried her suitcase to the bedroom while she'd stood in the living room like a first-time visitor, noticing how successfully her possessions and his had become blended. It seemed unlikely that a separation of their belongings could ever be made, but the idea failed to bother her, and that was another unsettling discovery. She couldn't seem to find within herself the passion with which she'd once viewed the prospect of making a permanent home for the two of them. The apartment was overrun with items she'd purchased to that end, and she'd looked around with detachment, wondering why she'd ever believed that knickknacks and curiosities could create an atmosphere of hominess. What she'd fashioned, in her fervor for nesting, was a themeless clutter of mainly useless objects.

To heighten her already festering fear, she realized she felt homeless. In an attempt to normalize the situation, she sat down with the daily newspapers and ran through the ads for executive secretaries. She lined up half a dozen interviews, retyped her résumé, then took herself off to the bedroom, where, in the unforgiving glare of midday light, she went to work with cover sticks and powder, hoping to devise some method of concealing the worst of the surgical tracks left indelibly etched into her face.

She painted and powdered, wet her face with a fine mist from the plant sprayer, then added another layer of makeup. The result was very like an Oriental mask, from behind which her undamaged eyes stared out: a Vincent Price movie with some murderous weirdo gazing through the eyeholes of a family portrait at potential victims. With some gray eye shadow and black mascara her eyes appeared larger, became more of a focal point. She brushed her hair forward, tried a center parting, then went for the scissors and cut a thick fringe to cover her forehead. The length of her hair helped hide at least part of her cheeks, but there was nothing more she could do.

She arrived early for her first interview, and sat in the waiting room trying not to squirm under the steady glare of the receptionist. Caley turned the pages of a magazine, telling herself she would not be thrown; she would not allow herself to be rattled by the truculent heat of the young woman's eyes.

When at last she was invited to go through to the personnel office, her clothes felt several pounds heavier and clung damply.

The woman who was to conduct the interview failed to look up when Caley arrived at her cubicle. She was in the midst of reading Caley's résumé and merely said, "Have a seat. I'll be right with you." Caley sat down and waited, longing for a cigarette, or something to do with her hands.

"This looks good," the woman said, raising her head with a smile she had to fight to hold onto as she saw Caley's face for the first time. She looked, Caley thought, like someone trying to keep a grip on a slippery fish. The smile faltered, but held. "Is that why it's been five months since you've worked?" she asked baldly.

"That's right." Caley had to clear her throat.

"What *happened*?" she asked, folding her arms over the papers on the desk and leaning forward with unfeigned eagerness.

"I was in a car crash."

"You must've gone through the windshield," the woman conjectured.

"That's right."

"What a shame," she commiserated. "And your qualifications are so good, too."

"Pardon?"

"Harding likes good-looking secretaries," the woman explained. "He'd take one look at you and have a coronary. I'm sorry to be so blunt, but there's no point to wasting anybody's time. I couldn't possibly send you up to see him. Are you going to be having plastic surgery?"

"I've already had it." Caley got to her feet.

"Here," the woman said. "Take your résumé. I know how expensive they are. And good luck."

She didn't add, "You're going to need it," but she might as well have. Caley folded the résumé into her handbag and retraced her steps to the reception area. She had originally planned to ask the receptionist to phone for a taxi, but that was out of the question now. She walked down to the lobby, where she'd spotted a telephone booth on her way in.

The next interview took place in a small insurance agency in Greenwich. She wasn't even invited to have a seat. The woman who'd been so friendly on the telephone took one look—Caley could almost see and hear the gears faintly whirring as the woman spoke—and said, "Gee, I'm really sorry. We just hired someone."

A definite pattern evolved. There were those who asked right out what had happened to her, expressing a morbid interest in the details of the accident. There were others who, upon sight of her, simply shut down and offered any excuse they could think of to be rid of her. The latter group appeared to be personally affronted, seething with infuriation that they should have to deal with someone who had misrepresented herself, who should have declared on the telephone that she was disfigured. She was spoken to as if she were simple-minded, or retarded; she was given a highly imaginative roster of lies that ranged from "The job's been taken" to "The personnel director just quit."

She got through five interviews and then declared a moratorium on her search for work. It was plain no one was going to hire her. She took to spending her days indoors with the curtains drawn, watching hated soap operas on TV and commenting aloud, in furious tones, on the stupidity of the feckless fools playing out idiotic roles in basically moronic scenarios. Between shows, refusing to give in to the hot tide of shame ready at any moment to drown her, she tried to think of something productive she might do with what remained of her life. Her anger and hurt were like raw sores on her body she told herself would go away, if she just didn't pick at them.

After five weeks of skirting each other with exaggerated politeness, Ron returned home one evening, smiling warmly, clearly bent on definitive action. He moved to take her in his arms. Gracelessly, she evaded the embrace.

"What's wrong?" he asked, at a loss. He'd imagined they'd make love. After all these months of abstinence, he'd hoped she'd see this demonstration of desire as proof of his affection. Aside from that, it had become for him a matter of undiluted need. They couldn't go on indefinitely sharing a bed without touching. He'd become accustomed to the sight of her; her features no longer jarred him each time he happened to glance over. Finally, he found her desirability unchanged. He'd overcome his initial revulsion, and had cast it away. Even though she was obviously still in a bad way emotionally, and he could often feel her rage and sorrow, he saw her now as being in need of all the support and caring he could give her. When he thought of her now—pausing in the course of his working day to consider her—he saw her as small and curled in upon herself, large-eyed with fear of further betrayals. He wanted very much to protect her.

In self-defense, she said the first thing that came to mind. "It's getting to the point where, when I wake up in the morning, I don't know where I am, whether I'm here or back in the hospital."

"Well, you're through with hospitals, for the time being anyway."

"Maybe for good." She reached to pick up an opaque glass vase with a pleasingly flat width she'd bought a year or so before on her lunch hour one afternoon in Greenwich. She looked around the living room, trying to think of what to say to him. "Why did you go out and buy all those flowers?" she asked.

"I wanted to."

She replaced the vase on the bookcase shelf, sat down, then at once jumped up to get her cigarettes. "Why?" she asked, returning to the sofa.

"I was excited about you coming home," he answered, sitting at her side.

"Why?"

"Why? Why was I excited? Because the place was like a tomb without you. Because I missed you. What's with all the questions, Cale?"

"Just curious," she said inadequately.

"I even," he admitted, "opened your closet a couple of times to remind myself how you smell."

"You could've just sniffed my perfume bottle."

"I tried that. It doesn't smell the same." His hand descended onto her shoulder and he lowered his head to her neck. "You don't have any on today."

"Not at the moment." He wanted to make love and she'd never been more reluctant. Yet she was curious, too. Perhaps if they did it, her love for him would reappear. "I could always put some on," she offered.

"Drink?"

"Sure. Why not?"

"The usual?"

"Sure."

He went into the kitchen to get the drinks. She sat a moment, smoking her cigarette, then got up and went into the bedroom. Did hookers feel this way? she wondered, despising her premeditation as she put out the cigarette before closing the curtains.

"Hey! Where'd you go?" he called from the living room.

"In here," she answered, stepping out of her shoes.

Pleasure darted in and out of her grasp. She couldn't involve herself in what was happening, even though Ron diligently worked to arouse her. She lay beneath him with her eyes closed, grieved by the mechanics of what had always, before, been the best part of their relationship. It had taken them months to get past their initial shyness and talk about what gave them each pleasure; months they'd spent learning to view one another openly, without self-consciousness. So much time and effort had gone into the weaving of an attachment, and now all she wanted was to have him finish and go away. Every thrust, each gasping breath he drew, generated only her despair and self-contempt. Yet when they were once more separate, she felt a terrible tenderness for him and had to stroke his arm until he got up and padded off to the bathroom to shower.

"I don't think this is going to work," she told him as he was pulling on his jeans. "It doesn't feel the same as it did. *We* don't feel the same."

"We're just out of practice, Cale." He reached beneath the sheet to fondle her breast. She stayed his hand.

"I'm not talking about that. I mean the two of us don't feel the same anymore."

"We both have adjustments to make." He tried to take hold of her hand.

"Oh, Christ!" she cried, in an exasperated scramble taking herself out of his range. Naked, cold, she stood by the bathroom door trying not to shower him with the rage she thought might spew from her mouth like lava. "I'm not in love with you anymore, Ron. I never thought this could happen. I thought the two of us would get married, buy a house, have kids, and live happily ever after. I really believed in that; it was my whole dream. Now, it's all changed. If I stay here with you, I'm going to end up destroying both of us. I need time to be by myself, to find out how I feel. I don't know what I think, who I am. All I feel, all the time, is angry and afraid."

"What'll you do?" he asked quietly. "What d'you want me to do?"

"I don't know." She wrapped her arms around herself for warmth. "I'm really sorry. I feel so awful about this. I thought if we made love again, everything would come right; we'd know each other again. I feel worse than I did before. I feel so dishonest. I think . . . I think I'd like to take the settlement money and go away.''

"Where?"

"I don't know. Somewhere. If you'd prefer it, I can go stay in a motel or something until the money comes."

"You don't have to do that," he said, looking hurt that she'd even think such a thing. "Anyway, the money came yesterday. The check's in my briefcase. I was going to give it to you after dinner, make it like a celebration. I don't understand this," he said somewhat angrily. "This is all part of blaming me for the accident, isn't it?"

"God! No, it isn't. I don't blame you. I honestly don't. I feel as if I blame myself, and that's not right either. I just . . . I want to run away. I want to get in a car and just drive. I want to find some kind of attitude I can live with, and maybe if I'm not out looking for a job, or wanting anything from people, maybe it'll put me on a different footing and I'll start to feel better about everything."

"You can't just drive forever. I mean, what kind of an idea is that?"

"Please," she begged. "I can't explain this. Let me have a little time to work out what I'm going to do. Maybe it would be better if I went to a motel."

The sight of her ruined face and thin, shivering body had a sudden, harrowing effect upon him, and he filled instantly with desolation. "Caley," he said, going to her, "don't even try to explain. You don't have to do that." He held her and shut his eyes as if his temporary inability to see might impede the progress of the understanding gaining ground in him. "Jesus, Cale! It's all fallen apart, and I tried so fucking hard to keep that from happening."

"I know that." She sighed, his body still warm from the shower thawing her. "I didn't know I was going to feel this way. I was counting on coming home, being with you, and putting things back to the way they were."

"How could you know how you'd feel? Nobody knows those things. I still love you."

"I don't want to hurt you, but I've got to get away. I have this feeling . . . it's kind of like wanting to get away from the scene of the crime. You know?''

"Maybe you'll change your mind and want to come back."

"Maybe," she allowed. "But I couldn't ask you to put your life on hold for me. The thing is, when I try to imagine any kind of future for myself, I can't see one. That really scared me, at first. Now, I'm scared, but it's different. I've got to get away, see where I'm going to go."

There was an ad in the next day's *Advocate* she kept coming back to. It was for a 1970 Cadillac convertible in good condition for thirty-two hundred dollars.

"It's probably a junker," Ron said, after reading the ad. "Why don't you go after something practical, Cale? Aside from everything else, those old Caddies get about three miles to the gallon."

"I'm going to phone anyway."

"It's up to you," he said, and returned to the paperwork he'd brought home.

The voice that answered sounded as if it belonged to an aging thug.

"I'm calling about your ad for the seventy Cadillac," she said.

"Yeah," the voice replied. "It's a great car, in good condition, clean. This for yourself, you're calling?"

"That's right."

"Great voice you got there. Tell you what, you come over take a look at this baby. You want it, I like the sound of your voice, I'll let you have it for twenty-five hundred. You look as good as you sound, you can drive away for two thousand."

"What's wrong with it?" she asked suspiciously.

"Nothin'. Me, I can tell people from the sound of their voice. You sound great. Come over, take a look."

She took his name and address, then went back to the living room to ask Ron if he'd mind driving her there.

"He said he liked the sound of my voice, so he'd let me have it for twenty-five hundred." She gave him an abridged version of the conversation.

"Sounds fishy."

"You know all about cars. If you think it's a dud, I won't buy it."

"Nobody in his right mind's going to sell you a decent

Caddy for twenty-five hundred," he argued as they drove toward the Cove area. "Guy sounds like a loony."

"He sounds like a thug, right out of Hell's Kitchen, with this gruff, gravelly, dese and dose voice. He probably is a thug. We'll know soon enough." She was curious to know what would happen when this man saw her. He'd probably refuse to sell her the car, and never mind his offer to knock five hundred off the asking price. Ron was undoubtedly right, she thought. People didn't start knocking the price down just because they liked the way you sounded on the telephone.

"I'll wait in the car until it's time for a test drive," Ron said. "My tagging along might put him off, if he's on the level and the sound of your voice got him all turned on." He parked at the foot of the driveway to a large waterfront house and reached for the newspaper she'd brought along.

Two men were standing outside the garage, and she couldn't decide which of them might belong to the gangster voice. Both men turned, catching sight of her, and she was able to watch the smiles vanish from their faces as she approached.

"I'm Caley Burrell. I just called about the Cadillac."

The larger of the two men recovered himself sufficiently to say, "You talked to me. C'mon, I'll show you the car." He turned and lifted open the garage door. "She's a beauty," he said, pulling down the cuffs on his plaid sports shirt as he turned back to her. "A coupla small patches of rust, and that's it. Mint condition."

If it ran, she'd buy it. The car was the embodiment of a dream she hadn't known she'd had until this moment.

"I want Ron to have a look at it. Okay?" She turned to discover pity creasing the middle-aged man's rugged face. On another day, she might have reacted to it, but just then she didn't have time. She signaled to Ron to come, then continued with her examination of the convertible.

"Only problem it has is the window on the passenger side doesn't want to work," the man told her. "Otherwise, she's perfect. You want to go for a drive, the keys're in the ignition."

Coming up the driveway, Ron emitted a low whistle. "Christ! That's something!"

"Got six more just like it," the man confessed with a grin and a shrug. "Took 'em as part of a deal. That's how come

I'm not asking more. I just want to move 'em.''

"Six more?" Ron asked, his eyes on Caley as she opened the driver's door and climbed inside.

"Your wife?" the man asked in a lowered voice.

"My friend."

"Had some kinda accident, huh?"

"Right." Ron moved to open the passenger door. "We'll take the car for a short test drive."

"Take a long one. Look under the hood. She's a beauty, I'm tellin' ya."

The engine started with a satisfying roar over which Caley stated, "I'm going to buy it! I love it!"

"Let's see if it runs first." Ron smiled as she swung her arm over the rear of the seat and turned to check that the driveway was clear.

"It's terrific!" she cried, steering the huge car down the street.

"It sounds pretty good. The shocks seem to be all right, and the interior's in okay shape." He ran his hand over the leather. "Head along here another couple of blocks, then park, and I'll have a look under the hood."

When they returned, Caley announced, "I'll buy it."

The man smiled. "Told ya. It's a beauty."

"I can bring you a cashier's check tomorrow."

"No sweat. I'll take your personal check, sign over the title here and now."

"She doesn't have insurance," Ron said.

"No problem," he said again. "Mine'll cover her until she gets signed on."

Caley had her bag open and her checkbook out. "Who do I make it out to?" she asked.

"Frank Longo," he said. "Gimme two thousand. You got a great voice."

There was a short somewhere in the wiring, which was why the passenger window failed to work, and why the battery was dead when she went to start the car the next morning. Ron solved the problem, once he'd jump-started the Caddy from his LTD, by showing her how to detach the cables from the battery.

"If you're only going to be leaving the car for a couple of

hours, it'll be all right. But when you're leaving it overnight, disconnect the battery and that way the short won't drain it. You can hook it up again when you're ready to go. Keep a small wrench in the glove compartment. Where *are* you going to go, Cale?" he asked, overseeing as she practiced disconnecting the battery cables.

"I don't have any definite plans. You don't think there's anything else wrong he didn't tell me about, do you?"

"I don't see anything. The points and plugs are good, the air filter's new, the fan belt's okay. The oil's right up, the exhaust's clean, no smoke or anything. I checked out the brake shoes and they're okay. You got yourself a bargain. You'll make up for it on gas, though. You'll be lucky to get fifteen to the gallon."

"I don't mind," she said, slamming closed the hood. "I love this car. I'm going to call her Clarabelle."

"Jesus!" He laughed.

"You've got a plan," Stan guessed.

"No, I don't. I've just got the idea that I'm going to get in the car and drive."

"Where to?"

"I don't know. North, south. Maybe I'll drive all the way from one end of the country to the other. I need to go."

"You're running away, Caley."

"That's right, I am."

"You're still going to have the same problems when you get back."

"You're assuming I plan to come back."

"Aaah!" He tilted back in his chair, his eyes on her. "I don't think I like what I'm not hearing."

"I only came to tell you I'm going, to say goodbye."

"And you're saying goodbye to Ron, too?"

"Right again."

"It's not worth making the effort to salvage what the two of you had?"

"I've tried." She lit a cigarette and recrossed her legs, holding the hand with the cigarette in front of her face. "I've tried so hard, I can *smell* myself trying. I still love him, but it's not the same. I can't get involved with loving him, not the way I used to."

"Can't or won't?"

"I don't *feel* involved," she amended. "Why was it I thought we'd just say goodbye and there'd be no inquisition?"

"I get the distinct impression you've got a very definite destination in mind, Caley. And I don't care for the impression I'm getting."

"You don't have to like it. It doesn't concern you."

"Sure it concerns me. I care about you."

"In your professional capacity."

"Don't give me that bullshit!" he snapped. "I don't segregate the professional caring from the personal caring. It's all just caring, and it bothers the hell out of me when someone I like sits here telling me goodbye and it has an inescapable ring of finality to it."

"I'm going on a trip, and using my settlement money to pay for it. What's wrong with that?"

"The trip part's fine. It's what comes after that worries me. What does come after, Caley?"

"Nothing. I can't get a job. Ron and I are out the window. Watching soap operas all day is rotting my brains."

"How hard have you tried?" he asked. "Half a dozen interviews and you've given up. There are jobs out there, but instead of digging in and seeing it through, you're running off on a major avoidance trip."

"Why do you have to put a name to everything?" she wanted to know.

"Why are you hell-bent on avoiding everything?" he countered. "Why are you so convinced your life isn't worth living? Why do you want to dump all your dreams in the garbage, write them off as trash?"

"I *hate* myself!" she raged. "I can't stand the sight of my goddamned face, and nobody else can, either."

"Nobody's one hundred percent happy with what they see in the mirror. It's not a good enough reason for killing yourself."

"As far as I'm concerned, it is."

He chewed on his lower lip and mashed his hands together. "You've shut down!" he said hotly. "You've made up your mind, and you refuse to listen."

"Look," she said, relenting. "I haven't completely made up my mind. I've just decided that going away is the one real option I've got at the moment. It's kind of comforting, Stan. If I have to sit around worrying about the rest of my life, and how everything's turned to shit, it makes me feel better to know that I don't have to stagnate.''

"You don't have to go out there looking the way you do, either. That surgery's still waiting.''

"Someday, sometime, some year. I don't want to discuss that now. I'm afraid, goddamn it!''

"You're just going to take it all with you.''

"Platitudes.''

"Nope,'' he said. "Truth.''

"Look, Stan. What I'm going to do is the right thing for me. You don't have to agree. I just know it's right. It's either get in the car and drive or put my head in the oven. Given the choice, I want to get in the car. I have a good feeling about it.''

"Will you do something for me?''

"What?''

"If you come right up to the edge, wherever you happen to get to, will you call me before you do anything? Will you just call me?''

"Why?''

"Humor me, and promise you will. I'll give you my card and write my home number on the back.'' He took a card case from his inside pocket.

"All right.'' She accepted the card. "I'll call you.''

"Make it collect, if you have to.''

At that, she laughed. "I've got plenty of money, Stan.''

"Then you won't have an excuse for not calling.''

The night before she was to leave, she was overcome by sadness. She hadn't expected to feel anything but relieved at the prospect of her departure, but when she put her arms around Ron with the intention of holding him a final time, she erupted into long-delayed tears, and clung to him feeling she might already be at the edge, her proposed trip nothing more than a tactic to delay the inevitable. She'd once loved this man, and a stinking traffic accident had killed off her ability to keep on loving him. He'd somehow managed to keep hold of his feelings for her, and it shamed her. Enshrouded in sadness and guilt, she sobbed on Ron's shoulder, trying to explain to him how responsible she felt for the loss of all they'd ever hoped to have together.

"You can always come home, Cale," he comforted her. "You might get out there and find you want to come back."

"I might," she said, wondering how offering even this slim possibility could deliver him such obvious pleasure. It was because he loved her, and this was the ultimate proof: he could be happy simply anticipating some future date when she might return. "Don't wait for me, Ron," she sobbed, holding on hard for the last time to all she was giving up. "I don't think I'm going to be back."

Chapter 14

GRACE HAD, for many years, rented a house in Puerto de la Cruz for the months of March and April. Located just beyond the old town with its narrow streets and overhanging wooden balconies, there was a typical central patio around which the house had been built. The patio was a cool refuge, with enormous potted ferns and flowering plants, where tables and benches and chaises longues sat invitingly on the square-cut paving stones. The interior rooms, kept shuttered throughout the day, were also cool, with rough, white-painted walls and simple furnishings.

Soon after they were married, Martin and Marian had come to Tenerife to spend a month with her parents, and Martin had spent most of his time in the Coach and Horses—a transmogrified British pub—drinking and talking with the British regulars, who seemed to derive comfort from finding a bit of England on this unforgivably foreign island. Old Hugh had frequently accompanied him, with the result that both Marian and her mother spent the entire month in a state of barely suppressed hostility. They had been joined, for those weeks, in common dislike of their husbands, and had sat together often on the patio, trading disparaging comments on the uselessness and consistently puerile behavior of men in general. Both women, as a result, had suffered from differing degrees of disloyalty, guilty at giving voice to their anger instead of quietly pretending that life was very much as usual. Grace had not invited them to return until now.

With a ravening need for the sight of his wife and children, Martin flew over three days ahead of time. Grace, driving the late-model Fiat that came with the house, collected him from the airport, amused by her son-in-law's impetuosity.

"Thought I'd just come ahead," he told her. "Couldn't see the point to sitting in that perishing bloody house twiddling my thumbs."

"Of course," she agreed, inclining her head. "I quite understand. How was your flight?"

"Bloody awful, naturally. Flying without a drink's like standing about in the middle of the M-1, just begging some twit to come along and run you down."

"You haven't brought much in the way of luggage," she noted.

"Didn't think I'd need much," he said. "Just my sketching gear, the camera, and some clean knickers."

She laughed, cautiously holding the car to a steady fifty kilometers. "Why is it," she asked, "that small boys, and you, Martin, are so preoccupied with knickers?"

"It's in our nature, isn't it?" He gave her knee a smooth pat. "You're looking jolly healthy."

"Thank you. It's the midday siestas."

"Is that what it is? I was hoping you'd say you'd taken up with some slick Spaniard."

She laughed hugely. "I'm a bit past it," she said. "Just a bit."

"I'll wager you've been over raiding the old botanical garden when no one's looking."

"As a matter of fact," she admitted, "I've quite a number of cuttings I plan to smuggle back in my sponge bag."

"They'll catch you at it one day, my girl, and then we'll be coming to visit you in the nick."

"Did you let Marian know you'd be coming ahead early?"

"Rang her before I left. What I want to know is why she's coming on this bloody charter flight from Manchester."

"She couldn't get seats," she explained. "It was the only flight with available space."

"She shouldn't have left it to the last bloody minute," he said, irked. "I told her to book seats before I went back to Canada."

"It doesn't really matter, does it?"

"I expect not," he said grudgingly.

While Grace took her siesta that afternoon, Martin went off for a walk through town. Sketching gear in hand, he strolled through the old town toward the main square, the Plaza Charco. The place was overrun with tourists, the outdoor café in the center of the square filled with nattering Brits sorting through their bargain-priced acquisitions. He continued on through the square to the Avenida de Colón, stopping to look down at the black sand beach of Playa Martianez, where well-oiled bodies lay baking in the sun.

He was surprised to remember as much as he did about the town, and walked along, glancing incuriously into the endless shops as he passed. On all sides, people were hawking their wares, everything from seashells to stuffed bloody alligators. The smell of fish and hot food cooking hung in the air. At the end of the Avenida, where the promenade became some other unpronounceable avenue, he stopped to sit down on a bench and watch the tourists troop past.

The sun bludgeoned his eyes. It danced in electric pinpoints off the water; it threw itself upon the shops and people with unremitting intensity; it insinuated itself through his skull, heating his brain. He sat, his hand shielding his eyes, staring at El Teide, the twelve-thousand-foot mountain, in the distance. No matter where one went on the island, the mountain was always in view, and he studied it now as the cool offshore breeze lifted the short sleeves of his cotton shirt. He was more tired than he'd realized, from his long hours of traveling. He had left Toronto in the middle of a snowstorm and had tried to ignore the shuddering lift of the aircraft as it had ascended through layers of cloud. He still felt queasy from the turbulence they'd encountered until they were well out over the Atlantic.

He'd come rushing across the ocean in order to expedite their reunion, but Marian and the boys wouldn't join him for another three days. He was both enervated and charged by the energy in the sun, the water, the tides of skimpily dressed people shopping. He saw nothing he wished to chart on the leaves of his bound sketchbook, yet he knew perfectly well that a short walk to the botanical garden would present him with enticing views. He well remembered the ancient fig trees with their grotesquely conjoined roots, the flowering riot of mimosa and bougainvillaea and jacaranda. Entering the garden was like gaining access to the fantasies of some elderly, slumbering giant, whose visions were entirely proportionate to the immensity of his personal structure. Everything was overblown, entangled, and almost insanely healthy. The trees and plant life proliferated almost as one watched, flowers shooting into existence as if to defy the natural order that pertained anywhere else.

He wished Marian would decide she'd had enough of the bronchial British winter and pile herself and the boys on a plane and come to the island early. He was beside himself every time he considered the hash the bloody Inland Revenue was making of his life. Redirecting his gaze to the dusty-coal expanse of sand, he watched two nearly naked, amply endowed young women slathering oil over each other's limbs. He found them interesting, but unappealing. All that youth overspilling the gaudy confines of a few snippets of fabric struck him as nothing more than a rude advertisement, a vulgar statement he had no wish to hear. The sight of the same two young women kissing, their oily hands held safely aloft, sent him to his feet. What people chose to do in the privacy of their bedrooms was entirely their own affair, but when they elected to perform publicly, he was offended. It made not a bit of difference to him that a woman should select, as the object of her desire, another woman. Homosexuality had never been a threat or an enticement to him. He simply disliked crude displays that could be overseen. To his mind, all emotions were rendered indelicate when, subjected to the scrutiny of strangers. Oddly enough, acts of an erotic nature depicted within the context of a film or play were capable of arousing in him a high degree of personal fire. He'd always thought this was because he viewed these performers while contained in sacrosanct darkness that allowed him to be viscerally involved, with that eight-foot breast, that twelve-foot thigh, that three-foot-wide mouth, all effectively lit to highlight what was ineluctably compelling. Women were exquisite creatures, marvelously unknowable in their fathomless self-possession.

Marian was a perfect example of everything that repeatedly
drew him to attempt, again and again, to pierce the enigma of
her containment within herself. It seemed to him astounding
that her eternally alluring externals were available to him, like
a puzzle he could play with ceaselessly, yet whose inner secret
would never be yielded up to him. There were times when, in a
certain light, he thought her smile and the glow of her eyes
were confirmation of how impossible it was for him ever to
solve the riddle she represented. He would have to spend—and
gladly—the remainder of his life turning the puzzle this way
and that, in a never-ending attempt to solve it.

The outdoor café, sheltered beneath the great palms in the
center of the square, was less than half filled upon his return.
He took a seat at a table on the periphery and ordered lemonade. Nearby, a bearded young man in walking shorts and a T-
shirt sat with one hairy leg propped over the other, an outsized
sketch pad balanced in his lap. He worked, pausing from time
to time, to drink some of the local malvasía wine. There was
something unforgivably contrived about his posture and the
convenient placement of the wine, even about the leather sandals fastened to his huge, not entirely clean feet. The man had
arranged himself like a still life, Martin thought contemp-
tuously.

There were artists who at once commanded respect, simply
by their obvious involvement with the subject of their choosing. Martin often paused to take judicious note of the work in
progress of other artists, even going so far, upon occasion, as
to offer his compliments on a line particularly well executed.
Then there were the poseurs, the draftsmen of little or no talent whose sole gambit in life was to position themselves prom-
inently in the hope of generating a sufficient daily dose of
attention. He could spot them at a hundred yards, and was
rarely wrong. Women were not exempt from this type of pos-
turing, but seemed less often given to flaunting their lack of
skill. Bloody hell! he thought, shifting his chair in order not to
have to look at the flagrant son of a bitch. Why, just once,
couldn't Marian take wing on an impulse and rescue him?
He'd take her and Grace and the boys off to La Riviera in
Santa Cruz for the best food on the island; he'd take them to
La Laguna to look at the churches, and to the forest of Monte

de las Mercedes, and to Englishman's Peak; he'd take them on that gut-wrenching cable-car ride up the old lady, Monte Teide. The boys would adore that. They'd shriek their hearts out. Years before, he'd almost passed out during that eight-minute ride to the top. But he'd go it again for the boys.

The lemonade tartly acid, it cut its way down his throat and arrived, a cool surprise, in his stomach. He sipped at the drink, his eyes recording the activity in the square. The light, where it fell unimpeded by the palms, cast a white glaze on everything that it touched so that, in brutal contrast, the shadows seemed to be lit from within, smoldering with color. This was a place that demanded watercolors, so that one could demonstrate with some degree of accuracy the way the light leached the tone in one spot, while infusing another area with hues of an intensity it was almost agonizing to see.

The bearded twit had finished his wine and was ordering another bottle. His American effusiveness knifed jarringly through the placidity of the café. Gulping down the last of the lemonade, Martin summoned the waiter, paid, and left the square, heading back through the old town to the house. He admitted to himself as he went that everything was a piss-off just now simply because he'd never had any real gift for playing a waiting game—for anyone or anything. Arbitrarily, because he was here three days early, he wanted Marian to be early as well. He needed to see her. Their telephone conversations had, for the most part, been taken up with logistics: Was this bill paid, had that letter been received, was he remembering to turn down the thermostat at night? The boys seemed not to know what to say when Marian turned the telephone over to them. Their voices lacked depth, as if they'd forgotten who he was and were merely being dutiful in saying their hellos. He wanted to see his wife and sons, to reestablish for them his reality, and to have them confirm his existence by the sheer substance of their bodies.

"I've never seen you quite so agitated, Martin," Grace declared on the evening before Marian and the boys were due to arrive. "For three days you've paced up and down, picked at your food, and, from the look of you, slept scarcely at all. Is there something wrong?"

"Too much undirected energy," he said, poking dubiously at the paella the maid had served up to him with a proud flourish. He'd refused the sopa verde, claiming that green soup had to have been concocted, in some part, from mold. "Absurd!" Grace had laughed. "It's parsley."

"I expect you'll be up at the crack of dawn to go to the airport," she said now, savoring an outsized shrimp.

"I expect so."

"I'm afraid you'll have to wait for me," she said equably. "I've no intention of leaving here a minute earlier than absolutely necessary. The flight's not due in until eight-o-four. If we leave at seven, we'll be there in ample time."

"Six-thirty. We'll leave at six-thirty."

She sighed, then shook her head. "We'll compromise and go at six forty-five."

"If we're late, I'll hold you responsible."

"We won't be late. Really, you should eat. This is simply delicious."

He pushed aside his plate and selected an orange from the immense bowl of fruit positioned in the center of the table. He peeled it, paying close attention to the many small fissures yielding juice as he cleaved the fruit meticulously into sections.

"Martin?" Grace asked. "Are you quite sure you're all right?"

He arranged the sections of the orange on the table, rearranging them as he attempted to put into words his inexplicable malaise. "Actually," he said, looking over at her with a smile, "I'm still trying to recover from the sight of you in that delectable bathing costume. Must drive the locals simply wild when you take to the beaches."

"Oh, quite!" She nodded, working to part the halves of a clam shell. "I daresay they're all home at this very moment taking good long whiffs of smelling salts to revive themselves. Seriously, Martin. Is there anything I can do to help?"

For a few seconds, as he gazed at her, Marian's features were superimposed upon her mother's. This older, deeply tanned edition of his wife comforted him. At the same time, he thought what a great pity it was that this exceptional woman had never been loved in marriage as she deserved, had never had the opportunity to divest herself of any consequential portion of her passion. Life, and a loveless marriage, had forced her to seek whatever physical pleasure she might find in the tending of an eternal garden. It seemed to him monumentally unfair, and a shocking waste.

"Have you ever thought," he asked, "what an enormously helpful social tool the old booze is? I've become a bloody bore since I stopped tippling. Rather cuts down on one's playtime establishments, to boot. The past few months, I've even found *myself* a frightful bore. I promised Marian I'd see to having the house repainted, and I haven't bothered yet to ring up and have them come round to give estimates." He selected another orange section and held it in his hand, examining it. "The truth, I suppose, is that I'm utterly useless without Marian around. I haven't the remotest notion, much of the time, what to do with myself. Can't begin to imagine how the washer and dryer function, so I've been carting all the laundry off to an inscrutable Oriental person who runs an establishment on Yonge Street. The oven, for some reason, doesn't respond to command and refuses to allow itself to be switched on. That puts paid to the old TV dinners. I've tried heating them on top of the stove. Filthy things got boiled on the bottom and were still frozen on top."

Grace chuckled as she helped herself to more of the paella. "You're simply not housebroken," she told him.

"I most certainly am. I've written out a list of all the places in the city that will deliver food, and I ring each of them in turn. Monday nights, I have some quite wonderful chicken from a place called the Swiss Chalet. They also, incidentally, do bloody good chips. Tuesday nights, I order pizza, or spaghetti, if I'm in the mood. Wednesday, I ring up for Chinese. Thursday, ribs arrive from Bar-B-Q Heaven. Friday, place on Bloor Street delivers me some of the hottest curry outside New Delhi. Saturday, the Lobster Kettle arrives with a succulent monster. And Sunday, the Princess of the South Pacific sends me over some Polynesian tidbits. All very organized. Occasionally, I cook up some eggs, brew a pot of tea. But the glory, you see, of living in a large city is the miracle of being able to ring up for a new delicacy every night."

"What sort of ribs?" Grace asked, curious.

"Piggy ribs. You know. From the back or the side. Very nice, they are."

"Piggy ribs. You're incorrigible."

"Not at all. Any number of people will confirm what a completely corrigible fellow I am. All this talk of bloody food's made me hungry," he said, pulling his plate back.

"It bothers you, doesn't it," she said, "being so dependent?"

"It certainly points up my general uselessness when it comes to matters of eating and cleaning. Why is it women are trained in the practical skills and men aren't? I'm going to see to it that Harry and Ian go to cookery school or somesuch. Undoubtedly, it's how you females entrap us. You've mastered the washer and dryer and the bloody oven."

"Oh, undoubtedly," she agreed. "It's all part of a subtle plot to keep you in your places." She patted her mouth with the serviette, then reached for her wineglass. "Would you care to go for a walk after dinner? There's an especially gifted guitarist at El Guanche."

"The old constitutional," he said, chewing fiercely. "Shades of the late departed Lady Bee, and the infamous nocturnal rambles to aid digestion."

"We'll have our coffee there," she said with a smile. "Good, isn't it?"

"It's all right. Do you ever regret any of it? I mean, all those years with that pompous old tyrant. Ever wish you'd dallied a bit on the side?"

Her deep blue eyes fixed on him for a long moment, and then she smiled brilliantly. "How do you know," she asked, "I didn't?"

"Half an hour ago they said the bloody flight was on time. Now they're saying it's behind schedule. What's going on?" Martin stormed.

"I expect the flight's simply delayed," Grace said calmly. "Try to relax, Martin. You'll have yourself worked up to a lather by the time they land."

"I like lather," he said. "I regularly lather up."

"Why don't you go along over there and have a word with the airlines people, see if they can't offer some explanation. I'll wait here."

Grace sat down and watched Martin go to the counter. He exchanged a few words with the woman there, then made his way back. "Toothy reassuring grin and a few basic platitudes," he said angrily, emphatically waving the hastily assembled bouquet of flowers he'd fashioned before leaving for the airport.

"Come sit down!" Grace ordered.

Martin perched on the edge of his seat, holding the flowers downward between his knees. "It's a bloody cock-up," he muttered. "Sorry, Grace, but something's gone wrong. I can feel it in my bones."

Unsure what to think, Grace put her hand on his arm and said, "This will all be sorted out any moment now, I'm certain."

"I'm confused," he admitted. "Just over half an hour ago, that arrivals board started flashing its light beside the Dan-Air listing. That means it was arriving. Now the light's gone off and the girl back of the counter says she's checking on it. Something's—" He broke off to listen to an announcement in Spanish that vibrated through the public address system. "What're they saying?" he asked Grace. "Did you get it?"

"I'm afraid I didn't. My Spanish isn't awfully good."

"Bloody hell!" he swore, looking around for someone who might translate for him. He noticed that the girl behind the counter was talking on the telephone, her features furrowed. Pushing the flowers at Grace, he hurried over to ask, "What's going on?"

"That was the control tower I was talking to." She pointed stupidly at the telephone. "They say the pilot requested permission to land and then they lost contact."

"When was that?"

"Thirty minutes ago."

"What does it *mean*?" he asked urgently.

"They think the plane has gone down in the sea, sir."

"Check the passenger list," he ordered frantically. "I want to know if my wife and children are on that flight."

"Certainly. What is the name, please?"

"Maddox. Marian, Harry, and Ian."

He stood and watched her punch into the computer terminal, knowing absolutely that she was going to confirm that Marian and the boys were on that flight. Dread cemented him to the spot and he waited, feeling all his internal systems threatening to shut down.

The girl nodded, directing large, liquid brown eyes to his. For a few moments, he was lost to the depthless empathy of her eyes. Then he managed to say, "Thank you," before turning to walk stiffly toward Grace.

She read it in his face. "Oh, dear God," she whispered. "The plane's crashed, hasn't it?" She stood up, the flowers falling around her feet.

He took her arm, thinking to direct her to the bar, then stopped himself. "I don't know what to do," he admitted barely audibly. "They think the plane's gone down in the bloody sea. They're sending planes out to look for it, notifying whatever ships are in the area. I don't know what to do."

"Perhaps it's a mistake," she began.

"It's no mistake. The pilot radioed in for permission to land, then they lost contact. *My wife and sons are on that bloody plane, Grace!*" His voice rose despairingly.

An airport official rounded up all those who were waiting to meet passengers on the Dan-Air flight and herded them to a small, private lounge situated to one side of the main waiting area. The half-dozen were offered drinks and coffee while the official promised to notify them the instant there was any news.

Martin and Grace sat side by side and drank the strong black coffee, trying to deal privately with their fear. At last, Martin jumped up, saying, "If I can't drink, I've got to do *something*," and went off. He returned a few minutes later with a package of American cigarettes. Grace refused his offer of one and sat back to watch as he began to smoke one cigarette after another.

At midday, trays of food were brought in. No word yet. No one ate.

Late in the afternoon, pots of fresh coffee and bowls of fruit were offered. Martin and Grace drank more coffee, sharing now an intense silence. Neither of them dared speak, nor were they able to look at each other. Side by side, barely touching, they waited.

More food was offered as darkness began to fall. It remained untouched and untasted on the trays.

Finally, the harried airport official returned to announce, first in Spanish and then in halting English, that the wreckage of the aircraft had been sighted on the mountain. He said that rescue workers were climbing to the site to search for survivors. As soon as any information was known, he would return, he promised.

"They're dead," Martin spoke for the first time.

"We can't be sure," Grace whispered.

"They're dead," he repeated. "All day I've been telling myself that. He just confirmed it."

There might be a miracle, Grace thought, as she got up to go in search of a W.C. Perhaps the children might still be alive. She took two steps toward the lounge door before the coffee, the stress, and her utter anxiety felled her. Martin flung himself forward to catch her and was borne to the floor by her weight. Crazed with fear, and uncaring of the spectacle they presented, he lay cradling his mother-in-law in his arms, weeping into her hair while someone went rushing off for medical assistance.

PART TWO

Chapter 15

UNCLE SAM RAN away just outside Ocala, Florida. Caley had left the cat in the car while she ran through a downpour to rent a room for the night. On her return, as she was unpacking, Uncle Sam hurled himself past her and streaked off. She called out, but he paid no heed: a sodden, overfat pellet shooting off on a preplanned escape.

She got her things into the room, then went out again, worriedly searching the parking lot. She hated the idea of the poor cat huddling somewhere, hungry and, perhaps, afraid. Why had he run off? He'd never been an adventurous animal. Maybe it had been wrong of her to uproot him, bringing him along as company.

Hourly that evening she stepped outside to scan the area, calling him to come to her. Her concern for the animal progressed to sadness for both of them. Sam was a house pet. How would he cope outdoors in unfamiliar terrain?

She slept poorly, and came fully awake at just past three from a dream that someone had come knocking at her door, refusing to respond when she'd asked, "Who's there?" She'd heard the menacing rattle of keys, and suddenly the door had started to open; unnaturally elastic fingers insinuated themselves between the door and the frame, attempting to unfasten the chain. She'd shoved hard against the door but the rubbery fingers had simply waggled, trapped, while she'd demanded again, "*Who's there?*" She'd wanted to telephone the police but feared leaving the door unguarded. At last, the sickeningly unreal fingers had oozed away as a man's voice whispered evilly, "It's your folly!" There was a pause, and then the rattling keys had been carried off.

She got up, lit a cigarette, and went to the door. The rain had stopped and she surveyed the puddled parking lot, softly calling Uncle Sam. Standing just outside the door, she smoked the cigarette, hoping he'd come into view. All that moved were the palms dripping in the tumid night air. She returned inside, fastened the chain, and tried again to sleep.

She dreamed this time that she'd parked the Cadillac in a vast lot before entering some sort of municipal building where she was to meet her old high school friend Barbara. It was the same Barbara who'd been on nursing duty in the emergency ward the night of the accident. Caley found her, and the two of them started toward the parking lot to retrieve the car, but couldn't seem to find their way. When they complained of this to a uniformed attendant, he smiled pleasantly and explained that they'd have to pay him, then follow the exit signs. The signs, oddly, were marked "Club" and led them up a circular ramp to a stairway. They climbed, following the signs, until they reached a top landing where the guardrail was missing, and a doorway set at least four feet above them was the end of the line. A discreet notice read, "Club." The door swung open and a businessman, clad in a raincoat and carrying a briefcase, smiled down at them, asking, "Coming to collect your sandwiches?" He smiled self-deprecatingly, commenting, "Ridiculous, isn't it? It's just about impossible to get in here." He offered to help them climb up, but Caley refused. Frustrated, and anxious to find the car, she turned to rail at Barbara, who backed away, saying, "I was just following the instructions he gave us."

She stayed in Ocala for three days hoping the cat would reappear. His running away seemed to symbolize the end of her attachment to home, to Ron. Without Sam, she had nothing to remind her of all she'd had, and lost. She'd been able, during the past month on the road, to put her feelings on hold. Now the cat had run away, and she was inundated by misgivings.

While there was a certain, almost mystical, isolation she experienced driving along, totally self-contained within the car, the frequent stops and attention she'd had to pay Sam had allowed her a nonspecific focus. All she'd had to do was drive, listening to the radio, and make routine roadside rendezvous with Sam's calls of nature. Faced with the prospect of continuing on without him, she had to reconsider just what it was she thought she might be accomplishing by this aimless, nomadic journey.

She'd managed to put part of it into words in her conversation with Stan. It all hinged on her being dependent only upon the car. She was seeking a state of being wherein she'd rely on strangers only for services, needing nothing more tangible from them in return. That was part of it. There was also, in her mind, the nebulous notion that she would learn about herself, about her strengths and weaknesses and her possible instincts for survival, as well as gaining some better insight into whether or not people would respond differently to her disfigurement when she appeared before them, not in the role of applicant for some position or emotion, but as someone with the wherewithal to purchase whatever it was they were selling.

She had, so far, garnered increasing pleasure from simply being on the road. She was going to have to find out if that pleasure would remain without Uncle Sam's insistent presence.

The manager expressed sympathy with her plight and said he'd keep an eye out for the gray Persian. Caley promised to call every few days, and got into the car, on her way to the Everglades. She drove, unable to relax, unable to take any satisfaction in the prospect of viewing the National Park. Giving up on her plan, she turned the car around and headed back to Ocala.

The manager of the Holiday Inn there wasn't surprised to see her.

"Thought you might be back," he said, sliding a registration card across the counter. "If you're gonna stay on awhile, I can give you a good weekly rate."

She couldn't decide what to do. She told herself it wasn't

reasonable to spend an additional week in this unpretty place for the sake of the cat. He'd claimed his freedom and was unlikely to return.

"I'll just stay tonight," she told the manager. "But if I change my mind, I'll let you know."

"Sure thing," he said, fishing a room key from one of the slots. "I understand these things." He smiled sadly. "The wife, she'd like to die she ever lost one of her Siamese."

She walked for hours looking for Uncle Sam while trying to come to terms with the fact that, from now on, she'd be completely alone. She tried to convince herself it was for the best. Nevertheless, every time she saw a cat, she had to stop and ascertain it wasn't Sam.

She performed a little ceremony of loss, consigning his dish and water bowl, the sacks of dry food and kitty litter, to the motel's dumpster. She hadn't expected to cry, but she did; standing empty-handed by a reeking refuse container, on the outskirts of a steamy Florida town, she wept, and then grew hardened, so that when she turned, finally, to the car and the continuation of her journey, she was determined to deal more level-mindedly with whatever came to pass.

To fill the gap left by Uncle Sam, she took to picking up hitchhikers. There was an appealing element of danger to inviting strangers into the car; she was toying now with her brittle mortality, with calculated indifference placing it in jeopardy. She'd see what, if anything, was in store for her. Perhaps she'd be relieved of the tiresome responsibility of her own future by some homicidal scavenger bent on adding to his collection of blood-spattered garments.

For the most part, she collected young soldiers from the roadside—boys who seemed inadequate beneath the weighty demands of their uniforms—who demonstrated a chilly politeness, who called her "ma'am," and who thanked her profusely with harried gratitude before nipping out of the car and marching smartly away in their spit-polished black boots.

In Valdosta, Georgia, she stopped for a pair of teenagers poised on the shoulder in the rain. Once ensconced in the rear of the car, the girl unzipped her nylon windbreaker to reveal a puppy she'd been sheltering. Charmed, Caley watched in the rear-view mirror as the girl played with the animal, and was disappointed when they asked to be let out at Cordele. As the boy was about to close the rear door, the girl said, "Did y'all see her *face*? Grossed me right out!" Caley gunned the motor, causing the tires to spit gravel at the witless pair as she shot past.

"*Fuck you and your puppy!*" she shouted, unheard, furious. Why couldn't the idiotic girl at least have waited until she was out of Caley's range before drawling out her complaints? She would not, in future, offer rides to any more females. At least the young soldiers affected good manners.

Alabama and Mississippi depressed her: too many mean dwellings squatting beneath the rain. She swung up into Tennessee, skirting Memphis on her way diagonally across the corner of the state into Missouri, and straight up through Missouri, headed for Iowa. Near the Iowa border, contravening her instincts, she pulled over for a young man whose looks —even from a distance, and especially close to—inspired trepidations. Thin, long-haired, and fully-bearded, he had Manson eyes and a nervous mouth. When she asked where he was headed, he mumbled, "Just along here a ways," and sat with his back against the door, glaring at her. They hadn't gone a mile when he said, "I'll get out here." She stopped the car and, before he closed the door, he bent in to smile, revealing horribly neglected teeth. "You're lucky you're so fuckin' ugly," he hissed, "else you'd be lyin' dead in the fuckin' ditch there." A gun materialized in his hand. Transfixed, she gaped at the gun for a moment, then some message managed to transmit itself from her brain and her foot went flat on the accelerator and she roared away, pulling into the first gas station she saw to call the state police and report, in a quivery voice, what had happened. She described where she'd left the young man and was told they'd send a cruiser right out there.

The station attendant listened slack-jawed to her end of the conversation. "You sure were lucky," he said, while he filled the Cadillac's tank. "You don't want to go picking up no strangers, a woman alone."

Still shaky from the incident, she bought a Coke from the faded old machine outside the office and drank it while the lanky attendant cleaned the car windows, then made change for her. As she was on her way back to the car, he admonished her again. "Don't go picking nobody up, now!"

"You can bet your life on it!" she replied. The encounter had managed to convince her she preferred not to risk a violent death. While death itself held few aspects of fear for her, and was, in fact, something she thought of often with something like fondness, she wanted to remain the engineer of her own fate. Her inability to sleep that night—each time she closed her eyes, seeing again those round, demented eyes and the filthy hand wrapped around the butt of the gun—confirmed she would take no more chances with strangers.

She liked Iowa, with its limitless cornfields and dusty heat. She checked into a Travelodge in Mason City and spent a week in the environs of the tiny swimming pool during the airless afternoons, and at a small table in the rear of a local bar in the evenings, listening to a trio play good modern jazz. There was an unexpected degree of affluence here, and nightly, over three or four drinks, she contemplated the regulars, wondering why she'd thought they'd be more rural in attitude and appearance than they were. Upon leaving the bar, she saw a number of the patrons climbing into late-model Cadillacs and Mercedes.

The regulars all dressed well in expensive casual clothes. The women either forced their bulk into designer jeans or opted for low-cut wraparound dresses and high-heeled slingbacks. A qualified makeup instructor might have earned herself a fortune in this town, Caley thought, because despite the blatancy of their wealth, the women seemed caught in a cosmetic time warp where blue eye shadow, black eyeliner, and silver-pink lipstick were still the rage. There was a lot of back-combed hair on view, to boot.

The trio, consisting of two black men who played piano and drums, and a white bassist, played for forty minutes of every hour, then disappeared into a back room for the remaining twenty minutes, becoming progressively more stoned as each evening passed. The higher they got, the better their music became.

Occasionally, embarrassingly, a local woman would insist on "doing a number with the boys." She'd hike up her skirts, climb onto the stage, clutch the stand-up mike with both hands, and render an impassioned, tuneless version of "Blue Moon" or "Everybody Loves Somebody Sometime" or "More." Her amorphous voice flirted tremulously, sidling near to notes before sailing right past them to land, with alarming vibrato, somewhere halfway between the appropriate note and the one directly above or below it on the scale. Her nightly search through several keys, combined with the feedback caused by her incautious fusion to the microphone, sent newcomers in search of the exits, while the regulars howled and emitted shrill whistles, and cried, "Sing your heart out, Sue-Anne!!" all of which the bleached, breasty Sue-Anne interpreted as approval. Behind the screen of a well-placed hand, Caley laughed herself to tears, picturing all the dogs in the immediate vicinity sitting on their hind legs, howling in direct response to Sue-Anne's winsome invitation. Sue-Anne clearly had her heart and frontal appendages set upon surpassing Dolly Parton's success, and nightly she thanked the audience with lethal seriousness for the accolades they'd elected to heap upon her worthy person.

What was even more interesting than Sue-Anne were the suffering expressions the trio of musicians tried to conceal while Sue-Anne slapped her claim on sounds no one had ever managed to chart on staff paper.

At the end of the week, Caley wrenched the battery cables back into place, filled the gas tank, and headed up into Minnesota. She felt better than she had in months; she'd learned something important during those hours spent in the Mason City bar: she'd come to understand that it was one thing to be visibly flawed, but it was quite another thing to climb into the spotlight and volunteer your private flaws for public consumption. Whatever she was, at least she wasn't deluded.

As she drove, the convertible top down, she sang "Blue Moon" at the top of her voice, allowing herself to slide up and down the scale in honor of Sue-Anne, then laughed loudly as the dust rose high in her wake.

Each morning, routinely, she ground beans, then boiled water for her coffee. While waiting for the water to boil, she showered. Then, the coffee dripping through the small filter into her mug, she tuned her recently acquired stereo radio/ cassette-player in for the local news. Coffee close at hand, the news in full swing, she did her hair and makeup. Dressed, she rinsed the mug, packed the electric mill, the coffee, and the hotpot into their carton, switched off the ghetto blaster, surveyed the room to make sure nothing had been forgotten, then carried everything out to be locked into Clarabelle's trunk. Her first stop of the day was the nearest McDonald's for an Egg McMuffin and a large coffee, consumed while she perused the local paper. After breakfast, she'd make a quick trip to the McDonald's ladies room, then go out to the car, consult the map, and head off. These evolving routines aided in establishing her sense that her life was, in fact, being lived rather than merely prolonged. She might be traveling by whim, but she was actively learning what she found acceptable or intolerable. She'd never before attempted to profile her feelings on the behavior of others, or of herself in relation to people at large. The exercise was most informative, and helped to substantiate her belief that, most often, people were willing to respond positively to a display of confidence and good manners. While they might, initially, react negatively to the sight of her, her dogged determination to speak quietly and succinctly, proceeding forward to her given goal of the moment, compelled those with whom she dealt to treat her with respect. Of course there were exceptions, people who simply couldn't get beyond the very sight of her. But she was able to discount them; they were, after all, not worth her time or energy.

She had acquired a number of items that facilitated her travels. Aside from the coffee-making supplies and the stereo, there was a down pillow, and a worn afghan throw she'd found in a secondhand shop in Dyersburg, Tennessee. She had a box filled with paperbacks and another, smaller, carton of food. For the most part, she ate in fast-food restaurants, but every so often she prepared some soup and nibbled on cheese and crackers and dried fruit. She had a Styrofoam cooler in which she kept cream for her coffee and a supply of Tab. Occasionally, she'd stop by the roadside for a picnic, popping a cassette into the ghetto blaster as she sipped on Tab and munched Wheat Thins and Jarlsburg cheese. The afghan did double duty both as a picnic blanket and as an additional layer of warmth in those motels that provided insufficient bedding and overefficient air conditioning. The pillow was purely practical since the majority of motels offered foam-rubber squares of unyielding rigidity that guaranteed a stiff neck and headache, come the morning. Her important papers and checkbook she carried with her in her handbag. Everything else had a place in the capacious trunk of the car.

Upon arriving in the outskirts of Minneapolis, she checked into a small motel directly opposite a shopping center consisting of a huge drugstore, a burger place that did only take-out business, a gas station, and a dry cleaner's. She unpacked what she'd need for a few days' stay. About to shut the trunk, she failed to give it a hard enough slam. The trunk lid bounced back, the handle catching her under the chin and nearly knocking her out with the impact. Blinking away involuntary tears, she managed to get the trunk locked and reeled indoors to the bathroom, where, with horror, she saw she was bleeding profusely, the front of her clothes soaked with the blood spurting from a deep gash in the soft underside of her chin. She couldn't stop the bleeding, and knew she was going to have to get some medical attention. Frightened at the prospect of once again finding herself at the hands of some unknown member of the medical profession, she pulled a cotton jacket on over her ruined shirt. Holding a washcloth to her chin, she ran across the parking lot to the manager's office.

The manager, in this case, was a burly woman in a man's plaid sports shirt. She looked up as Caley entered and said, "Jesus Murphy! What happened to you?"

"The trunk lid," Caley explained.

"We better get you over to the hospital." She stepped back into the doorway of her apartment to bellow, "Fred! Hustle your buns out here and look after things! I gotta go out for a while."

Caley immediately trusted this hefty woman with the salt-and-pepper hair and huge biceps.

"You come on now." The woman took Caley's upper arm and directed her outside to a pickup. "Get yourself in there," she ordered, waiting to make sure Caley was settled before tossing the door closed. "Probably gonna need a few stitches," she said, handling the pickup with the kind of effortless grace men usually displayed behind the wheel of a truck. "What's your name, anyhow?" she asked. "I already forgot. Never do take much notice what's on those registration cards."

"Caley."

"Oh, yeah. Right. I remember seeing that. My name's Louise." She glanced over, her stern features suddenly redeemed by a grin. "You must be prone or something, Caley. Had yourself a couple accidents a time or two before, huh?"

"A couple," Caley admitted.

"Must've been a real bad one, from the looks of you. Went through the windshield. Right?"

"Yes."

"Jeez!" Louise shook her head. Looking over again at Caley's bleached features, she said, "You gonna pass out? You look as if you might."

"I might," Caley allowed.

"See if you can't put your head down there on your knees. We don't have all that far to go now."

Caley bent forward, still holding the saturated washcloth to her chin. "This is very kind of you," she said, the words distorted by her posture.

"Oh, hell!" Louise dismissed that. "You're in no fit condition to drive that audacious car to no hospital."

In spite of her nausea, Caley smiled to herself at Louise's description of Clarabelle.

"You got medical insurance?" Louise asked as she was helping Caley down from the cab of the pickup. Caley nodded, surprised by the woman's strength as she was lifted to the ground, then held upright by one solid arm as Louise slammed the truck's door. "Nothing to you," she declared, leading Caley in through the emergency room doors. "You want to eat more."

Louise took charge. It was, in many ways, one of the most comforting experiences Caley had had in years, and all because she'd suffered a mishap. Louise explained to one of the nurses what had happened, and oversaw the initial examination of Caley's chin, deftly disposing of the blood-soaked washcloth once it was no longer needed. She also filled out the hospital forms, finding the appropriate information in the wallet Caley simply handed over to her. Having settled Caley in the waiting room, Louise went off briefly, returning with two paper cups of coffee.

While Louise was gone, Caley looked around at the others assembled. One young woman, in a supermarket coverall and cap, held her towel-wrapped hand in her lap and looked repeatedly at her wristwatch. Another young woman had her enormously swollen, shoeless foot propped on a chair. A man in his late twenties who appeared to have suffered a terrible beating sat half-slumped in a wheelchair. An elderly couple sat together, and Caley couldn't determine which of them had come for treatment. Directly opposite were two kids who didn't look more than sixteen, the girl with an infant on her lap. The baby snuffled and wheezed, laboring to breathe. No one seemed to take any notice of Caley, although everyone looked up when Louise came marching back with the coffee. Her robust good health seemed misplaced here, while Caley was simply another of the wounded. Oddly enough, Caley's apprehension dissolved once she'd surveyed the others assembled.

"Drink this," Louise told her, dropping into the seat beside her. "So," she asked, after her first swallow of coffee, "where you on your way to? Connecticut's a long ways from here."

"Nowhere in particular," Caley told her. "The only reason I stopped in Edina is because I read somewhere that the woman who wrote *Ordinary People* lives here. I thought I might stop in Indianapolis sometime, too. Booth Tarkington lived there, and so did Kurt Vonnegut."

"They're all writers, huh? You a writer, too?"

Caley gave a weak laugh. "No. It's just kind of interesting to see the places where well-known writers lived. It's an excuse, I guess; something to justify my being wherever I happen to be."

"You need an excuse for that?" Louise turned to examine Caley with renewed interest. "How come you'd think that? Because of the way you look?"

"This is probably going to take ages." Caley took stock again of the others waiting. The baby seemed to have gone to sleep, its frail chest fluttering with its efforts to breathe. The mother, if indeed she was, had deeply bitten fingernails and acute acne she'd tried to hide beneath a thick layer of dark pancake makeup. The father lounged with sprawled legs, one arm lazily extended along the back of the girl's chair. He looked bored, or drugged, or both; his eyes heavy-lidded, his mouth slack. The young woman in the supermarket coverall was now gazing steadily at her watch and whispering to herself.

I don't want to be here, Caley thought, deluged by that feeling of helplessness that only hospitals seemed to trigger in her.

A resident appeared in the doorway and read a name from his clipboard. The elderly couple both creaked to their feet and followed after him. As they were going, there was a sudden commotion in the corridor, and Caley turned to see several nurses and doctors speaking sharply to two youthful blacks who were gesticulating in the direction of a third black on a gurney one of the nurses was endeavoring to wheel into a cubicle. The commotion came to an abrupt halt as a pair of uniformed police officers stepped into view, beckoning the youths to go with them. As the nurse and one of the doctors hurriedly pushed the gurney into an examining cubicle, blood overran the elevated stretcher and spilled to the floor. The gurney's wheels left blood impressions on the neutral linoleum.

"Knife fight," Louise commented knowingly. "How's the chin?"

"Sore."

"Don't much like hospitals, do you? Me, neither. Seem to spend a hell of a lot of time in them, though, for one reason or another. I'll bet I've put in a month's worth of days in this waiting room. The kids're always breaking an arm or a leg in the pool, even though we always warn the parents to keep an eye on them. Or Mike, my boy, he'll have some kid over likes to play with knives and winds up cutting his hand half off. This one time, we had a guy in one of the units, came for the Series in '66 when the Twins were playing. Got himself so blind on Wild Turkey he slipped and fell going into the unit, put his head right through the glass in the storm door, then damn near cut it off trying to get loose. I was here the entire night with that one."

"Why didn't you call for an ambulance?"

"He'd of bled to death if I'd waited," Louise said matter-of-factly. "I figure it's better to get in the pickup, lean on the horn, and just get the hell on over here. They told me when I brought him in I did just the right thing. He'd of bled to death."

"My God!"

"Oh, that's nothing," Louise went on, unperturbed. "This one time, one of our maids, it must've been Lucy, she slipped on this bathroom floor she'd just finished scrubbing, legs went every which way, banged hell out of her head on the corner of the sink and wound up with her head in the toilet. We had to give her artificial respiration. My Fred did that while I phoned for the medics. I'll tell you, there's not a hell of a lot you don't see running a place like ours."

Another name was called, and the couple with the baby got up and, in slow motion, trailed after the doctor.

"Those two don't look old enough to have a kid," Louise echoed Caley's own thought. "Probably don't know which end of that poor baby's which." She looked closely at Caley, then patted her on the arm. "Won't be too long now. You hold on, they'll get you fixed up."

"I'm all right," Caley lied, checking the time. They'd been waiting in this small room for close to an hour. "I'm just tired out from driving. I started at eight this morning."

"Where'd you come in from?"

"Iowa." She was definitely feeling the effects of the day's drive; there was a buzzing in her fingertips, and her body seemed to want to sway to the car's motion. Nausea gripped her again, and she had to rest her head on her knees. Louise's hand had a tranquilizing effect as it stroked Caley's hair. Her kindness, her instincts for nurturing were baffling. This woman seemed not in the least bothered by Caley's disfigurement. She'd delved at once beneath the surface, readily able to locate the recognizable person within. She went for water and came back to present the cup into Caley's unsteady hand, putting an immediate stop to Caley's stream of grateful phrases. "Just drink that down," she said, her eyes deep with kindness. "There's no need to keep on thanking me. We'll get you squared away here, then take you home and get some decent food into you. Seems like you could use some looking after."

After two and a half hours, Caley's name was called.

"Want me to come in with you?" Louise offered.

"No, that's all right, thanks." Caley followed the doctor into one of the curtained cubicles, where she was invited to have a seat.

"Now, what've we got here?" he asked, peeling away the temporary dressing the nurse had applied. "Hmmm. How'd you manage to do this?"

She explained, and he said, "That's different." With a smile, he asked, "Had a tetanus shot lately?"

"Seven or eight months ago."

"That's good enough. I'm going to have to put a few sutures in to close this up. Okay?"

"You're not going to give me a general, are you?"

"Had a little too much of that, huh?" Again he smiled. "There's no need. A local'll do it. Get you stitched up and you'll be on your way in no time flat." His eyes scanned the clipboard as he selected the instruments he'd need from the sterilizer. "You're a long way from home, Caley," he said without looking up. "Visiting?"

"Just passing through."

"The surgery's pretty recent, isn't it?" He looked up from the tray he was preparing. "Scheduled for more?"

"No. I bowed out." She stiffened, prepared for a lecture, but to her surprise, he said, "I wonder, a lot of the time, that more people don't bow out after climbing up on the table half a dozen or so times. Are you going to want a prescription for some painkillers? You're going to feel the bruising for a few days."

"I'll tough it out."

"Figured you would," he said, almost admiringly. "We'll just get you to lie down here now." He had amazingly gentle hands, with which he eased her back on the table. He swabbed her throat and the underside of her chin with alcohol.

"Why did you say that?" she inquired.

"The truth?"

"Sure."

"You've got some of that same look the guys used to have coming back from Nam: battle fatigue. A lot of them wore their wounds like medals, like they were just daring people to say word one and they'd let them have it with both barrels. Mind if I say something else?"

"No."

"I hope you won't let yourself fall into that trap. Okay, now. This'll sting a bit."

Chapter 16

THE WALLS CAME down in gratifying gusts of plaster. The brittle lathing beneath the Victorian plaster and dozen or more layers of paint, splintered into jagged tusks Martin sheared neatly to the gumlines of the mouths he was shaping; apertures yawning a welcome. He used a wheelbarrow to carry the debris out of doors to the commercial receptacle he'd hired and had placed on the lawn. Rock music from CHUM blasted into the hollows left by the temporarily silenced electric saw. His hammering beat a steady underscore to the bass-ridden throb, the whiny bleat of nonsensical lyrics.

His head covered by a knotted white handkerchief, clad in plaster-heavy tattered jeans and shirt, his feet bare inside torn tennis shoes, he took aim at the walls, felling them, one by one. His toil, arduously incessant, was his sole focus. Nightly he showered away the day's sweat and plaster grime before collapsing onto the bed, where a deathly sleep mercifully overcame him. If he dreamed, he retained no memory of those dreams upon waking. He would rise, drag on his filthy uniform, and carry his morning coffee with him as he viewed his progress.

Already the wall separating the living and dining rooms was gone, as was the one that had stood between the hallway and the living room. The conservatory remained, approachable through the paneled door, still intact, at the far end of the dining area. The open space he'd envisioned was a reality, enclosed only by retaining walls.

He stood inspecting the last remaining first-floor wall, the one before the kitchen. If he removed it, he'd be bound to replace the kitchen fittings altogether. The yellowing cabinets and appliances begged to be scrapped in order to make way, perhaps, for some of those fine Scandinavian or Italian fittings. He could readily see the light that would accumulate in these rooms, with that last wall taken down.

It would be solid, contained, permanent, created from within, this light. No more would those bewildering, geometric slabs fling themselves across his vision. It would, he knew, appease him to enter this place and each time become an integral part of the light, rather than a detached interpreter of it. No secret seams of dirt, no angular traps where light might become caught, and lost. It was what he wanted, he decided, and set down his cup in order to test the potential mobility of the stove, and then the refrigerator. They refused to be moved. Instantly outraged, he struggled to shift each one and, failing, felt his fury beginning to pound against his eardrums.

"No fucking cooker's going to stop me!" he ranted, bringing his clenched fist down on the grease-spattered surface.

He flew to the telephone to call his old friend Mickey McEllimore.

"What're you doing?" he demanded.

"What d'you mean, what'm I doing? I'm sleeping, you daft, fucking Brit. What the hell d'you think I'd be doing at seven in the bloody morning?"

"I mean, are you working at present? Have you got something on? If not, I need you to come lend a hand here."

"Lend a hand at what?"

"Work! Physical labor. Something you tatey-diggers wouldn't know about, but for which I'll *pay* you."

"Physical labor, and you'll pay me?" Mickey asked skeptically. "What sort, specifically, and how much?"

"Fifty a day and all the beer you can swill, to help me with the renovation."

"You're renovating the house?"

"Isn't that what I just said? Yes or no?"

Mickey groaned. "I'm in no fit condition for renovating."

"I'm not interested in your hangover. Yes or no?"

"Well, all right. I suppose you want me straightaway?"

"You suppose bloody right. Get dressed and get over here. And bring a dolly."

"A dolly?"

"To move the appliances out of here."

"The appliances? What're you going to do with them?"

It was Martin's turn to groan. "They're going into the trash!"

"Don't be a complete fool, Maddox. Ring up the bloody Sally Ann or the Goodwill and they'll come cart the lot off."

"Oh! Right! Good idea. I'll expect you within the hour."

"I'll bring me own suds," Mickey said, and hung up.

Mickey was a round, redheaded Irish writer, a premeditated fanatic who'd authored several salacious science fiction novels and paid the rent by stringing for several American publications, as well as writing the occasional guest column for the *Star*, which would generate a volume of hate mail that filled him with pride. "I'll take the opposing side to any issue," he'd stated regularly throughout the more than eight years of their friendship, "just to see those letters come in. Drives them wild, it does." He loved to inspire dissension, and he worked hard at it. There were exceptions, of course, to his perennial invective, and Martin's work was one of them. Mickey had, in no small way, been responsible for the popularization of Martin's paintings and their attendant rise in value. "For a cretinous, alky Brit, you're a fucking good painter!" Mick had declared upon seeing for the first time a showing of Martin's canvases in a fashionable downtown Toronto gallery. Martin had laughed heartily, appreciatively, and they'd gone off together that same evening to get drunk. They'd been drinking companions until Marian had left to take the boys back to England.

He arrived at the house carrying a six-pack of Carlsberg and knocked at the door until his knuckles were bruised, failing to make himself heard over the rock music and the incessant hammering from within. At last, he simply opened the front door and stepped inside to stare at what Martin had done.

Sensing his presence, Martin turned and shouted, "It's

about bloody time. Get a shot of that''—he nodded at the six-pack—''and grab some tools. We're taking down the kitchen wall today.''

Mickey walked over to the mantel to turn down the volume on the radio. ''The kitchen wall, is it?''

''Right. It was too early to ring the Goodwill, so you might just as well stow the beer in the refrigerator for the moment. I can't shift the bloody thing to unplug it anyway. We'll let the lads who come for it worry about that. Coffee's made, you fancy some.''

Swallowing the numerous questions he'd have liked to ask, Mick went off to the kitchen to put the six-pack into the otherwise empty refrigerator before pouring himself some coffee. He took a mouthful, speculating on the reasons why Martin had elected to act out his grief in this manner. Mickey had read about the crash; word of what happened had reached all Martin's friends. None of them had known quite how to display their sympathy, which was why Mickey had agreed to come along this morning.

''I don't know sweet fuck-all about renovating,'' he told Martin upon his return to the front of the house. ''I didn't know *you* did.''

''Doesn't matter.'' Martin dismissed this. ''There's not a lot you need to know. We'll get that last wall down, trim back the lathing, then get on to the plastering. I'll fill in the undersides of the headers, lay in some wire mesh to hold the wet plaster, then we'll have a go at smoothing it all down before replacing the trim. Simple. Grab that crowbar there, and we'll get on with it.''

''You don't mind, I'll finish my coffee first.''

''In that case, I'll just go ahead and get this wood cut to size for the headers.''

''Planning to do the entire house, are you?'' Mick asked, his elbow resting on the mantel as he took leisurely sips of his coffee.

''Only the downstairs,'' Martin explained curtly, ''for the moment.''

''How long've you been at this, then?''

''Quit nattering and finish your bloody coffee. I need help here, not a meeting of the ladies' auxiliary.''

"Humbly begging your pardon." Mick drank down the last of the coffee, wedged a cigarette between his lips, lit it, took a long drag, then said, "Right-o. Let's toot."

At noon, Mickey insisted on stopping for lunch. After a thorough check of the kitchen, he said, "There's no bloody food! C'mon, we'll go get something to eat."

"I'm in no mood for a chinwag with your crowd," Martin warned.

"Christ!" Mick exclaimed, examining his blistered palms. "My car's in the drive. We'll go over to the diner."

Martin didn't respond for a moment, preoccupied with his inspection of the partially demolished wall. Taking his hand over the still-standing, painted part of the surface, he considered the idea of leaving the house, going somewhere public for a meal. It seemed such a simple, ordinary thing. Yet he felt a small twinge of fear at the prospect, and this struck him as abysmal. "Fuck it!" he decided. "Let's go eat."

"I was sorry to hear about the accident," Mickey said as they awaited their food in the diner. "Tried to ring you a few times, but there was never an answer."

Martin nodded, his eyes fixed on the middle distance. "I only reconnected the telephone this past month," he said. "Didn't fancy taking any calls."

"We've been out of touch awhile," Mickey commented. "What is it, eight or nine months, at least."

"I went over to fetch them back, and stayed six months," Martin said, as if dredging his memory for details of events that had occurred many years before. "Had to leave, finally, because of the sodding Inland Revenue. Came back and couldn't do one bloody worthwhile thing. We were meeting up in Tenerife, you see. The plan was they'd all be coming home when school broke up in July." His eyes slowly came to rest on Mick. "They gave me a special bloody dispensation," he said rancorously, "so I could see Grace safely home and stop with her a few weeks." He moistened his lips and looked down at the water glass as if debating its worthiness to quench his sudden, dreadful thirst. "It turned her old overnight," he said softly. "Terrible to see."

"I'm sorry, mate." Mickey lit a fresh cigarette and offered

one to Martin, who failed to acknowledge the gesture. "I'm sorry as can be."

"I haven't been able to paint since I returned, so I've been going about town taking photographs; set up a darkroom in the basement, but I seem to lose interest by the time it comes to do the actual work."

Mickey smiled. "I thought you considered photography just a notch above sodomizing farm animals."

Martin returned his smile. "It keeps the old mind functioning. Just this past fortnight I started putting some of the films through the process."

"I'll have to see this!" Mickey declared with enthusiasm as the waitress arrived with their food. "Ah!" He rubbed his hands together. "Cheeseburgers, greasy chips, and wilted cole slaw. My favorites!"

Martin laughed, so unaccustomed to the activity that he wouldn't have been in the least surprised to see a puff of dust issue from his throat to accompany the sound. "Silly bastard," he said fondly. "It's a tonic, seeing you."

"Can't say the same for you." Mickey spoke with a full mouth. "Getting me up at the crack of bloody dawn to do physical fucking labor."

"Work off some of that revolting beer gut."

"Leave off!" Mickey protested. "Took me years of concentrated hard work to build this." He laid a protective hand over his belly. "Those beer adverts on the telly are my life-support system. All you Scotch drinkers look down upon those of us who are connoisseurs of the yeasty brew."

"I've given up drink," Martin confessed. "Haven't touched a drop in three hundred and twelve days."

"Jesus, Mary, and Joseph! Well, doesn't that explain it all! No wonder you're knocking down bloody walls! Three hundred and twelve days. It's bloody awesome!"

"I'm rather awed myself." Martin picked up his knife and fork, then replaced them in favor of the water. He drained the glass, then started on his hot hamburger platter. "Tell me who you've offended lately, Mick. Bring me up to date on your hate mail. Writing another esoteric space epic?"

"Just sold the new one in New York." Mickey swung avidly into one of his favorite topics. "That useless goddamned agent finally got off his arse and made a halfway decent deal. We got fifteen thousand U.S. advance on the hardcover. He imagines I might get as much as twenty-five for the paperback reprint rights.''

"More fun and frolic in the galaxies." Martin wrinkled his nose. "Hermaphrodites from outer space."

"Mind how you go! I'm becoming a bloody underground *cult* figure, Maddox. The college kids go mad for my stuff. And this one's a little different."

"Let me guess. Hermaphrodites in *inner* space."

"Fuck you!" Mick calmly continued eating. "Aliens in the form of a lethal virus. Political comment, social satire, and lesbians."

"Jesus!" Martin popped a gravy-laden french fry into his mouth. "Local lesbians or intergalactic?"

"One of these days, I'll be on the *New York Times* best bloody seller list and then we'll see!" Mickey chewed, swallowed, then asked, "You're not painting at all?"

"Not at the moment. How are Esther and the kiddies?"

"Esther's gone off to 'find herself.' She'll need both hands free to do that, the skinny bitch. Brendan's away to McGill, and Liza's home with me for another month before she starts sharing digs with a chum. Esther rings up every night. She's got herself an apartment downtown in one of our less savory neighborhoods, and she's working at some frightfully elegant frock shop in the Eaton Centre. I'm waiting for her to start talking about divorce. It's been six months and so far no talk."

"You don't seem brokenhearted over it."

"Best thing that ever happened. I can sit down at the machine and write whenever I damned well please, without worrying about disturbing Esther's eight hours of bed rest. I've been writing better than ever with her out of the house. Come and go as the feeling takes me, and no running commentary to meet me every time I set foot inside the front door. Lousy cheeseburger. Not enough cheese, for chrissake! Wouldn't that be a fine idea, now, for one of my columns? I'll rate the bloody hamburgers in town. That'll get everyone's blood racing nicely."

Mick expounded on his ideas for the column, and Martin

ate automatically, without tasting. The food might have been dry fodder, and he an enervated beast of burden yoked for eternity to a wagon he couldn't see. He was finding this, his first exposure to a friend since the plane crash, a tedious enterprise. Even the most rudimentary level of communication seemed to require more than he had to give. He knew his contacting Mick was a healthy sign, but what he'd failed to prepare for was the tiresome chore of conversation. People required words, reactions, thoughts; he lacked the interest to perpetuate conversation. After only a few returns, trading information, he longed to revert to his previous silence, and remain in it. There was one good point to all this, though: Mick had actually made him laugh. He'd thought, until now, he'd probably never again find anything humorous. But Mick had made him laugh.

The Goodwill truck came the following morning. The driver and his helper grunted, tugging and heaving, and finally managed to uproot the appliances, along with a substantial amount of the linoleum.

"We'll have to take up the rest of the lino," Martin announced, secretly pleased at having yet another task to perform. "After this wall's well and truly down, we'll get those cabinets ripped out, then take up the lino."

"What's all this in aid of?" Mick asked, adeptly uncapping the first bottle of a fresh six-pack.

"In aid of? I'm fixing the bloody place up," Martin said, with mild exasperation.

"I *know* that," Mick said, wiping his mouth with the back of his hand. "But what're you going to do once it's all done? Or do you intend to become a male Penelope and spend the rest of your worthless life mucking about with this Victorian crap heap?"

"How the hell should I know?" Martin shot back, flustered by Mick's quick perception of his fixation. "Maybe I'll take a bloody trip or something. Right now, I'm concerned only with the job at hand. Let's get this wall down!"

That night, long after Mickey had departed, Martin lay on top of the bed and considered the question of his spiraling involvement in the renovation, and what he'd do once it was complete—if he allowed, at any point, that it *was* complete. He had, since returning to the city, been getting through each day as it came. Plans were something he'd abandoned with the wreckage strewn in the crevices of the mountain on Tenerife. The very idea of the future, the most tentative thoughts tending in that direction, resurrected his dread. He simply couldn't contemplate anything that fell beyond tomorrow.

He closed his eyes and watched his wife and sons in diastatic action, consigned for all time to immutable distance. He could see them, address them, compel their regenerated figures to respond with mime action, but he couldn't touch them except, perhaps, in dreams. And he no longer dreamed. He was no longer able to travel, in alpha, beta, or any other state, to be with them. All he was able to do was project these disseminated home movies on his interior screen. His life had been severed, his bloodlines slashed; he was a functional robot, programmed for menial work. Today, though, he'd invaded his own program, and had laughed. He couldn't decide if his laughter was a demonstration of the worst sort of treachery, or the insistence of his spirit on asserting its right to life.

He thought constantly of the blissful amnesia he might attain with a few drinks, and as constantly rejected that tantalizing offer. He'd given his word, and he'd keep it, whether or not the person to whom he'd given it was there to witness the fulfillment of his promises. He was intrigued by his old-maidishness, and watched Mickey daily work his way through half a dozen or a dozen bottles of beer, with something akin to fascination. Each time Mick opened another bottle, Martin was prompted to comment to himself upon the nature of addiction. Mick opened bottles, drank his beer, as automatic actions. He smoked cigarettes in the same manner, lighting them each time he realized that his hand was empty, that there was nothing smoldering in the nearest ashtray.

Martin was enormously pleased with his abstinence. It was his only active pleasure; proof of his fidelity, his honor. It would have been too easy to succumb, allowing himself to sink without resistance into a stupor. He preferred to remain sober; it was his penance—for anything, for everything; it was the daily reminder of losses sustained. Were he to drink, he might forget certain of the scenes and images that were the amalgam that filled his private gallery. Never mind that his sleep failed to generate dreams—a fault, no doubt, of his failure, in waking life, to find anything of value. He had no need of them for now. He was too absorbed in the indexing of his memories, in the preservation of every word, every gesture, every moment he'd shared with his wife and sons.

"You're going to make the place into a fucking shrine!" Mickey was flabbergasted.

"Not quite," Martin said coolly. "I simply intend, someday, to hang the portraits of my family on these walls."

"It's too goddamned Gothic!" Mickey protested. "They'll come for you with the nets, my boy."

"They're my finest pieces," Martin explained. "They deserve to be hung to their best advantage. This will be the place."

"Well, bugger me!" Stumped, Mick reached for his beer and took a long swallow. "You don't *seem* crazy, but you've fucking well gone over the edge."

"That's entirely possible," Martin averred, stepping back to examine a freshly plastered header between the living and dining areas. "I'd take it most kindly if you'd pick up your bloody trowel and help me finish before the plaster goes dry. I want you to come with me to the showroom this afternoon to look at new cabinets and fittings for the kitchen."

"What about furniture? What do you plan to sit on, of an evening?"

"All in due course. The kitchen first."

"Fruitless, it is. You'll probably use the stove as a planter."

"What a jolly clever idea!" Martin flashed him a smile. "Clever you are, for an aging Irish reprobate overeducated for his station."

"Talk of aging reprobates, I ever tell you about Donleavy? Jesus Christ, but the man was the ultimate bloody irony, stepping oh-so-sprightly over the turf at Trinity, all rigged out in gear no self-respecting Irishman would ever be caught wearing to his own wake. More Irish than the bloody Irish, he was. We all thought the bastard was a simple fool, and here he went and turned out all those bloody books. My God, you should've seen him, though! Gingerly picking his way across the commons in his Donegal tweeds, walking stick and all. I ever tell you about him?''

"Only eighty or ninety times,'' Martin said. "Why is it he irks you so?''

"Because the man was a fucking fool! It isn't right that such a fool should be so goddamned successful. It offends me,'' Mick said with wounded dignity, noticing that Martin seemed to be more himself each day. While Mick loathed the labor and would've given almost anything to be free to sit on the sidelines and watch Martin do all the work, it was worth the price of admission to hear his infrequent laugh and to have him exercise his sarcastic wit. "He could write, as well,'' he added. "That's the part that really hurts. The bloody man was truly gifted.''

"Was it just his gear that offended you so? Or was there something more to it?''

"The gear and the great pretense of it all. After we've finished at the kitchen place, why don't we buy you a refrigerator and some food? The novelty of eating indoors might appeal to you.''

"It's bad enough I've been coerced into going with you to that filthy diner every day for lunch. Weeks on end of watching you eat those foul cheeseburgers and chips. I intend to maintain the status quo until this place is finished. Feel free, however, to bring your groceries with you, if you've a mind to work with a wadge of Wonder Bread and fish paste stuffed in your maw.''

"Piss off!'' Mick said good-naturedly. "I bring the food, you'd bloody eat it.''

"I hadn't thought of that.''

"You would and all.''

Martin took several rolls of film of Mick putting the finishing touches to the first completed area. Mick clowned for the camera as Martin clicked away. The best shot was one of Mick sprawled on the living room floor with his back against the marble perimeter of the fireplace, a beer in one hand and a cigarette in the other, his features suffused with humor. Martin took the negative to a commercial reproduction house to have a three- by four-foot blow-up made, and presented the dry-mounted end result to Mick on their last day of work together.

"Don't go forgetting to call me!" Mick reminded him, going off down the front steps carrying the poster and the last of the empties. "We'll go out and diddle the local nymphets."

Martin waved him off then closed the front door and turned to look at the excellent work the two of them had done. There was still the painting of the walls to be done, the refinishing of the floors and trim, and the installation of the new kitchen cabinet and appliances, but it was all there, just as he'd visualized it. Marian, he thought, would have approved.

Chapter 17

LOUISE OFFERED CALEY a job: seventy-five dollars a week and her room in exchange for cleaning the motel rooms. With no real reason to refuse, Caley accepted. It was very like signing on for an apprenticeship in detection. There were all sorts of clues to indicate not only the gender of the former occupants but also qualifying indicators as to the type of people they were.

For the most part, men left the rooms less messy. Aside from beer cans or empty liquor bottles, they left behind little impression but for the telltale quality of aftershave or cologne clinging to the still-moist bathroom air. The women, perhaps aware that another woman was going to have to clean up after them, seemed to make a vengeful point of using every towel and leaving them in soggy heaps in the tub, on the bathroom floor, even under the bed. In their wake remained varicolored strands of hair on every surface, and talc footprints showed their progress from bathroom to bed to television set to chair: a ghostly trail Caley erased with the vacuum cleaner.

The men left numbers and partial names written on the telephone book cover, on the notepads beside the telephone; the women rarely seemed to make calls. The majority of guests stayed only one night and were gone early in the morning. A few, mainly salesmen, stayed two or three nights. By the weekend the salesmen were always long gone; they traveled Monday through Thursday and set out for home on Friday. Teenagers frequently rented a room for a Friday or Saturday night, and brought along half a dozen friends for a beer-and-pizza party. Fred and Louise, indulgent of these goings-on, usually tried to put the kids at the far end of one of the two buildings in order not to disturb the other guests, who were most often families breaking a long trip and trying to save on expenses by cramming themselves, kids and all, into one double-bedded room.

The walls were reasonably well built, but not so thick that, upon occasion, Caley couldn't hear the rhythmic heaving of the bed in one of the rooms adjoining hers. She drowned out the sounds by getting up and turning on either the television set or the ghetto blaster, and smoked a cigarette, waiting for silence, made lonely by the proof of others' ardor. Came the morning, she'd stare at the vacated bed for a long moment before, with averted eyes, stripping the lovemaking arena of its soiled linens.

There was one morning when, failing to receive any response to her knock, she entered one of the units with her passkey to find two leftover teenagers from the previous night's party engaged in some fairly startling acrobatics. She withdrew hastily, unnoticed, and collapsed in laughter against the cleaning trolley.

Many times she emerged from one of the rooms to get fresh supplies from the trolley, only to catch one of the departing guests in the act of pilfering toilet paper or boxes of tissues or plastic-wrapped drinking glasses or towels. Once or twice, boldly, they completed these acts of theft and walked off across the parking lot to their cars, silently defying her to do something. What she did was to take note of the license numbers and then check with Louise on how these people had paid. More often than not, they'd used a credit card. Louise would list what had been taken, figure the cost, then add it to the charge slip. "They never come back at us," Louise told her. "They know damned well they're petty thieves." When the payment happened to have been made in cash, Louise just shrugged and entered the losses in the books under pilferage.

Aside from the bold thievery by these otherwise ordinary people, they lived on a level where they failed to recognize the existence of a wide range of people. Since accepting Louise's job offer, Caley had joined the ranks of those who went

unrecognized: waitresses, cleaning and maintenance staff, gas
station attendants; an entire population of people who performed the less pleasant duties of serving up, cleaning up, filling up. Mainly, they were a legion of unacknowledged souls,
and initially Caley was disturbed by motel guests who'd
dismiss her with a wave of their hands, without even bothering
to look at her. She was shouted at through closed doors, told
to go away and come back later. The treatment accorded her
by guests bordered on incivility. After all, she was a drudge,
someone paid to clean up a ceaseless accumulation of detritus.
Since no self-respecting, well-educated woman would ever
consider taking on so lowly a job as the cleaning of motel
rooms, it was safe to ignore her, to treat her as if she were
barely subhuman.

She had two choices: either she could be offended and sum-
marily quit, putting an end to the ongoing humiliation; or she
could take advantage of the inbuilt prejudice she met daily and
take close notes on the human condition as she perceived it.
She opted for the latter, being careful not to fall into the trap
of viewing those who would not see her as being ignorant,
uncaring, ill-bred potential petty thieves who were no more
worth the time of day than they thought she was. It was all too
easy, she saw, to become embittered when one suffered daily
the curse of invisibility.

She became a full-fledged detective, putting together com-
posite images of those who came to rent the rooms. She grew
quickly adept at spotting the leavings of the illicit couple, the
family pack, the teenage gang-bang, the lonely salesman, the
alcoholics who came solely to dabble with the rapidly unraveling perimeters of their awareness. Knowingly, she assessed the
clues and, satisfied, got on with the job of restoring the rooms
to impersonal order.

Only once, upon entering a unit, was she all but over-
powered by the essence of the recently departed occupant. It
happened in October, almost three months after she'd started
the job. She opened the door, turned on the lights, and
breathed in the lingering fragrance of an expensive perfume.
The room was scarcely disturbed, the blankets on one side of
the bed neatly folded back, only the slightest indentation in
the pillow. The scent was stronger in the bathroom, where the

towels hung on the racks, damply correct. The wastebaskets contained the discarded packaging of a pair of Christian Dior pantyhose, tissues and several cotton puffs tinted with makeup, an empty Tampax package, and a depleted box of English cigarettes. Several lipsticked cigarette butts were in the bathroom ashtray, and only a few dots of face powder and one long, blond hair were in the sink. She was reluctant to begin cleaning, and stood for some time breathing in the perfumed air, trying to construct the image of the woman who had spent the night here. She was someone with money and good taste, someone thoughtful and considerate, someone almost suicidally lonely. In view of the nearly palpable essence of the woman lingering like a shadow, it seemed somehow a sacrilege to eradicate her with Windex and Ajax and the Electrolux. She was sidetracked by the question of why the names of so many products ended in *x*. Caught up in this, she began automatically to clean the room.

Until the weather turned and it became too cold, Caley and Louise met up most afternoons in the pool enclosure. They'd sit, either at one of the tables or together at the deep end with their feet in the water, and talk. Louise willingly revealed her history, claiming it wasn't worth the hearing, but if Caley was interested, she was glad to tell.

"It's a boring story, you know. I'm just a farm girl from Wisconsin. Grew up knowing there was no such thing as 'spare time.' Always chores to do on a farm—feeding the chickens, muckin' out the barns, one harvest or another ready for planting or reaping, cows to be milked, and food to put on the table for the family and the hands. I figured I'd finish school and go off to the city; that was the whole plan. Me and my sister, Ella—she was two years older than me—we planned for years how we'd go live in Madison or maybe Racine, get ourselves jobs, and have some adventure in our lives.

"We did it, too, the year I was eighteen. We tried Madison for about a year and didn't like it all that much, so we came on to St. Paul. Ella got herself a good secretarial job—she had brains, Ella—and me, I went to work in Dayton's downtown Minneapolis, selling notions. I used to sew a lot when Mike was younger, made all his clothes, a lot of Fred's and mine, too. Don't have the time or patience for it, these days, but back then, I did. Anyway, we had a nice place upstairs in this woman's house in St. Paul, and things were going real good. We went out on dates together, or we'd go bowl on a Saturday night. We were sending money home every week, and feeling real good about that, too.

"Anyway, what happened was Ella started getting all quiet and kind of moody, and didn't want to talk about whatever it was that was bothering her. It turned out she got herself involved with her boss and was meeting him after work here and there, you know. The upshot was she got herself pregnant and, naturally, the boss didn't want to know about it.

"You have to understand the kind of family we had to know why she just flatly refused to go home. If my mother wouldnt've killed her, my dad sure would've. Lutherans with a vengeance." Louise shook her head. "Well, she took herself off to some back-door quack and had an abortion. By the time I got her to the hospital, she was so paper white I just knew she wasn't going to make it. They took her off to one of those little rooms—like they took you—and I sat there and waited. She never came out. She just bled to death, and everybody forgot about me, forgot I was sitting there waiting. It must've been three, four hours before anyone thought to remember somebody had brought her there, and that somebody was sitting in the little waiting room chewing on her fingernails, waiting.

"Funny thing of it is, that's how I met Fred. He'd been working upstate on a surveying team, and some stupid ass went'n put a hatchet right through his own foot. Fred came in to wait with him while they sewed up his foot. We both sat there. People came and went, and in the end it was just the two of us. I guess he saw how upset I was getting, and he went off and brought me back a Coke. It was the first human thing anybody'd thought to do for me there, and I just broke out crying. He was the kindest man I ever met, looked after me and, afterward, helped me make all the arrangements for Ella. Made me write down my name and address and said I'd be hearing from him. Of course, I didn't think I would, but one night a few weeks later, I came home from the store and there he was, sitting on the front steps in his red wool jacket and his cap, waiting for me. That was twenty-nine years ago. Can you believe it? It's just amazing the way time gets away from you.

"We got married when I was twenty-one, then we started saving up to buy this place. Took us eleven years to scrape up enough for the downpayment, with Fred working surveying crews all over the state and me working days at Dayton's and nights bartending a place over in St. Paul. We hardly ever saw each other. It's probably"—she laughed—"how come we stuck it out so long. Didn't get a chance to get bored with each other. Anyway, that's the whole thing. We bought this place, moved in and started running it, and a year after that we had Mike." She laughed. "How'd you get me going on all that ancient history? C'mon. Let's go see about some supper."

Most evenings Louise invited Caley to eat with the family. After dinner, she'd help Louise clean up the kitchen, then they'd all sit in the living room and watch TV or play Scrabble or Monopoly. Caley felt very at ease with these people. Fred was a quiet man, tall and lanky, who seemed content to do the chores around the place. He maintained the heating and air-conditioning units, and fixed the TV sets, as well as repairing the occasional broken window or door. He seemed always busy with some piece of work, yet he failed to have the preoccupied self-absorption men usually carried with them like shields. He was invariably warm and had a good smile, one that sent the otherwise smooth surface of his features into countless creases. He had quite a sophisticated sense of humor and liked to watch shows like "That's Incredible" or "Real People" and guffaw loudly from start to finish at the ludicrously mawkish sincerity with which the witless and bizarre offerings were presented.

Mike embodied an interesting combination of his parents' qualities. Like Louise, he was forthright and conversational, and like his father, he found enormous humor in what was offered up as daily fare on TV. He was a tall, handsome boy, with a direct gaze and his father's summery smile.

"He's a whiz with computers," Louise explained early on, "spends hours after school fussing with them floppy disks, whatever they are."

"One of these days," Mike informed them, "everybody's gonna have a computer. *Everybody*," he added emphatically.

"You don't want to, you won't even have to leave your house. The computer'll do everything: tell you when to get your car serviced, pay all your bills, keep track of stuff like insurance and recipes, everything. It'll even keep you company and play games with you. It's gonna happen, boy, and are they ever gonna need people like me to show how they work and what-all they'll do for you. I've already written one handbook, and my computer sciences teacher thinks he might be able to get it published."

What Caley liked most about this family was their steady interest in one another. Louise rarely had to reprimand Mike. A quiet reminder was all it seemed to take to redirect her son's energy. "That room of yours could use some attention," she'd say, and Mike would go off to attend to it. "I've been blessed in that boy," she confided to Caley. "Doubt the mothers of some of his friends could say as much. Some of those boys're downright half-witted, can't do the simplest things. Mike's gonna be all right. He knows how to look after himself, knows how to fix a meal or clean up a place."

They liked each other, and they liked Caley, too. As the winter came on, with nights when fog fell with the swollen density of something malevolently alive, Caley's presence at the dinner table was expected. She and Louise went to movies together, and to the occasional bingo game where Louise cursed roundly each time she needed just one more number and somebody called bingo. Louise came of an evening to visit with Caley in her room, and there'd be more talk.

"Hope you don't mind my asking," Louise said, "but I can't help wondering about your finances. It's expensive, living on the road. How d'you manage that?"

"I got a settlement, from the accident. Originally, I thought I'd just buy a lot of traveler's checks and pay as I went. But when I went to talk to my bank manager, he had a quiet fit and told me I'd be out of my mind to do that when the interest rates were so high. He talked me into buying commercial bank paper—don't ask me what it is, I couldn't tell you. He invests the money with some company like J. C. Penney, something like that, for sixty or ninety days and then deposits the interest into my checking account, and rolls over the principal for another sixty or ninety days. They set it up so I have a big credit limit on my Mastercard, and I pay everything with the card. Every month the bank takes whatever's due out of my account; they pay my Blue Cross and anything else I owe; and they let me use their office for a mailing address, so if there's anything important, they can take care of it."

"Must've been a lot of money," Louise said.

"Fifty-eight thousand dollars," Caley told her. "I had some savings, too. It sounds like a lot, but when you think that it's probably all I'm ever really going to have in the way of a nest egg, it's not that much. Luckily, with the interest rates so high, it's been earning good money for me. When I called in a couple of weeks ago, he said I was accruing too much in my checking account, so he'd added some of it to the capital. It's working out really well, for now."

"That's not a whole lot for a settlement," Louise said. "I've heard of cases where they paid hundreds of thousands of dollars for injuries like yours."

"I just wanted to get it over with."

"I can understand that, but it doesn't seem altogether fair."

"Who knows what's fair?" Caley said. "It doesn't matter."

"No so long as you're satisfied, it doesn't."

"I'm satisfied."

"Business is gonna slow way down now," Louise said. "We book out a few of the rooms by the week to musicians playing around town, get some of the salesmen, but they mostly stay in the motels closer to downtown in case the roads close."

"Maybe I should think about moving on," Caley offered. "I hadn't planned on staying so long."

"Now, where you gonna go?" Louise wanted to know. "You don't want to start driving aimlessly this time of year, this part of the world. You get caught in some storm and you'll wind up in big trouble. Just stay put," she advised. "Time to go's when the weather breaks, around April."

"I'll start paying for my room," Caley began.

"No, you won't!" Louise cut her off. "You're the best girl we ever had, and truth to tell, it's been a long time since I had someone to visit with. You just put that thought straight out of your head. And drink that coffee you went to all that trouble to make, before it goes cold."

•   •   •

The air acquired a lacquered, lacerating edge, and then the snow came, accompanied by a wind that sang at the edges of the windows and doors; a harsh, whistling music whose volume increased to a moan in the night as it sculpted the snow, driving it into exotic formations. The snow was blinding, a massive assault on all the senses. Simply attempting to cross the parking lot from her room to the motel office became a major expedition, its successful completion to be greeted by congratulatory smiles as she struggled into the aching warmth of the apartment behind the manager's office.

"Don't have winters like this back east, I'll wager," Fred ventured, pouring her some coffee.

"Nothing like this," she confirmed. "I'm going to have to buy some warmer clothes, and a new coat."

"I'll take you downtown," Louise declared. "Those rubber boots'll see you with a case of frostbite. You want some with a good, thick lining."

The following morning, the two of them drove into the city in the pickup.

"I've got nothing against that car of yours," Louise said, "but I sure wouldn't recommend trying to drive it on these roads. That's a recreational vehicle if ever I saw one."

Caley laughed. "I had it out yesterday. I was all over the road. I guess I should buy some snow tires or something."

"Good idea. Till you do, feel free to borrow the pickup. It's a whole helluva lot safer."

They parked in an indoor garage downtown and went to Dayton's. "It's a good store," Louise said, proudly loyal. "They always treated me well, the years I worked here."

In the women's coats department, Louise wandered around while Caley went through the racks, setting her bag and old coat on the floor to try some on. As she was studying her reflection, trying to decide on a heavy navy duffle coat, her eyes connected in the mirror with those of a small girl of four or five. The child's eyes widened and, in a shrill little voice, she asked, "What's the matter with her face?" The mother, who was pushing through jackets on one of the racks, ignored her.

"What's the matter with her face?" The child was pointing

now and trying to free herself of her mother's grip on her hand.

"Shush, Barbie!" The mother tugged sharply on the child's hand, still examining the jackets and their price tags.

Undaunted, Barbie managed to extricate herself and, pointing accusingly, one little finger relentless and unwavering, moved toward Caley. "What's the *matter* with your *face*?" piped her little voice, gaining in courage and volume; she closed in until she was standing directly in front of Caley, gazing round-eyed up at her.

Unable to avoid the accusatory finger and piercing tones, Caley leaned down and whispered, "Go away or I'll rip your tiny throat out!"

The finger was removed, but the child remained, clearly not able to decide whether to laugh or be afraid. This might be some new kind of game, and Barbie wanted to play it. Caley had no means of defending herself from the child's ruthless determination to have her question answered. Her chubby, indeterminate features were obstinately set as she again asked, "What's the matter with your face?" Her hands now safely clenched behind her back, she took another step forward, peering up at Caley with unblinking steadiness.

Hotly mortified, seething with frustration, Caley looked around for Louise. She was nowhere in sight. Caley took off the duffle coat and bent to retrieve her old coat and bag. She straightened to find little Barbie hadn't budged an inch. "What's the matter . . ." she started again.

Caley did the only thing she could think of. She drew back her lips, bared her teeth, and snarled, thinking to scare the kid off. She succeeded. With a terrorized, astonishingly loud scream, Barbie stood her ground a moment longer, then turned and bolted back to her mother, throwing her arms around the woman's thigh, her high-pitched screams rending the air, her eyes fearfully tracking Caley's every move.

"Will you stop?" the mother snapped, trying to disentangle herself.

"That lady!" Barbie shrieked, pointing again. "She *scared* me!"

At last, the woman looked up. Her eyes found Caley and she shot her a look of excessively violent animosity as her arm closed protectively around little Barbie. The look said, "How dare you show that face in a public place? How dare you show it to my child, and frighten her?"

Trembling with chagrin, Caley held her ground, just dying to have the woman say even one word to her. The air between them expanded, elastic, and then the woman turned and led the child away. Caley took several deep breaths, battling down her rage and humiliation, grateful no one had been around to witness the incident. All she wanted was to hide somewhere. The idea of again encountering that mother and that child somewhere else in the store unnerved her.

"Find anything?" Louise asked, appearing from behind one of the racks. "That looks good." She took the duffle from Caley and held it up for examination. "My God, the price of things!" She shook her head over the price tag. "You gonna get this?" she asked. "I'd get this," she went on without awaiting a reply. Linking her arm through Caley's, she said, "There's assholes born every minute, breeding more little assholes every other minute. Neither of them're worth getting yourself worked up over. Sales desk is this way."

"I'm going to buy you lunch," Caley announced.

"With your little plastic card, right?"

"That's right."

"And your bank in Connecticut's gonna pay the tab. Right?"

"Right again."

"Well, I don't mind if I do. But first we'll get you some decent boots. Then, if you really want to buy me lunch, there's a nice place Edina-way I wouldn't mind."

The Camelot had a moat and a drawbridge, stone walls and turrets. Caley was amused by the look of the place. "How's the food?" she asked doubtfully.

"Just you wait and see. Me and Fred, we came here our last anniversary. Had a swell time. They got this Jester's lounge upstairs, with live entertainment. Years back, when Mike was just a baby, we used to come down for a drink now and then. They had this girl up there. Funniest damn girl, sang real nice, too. They were lined up all the way down them stairs there, waiting to get in. What she did, she'd say, 'You got any requests, write 'em down on small pieces of money and send 'em up.' You wouldn't believe the money people paid, asking for songs she never heard of, half the time, so she'd make them up on the spot. We came a few times to hear her. Had a real pretty voice, she did, nice and low. She got a big write-up in the paper, in Will Jones's column it was. Wish you could've seen her. She was something.''

The service was very good, the food was excellent. They shared a bottle of red wine, and by the time they left the restaurant to drive back to the motel they were both a little high and found everything, including the onset of fresh snow, funny. Louise went in to take a nap before dinner. As she carried her purchases across the lot to her room, Caley noted four cars in the lot, two more than they'd been averaging. After hanging away the new duffle coat and placing the boots on the floor underneath, she went on impulse to the telephone.

"I'm going to make a long-distance call," she told Fred when he picked up at the switchboard in the office.

"Sure thing, Caley. Just you hold on now and I'll get the operator for you."

She called the office number, identified herself to the secretary, and Ron came on the line at once, eagerly asking, "Hey, Cale! Where are you?"

"Minneapolis. I thought it was about time I checked in to see how you are."

"Minneapolis. Jesus! What're you doing out there?"

"Believe it or not, I'm working as a chambermaid in a motel."

"You're kidding! Cleaning up, that kind of stuff?"

"I've been here almost six months, working for a really nice family. They've been so good to me, Ron. You'd love them."

"Are you going to stay there?"

"I don't think so. I'll probably move on in the spring. How are you?"

"Oh, same as usual. How are *you*?"

"I'm okay, better than okay really. Oh! Guess what! Uncle Sam ran away, in Florida."

"Maybe he wanted to retire." He laughed.

"Maybe. How're things at the office?"

"Same. Where d'you think you'll go in the spring, Cale?"

Hope rounded the edges of his words.

"I haven't thought about it all that much. Maybe Canada. I was thinking I might head north and drive right across."

"And after that?" he asked. "Think you might be heading this way?"

"I don't know, Ron."

"A chambermaid," he said. "Are you serious?"

"Honest to God. I'm very good at it, too. I can tell you all about someone just by cleaning up after him."

He laughed again, then said, "Listen, stay in touch, will you? Don't wait months before you check in again. Okay? I was starting to get worried."

"Don't worry. I'm fine."

"Car holding up all right?"

"So far. I haven't been driving it much lately. The roads're really bad and I don't have snow tires."

"It's been deadly around the apartment," he said, hopeful again.

"I can imagine. You ought to start getting out, socializing."

"Well, I've done some. It's a hassle."

"You stick with it. I'd better go now."

"Is there a number where I can reach you?"

"Sure." She gave it to him, then said, "I'll call you again soon."

"Don't forget. And send me a postcard or something."

"Take care, Ron."

"*You* take care, Cale. I'm thinking about you."

The connection broken, she felt suddenly adrift, self-exiled from everything familiar. She had to wonder why she refused, for the moment, even to consider going back. Ron still wanted her, was evidently hoping she'd return. She could go back. He was decent, and kind, and he loved her. "It's not time yet," she said aloud, sitting on the end of the bed to watch the snow blow past her window.

Stan would have had a lot to say about her decisions, she thought. He'd have dragged out some of his favorite words like "avoidance" and "aversion" and flung them into the air with panache. And maybe he'd have been right. But Stan, she thought, couldn't possibly understand how it felt to be the one inside, the person who had to keep on living somehow behind the damaged mask, at the end of the accusing finger. Louise understood, though, and her displays of compassionate understanding inspired in Caley a gust of emotion as sudden and complete as the ferocious winds that wailed their accompaniment to each night's passage.

Chapter 18

HIS MOTIVATION, CAPRICIOUS and unreliable, abandoned him. Martin had to stop in his efforts to match the Victorian moldings where the newly built arches demanded them. He simply had to stop. On his knees, surrounded by lengths of quarter-round and one-by-six and decorative, notched, half-round, he gazed at his hands and then at the stockade he'd erected around himself.

Beyond the denuded windows the snow fell; its accumulation produced a glare that reflected inward so that the house appeared to be lit from outside. He felt like something small —a child's pet mouse, perhaps—trapped within the confines of a solid-walled cage. Rising, he walked to the window, to stand with his hands braced on the damp wooden sill, watching the snow swirl, eddying. He'd always loved snow, but he felt now as if the steady downfall were cotton, packed tightly around the house, to prevent its being damaged. He was being preserved within these walls, an unwitting captive.

Mickey had left behind a package of cigarettes, months old, stale and acrid-tasting. Martin smoked one of the Export A's. He stood now by the fireplace, tipping his ash into the grate, his eyes on one section of the vacant bookshelves that flanked the fireplace. He could no longer ignore the fact that he was letting this project drag on and on. Given his present rate of progress, completion might be put off for months, even years. To what end? he wondered, glowering at the scrolled ceiling centerpiece he'd thought he'd strip so that its detail would attain a clearer definition.

Initially, he'd undertaken the renovation out of anger, and fear, because of Marian's leaving him. He'd returned to the task with the idea of fabricating what Mick had termed a "shrine." He'd immersed himself in the work, determined to think only of the job at hand, and he'd been successful. For months on end, he'd directed his roiling energies into making perfect even the slightest detail of the job at hand. Now he was faltering, in the grip of a mounting sense of dispossession. Perhaps it was because he'd violated the integrity of his ambition by inviting an outsider, Mickey, to participate in the project. Perhaps he'd soiled the intent by exposing it to the jaded views of someone who failed to understand why this project had been undertaken.

"Rubbish!" he said, tossing the cigarette into the grate. This had nothing to do with Mickey, or with any nebulous concept of lost integrity. The truth was, he thought gravely, that he'd unknowingly entered into a new phase, one that was demanding, more and more, he try to reestablish some more rational form of existence.

It was hell being sober. With the aid of drink he might have been able to go for years painstakingly duplicating lengths of Victorian trim; he might have floated along on liquid forebearance, daily rallying the vitality needed to commemorate what had been lost. Abstinent, what was overtaking him now was undiluted impatience, an urge to see this labor ended. He was also beginning to see a degree of unworthiness in his immersion in the project. While he'd never cared overmuch for what others thought of him, he was nevertheless able, dispassionately, to see that from the outside, looking in, he could be deemed obsessive. And it wasn't the viewpoint of others that was distressing so much as his sudden, calamitous capacity to see himself in this light.

He hadn't even tried to sketch. He'd told himself his talent, or at least his curiosity, had died along with his family. And so he'd relegated his prior occupation to a mental dustbin, along with all the emotions that no longer had an outlet. The most he'd done was to walk here and there in the city, taking black-

and-white photographs; and despite the novelty of this occupation, he still privately regarded photography as considerably
less than art. To be fair now, he thought he ought to try his
hand, see if the sureness was still there.

It could have been the inhalations of stale smoke that were
responsible for his light-headedness, but more likely it was the
combined fear and excitement aroused by the revival of his interest in documenting the people and objects and scenes that
existed beyond the safe anonymity that concealed him within
this house.

He didn't want the house to become an albatross, instead of
the haven it really was. In order to prevent that happening, he
was obligated to go out so that he might, upon his return, appreciate again all this place signified. If he didn't go out, if he
didn't make the effort, he knew he'd begin to deteriorate. It
was inevitable. Madness awaited him in the sacks of plaster
and gallon containers of paint; it beckoned to him from the
boxes of nails and the uncut lumber; it lurked in the pristine
kitchen with its white-tiled floors and empty cabinets. He'd
disposed of everything that had once had a place on this floor,
except for the television set, which he'd wrestled down the
stairs to the cellar. He'd cleared the conservatory of its inven-
tory of dead plants, having made quite a number of trips back
and forth to the commercial dumpster he'd hired during the
initial phase of the renovation. He'd scavenged, pouncing
upon any item that had belonged to that time when a family
had been in possession of these rooms. Everything was gone,
even the old china and silverware. Now, contemplating the
profound emptiness of his cage, he knew he'd go right round
the bloody twist if he didn't leave off for a time and verify that
the world was still out there.

This insinuation into his brain of worldly obligations rechanneled his ever-present grief. He *wanted* to go off his fucking nut, wanted to be found dead and rotting in here: a
skeletal testament to his devotion. The world and his knowledge of it was interfering with the homage he sought to pay
dear old Marks and Spencer, and Marian. It wasn't fair, he
thought, returning to the window. It wasn't bloody fair that
some damnable part of him was insisting he have a life. He
wanted to choose the coward's way and lose himself in brain-

lessly fitting old lengths of wood to new, doing so clever a piece of work that no one would be able to detect the joins, or to determine which the original and which the reproduction.

It had been a very British spring, he recalled, with rain day after day, well into June. The temperatures had stayed low, only inching upward in late July. By the end of August, the days had started turning cool. In mid-November, the rains had returned. Leaves had lain in sodden blankets on the lawn, too heavy to be shifted by the wind. The weather, at least, had remained faithful to his mood. The proof was the present early snowfall.

Even worse than his lamentable instinct toward life was the recent perfidy of his body. Several mornings in a row he'd awakened in a state of need, his erections a shameful denial of his ongoing love for his wife. His body enraged him, and he punished it with icy showers and long hours of exertion, unrelieved by breaks for food or anything more nourishing than coffee. The preparing and consumption of coffee were his only actions in the new kitchen, and he cleaned up afterward with manic scrupulousness. By the end of a day's work, the coffee had set his hands vibrating and his heart racing; his back and stomach ached in concert, and he could no longer ingest more than minute portions of food. Perversely, he took satisfaction in his ability to dominate his loathsome body. Given his head, he'd torment this sinewy housing until it died of neglect. Instinct, however, refused to allow that, and, periodically he'd ring up one of the numbers on the list and have a meal delivered hot.

Turning from the window, he contemplated the work remaining to be done. Working flat out, this area could be finished in as little as six weeks. Going at it part-time, it might take three or four months. With a sigh, he pushed away from the window and went to drag his cardigan from the foot of the hall banister.

He was assaulted by the wind as he opened the kitchen door and stepped outside. "Bloody cold," he muttered, his feet sinking into the several inches of snow. The teeth of winter were set firmly in the wind; they chewed savagely at the trees; disdainfully, the wind spat now into his eyes.

As if it were the actual embodiment of neglect, dust lay over everything in the studio. It seemed even to adhere to the light, so that Martin blinked repeatedly, trying to refine his vision. On the far wall, still in their crates, were stacked the English canvases. Like wearied soldiers marooned on a parade ground, they leaned in to the wall, awaiting a call to arms. Purposely, Martin ignored them, going instead to the table where his supplies sat in stolid diffidence.

The act of reaching for the sketch pads and pencils affected him in the same way the placing of his hands upon the acquiescent flesh of some unknown woman might have. Alarmed, he swept the dust from the pad with his hand, then absentmindedly wiped his hand on his trousers. It was hard to breathe. His desire to be casual was outweighed by his awareness of the moment's significance. Possibly, he'd discover his talent had acquired its own patina of disuse, and then his grief would burgeon in yet another area; but he had to risk it. His options had narrowed critically. Whether he wished it or not, his common sense had begun dictating to him, a rattling tickertape of logic declaring he hadn't the right to discard his life, or his body, as atonement for the deaths of the people he'd loved. He wasn't responsible for their deaths, no matter how hard he had tried to bury himself beneath a conjectured avalanche of what-if's. The simple truth was, they'd died through misadventure, and nothing he might have done would have prevented it. If he chose to abandon his own life as a result, while it might be readily understandable as a by-product of his sorrow, it was nevertheless unacceptable and, on too many levels, unforgivably self-indulgent. If he'd wanted to die, the appropriate time for it had long since passed. He was going to have to live; there was nothing more to it.

He could only remain in the studio for a few minutes. The proximity of the paintings was more than he could bear. He switched off the lights and went to the door at the head of the stairs, where he stood for a few seconds, listening, as if he could hear the dust settling—it would make small, tinkling sounds—on those surfaces he hadn't yet dared approach.

The snow had already filled in his footsteps, leaving behind only shallow indentations that were rapidly blending with the unbroken carpet of snow covering every surface. His lungs fluttered, protesting the air's savage edge, as, head down, he flung himself forward toward the house.

He carried the fistful of pencils and sketching blocks to the living room, where he placed them on the mantel before backing away, garnering strength for his second, more important trip out of doors. Smoking another of Mick's stale cigarettes, he kicked at the small pile of debris in the middle of the room—tag ends of quarter-round, bent nails, and sawdust—gripped by the odd feeling that he was in the throes of birth-giving labor, about to deliver himself of himself. He imagined himself slipping the wet length of a birth canal to arrive on the outside, bloodied and gasping, fighting to draw in air to replace the amniotic fluid in his lungs.

"Fuck this for a lark!" He stormed over to the telephone. "Listen!" he bellowed upon hearing Mick's voice. "I've got fucking agoraphobia or somesuch bloody nonsense! Come collect me and I'll subsidize your night's drinking."

"You wouldn't be telling me the shrine's completed, would you?"

"I didn't ring you up to discuss that. Come collect me, you steaming Irish git!"

"There's a fucking blizzard out there. Or haven't you noticed? You gone off the wagon, Maddox?"

"I'm not off the wagon, and I know what's going on out there. Will you come?"

"On my way, old sport."

"Be quick about it, will you?" Martin said more quietly. "I'm already losing my nerve."

"Half an hour," Mick promised, and hung up.

"I learned, years and years ago," Mick said, "that it's all too easy to see ready solutions to other people's problems. In view of how easy it seemed to be, I decided the wisest course was to keep one's gob shut and reserve judgment. So, mate, I'll just sit here and enjoy me boilermakers, and you do whatever it is you do with your pencils and paper."

"A fine idea," Martin agreed, and set to work. He sketched frantically, turning page after page, for several hours. When at last he emitted a huge sigh and reached for the glass of Perrier he'd ordered hours before, Mickey said. "I don't know how you can drink that filthy stuff."

"I don't know either. Still, it's thirsty work." He drained the glass, then plonked it down on the table. "Let's go get something to eat."

"Perfect." Mick insisted on paying the tab. "All you had was that revolting gnat's piss. I wouldn't dream of allowing you to spend good money for it. As a matter of fact," he said, grunting as he reached into his back pocket, "I'll buy you a meal, to boot."

"Won the pools, have you?" Martin asked, eyeing the wad of bills Mickey recklessly revealed.

"Got the last part of my advance," Mickey confided. "This'll have to do by way of celebration. Not quite what I had in mind, but what the hell."

"Where shall we go?" Martin asked as they stood in the doorway of the bar, surveying the untrammeled snow in the road. "What do you fancy?"

"Switzer's," Mickey decided. "I wouldn't mind some corned beef."

"Your idea of a celebration, is it?"

"Didn't I just tell you it wasn't what I had in mind? I know for a fact I said those words not five minutes past. Unless of course there's an echo." Turning up his coat collar, he said, "Come on," and started off in his rolling run, toward the car.

"Given up driving?" Mick asked as they headed along Queen Street toward Spadina.

"Not intentionally. I simply haven't given it any thought recently. I expect I should take the bloody thing in for servicing before it falls to pieces."

"Wouldn't be a bad idea. Then I wouldn't have to chauffeur you about when I'd prefer to be happily, irresponsibly pissed. The local constabulary tend to frown on that sort of thing. You look pathetic, Maddox. I'll wager you haven't eaten a proper meal since I left."

"Been too busy," Martin alibied.

"Too busy, my old Aunt Fanny. You've been trying to commit legalized suicide, you dumb fuck. I may be Irish, but I'm not stupid. You, on the other hand, could win awards for your carryings-on in recent times. I could see it now if you were Bobby Sands, or one of those other lads starving in protest. But you don't have a good enough reason to be doing this to yourself.''

"Are you planning to take on the role of my mother?"

"Don't go all caustic on me, Maddox! It's all to the good you rang up, because I was about to come round and drag you out by the scruff. I'll be blessed!" he exclaimed. "There's a parking spot, and right in front, no less." With a quick look to be sure he was in the clear, he made a sweeping U-turn across Spadina and pulled in at a meter directly in front of the delicatessen. "It's not a night for walking more than a few steps, if it can be avoided," he told Martin, on their way in through the door.

The spicy, heated air accosted them as they entered. Martin's stomach recoiled. He looked at the food—the salads and pickles and cold cuts—behind the counter as they went to a booth, and wondered if he was going to be able to eat.

"What's the news of Esther?" he asked, watching Mick scan the menu. "And how are Liza and Brendan?"

"Brendan's in love," Mick said, holding aside the menu. "Liza's in love. And fuck me if Esther's not in love, to boot. She's filed for divorce, and rings me up every few hours to check for signs of jealousy while regaling me with tales of her daring escapades. I can't tell you how grand it's going to be when the whole thing's over and I can put the blower down in her fucking ear. She's found herself a young stud. If she's got anything to do with it, he won't be young too much longer. Rutting herself into the ground, the stupid cow, and thinks I'm interested in the details. I'm having potato pancakes, corned beef on a kaiser, a side of slaw, and a Carlsberg," he told the elderly waitress who'd listened to all he'd said with unfeigned absorption. With a smile, he slipped the menu back into place between the cluster of condiments and the wall. "What time do you finish up here, my old darling?" he asked her. "Or don't you fraternize with the customers?"

She bestowed a yellowed grin upon him and gave his shoulder a push with the flat of her hand. In a thickly Slavic accent, she turned to ask Martin, "What you have?"

"Pastrami on a kaiser, chips with gravy, an old dill, and a cream soda."

"Goot!" She wrote briefly, then walked to the kitchen door to shout out her order for the potato pancakes and the fries. Then, stuffing her pad and pencil into her apron pocket, she went behind the counter and began dishing up cole slaw as she ordered the pastrami and corned beef from the young man doing sandwich duty.

Mick followed her progress until she reached into the refrigerated cabinet for the dill pickle, then turned back to Martin. "How was it, the sketching?"

Cautiously, Martin said, "I am not without hope. The joints could do with some oiling, but the hand-eye coordination's still there." He helped himself to one of Mickey's cigarettes and lit it, paying close attention to the placement of the spent match in the ashtray. "It was good of you to come fetch me, Mick."

"Happy to oblige."

"I had myself convinced I had to get out of the bloody house but couldn't seem to make myself go."

"You want to watch out." Mick frowned. "You're on your way to creating some serious problems for yourself."

"What really had me going was the idea that I'd pick up a pencil and nothing would happen."

"Surely not after all these years? You don't lose it all that easily, no matter what you might think."

"I'm not entirely convinced of that. Let me tell you something. Directly after we'd heard about the air crash, Grace and I got into the car to drive back to the villa. Grace was in no fit condition, so I drove, and as we went along, all the color gradually bled away out of everything. It was rather like watching a color film that goes suddenly to black and white. Everything turned to shades of gray. I took it as a sign."

"What of?"

"I don't know. Perhaps that, without them, I literally had nothing left. It felt that way," he admitted hesitantly. "I believed it had come to that."

Mick forced air between his teeth in a hissing sound that, with accuracy, reflected his dismayed response to what Martin was saying.

"Then today," Martin went on, "there I was sawing away at those bleeding endless lengths of trim, and I suddenly couldn't keep on. I had to stop then and there or I'd have turned into a complete nutter.''

"Maybe," Mick thought aloud, "it's come time for you to rejoin the living." Martin's head came up sharply, his chin jutting forward, and Mick added, "No offense intended, but I'm dead serious, mate. It's time. Sooner or later, we all have to accept whatever's done is done; it's final, and we're still here. A time comes when you've got to get on with it. For all my jokes, it's taken me bloody months to come to terms with Esther's buggering off on me. The first little while, I kept thinking she'd come to her senses and bring her bits home. Then, when I saw that wasn't going to happen, I got on with it, trying to make the best of a bad situation."

This was a conversation he'd engineered, yet Martin was so unaccustomed to intimate dialogues with other men, so unfamiliar with the protocol, if any existed, that he simply had no idea where to go with the confirmation Mick was lending his own sentiments. In part he was embarrassed by Mick's revelations; in part he wanted to crack jokes to get them both past this moment; and in part he wanted, even yearned, for the privilege of unburdening himself. The public-school, establishment Martin was fairly repelled by Mick's admissions; the experienced adult and artist Martin was envious of Mick's ability to be truthful about his feelings.

He gave an awkward laugh, his fingers toying with the cigarette. Self-conscious, he wished he'd never uttered a word. Simultaneously, he knew that if Mick extended even the slimmest further invitation, he'd start recklessly spewing out words.

"Are you planning," Mick asked, "to spend the rest of your life locked up in that house?"

"I had thought I might," Martin began tentatively, feeling his way. "It does seem I'm no longer quite up to the job. Christ, Mick! They died, and I'm saying, and doing, things I wouldn't have believed myself capable of, even a year ago. Why does it feel so fucking demoralizing to talk about one's feelings? Why is that? Why is it we're told not to reveal emotions? Women do it all the bloody time, and we make light of them for it."

"I don't see that it's all so terrible," Mick said. "I mean, it's the truth, what you're saying. And if it didn't seem to me you were in such abominable shape, I probably wouldn't have admitted to being pissed off with Esther. It's only at the worst of times any of us seems willing to admit to having any feelings at all.''

"Surely to God you're not going to try to tell me what happened is for the best?''

"What kind of fool do you take me for? Of course I wouldn't tell you a load of old shit like that. That's bloody obscene. I've got the idea you've a few things on your mind you'd like to talk about, and I'm telling you, in my way, I'm not averse to hearing you out. Jesus, Mary, and Joseph! We're fucking inept at this!

"What I'm trying to tell you is: think back on the number of times over the years you've kept me company in the bottle, then taken me home and put me to bed. I'll be fucked if I could give you an off-the-cuff definition of it, but I've always thought of the two of us as friends. I'll have you know I don't leap to attention for every moronic Brit who happens to take it into his head to ring me at the crack of bloody dawn to come do physical labor. I'd like to help, and I'm sorry if my years at Trinity come as a parallel to yours in public schools. We're cut from the same fucking loaf and I'm as bloody embarrassed to be sitting here nattering like an old woman as you are. It's just there comes a time when maybe it's the only course left.''

"You're not drinking your beer,'' Martin said quietly.

Mick wrapped one thick hand around the sweating bottle. "I went dry once,'' he said, watching Martin pull the tab from a can of cream soda. "Fucking horrible, it was. Felt like me chest was filled with monstrous little demons all poking away at my innards with tiny pitchforks. That stupid cow!'' he said acidly. "Ringing me up to narrate her sexual exploits. I'd like to tear her fucking tongue out.''

"Actually,'' Martin said, "I quite admire you, for being able to talk of it. How long did you stay dry?''

"Four entire days. Then I had a drink to celebrate.''

Their eyes met and held, and then they laughed loudly.

In the next day's mail, Martin received a letter from Grace.

My dear Martin,

I had hoped I might hear from you, but cannot claim to being surprised by your long silence. I haven't felt up to dealing with people, either, in recent months. I've done a great deal of thinking, and remembering, and have been frightfully remiss about the grounds. They've rather gone to ruin, I'm afraid, but I simply haven't the interest I once did.

I decided it was time to write for a number of reasons, not the least of which has to do with the house here. In September, I had a letter from a firm of solicitors who are handling the estate of Mr. Mendoza, who owned the house we've rented all these years on Tenerife. Mr. Mendoza died in early August and one of the conditions of his will had to do with offering me the privilege of purchasing the villa at a most reasonable price.

In view of how cumbersome I've found the house and grounds since returning here last April, I decided I might be happier in a smaller place, in a better climate. I listed the house with estate agents and it sold quite quickly, actually more quickly than I'd imagined it would.

In an odd way, the prospect of living out my life on the island seems to bring Marian and the children closer. I am hoping that you won't find this morbid or fanciful, but rather, simply practical. They *are* there, after all, in one sense, and what with the simply wretched weather we've had in England this past spring and autumn, I'm very much looking forward to returning there.

The new owners take possession here a week Monday, by which time I hope to be in Tenerife. For the first time in too long, there's something to which I'm looking forward. Martin, I do hope you'll come to visit with me on the island. I think of you often, and miss your frightful jokes. Please let me know how you are.

With all my love, Grace.

The letter cheered him. He reread it several times, then sat down to reply. He wrote truthfully of the guilt he felt at starting to emerge from his benumbed state, and told of his work on the house, and his renewed efforts at drawing; he confirmed his intention of visiting her in the not-too-distant future once he had a bit more of an idea what he hoped to do next. He concluded by stating, "It makes perfect sense to me that you'd choose to return to the island. I'm not all that enamored of the wretched Canadian weather, and will look forward to seeing you, and soon. I imagine you'll have taken up the paving stones of the patio in favor of grass and half a dozen flowering beds, and you'll be up to your filthy tricks with the gardening shears. I miss you, too. All my love, Martin."

He sealed and stamped the envelope and went directly out to post it. As he walked back through the snow to the house, it occurred to him that the first half of his life had ended. He was free now to move into the second half, and to create of it what he wished. Smiling, he returned indoors.

PART THREE

Chapter 19

I T WAS TIME, Caley decided, to move on. The mornings still arrived bearing testimony to winter's reluctance to ease away gracefully, but by early afternoon there was sufficient warmth to allow going without a coat. Freed finally of boots, her feet felt oddly light. For a week or more her initial steps of the day were ungainly as her body sluggishly anticipated the impediments that had become habitual. By the second week of April she'd at last grown accustomed to the renewed weightlessness of her body. Her legs no longer felt quite so stemlike; her arms cut easily through the air; she hurried through her housekeeping duties, anxious to get on with the preparations to be made for leaving.

Throughout the winter she'd visited the local library, returning to the motel with armloads of travel books. She was going to go to Canada, in advance, she hoped, of the seasonal tourist traffic. It was her intention to go to the very edge of the country, and she was preoccupied by an image of herself standing boldly on some ragged precipice, gazing at the horizon. She imagined the Atlantic curling in on itself as it collided with the shoreline far below her; she could almost smell and taste the salt, the ozone-laden air. In more fanciful moments, she even pictured herself taking up residence in a small cottage positioned imprudently near the edge of the precipice, where the ceaseless wind—sometimes gentled by the heat of the sun, and sometimes ferociously encumbered with unshed moisture—would batter at the walls and roof, tossing aside unsecured shingles in its efforts to unseat the place and send it toppling into the violent foam. She admitted to herself that these overtly romantic images had in no small part been inspired by Daphne Du Maurier's descriptions of the Cornish coast, and by her late-night consumption of frivolous gothic novels. Nonetheless, she was determined to make her way to the end of the continent. It was her only destination. Everything she might see along the way would be purely incidental, dry fodder for her curiosity. Her ultimate option lay at the water's edge. Her future would be determined upon her arrival there.

She took the Cadillac in for an oil-change and a tune-up. She packed away her winter garments and stored them in a far corner of the trunk. She delivered several shopping bags of books to the nearest Goodwill box, and stocked up on new reading material she'd get through during her evenings on the road. She spent an afternoon washing and waxing the car, then vacuumed the interior. She polished the supple leather seat covers and hung an air freshener from the tuning knob of the radio. Her entire being hummed with excitement. Her benign sojourn had come to an end.

"Just about set to go, huh?" Louise noted.

"I've stayed a lot longer than I thought I would."

"I know that." Louise watched Caley polish the window on the driver's side. "Any idea where you're headed?"

"Canada."

"And after that?"

"I haven't thought that far."

"You're gonna be cruising around in this machine when you're an old lady," Louise said with a laugh that didn't quite conceal her concern.

"That's possible." Caley returned her smile. "There are worse things."

"Oh, sure there are. But don't you think one of these days you're gonna want some kind of organized life for yourself? You're not a wanderer by nature, Caley. Some folks are, and you can see it all over them. You don't have that kind of stamp on you."

"I've given up thinking about the future," Caley said, paying close attention to cleaning the rear-view mirror.

"For the time being, maybe. But sooner or later everybody's got to consider where they'll be in five or ten years' time. Don't you have any family somewhere?"

"Nope. No family, no one."

"Well, I guess that helps, if you're planning on spending the rest of your life living out of a car."

"Maybe not the rest of my life," Caley said a little uncomfortably.

"We all need a home, girl. Everybody has to have one, just like we need to have other people around."

"I used to believe that. Not anymore."

"I guess I'm just being selfish, trying to think up ways to talk you into staying around."

"That's not selfish," Caley disagreed, finally stopping her work on the car to look at her friend. "I'm touched that you'd want me to stay."

"But not so touched you'd stick around."

"Not because I don't care about you, Louise. You've been wonderful to me. You're probably the best friend I've ever had, and I'll come back to visit. We won't lose touch, I promise. I just can't stay here."

"Hell! I know you're more than a chambermaid. I know you've got education."

"It isn't that. It's been good for me, doing the work. I'm grateful that you let me do it. It's just that since the accident, everything I ever planned has moved out of reach. I don't know what to hope for anymore, or even if I hope for anything."

"And you think driving around aimlessly you'll find something?"

Caley wanted to tell her that in spite of how it looked her travels weren't aimless, but she didn't know how to put the thought into words without sounding crazy. She had an appointment at the end of the line, and all she had to determine was whether or not she cared to keep the appointment. "I might," she said, "find out that going from day to day is all there is."

"You're dead wrong," Louise said unhappily, "but I guess I'm not the one to convince you of that."

"You've convinced me of a lot of things, I'll tell you. I've looked at you and Fred and Mike, and I've seen how the three of you treat each other, the feelings you have for each other. It's told me a lot, and it's been important for me to see it. I'll never forget you, and I'll never forget the way you've included me, made me feel like a part of what you have."

"You're welcome to stay."

"I've thought about it," Caley conceded. "There's a voice in my head that says I'm crazy to leave here. But there's another voice that says I'm crazy if I don't." She hugged the older woman, saying, "You have my promise, I'll stay in touch."

"One thing I'll say," Louise spoke guardedly, "you don't have the same look you had when you first rolled in here."

"What d'you mean?"

Dropping her guard, Louise said, "You don't have that whipped dog look to you anymore. You carry yourself proud now."

"Well, if I do, it's because of you."

As she drove across Wisconsin, she admitted to herself that she'd grown fearful of attachments, Louise and her family aside. Her capacity for commitment had undergone a radical change. Much of the time she felt as if she didn't give a damn about anything, as if the part of her containing the roots of her emotions had grown its own thick scar tissue. Perhaps, mistakenly, it had been excised during one of the surgical procedures. Whatever the reason, she certainly no longer cowered in the public eye, as she had. Louise was right about that. If people stared at her, her silent response was, "Fuck you!" So they stared, what did it matter? When she got to the edge of the world, when she was standing on that precipice, she'd make up her mind once and for all what there was left worth caring about. For the present, she was engaged only with the mechanical action of getting from place to place. She'd become cocooned once more in the attractive isolation that came in being on the road.

She saw what there was to be seen and availed herself of the comforts for hire along the way. It was one-way traffic: she purchased shelter and was obliged to offer only money in return. Impersonal traffic, she was merely one more set of head and tail lights, one more highway traveler. Nobody really cared, nobody really noticed much, and that suited her perfectly. This mode of existence compounded her sense of living concealed behind a misrepresenting mask, just as being a member of the invisible sect of service purveyors had. She'd even found a certain security behind the mask, because so few people were interested or willing to poke at the rims of her concealment, on the offchance someone might be hidden back there. She was backstage, and the action took place out front; she ran the lights, the sound, and the curtains, and no one thought to question how it all managed to go so smoothly.

Throughout her life everything she'd had to offer had been on display in her face, and she'd lived according to that display. Like goods on show in a store window, she'd advertised her amiability, her sincerity, her reliability and competence, and all her other marketable qualities. She'd always understood that her externals, her mode of behavior, would draw to her the man who'd provide home and family, a lifetime's security. Since it was no longer possible for her to dress the window to its advantage, she'd abandoned the effort altogether. The care she took with her hair and with the minimal amount of makeup she applied were strictly for her own benefit. She knew that where others were concerned, her eyeshadow and mascara were construed as an outrage. How dare she highlight any aspect of the mask! She dared and, more and more defiantly with each day, challenged anyone to argue her right to do whatever she chose. She hadn't yet, though, reached a point where her "Fuck you!" attitude held firm. She was alternately fatigued and infuriated by the reactions of strangers, and could never accurately predict whether she'd be offhand or offended. She hadn't the energy to be defensive full-time; therefore, being on the road allowed her to relax.

She drove, attuned to Clarabelle, aware of the slightest nuance of alteration in the car's performance—a hesitation when she accelerated, a tiny tug to the left when she applied the brakes. She stopped at once at the nearest dealership to have the problems set right. The car was her ally, her companion, her home, and she was responsible for its maintenance. Fondly, she oversaw the repairs, as if the vehicle were something alive and not just an outmoded mobile collage. Nightly, she disconnected the battery cables; each morning, wrench in hand, she hooked them back up. The car started every time with reliable complicity. At night, while she slept, the car stood sentry outside her rented room.

At the border, the Canadian customs officer looked for a long time at the car before directing his eyes to her. He seemed disturbed as he rapidly asked her her citizenship and the purpose of her visit to Canada. He stood with his hand on the door, leaning in to scan the car's interior, and appeared to want to say something to her. He didn't bother to ask if she had gifts, cigarettes, or liquor. He was lost, for several ponderous moments, in private ruminations. She waited, fully expecting to be asked to pull to one side while the car and her identification were checked.

The man, middle-aged and tired-looking, drew himself together at last and looked fully into her eyes. She saw in their faded blue the images of inept smugglers and cocky children; she saw a history of personal pain and much-abused sympathy. She and this man could have gone somewhere together and, over a cup of coffee, silently communicated their mutual knowledge of the blacker aspects of humanity.

"How long are you planning to stay in Canada?" he asked.

"Six or eight weeks. I'm not sure."

"Your destination?" *Are you well? Are you happy?*

The rocks lining the Atlantic coast. "I thought I'd drive right to the end."

"The end of what?" *I'm glad to see you've got a sense of humor.*

"The end of the country. Nova Scotia, I guess." *You're a nice man. I like your smile.*

"And you're going to stay six or eight weeks?" *I wish I had your guts. The crap people have probably handed you!*

"Is there a limit to the time I'm allowed to stay?" *Are you going to turn me away because you can read my intent?*

"Well." He drew a deep breath, considering. *I'm not going to be the one to interfere. You've got the right to go wherever you goddamned please.* "Long as you're not seeking employment here, I guess you're welcome to stay however long you like."

"Okay." She smiled. "Then I think I'll stay as long as I

like." *You'd understand, wouldn't you, if I just stepped out over the edge, into the air? Just seeing you, talking to you, changes my mind about that.*

There was a pause, and then he bent farther so that their faces were no more than a foot apart. *I could put my hand on your cheek and say soft things. When does it stop? When do we quit defrauding people?* "You stay as long as you like," he told her, starting to smile. *Maybe it stops here, even if just for a minute.* "And make sure you have a good time."

"Thank you." *Thank you thankyouthankyou.*

"You drive carefully now." *I'll think about you tonight, on my way home; I'll hope you're finding what you're looking for.* His smile was enclosed by myriad small creases as he tipped his cap to her.

Her Connecticut license plates seemed to intrigue the Canadians. Often, while stopped for a light, or at a crosswalk, the pedestrian traffic would gaze with a slight furrowing of brows at the picture plate at the front of the car that, in green and white and brown, showed a large tree and read: *Connecticut, The Constitution State.* Sometimes, they'd glance up to take a look at her, but for the most part they continued on their way, looking puzzled.

In Niagara Falls she saw cars from all over the States. Here, no one seemed to find anything unusual in yet another American car. She parked between cars from Ohio and Pennsylvania and got out for her first look at the Falls.

She held her breath and gazed through the heavy mist, enchanted. She was immediately soaked by the spray, but remained for close to an hour watching the water plunge over the horseshoe edge. Such a massive display of power, with its accompanying, ceaseless angry roar, was mesmerizing. It astonished her to think that there was no way to stop any of this; the water would go on and on, forever falling.

In her hotel room that night, even with the windows closed, she could still hear the tremendous rage of the Falls. She fell asleep visualizing the water moving along the river until it arrived at the end. In the morning, after breakfast, she returned to the viewing area to lean against the wet gray-stone retaining wall and gaze at the gushing, shuddering liquid mass. She wondered at the foolishness of anyone trying to go over those falls in a barrel, or across them on a tightrope. No one could defy something so eternal, so tumultuous. She passed the morning shifting from one viewing area to another, watching the hypnotic torrent until she was shivering from overexposure.

For a week, she returned daily to take up her post at the wall, where she gazed contentedly at the water. Her reluctance to leave this place was overwhelming, but the onset of a cold, induced by her many hours of standing, drenched and chilled, at last induced her to go.

Back on the highway again, with the heater going despite the mild temperature outside, she lit a cigarette and tried to comprehend the impact the Falls had had upon her. Perhaps it was the simple fact of their existence and nothing more. She only knew that she personally represented very little when viewed next to something so immense. Rather than feeling diminished by this knowledge, she was heartened. She'd seen something vital, something primal, something that would continue whether or not anyone was there to witness its existence. It was a constant, superb and complete in its own right. They could festoon it with colored lights and sell postcards and slides of it, but they could never alter it. Perhaps honeymooners went there seeking confirmation of permanence, hoping they might, with their presence, place a similar stamp of stability on their marriage.

Canadians didn't laugh in public places. They seemed not to want to draw attention to themselves, and so they dressed and behaved with what might have been inbred conservatism. On the one occasion, in the hotel restaurant in Toronto, when she heard the rich, mellow laughter of a woman, she, and everyone else in the place, turned to see who was responsible for the full-bodied musical gusher. Caley smiled in automatic response, but noticed that everyone else looked irritated. She put it down to the hotel and its generally subdued atmosphere. But it was the same when she went to the movies. She laughed aloud, and the people seated nearby all turned to look at her, or laughed several beats behind, as if she'd been appointed leader of the squad. Her pleasure in the film was ruined.

The city was beautiful but it gave her the willies. It was the cleanest, most well-tended place she'd ever been; the streets were crowded with nicely turned-out people; it draped itself comfortably along the shoreline of the lake, sprawling in orderly fashion. It was huge, yet tidy, and, overall, gave her the impression of coldness. She became once more invisible here, as she wandered along Yorkville, just another passenger on the tourist train. Instead of the two weeks she'd intended, in three days she was back in the car, on the MacDonald-Cartier Freeway, headed east.

She stopped for lunch on the highway and, within three hours, knew she'd contracted food poisoning. Her insides clutching themselves in spasms, she left the highway at Brockville. She stopped at a drugstore, where she bought several over-the-counter remedies before finding a motel near the highway. After dosing herself with Pepto-Bismol, she lay down on her rented bed in the dark, vowing never again to eat a tuna sandwich prepared by anyone as patently feebleminded as the boy who, gawking, had had her repeat her order three times while those queued up behind her in the roadside cafeteria had tutted and clucked impatiently.

She reclined on the bed, the Pepto-Bismol bottle in her hand, swearing she'd write up a list of things she must never again eat in roadside establishments. Tuna would head the list, and mayonnaise would come second.

She fell asleep and wakened late in the afternoon, her hand still holding the bottle, which was now half empty. Moving apprehensively, she went out to bring a few things in from the car. Outside, menacing clouds were collecting for a storm. She worked quickly and got everything inside just as the first splashes of rain began to fall.

Immersing herself in a tubful of hot water, she felt sorry for herself, and thought longingly of Ron, wishing he could be there to comfort her. She had to remind herself of how poorly he coped with illness. This failed, though, to dislodge her momentary yearning to see him. He'd written twice, once at Christmas, enclosing a note inside his annual Unicef card, and once at the beginning of March. In the second, longer letter, he'd advised her he was moving. He'd bought a two-bedroom condominium apartment just up the road on Strawberry Hill.

He'd also started dating, but claimed to be depressed by the women with whom he socialized. "I invited women to come back to the apartment for coffee or a drink, on two different occasions. Both times, when I came back with the drinks, they'd taken their clothes off. I didn't know what the hell to do. I mean, it wasn't what I'd invited them for." He wished she'd pack up and come back; he missed her. "I even thought about buying another cat, just to make it more like it used to be around here."

His letters had saddened her; it had been like reading about someone she'd known a very long time ago. She couldn't make the connection, then, at the time of reading, between the man upon whom she'd pinned her hopes of the future and the plainly lonely man who'd put his unhappiness into words for her to read.

She'd written just before leaving Minneapolis to say she was about to go on the road again, and had encouraged him to keep up his social life. He was bound to meet someone compatible. After all, he was a decent person, and good-looking, as well as trustworthy and solidly responsible.

Now, ensconced in a bathtub in a motel room in another country, with yet another case of food poisoning—she'd had three previous bouts in her travels—she had to wonder if she hadn't been seriously mistaken in refusing to offer Ron even the possibility that she might, someday, come back. She wished she felt more than merely fond of him, but no matter how she scoured the most distant recesses of her heart, she was unable to locate more than sisterly feelings for him. One man's love and one woman's fondness didn't constitute sufficient grounds for a long-term commitment. It was a pity, though. He'd demonstrated a love for her that shamed her with its durability.

"Forget it!" Her voice was an unnatural whisper that bounced off the mildewing tiles. In the morning, she'd be on her way again. There was a pioneer village to see, and all of French Canada. "I'll eat snails!" she told her pallid feet. "Everybody should eat snails at least once. And frog's legs, too." She started to laugh, ignoring the tenderness of her stomach. She'd eat snails and frog's legs and then either crawl, or hop, back to the car.

Chapter 20

THE RENOVATION OF the ground floor was physically completed. All that remained to be done was the painting of the newly plastered walls and ceilings. Gallon containers of flat white latex paint sat on the dropcloth in the corner, waiting to be used. The perimeters of the windows had been covered with masking tape to reduce the amount of paint that would later have to be scraped from the glass. The drop cloth concealed the floor. A lightweight aluminum, six-foot ladder stood splay-legged in the center of the room. Today, on this early morning in June, he was going to start the final phase.

Recently, he'd begun to take an interest in furnishing the place and had visited various furniture showrooms around town. Just the afternoon before, he'd gone for a long walk up Yonge Street that had culminated in his arrival at the Art Shoppe, where he'd studied the model rooms on display in the windows for a time before pushing inside to take a slow, thoughtful tour of the store. He'd dismissed the section with the bona fide antiques and expensive reproductions in favor of an examination of the modern furniture—sample groupings of Roche Bobois sectionals, and pieces of Italian lacquer, exotically curved rattan chaises, and matte-finished golden oak tables. Twice he was approached by effete salesmen who languorously asked if they might assist him. Their faintly lifted eyebrows and disdainful attitudes prompted Martin to play out what he called his "Duke of Derision" role. In an accent dripping with Etonian decadence, he'd said, "Thanks awfully, old chap. One doesn't see anything one fancies at the moment," and then watched their lethargy and distaste vanish, replaced by oily obsequiousness. "I'll be nearby if you have any questions," both men had volunteered, and Martin had nodded dismissingly. It worked every time. The only people he'd ever encountered who were more smitten by a British accent than the Canadians were Americans he'd met on his infrequent visits to New York. He'd watched shopgirls in Saks Fifth Avenue melt into attitudes of devoted attention when he'd gone there to shop for gifts for Marian and the boys. He'd always find it bizarre, to say the least, that people could become instantly enamored of him simply because he spoke with an accent that declared his English antecedents.

He lost his poise as he inadvertently wandered into an upstairs area designated for children's bedrooms, and stood for quite some time staring in at a room Marks and Spencer would have adored: bunk beds complete with hidey-holes and a ladder, twin desks back to back with sturdy chairs tucked into the kneeholes, chests of drawers, and a brilliantly colored Oriental kite mounted on one wall. The high-gloss, white-enamel-painted furniture would soon enough have borne the fingerprinted evidence of the boys' traffic. Had they been present at that moment, they'd have set up a clamorous din, begging to have this room transported all of a piece to the Rosedale house.

It took considerable effort for him to leave. He was overcome by the suspicion that were he to stretch out upon the lower bunk, he'd be able to feel the warmth, and breathe in the grassy scent, of his sons. He had turned and fled from the store, and as he'd marched back down Yonge Street, he'd looked closely at the taverns he passed, feeling more strongly than ever, the deprivations of his life: no Marian, no Harry and Ian, no booze. He'd quickened his pace and made it home in just over half an hour. By the time he arrived, he'd succeeded in recovering his sense of purpose and had gone about readying the rooms for painting.

Now he pried the lid off one of the gallon cans and cautiously tipped some paint into the tray. He looked around for a moment, measuring visually the size of the job to be done, then began applying the paint to the walls.

• • •

During the long months of the winter, he'd made it a point
to leave the house daily, going out in any sort of weather to
sketch. He had positioned himself on streetcorners, on
benches in downtown parks and at the lakefront; he'd leaned
against walls in subway stations and against telephone poles at
busy intersections; he'd parked his bottom on the bonnets of
automobiles; he'd loitered after dark in the environs of lower
Yonge Street; he'd looked, and studied, and transposed what
he saw onto the pages of one book after another. He'd examined those men outside the hostels on Jarvis Street, attempting
to fix their displacement on his pages. He'd given one touching couple ten dollars to pose for him: a man and woman of
indeterminate years, with bad teeth, shabby clothing, and
lusterless hair. He'd spotted them shambling up Church
Street, holding hands, and had been moved to ask them if
they'd consider posing only for a few minutes. They'd agreed,
and had stood, staring in bemusement at him, their hands remaining linked.

He'd gone to the St. Lawrence Market and to the Kensing-
ton Market; he'd staked out shops in the Greek area, the
Italian area, the Portuguese area, and in Chinatown. He'd
done renderings of the storefronts on Queen Street East, and
of houses on Crawford Street; he'd tramped through the snow
in High Park in order to sketch one naked tree at the edge of
Grenadier's Pond. He'd covered the city, traveling on street-
cars and buses and subway, trying to gain insight into the
tightly woven fabric of other lives. And throughout all this,
he'd carried with him, like old snaps in the yellowed cello-
phane of an outworn wallet, pictures of everything he'd
valued without ever pausing to realize the risks involved in
love, and in family life. It was only after the fact that he knew
he'd wasted more time than anyone had a right to. As if to
atone, he worked to document what he now knew to be valuable: the human condition, in all its forms, and the dwellings
that gave it shelter.

He felt, finally, that he'd redeemed himself, at least in part,
and that his winter's work would, eventually, find its way onto
canvas. He wasn't yet ready to make that final transition.

• • •

He was on the top of the ladder, dabbing at the center molding in the ceiling with a small brush, when the doorbell rang. Startled, he twisted involuntarily in the direction of the door, and began to fall. He tried frantically to right himself. The paint tray and the brush flew from his hands as both he and the ladder tipped, turning, and he crashed to the floor. The ladder, spiraling, bounced; the feet struck his face and leg, bounced again, and was still. The noise of his falling seemed to him tremendous; it echoed in his ears as he rested, unable to move for a moment, on the floor. The doorbell went again and he turned, lifting his torso to extricate his left hand, which lay caught beneath him. He opened his mouth to speak, thinking to summon whoever was out there to come inside, but found he could make no sound. Anxious for the help he knew he needed from the person at the door, he managed to get to his feet, and hobbled to the front door, getting it open with his uninjured right hand.

"Jesus, Mary, and Joseph!" Mick paled at the sight of him. "What's happened to you?"

"Fell off the ladder just now. Have to lie down," Martin gasped, staggering into the living room where he stretched out on his back on the floor, swallowing down the nausea that was threatening to take him under. Apologetically, he said, "Feel a bit ill, have to rest a minute or two."

Appalled, Mick squatted beside him, asking, "Are you badly injured?"

"Don't know. I'll check in a moment. Christ!" He exhaled through his teeth and closed his eyes, aware of pain in his leg, his face, and, most especially, his left hand.

Mick rose and went to the downstairs bathroom to soak a hand towel in cold water. Returning, he draped the towel around Martin's face, then sat again on his haunches, waiting. When, after five minutes, Martin was at last able to sit up, Mick watched closely as Martin lifted his right trouser leg to see two deeply bruised, bloodless gashes on his inner calf.

"Those're bad," Mick said quietly. "You're favoring your hand there. D'you think you've broken it?"

"The foot of that fucking thing"—Martin pointed a wildly trembling finger at the ladder—"hit me square in the face, and then caught me in the leg. See anything?'' he asked, letting the wet towel fall away.

"It's not cut, probably just bruised. What about the hand, though, Martin? I don't care at all for the look of it.''

Martin cradled his left hand in his right and experimentally turned it, attempting to flex his fingers. The resulting explosion of pain confirmed that bones indeed had been broken.

"Come on.'' Mick helped his friend to his feet. "I'll run you over to the hospital; we'll get that seen to.''

Martin couldn't remain upright. "Sorry,'' he said, seating himself once more on the floor. "Not quite ready yet.''

"Hell!'' Mick said worriedly. "If you weren't dry, brandy would do just the job here.''

"It is a pity, isn't it?'' Martin tried to smile, but his teeth, stupidly, were chattering.

It was more than an hour before Mick was able to get him out of the house and into the car.

The several broken bones in his hand put paid to his painting of the ground floor.

"I'll finish the job for you,'' Mick offered. "Keep me supplied with Carlsberg and a running commentary, and I'll have it done in no time.''

Resigned, Martin sat tailor-fashion on the hallway floor, his clumsy, cast-enclosed left hand nestled in his lap, and watched Mick work. "One thing's for certain,'' he said. "You're a far better painter than you are carpenter.''

"Try to hold off on the praise. We don't want me turning swell-headed now.'' He ran the roller dry on the wall, then carried it over to the paint tray. "What I think,'' he said, "is that you threw yourself off that ladder with malice aforethought. You wanted an excuse not to have to muck about in here any longer.''

"Oh, indeed!'' Martin agreed. "Most effective subterfuge I could think up on such short notice. The doorbell went, and I thought to myself, 'That'll be Mick. I'll fling myself from the ladder, break half a dozen bones in my hand, and, out of sympathy, he'll offer to complete the job for me.' ''

"I wouldn't put it past you. You've always been a devious

bastard. I'd say you overdid it this time, though. I wouldn't have thought it necessary to damage yourself to the extent that it's going to take a plastic surgeon to set your hand to rights.''

"What can one say?" Martin shrugged humbly.

"*One* could get off *one's* arse and fetch *one* another bottle of brew."

"How frightfully remiss of me!" Martin got up and went to the kitchen, where he stood for a moment, suspiciously eyeing the light. Satisfied it was of an even, nonmathematical quality, he returned to Mick with the beer. "I've been thinking," he said, "that I might have a break."

"That's good, very good! I would've said you'd already had a break."

"Leave off," Martin said, handing over the Carlsberg. "I fancy getting out of the city for a fortnight or so."

"Where will we go?"

"We?"

"You don't expect to get about on your own, do you?" Mick presented an expression of utmost reasonableness. "You can barely dress yourself without a valet in attendance. How, might I ask, do you expect to travel unaccompanied? And did you have some place in mind?"

Breaking into a smile, Martin resumed his seat on the floor. "As a matter of fact, I do. Does Quebec hold any interest for you?"

"Not Montreal!" Mick said flatly. "I hate that bloody city now they've driven out all the really interesting people with their rabid separatist notions." He drew a sharp, angry breath. "There was a time when I'd go for a weekend on a moment's notice. Not any more. They're all so bloody anti-Anglo."

"I was thinking of Quebec City."

"Ah, now! That's an entirely different matter. Quebec." Mick mulled this over as he downed half the Carlsberg in one gurgling go. "Haven't been there in, it must be ten years. It'll be chockablock with tourists, don't you know."

"I've booked us into the Chateau Frontenac."

Mick halted mid-swallow. "Well now! Aren't you the cunning little fellow? Had it all planned, did you?"

"I expected you'd invite yourself along."

"To do the driving, if I'm not mistaken."

"You are not mistaken. I thought it was time to give the XKE a run before it dies a quiet death in the garage."

"We'll have no need of a car in the city."

"Then we'll park it and go about on foot."

"The Chateau, is it?" Mick smiled approvingly. "One thing I'll say for you, Maddox. You don't do anything on the cheap. When do we leave?"

"When you've done with the painting."

Mick looked around, trying to gauge how long it would take him. "How long were you thinking to stay?" he asked.

"A week or two. I booked in for a fortnight, but that's easily changed. Why? Is there some problem?"

"It'll have to be a week for me. I've got to go to New York to do a bit of business."

"A week, then," Martin agreed. "If I choose to stay on, you'll drive the car back."

"Sounds fair."

"Done!"

My dear Martin,

Life at last seems to have settled into something of a routine here, and I must confess that I have nowhere near the amount of free time I anticipated.

There are quite a number of expatriate English who've retired to the island. They socialize on an alarmingly regular basis, and have taken to inviting me. It's fairly difficult to resist without giving offence, but I've managed to be indecently creative in the number of excuses I'm able to offer at a moment's notice. I have joined a bridge group, and play three times a week, and there are occasional dinners given and received. All in all, I'm finding my existence here every bit as pleasurable as I'd anticipated. And, yes, I have done a minor amount of gardening, but have only appropriated one small area of the patio.

The weather is simply splendid, day after day of temperatures in the mid-eighties. I go early each morning to the beach, to swim before the crowds arrive, and then return to do the marketing. Maria has been teaching me some of the local dishes, and I'm now quite adept at the infamous "green soup" you were so suspicious of. The paella is far more difficult, and my two attempts thus far were entirely inedible. However, you have my promise that I'll allow Maria to do the cooking if and when you choose to come visit.

I'd adore to see you. Perhaps you might be tempted to come this autumn or winter when, as you say, the weather there turns foul. You would, of course, be welcome to stay however long you like. I doubt you'd find the bridge club to your liking, but I expect you'd find sufficient activities to keep you occupied. Please do think about it, won't you? It's been more than a year and I'd hate to see too much more time pass before we see one another again. Just let me know when you'd care to come and I'll collect you from the airport.

With all my love, as ever, Grace.

My dear Grace,

Believe it or not, I'm actually, finally, going to leave the house for a bit and take a brief vacation. My old friend Mick and I are off to Quebec City for a fortnight. I hope to do a fair amount of sketching, but primarily, I feel the need to get away for a time.

The renovation on the ground floor of the house is complete, and my invitation to you still stands. There are any number of bedrooms going begging, and I'm sure you'd find at least one to your liking. Perhaps you could be seduced into considering a visit as a relief from all that perfect weather.

Of course I'm tempted to come visit you. And of course I'll be bound to consider it once October rolls around and everything turns terribly dreary. I expect I'll ring up the airlines and come flying over just to accompany you on your morning splash. I never could resist the sight of you in a bathing costume.

At the moment, I'm slightly incapacitated due to a silly accident—fell off a bloody ladder, no less, and broke a number of bones in the old left hand. Luckily, I'm still able to work, and Mick's doing the driving to Quebec.

Things seem to be changing. I'm not entirely certain what I mean by that, except to say it appears I'm coming out the far end of the tunnel. I'll admit I feel rather newly hatched and unsteady, but it has to be done; one has to move on, despite the guilt one feels at discovering there's a life to be lived after all.

I'd adore to see you, too. As I said, in all likelihood, comes the first filthy day and I'll be on to the airlines people. I am glad you're so frightfully popular with the expatriate set, and that you've left at least a bit of the botanical garden intact. Undoubtedly I'll write again to regale you with tales of my adventures upon my return from Froggy-land.

All my love, Martin.

P.S. Try not to drive the locals wild with your extraordinary bathing costumes, you naughty thing!

A pad propped up on his cast, Martin rested against the shadowed wall of the Chateau. The object of his drawing was a horse-drawn calèche, the services of which were being flogged by a gaunt young man who assailed passers-by. The horse, emaciated and overworked, stood, head bowed, awaiting its next tour of duty. Martin's instinct, upon first seeing an entire procession of these abused creatures, was to take the offending proprietors by the scruffs of their necks and shackle them into place, forcing them to draw the burden of tourists upon their own shoulders. Since he was in no fit condition to take on the task, he'd rechanneled his angry energy into a series of harshly exaggerated sketches. The drawings had an ominous aura, showing horses driven beyond all reasonable limits, carriages in advanced stages of decay, and drivers with avid, haunted faces and tattered clothes.

Mick had taken himself off to the boardwalk fronting the Chateau for a look at the tourists, saying he'd be back in fifteen minutes. "Do me a favor and finish that dismal lot by then, would you? You can ring up the RSPCA or whatever from the restaurant. I'd like some food, if it's all the same to you."

A constant flow of people moved between Martin and the

row of calèches. His hand worked furiously, creating vignettes charged with umbrage. Beyond the immediate queue of carriages for hire were buses into which people filed, to be driven off on sightseeing tours of varying duration. In the Place des Armes, immediately in front of the hotel, two street musicians had collected a crowd, to which they performed with self-absorbed tunelessness on bongos and trumpet. Completing his latest sketch, Martin's eye was caught by a young male mime, clad in an assemblage of outrageous castoffs, who was successfully diverting the audience's attention from the irritating thump and whine of the two musicians.

Closing his pad, he transferred it to beneath his arm before making his way across the road and into the Place to get a better view. Many of the tourists were taking photographs, several of them volunteering their children into the frame with the mime, who, for the most part, managed to frighten the kids witless with his black-and-red-painted eyes and overdrawn scarlet mouth.

Seating himself on the curb, Martin watched the trumpeter and bongo-basher try to maintain their decorum as the mime danced an out-of-tempo jig, juggled a single Ping-Pong ball while standing on one foot, made a series of lunatic faces, produced golf balls from the musicians' ears, and played, finally, accompaniment on a spangled kazoo. Martin thought him magnificent and loudly offered his approving laughter along with several dollar bills, which the mime made disappear into the voluminous depths of his moth-eaten lime-green dinner jacket. The children seated on either side of Martin watched this exchange with unfettered enthusiasm, squealing with delight when the mime rewarded Martin with a squirt of water from the flower on his lapel.

Martin laughed, finding within himself the boy who'd always been enchanted when the circus had come to town. His laughter, when he became aware of it, surprised him, returning him, in memory, to occasions when Mrs. Rogers, his grandmother's housekeeper, had been appointed his guardian at the circus, or a Christmas pantomime. Mrs. Rogers, a round, flushed woman in her fifties, had been the one person in his childhood with whom he'd been allowed to express his boyish impulses. The two of them had wept with laughter at the pantos and had applauded, open-mouthed, the daring feats performed by the acrobats and tumblers. He'd known happiness then, and had lived for those moments when Lady Barnes would impatiently signal her permission for another outing.

"I thought you were going to stay where I left you," Mick complained, positioning himself at Martin's side on the curb. "Might I ask why you're laughing yourself into a state of hysterics?"

"Watch the mime!" Martin urged. "He's wonderful, taking the mickey out of those two buffoons for all he's worth."

"I'm *hungry*, Maddox."

"We'll go in just a moment. Watch!"

Standing to one side behind the bench where the musicians were seated, the mime, his tongue extended, was beating time on two striped drumsticks. Hopelessly out of synch, his eyes rolled, his tongue lolled, he danced from side to side, emulating the bongo player's concentration.

Mick laughed, his enormous belly bouncing against his knees.

"Didn't I tell you?" Martin exclaimed, one-handedly freeing the camera from its carrying case. Holding it braced against the cast, he removed the lens cap, fixed the focus, and took a number of medium shots. Then he changed lenses, fitting in place the bayonet-mounted telephoto, and took half a dozen close-ups of the mime. There was a painting here, a comment—perhaps about childhood—he wished to make. The photographs would serve as reference points. The lens cap back in place and the bulky telephoto once more inside the case suspended from his belt, he announced, "Ready to go now."

"Half a minute," Mick protested, enjoying himself immensely. "By Christ, he's funny!"

The music ended at last, and the two musicians passed a hat, but people were already moving off. It was the mime who'd held them; the musicians were of no interest. Certainly they were talentless compared to the boy Mick and Martin had discovered playing the flute, the evening before, at the foot of the steps leading to Le Petit Champlain.

Mick hefted his bulk upright and waited for Martin to fall in at his side. "There's an outdoor caff midway down that street at the bottom of the steps. Thought we might give it a try, eat, and watch the parade."

"Whatever you like." Martin felt alive and well, despite the ongoing pain in his hand, for the first time in more than a year. His feet felt springy inside brand-new tennis shoes; his entire body was alert to new sensations. "Had you given any thought to the fact that we're going to have to climb all these steps to get back up again?" Martin asked on their way down.

"Don't be a complete fool! We'll take the funicular."

"I should've known you wouldn't make the trip if you didn't have an easy route in mind to get you back."

They found a table close to the street and, at once, both turned to watch the tourists walking past. They ordered, and then Mick said something, but Martin failed to hear. For a moment, the heat of the sun on his head, and the flow of people, transported him back to Tenerife. He could see and feel again that afternoon, could recall every detail of the time he'd spent on the promenade looking alternately at the expanse of black sand beach and the tourists flocking in and out of the shops; he could feel the welling need he'd had to see his wife and boys. It was over in a few moments and he was aware again of Mick, and the busy waiter, and the astonishing number of immensely fat people going past.

"Do you suppose," he asked Mick, "these people know how monstrous they are?"

"I reckon not." Mick watched an enormous woman with badly bleached hair, in a tight, hot-pink terrycloth jumpsuit from which her globulous thighs protruded like hams. "D'you see that?" he asked. "In-croy-a-bull, as they say. Imagine crawling under the sheets with that! The mind boggles."

At the table to their right sat a couple with a child. The man, his long, greasy-looking curls caught up in a ponytail, wore a leather vest over his bare chest, adorned with buttons advertising, among other things, women's rights, the pro-abortion lobby, Eugene V. Debs, Joe Clark, and the benefits of pot. His thin legs were enclosed in black leather trousers; his filthy feet supported leather thong sandals. The woman wore a low-cut black evening gown and very high-heeled backless sandals; around her neck and wrists sat a volume of rhinestone jewelry; from her ears dangled thick silver hoops. Her face was almost as white as the mime's with makeup; twin swathes of rouge defined slanting cheekbones. Her dark hair had been cropped close to the scalp, but for one long curl that dangled at the back of her neck. The child, a girl of six or seven, was outfitted in a cotton print dress several sizes too large that hung almost to her ankles. She was absolutely filthy, and had the huge, staring eyes seen often in photographic portraits of groups of starving children in Third World countries. She was, with great delicacy, eating an enormous slab of French bread slathered with butter and jam and, between bites, drinking a bowl of café au lait.

"Aren't they extraordinary?" he told Mick, indicating the family. "They're straight out of Haight-Ashbury, American neo-Gothic." He was already at work, surreptitiously sketching the trio, using faint, feathery strokes to capture the child's soiled fragility.

"Sit here long enough," Mick wagered, "and you'll see everything. They're taking their sweet time with our food," he added.

"It's an abomination," Martin said hotly under his breath. "People like that shouldn't be allowed to breed indiscriminately. The child needs a hot tub and a good scrubbing. She ought to have a proper meal and some decent clothes."

"You're not going to start again, are you," Mick pleaded, "the way you did about the horses? You'll spoil me appetite."

"Nothing would spoil your appetite," Martin said. "And in any case, it's a French tradition." He continued to work, his eyes moving back and forth between the page and the family. "One doesn't hurry when it comes to food. A meal is a leisurely enterprise."

"At least he could bring the bloody beer and let me be leisurely with that."

"All in due course." Martin was beginning to find Mick's engrossment with food and drink somewhat of an impediment to his own need to work. He wished to be free simply to stare and study, or to make drawings as the whim took him. Mick seemed to see things only when they were pointed out to him, and usually he opted to view women, making sexual references Martin found adolescent and irksome. He was grateful that

Mick was leaving later in the afternoon; he didn't want to place their friendship in jeopardy with these fundamental differences between them.

The sketch completed, he was considering how he might broach the subject of his going off on his own after lunch, saying goodbye to Mick here. Placing his pencil atop the closed sketchbook, he looked across at Mick, and then beyond him.

For a moment, there was no sound. Silence engulfed him and time ceased its movement. Everything was a frozen frame as his eyes took in the woman descending the last level of the Break-Neck stairs. Riveted, he watched her approach along the cramped street, and as she drew closer, sound and movement resumed. He found he was holding his breath. The woman would, he knew, continue on her way past him in the next few seconds, and he might never see her again. It was imperative that he follow. There was no question of choice: he had to go at once.

"Listen, Mick," he said quickly, pulling some bills from his pocket and dropping them on the table. "There's something I have to do and I don't know how long it's going to take. If I don't make it back in time, thank you for coming along, and have a good trip back. Have a care driving, won't you? I'm going to stay on a bit longer, do some more work." He snatched up his sketching equipment, readjusted the camera around his neck, and danced off between the tables, his eyes still fastened to the woman, his feet light with renewed purpose.

Dumbfounded, Mick started to say something, thought better of it, and sat back watching as Martin flew off down the street, becoming part of the tide of people drifting toward the bottom end of the Petit Champlain. "Bugger me," he said softly, confused, then smiled happily as the waiter finally arrived with his beer and the food.

Chapter 21

A YOUNG WOMAN of medium height, with a slender build, she carried herself with an impressively defiant grace. Keeping sight of her, Martin stayed some yards behind, pausing when she did. She had shoulder-length auburn hair and wore a wide-brimmed straw hat. Her dress was a simple blue shift, her sandals an assemblage of thin white straps. From her right arm hung a capacious canvas bag. She moved as if either uncaring or unaware of the heads that turned as she passed, of the chittering whispers her passage inspired. People were shocked by the sight of her, and he noted the reactions, as well as her unheeding progress along the street.

The sun was at its peak, creating shimmering heat auras that rose from the pavement to envelop the people who trod its length; it was laden with the aromas of popcorn and sticky candy floss, fresh-ground coffee and just-baked bread. Entrapped amid the smells of food were strands of perfume trailing in the wake of the women who picked their way along the uneven street. Martin breathed it all in, as if aware for the first time of the countless threads that went into the weaving of any single day. He followed the woman with single-minded dedication.

She stopped once to enter a basement-level clothing shop, and he rested against the blue-painted brick wall of the building opposite, to wait. She reappeared less than five minutes later carrying a white paper bag, which she tucked into the canvas carryall. He was profoundly curious to know what she'd bought, but guessed, happily, that he'd know before this day had ended. He remained where he was, waiting to see where next she'd go. Her eyes passed over him and he thought, impossibly, there might be some recognition, which was absurd. They didn't know one another, had never met. Yet he was overwhelmed by the idea that he did know her; even the destruction of her face was familiar. Her large eyes were just as they should be: quick and appraising and intelligent.

He considered, and discarded, any number of ploys he might make use of to meet her: she'd take a seat in one of the many crowded outdoor terrace cafés and he'd ask if he might join her; she'd elect to ride the alarming funicular up to boardwalk level and he'd offer her a humorous commentary on the fearsome aspects of the juddering ride. He was determined to make her acquaintance, and never mind the difficulties. It would be, he knew, tantamount to convincing someone with black skin that he, Martin, was not a racist. The same perils were involved; the same pernicious doubts were bound to be spawned when one was on the receiving end of doubtful attention. Nevertheless, he would find some way to speak with her.

She turned at the end of the street and retraced her steps, looking now at the artists' and crafts-peoples' dwellings on the opposite side. She paused to read the plaque affixed to a large boulder in a grassed area just beyond the café where he and Mick had planned to have their meal. He read over her shoulder. She seemed unaware of him, although he was close enough to appreciate her scent, a light fragrance redolent of spring flowers. He felt, for a moment, something like love for her—for having the courage to wear cologne and mascara, for daring to face down the eyes of strangers. He was in awe of her defiance. She moved on; he went with her, a dogged shadow. Curiosity, a stranger's fondness, and a mounting eagerness, all combined to energize him, so that when she began to mount the Break-Neck stairs instead of riding the funicular, he was scarcely winded by the climb, and kept pace with her as she moved steadily upward. He watched the flexing of her calf muscles, and noted approvingly the fineness of her ankles. He was only a few yards to the rear as she headed toward the final set of stairs that would deliver them into the far corner of the Place des Armes.

His legs were aching in protest when he arrived at the top of the stairs, and stood for a moment, scanning the area. He'd lost sight of her, and told himself his sudden twisting panic was ludicrously disproportionate. Like some fuzzy-brained, gormless twit, he was chasing after a woman for no known purpose. He simply knew he had to stay close to her. He hadn't taken the time to analyze why, or what it was he thought he might discover; he just had to remain within sight of her.

He spotted her at the entrance to Du Tresor Street and ran forward as she began to work her way through the dense pack of tourists examining the paintings and etchings, the prints and lithographs on display on both sides of the short alley. It would be all too easy to lose her here, in the mass of people either purchasing pieces of art or contemplating one. Fortunately, she was taking her time, and he was able to keep her in view.

She stopped before a group of especially well-executed etchings, and he took advantage of the opportunity to commend the artist, a young woman from Montreal, on the quality of the work, and the mounts and framing. He promised himself he'd return for another, longer viewing once his sleuthing was out of the way. He'd intentionally been avoiding this street, positive he'd find nothing of value here. He'd been quite wrong. There was a great deal of quality effort to be seen, despite his having been prepared to be repelled by the amateurish and/or rubbishy commercial trash put out on display. Naturally, there was some of that, but the majority of the work had been executed by talented professionals, some of whom he knew personally, and some he knew by reputation.

The woman was on the move again, and he continued his pursuit of her out the far end of the alley and to the left, along Buade, to des Jardins. She came to a stop outside the Café de la Paix, and he could sense her deliberation. Go in! he silently urged. Find yourself a table and have a drink or a bite to eat!

As if heeding his unuttered command, she went forward, stepped up into the outdoor café, and looked around. Spotting a shaded table in the far corner, she made her way toward it. Immensely pleased, Martin saw there was a free table near the entrance and at once sat down. He ordered a salad Nicoise and some Perrier with lime, then removed the camera from around his neck and circumspectly fitted on the telephoto lens. Through it he was able to establish a good close-up frame of her, and hastily he made several exposures, a little afraid she might hear the click/whir of the motor-driven film advance. Fearful of exposing himself, he returned the lens to its case and set the camera down on top of the sketch pad. There was no way he could possibly sit and sketch her without attracting attention, and the last thing he wanted was to upset her.

He was close enough to hear her voice and to decide that her accent was American, probably eastern. There was a slight flatness to her vowels that told of New England and, at once, he worked up several little background scenarios for her: she was the reckless daughter of some eminently successful banker, and had crashed her Porsche while driving sixty or seventy miles over the speed limit; she was the widow of the son of some banker, who'd managed to kill himself while driving his Porsche sixty or seventy miles over the speed limit; she'd survived the crash only to bury her husband and was now aimlessly touring the world as she tried to piece together what remained of her life; she had attempted to kill herself via vehicular suicide, and had failed.

None of these ideas was to his liking, and he abandoned the effort in favor of contemplating her and trying to pin down the reasons for his instant obsession.

As he nibbled disinterestedly at his salad, he scanned the café, his eyes returning constantly to her. The broad brim of her straw hat successfully shielded much of her face so that he was unable to see her expression, but everything else about her, from the way she smoked a cigarette to the way she sat slightly away from the table with her legs crossed and one sun-tanned arm resting on the tabletop, confirmed his first impression of defiance and grace.

She was a woman alone, situated clearly beyond the mainstream. Perhaps her disfigurement had placed her there initially, but it had been a conscious decision on her part to play the maverick, pushing her way past whatever boundaries had been set up for her, in order to establish herself in that region beyond the perimeter, that wasteland usually reserved for souls with no hope of redemption. She'd acclimated herself to isolation and had found a way to make it work for her. She seemed not in the least dejected, but rather, in control and purposeful. She drank two cups of coffee, tore a croissant into a number of small pieces, which she consumed with gusto. She had appetites, he thought; it was a healthy sign, one that went with the intelligence in her eyes.

Of course he knew her! he thought, stunned by sudden recognition, and by his failure to see it sooner. Had he been a woman, he would have been her. All at once, he knew positively how he had to have appeared to others throughout the previous year, because he was readily able to see it in this woman. Bloody hell! he thought anxiously. Please God when he spoke to her she wouldn't be some dull-witted, inadvertently gracious-seeming embodiment of his own sentiments, but the brightly bitter person he wished her to be!

Once her coffee and the cigarette were finished, she signaled to the waiter and reached for her canvas bag. Martin followed suit and, minutes later, he was again following as she left the café and proceeded along des Jardins to Saint-Louis, in the direction away from the Chateau.

In the middle of the next block was a booking office for mini-bus tours. This was her destination. She climbed the several steps up to enter the office, where she waited for the agent to complete a telephone conversation. Martin eavesdropped from the sidewalk, glancing now and then through the open door.

The tour of the Île d'Orleans had been canceled, she was told. If she was interested, there was a bus going to Montmorency Falls and Sainte Anne de Beaupré in less than half an hour.

"There isn't anything else today?" she asked.

"That is our last tour of the day," she was told. "But tomorrow, if you still wish it, you could go to the Île d'Orleans."

"What's at Sainte Anne de Beaupré?" she asked.

"Ah," the agent spoke in reverential tones. "This is a shrine, eh? Like Lourdes. You have heard of this?"

"A shrine?"

"Also there is the cyclorama. Very wonderful, showing Christ being put away from Jerusalem. The shrine is very famous."

"All right," she agreed in a doubtful tone, and opened her bag to find money for the fare. "How long is this tour?"

"Three hours. You will have stops at Sainte Anne des Plaines where they make the bread, and at craft shops." He accepted her money, gave her a booklet on the shrine, and assured her she would enjoy the tour. "The bus will be returning soon now, if you will wait."

Martin had no alternative but to go into the booking office and purchase a ticket. Leaving the office, he saw she'd opted to wait on the small bench out front. He'd have liked to sit beside her and commence a casual conversation, working up to the coincidental aspects of their common destination. He didn't have the nerve, and, instead, paced on the far side of the driveway where the mini-bus would turn around. As he completed each lap, he began to wonder what in hell he was doing following a woman he didn't know to, of all things, a shrine. It was absurd! He could put a stop to it simply by going over, introducing himself, and inviting her to tea. At which she'd tell him in quite precise terms the anatomically impossible things he was free to attempt to do to himself. Damn! He trudged back the way he'd come, counting out thirty steps before returning. When he checked the time, he saw that the bus was running late. It should have arrived ten minutes ago. Not only was he about to go off to visit a shrine, but at the rate things were going, he might spend the rest of his bloody life doing it.

Seven or eight more people were now waiting on the sidewalk, looking up and down Saint-Louis hoping to sight the bus. Only two of the people seemed to be together, a very ordinary middle-aged couple. The rest were a dreary, mismatched lot: two men both hopelessly overdressed for the weather, one in something horribly like a polyester leisure suit, and the other in wool trousers, a heavy plaid shirt, and knitted vest. The one in polyester was suffering from an advanced case of dandruff and looked as if he'd just come indoors from a snowfall. Martin rolled his eyes as he turned to look at the others. There was an enormous woman shrouded in a drably voluminous raincoat, and a small, elderly woman whose expression was furled like a closed umbrella. The mini-bus finally pulled up before the booking office, and a last-minute passenger came bustling up the street from the direction of the Chateau.

This was it. Martin hung back, allowing the others to board the bus ahead of him. Then he climbed aboard and looked for her. She'd taken the seat at the rear. The seats ahead of and beside her were vacant. What good luck! But which to choose? He decided on the one ahead of her, reasoning he'd be in a better position to institute casual chat were he to turn at some point and comment on this or that. He slid over onto the window side of the seat, and again was aware of her scent. He breathed slowly, fully filling his lungs, stricken by nervousness.

This wasn't the tour she'd wanted to take. Caley settled herself in the rear of the mini-bus, fighting down an impulse to get up and leave. She hadn't been to church since her adoptive parents had died, and the idea of touring a shrine didn't have much appeal. She imagined, with a sinking feeling, there'd be legions of the maimed seeking miracles; copious tears and murmured imprecations when those miracles failed to occur. To make matters worse, the sky was rapidly clouding over and rain would undoubtedly pour all over this little band as it filed into the various crafts emporiums, the shrine notwithstanding. And if all this wasn't bad enough, every time she turned around, this guy popped up. She'd seen him down on Petit Champlain; she'd caught sight of him again when she'd gone to look at the artwork in the alleyway across from the hotel; and now here he was sitting smack in front of her on the bus.

He didn't look creepy or weird, but he did have a cast on his hand and wrist. Maybe he was trekking off to the shrine hoping to be healed, or something. God! This was nuts. She really hoped he wasn't going to try to start a conversation—something cozy like how they were both en route to Saint Anne de Beaupré seeking magical cures. Still, he didn't look as pathetic as some of the other guys on the bus—the one with the dandruff and the leisure suit, or the one dressed for the Arctic. This guy's clothes were well cut and expensive-looking, as was the camera around his neck. Even blond guys with big gray-blue eyes could be total fruitcakes, though, and she was pre-pared to deal with him if she had to.

He really was good-looking, she thought, glancing at his profile as he gazed out the bus window. About thirty-five, maybe. He was probably a professional photographer, what with that big lens in a case threaded through his belt, and the books and stuff on his lap. He had a pocketful of pencils, so maybe he was an artist, and he was along on this trip to take photographs. He did have good, strong features, and a smooth complexion. A rich tourist, she decided.

Happily, smoking was allowed at the back of the bus. She lit a cigarette as the bus pulled away from the curb and the driver began a narrative, first in English and then in French. She tuned him out and gazed through the window. She'd been in the city for two days and had, so far, found a lot to like. Everyone spoke English, which made all transactions simpler than she'd anticipated, and the items for sale in the shops weren't the usual tourist crap. Of course, if you wanted tourist crap, it was around, but there was a choice. She'd been very impressed by the artwork, and had debated buying a small etching, but talked herself out of it. After all, she didn't possess a set of walls upon which it might be hung, and she could hardly start hanging pictures in the car.

Until now, the weather had been perfect, and she'd walked one afternoon for miles across the Plains of Abraham. Except for this walk, she'd stayed within the limits of the Old Town, and thought she might venture beyond the walls tomorrow. In spite of the hordes of tourists, the city had what she believed was a European attitude, something that certainly hadn't been the case in Ontario. Here, the atmosphere was relaxed, the pace unhurried. It was the first place she'd been to that relied heavily on tourist trade yet seemed in no way resentful of that dependence. The natives had been helpful without a trace of antagonism; they'd shown pride in their city, and appeared happy to share the place. The previous day she'd spent several hours at a table in the café situated in the middle of du Tresor

Street, drinking coffee and watching the crowds as they looked at the artwork, and no one had hassled her to move on and free up the table for others. Periodically, the waitress had drifted past to ask if Caley wanted more coffee, but had otherwise left her alone.

Even Montreal hadn't had this degree of ease, and it certainly hadn't had the same quality of open friendliness. She'd felt pressured there, less acceptable, not because of how she looked, but because of her inability to speak the language. The French in Montreal had been pretty hostile, and the city had struck her as being kind of grimy, seedy. Here, she might live for years and simply blend into the mix of people who habituated the cafés and resided in the old gray-stone buildings with the pots of flowers on the windowsills.

The man in the seat ahead was turning. His face presented itself, and she tensed, thinking, Shit! I knew it! He was going to turn out to be a creep, after all.

"Forgive me," he began with a smile that displayed strong white teeth. "I'm afraid I'm following you."

"*What?*" Oh, Christ! She was about to be saddled for three hours with a loonie.

"I saw you on Le Petit Champlain and I thought I simply must meet you."

She was distracted for a second or two by his English accent, and by his expression, which was ripe with unconcealed enthusiasm. But for what? Did he think she might be one of those spooky women who liked to get into weird sexual things with strangers? "Oh, fuck off, will you?" she sighed wearily.

He turned away and at once commenced playing both parts of a two-part conversation she listened to with disbelief.

"What *is* the matter with you?"

Shifting to the far side of the seat, he answered: "I simply told the truth. I saw nothing wrong in that."

"Well, you really shouldn't go about inflicting yourself on strangers."

"I'm *frightfully* sorry. I didn't consider it might be an infliction."

"You weren't thinking, were you? I believe you owe the woman an apology."

"That'll only make matters worse, I should think."

"Nonsense! You were unforgivably rude. Apologize at once!"

Abruptly, he turned and, in perfectly aggrieved little-boy tones, said, "I apologize!" then looked forward and continued with the two-way conversation, but in lower tones.

"There! I did it! Are you happy?"

"*Happy?* I'm mortified. Imagine carrying on in such a fashion! It's simply *not on!*"

"You're going to go on and on about it, aren't you? You're not going to give it a rest, are you?"

"Most likely not."

He groaned and sank lower so that only the top of his head remained in view, but he kept up his muttered conversation, and she began to laugh, quietly at first, and then more loudly.

"You *see* that!" his one voice told the other. "You've made a complete and utter laughingstock of yourself. I don't know what's to be *done* about you."

"No one *asked* you to come along, so you can jolly well shut your cake-hole!"

"Isn't that lovely! Isn't that just charming!"

"Belt up, twit!"

He was incredibly funny and, without thinking, she reached out to place her hand flat on the top of his head. At once, he sat upright and turned around, his eyes wide with expectation and humor.

"You're out of your mind!" she laughed. "Do you always carry on conversations with yourself?"

"Only when I run the risk of coming over as somewhat more than slightly demented." He smiled, saying, "I wanted to talk with you and couldn't think of any other way. Quite likely, I am indeed out of my mind."

"Why would you want to talk to me?" she asked.

"Haven't the foggiest," he admitted. "I happened to see you, and thought I really must meet you. I suspect it's one of the more bizarre things I've ever done sober."

"Does that mean you do bizarre things when you get drunk?"

"I expect I did. I gave up drink fourteen months ago."

"Why?"

"Aside from all the other considerations," he answered, "I do believe I was well on my way to becoming an alcoholic. If I wasn't already one. So I gave it up."

"Wasn't it hard?"

"Oh, horribly. At first, I counted the days. You know: it's now been twenty-six days dry; it's now been forty-seven, et cetera. Once I got past the year mark, I switched over to months. Eventually, I suppose I'll deal in terms of years."

"You're never going to drink again?"

"Never!" His smile widened.

"That's very impressive."

"Not at all. My drinking was far more impressive. Enough of that! Tell me, are you on the way to this shrine for religious reasons?"

"God, no!" she exclaimed, then laughed. "The tour I wanted to take wasn't on today. I'm not so sure this one's a good idea. I don't know how I feel about things like Lourdes, the whole idea of miraculous events."

"Really? What do you think?"

"I'll know once I've seen the place. I just hope we're not going to have to stand by and watch dozens of people climbing steps on their knees, that kind of thing. I saw a movie, years ago—what was it called? I know! *Mondo Cane*, that was it—and they showed all these strange religious rites people all over the world got into. I remember mostly the part about going up the steps on the knees, close-ups of the blood."

"That *would* be dreadful," he agreed. "I'll tell you what. If we catch sight of anyone doing anything of the sort, I'll whisk you right away and we'll go have tea somewhere."

"Why are you going?" she asked.

"Because you are. I told you: I'm following you."

"Seriously?"

"Quite seriously."

"I thought I kept seeing you, but I really didn't think you were *following* me."

"Well, good for you! No signs of paranoia."

"Why would I be paranoid?"

"Don't misunderstand. I wasn't implying that you might be."

"Good. Because I'm not."

"Never!" he agreed earnestly.

"You don't live here," she guessed. "Are you visiting from England?"

"Visiting from Toronto. I live there."

"I didn't like it as much as Quebec."

"It's different," he allowed, "but it has its own flavor. I'll wager you didn't stop long enough to get an accurate impression."

"Just a few days."

"There! You see? You need more than that, a week or two, at least."

"Nobody laughed," she said. "And the one time somebody did, everyone turned to stare as if laughing was illegal or something."

"How very perceptive of you!" he said admiringly. "I've often wondered about that, myself. There are days when I fully believe English-speaking Canadians feel public laughter lacks decorum. One should, at all costs, reserve one's humor spasms for the privacy of one's home. I suspect they think it's more British if one maintains a posture of serious sobriety. Naturally, it's not. We Brits are reknowned for our humor."

"Are you?" She started to smile.

"Oh, absolutely! Ask anyone and they'll confirm it. The British are, without question, the funniest people on earth."

"Depends on what you consider funny."

"Precisely! Now, tell me! Where are you from?"

"Connecticut, originally."

"Originally. But no longer?"

"Lately, I'm not from anywhere. I've just been driving around, looking at things, being a tourist."

"I see. Are you by any chance the daughter of a wealthy banker?"

She laughed and shook her head.

"I should introduce myself, shouldn't I?" He extended his hand to her over the back of his seat. "Martin Maddox."

"Caley Burrell."

"Caley. Are you Irish?"

"I might be. The man I was named for was, definitely."

"And who were you named for, may I ask?"

"The policeman who found me."

"You were *found* by a *policeman*?"

"I was abandoned as an infant outside a hospital in New York."

She'd thought he'd find humor in this but, if anything, he seemed upset. His brows drew together, his mouth thinned, and he said, "I am sorry. That's frightful, simply frightful."

Baffled by the depths of his reaction, and eager to change the subject, she asked, "What do you do, Mr. Maddox?"

"Martin. Do? I'm an artist. At least, I'm attempting to get back to it. I haven't done any serious work in more than a year."

"Because of that?" She nodded at his cast.

"No, no. Nothing to do with this. This happened fairly recently, fell off a ladder when the doorbell went. Bloody ridiculous accident, broke half the bones in my hand."

"Oh. I thought you might be going to the shrine . . . you know."

"Hoping to be cured of my 'affliction'?"

She shrugged, smiling.

"Not at all. I told you: I'm *following* you."

"But why?"

"Do you think I might have one of your cigarettes?"

"Oh, sure." She found the pack in her bag and offered him one along with a book of matches.

"Thank you. Why am I following you? Why *am* I following you? I've been asking myself that same question for several hours now, and I'm not in the least sure I have a satisfactory answer." He drew on the cigarette, turning aside to exhale the smoke. "I was taken by your bearing, in the first place. And in the second, once I was able to get close enough to see, by your eyes."

"My eyes?" The man was an artist, and artists had different vision, special ways of seeing things. She'd always been somewhat awed by people with the talent to draw and paint well; she'd believed they were gifted with a kind of clarified vision, one that dispensed with the trivial, and homed in on what was true.

He leaned slightly closer to her over the back of the seat. "I expect you'll think this absurd, but since the moment I saw you I've had the oddest feeling that I know you. No, no, we've never met. It's just that, without ever having clapped eyes on you before today, you're someone I seem to know." Impatiently, he said, "That's no good. It doesn't explain a thing. You must understand that I'm not given to following people, women, about. I was curious," he wound down, dissatisfied with his inability to justify his behavior.

Automatically, she covered her lower face with her hand and gazed at him a moment longer before directing her eyes to the window. She felt like a fool, duped by her craving to endow talent with mysticism.

"Damn!" he swore softly. "Now I've offended you. You suspect me of being kinky."

Fuck off! she thought, furious with herself for forgetting she was no longer an ordinary woman, but a freak who'd attract the odd and the curious.

When she failed to respond, he reached out to move her hand. "You really musn't do that, you know. There's no need."

Thrown by this display of sensitivity, and unsure how to deal with this odd Englishman, she reached into her handbag for a tissue and dabbed at her nose, which had begun to run due to the air conditioning on the bus.

"Have you a cold?" he asked caringly.

Why the hell would he care? she wondered. "It's the air conditioning," she explained, with the hope of somehow grounding the conversation. "What do you want from me?"

"Do I want something from you?" he asked himself aloud. "I truthfully don't know. Do you want something from me?"

"I don't even *know* you. Why would I *want* anything from you?"

"People are always wanting things from one another. Strangers expect courtesy; those we know want respect and caring. All human intercourse is predicated on attempting to satisfy the wants of others in the hope we'll benefit from a reciprocating act. I give to you; you give to me. You need something, I try to supply it, in return for which you try to supply me with something I need. You do have fine eyes," he observed disarmingly, "very fine eyes."

"How," she asked, "do you manage to dress yourself with one hand out of commission?"

He laughed delightedly. "Perhaps all this chat has been in aid of soliciting your assistance in the process."

"You're nuts!" she declared, reacting positively to his laughter. "Completely nuts."

"Oh, I wouldn't deny that," he said. "I wouldn't dare."

Chapter 22

"I LOVED NIAGARA FALLS," she confessed to him as they stood on the belvedere looking over at Montmorency Falls. "I spent hours on end looking at them."

"It's about to pour," he said, his eyes on the sky. "I'll wager we won't make it back to the bus before it starts pissing down."

She looked up to confirm that the sky had indeed gone very dark.

"Come on!" He took hold of her hand and began to run with her back to where the mini-bus was parked at the end of a long line of tourist vehicles. Halfway there, the rain descended as if someone had overturned a cauldron. It fell with such force that they were both instantly drenched.

Once inside the bus, Martin sat down beside her, both of them shivering in the cold air blasting out of the vents.

"I say!" Martin called out to the young driver. "Do you think you could lower the air conditioning or turn it off? It's bloody perishing in here!"

Without a word, the driver flipped a lever and the interior of the van went suddenly quiet.

"Thank you." Caley opened her bag, looking for something with which to dry her hair. She found a cotton scarf and rubbed it over her hair, then brought out a white paper bag and a cigarette. She let the bag sit in her lap while she lit the cigarette and then, as an afterthought, offered the pack to Martin.

"Thank you, no. I smoke only occasionally. What did you buy?"

"This? It's a kind of sweatshirt."

"Let's have a look," he said eagerly. "I was dying to know what you'd bought."

"That's right. You were following me." She pulled from the bag a heavy white sweatshirt with a cotton eyelet insert and collar, and held it up for his inspection.

"Very pretty. Put it on, why don't you? Keep you from getting a chill."

"Good idea."

He held her cigarette while she dragged on the shirt, then accepted the cigarette back from him. "That is better," she said. "I completely forgot I had it."

The driver put the bus in gear, and she looked out the window at the manor house, disappointed they hadn't had longer here. "It's too bad they wouldn't let us look around inside the house."

"Not to worry," he said cheerfully. "I expect they'll allow us hours to tour the shrine."

"I'm really not looking forward to it."

"It might be quite spiritually uplifting," he said, although, if anything, he expected the reverse would be true.

As the mini-bus started forward along the drive she took a final look at the lovely old white house with the dormers on the upper story, and at the empty chairs on the front porch.

The driver had resumed his French and English travelogue, explaining they would soon be viewing some of the best examples of early Canadian domestic architecture as they drove along the shore. Caley listened for a minute or two, then allowed his voice to fade into the background of her thoughts.

"Why d'you think they turned that place into an old folks' home?" she asked Martin.

"No idea. Seems rather a nice place to potter about, although I can't say I'd fancy being penned up with a gaggle of old duffers. I'd prefer something more private when I come down with the old inevitable Alzheimer's."

"What makes you think you're not already prematurely senile?"

"Good point. I was hoping I had a few more years, but they

do say you're completely unaware of it taking you over." He let his tongue loll and faint tremors shook his head. "Good God! You may be right! Have I done anything in the last hour I don't remember?"

"You're married, aren't you?"

He looked down at the gold band he still wore on the ring finger of his left hand. "I was."

She was going to ask if he was divorced, but something cautioned her not to pursue the matter.

"Have you been married?" he asked.

"No. I lived with someone for a few years. We used to talk about one day getting married. . . ." She shrugged, and they fell into a silence that wasn't broken until the mini-bus pulled over to the side of the road and the driver explained they would be stopping here for half an hour to sample fresh-baked bread and maple butter, and to purchase homemade jams and jellies, should they wish.

"That sounds good," Martin said. "Are you going to come along and join the queue?"

"Sure. Why not?"

They sat on rough benches at a large wooden table in a room filled with people from other tours, all of them eating the thick slabs of still-warm bread coated heavily with maple butter, and drinking coffee. The air was steamy with the moisture drawn from damp outerwear, and the aroma of fresh coffee and maple rode upon the steam, wafting forward in gusts every time the front door opened and one group departed as another entered. It had the effect of making Caley sleepy. She ate slowly, her jaws leaden, and paused now and then to sip the good, strong coffee.

"This is nice," she said dopily, watching Martin's jaws work as he quickly devoured the bread. "I'd love to be able to bake bread."

"I'm sure you could, if you tried."

"What makes you say that?"

"I simply know you could."

Holding her paper cup of coffee, she looked around the room, becoming aware that something unusual had happened. Where in the past people would have stared at her remorselessly, they now looked at her, then at Martin, and then away.

She cocked her head to one side and looked at this man, working it through. He had an impressive presence, so that even silent, he commanded respect. Part of it had to do with his handsomeness, and part with the obviously high quality of his clothes and demeanor. This man was wealthy and likely always had been; he seemed to glow with prosperity, and had the habits of someone who'd been accustomed throughout a lifetime to having entreé to people and places others might never gain. Martin had this, and something more. He had, she decided, the gift of authority; a natural, authentic command of people and situations. When he spoke, others listened, and it wasn't due only to his terrific accent and clear, well-modulated voice. It had to do with credibility. He said a lot of fairly peculiar things, and used uncommon words, but this simply amalgamated his impact. People would think twice about defying him; he had an almost visible integrity. And being in his company had an overlapping effect: people assumed they were a pair and, because of it, stepped up their respect for her. They still gaped, but it wasn't the same as it had been. Martin was causing people to think about how they reacted to her. It was as if, since he found her worthy of his time and attention, she must be something more than merely a disfigured woman. He was endowing her, simply by his presence at her side, with renewed credibility. It bowled her over. Out in public with Ron, and even with Louise, she'd been very aware of their defensiveness on her behalf, as if they were always at the ready to leap between her and anyone who might dare stare too long at her. This man gave off none of that; he appeared perfectly content simply to be wherever he happened to be.

The effect he had, both on others and on her, was extraordinarily tantalizing. He made her feel safe.

"Aren't you bothered being seen with me?" she asked bluntly.

"Why? Is there something wrong with you?"

"Be serious! I bother the hell out of people, and don't tell me you haven't noticed."

"I noticed," he acknowledged. "I saw it straight off. What interested me more was how you manage to maintain your dignity."

"And another thing," she pushed on, "how come you haven't asked me for all the gory details of what happened?"

"That would be in very bad taste. One doesn't question people." He crumpled his paper cup. "Would you like me to dispose of that for you?"

She looked down at her empty cup and paper napkin. "Oh! Sure, thanks."

As they were running back to the bus, the rain still falling torrentially, he again took hold of her hand. It felt, as he did it, as if he'd reached into the interior of her chest and squeezed her heart. She was waiting for him to make a declaration of what it was he wanted of her. Perhaps he'd ask her to take off her clothes and lie down beneath him. She'd be willing. Why not? He had to want something, she reasoned. Why else would he be paying so much attention to her? Perhaps cripples aroused his sexual appetites.

Dutifully, they admired the houses the driver singled out as worthy of note, although it was difficult to form any clear impressions through the rain washing down the bus windows. As they were approaching the Basilica of Sainte Anne de Beaupré, she asked, "Do you believe in miracles? I mean, what do you think about people who make pilgrimages to places like this?"

"I can't honestly say I've ever given it any real thought, but I don't believe I subscribe to it. There's really only one true miracle, and that's life itself. It strikes me as presumptuous that people would have the temerity to hope for more. I mean to say, given there is a God—regardless of one's personal religious concepts—I should think He'd done quite enough simply by allowing us to create lives. To anticipate any more than that smacks of greed and an instinct for preferential treatment. So yes and no. I believe life is a miracle. Therefore, I do believe in the possibility of them. But no, I don't believe in what you might, for want of a better term, call minor miracles." He paused, then asked, "Are you quite sure you're not catching cold?"

"It's just a runny nose," she said, concealing a tissue in her palm. "You know, I used to think being able to have a baby was a miracle. I mean, it seemed to me that two people making a third person was an incredible thing. I guess I still think that."

"It is," he stated firmly, "most definitely a miracle." Of course it was, he thought. All he had to do was close his eyes and twin miracles danced on his memory's screen, scrambling in the sunlight of an eternal garden. Marks and Spencer had lived for a time, after all, and nothing could alter the joy he'd known in them.

"What happened?" she asked quietly.

"Might I have another of your cigarettes? I'll buy you a fresh pack when we arrive."

Silently she gave him a cigarette and waited, guessing he was about to reveal to her the scope of his personal tragedy. It was, she now realized, his tragic aspect, camouflaged by ready humor, that was the final element of his authority. Only someone who'd suffered terrible pain could have responded as he'd done to the details she'd offered of her origins.

"My wife and sons died in an airplane crash," he told her. "It happened last April."

She stared at his profile, and it lost its definition as she wept without warning, in immediate understanding of his loss. Her tears overflowed as she cast about for something that might adequately communicate how utterly she sympathized. Nothing had ever cut more directly to the core of her feelings than his quiet statement.

Looking up to see her in tears, he was astounded, and at once put his arm around her shoulders. She forgot they were strangers, and that she was no longer the same as she'd once been, and allowed herself to find solace in the gesture. The cast on his hand pressed heavily on her shoulder, and she didn't mind in the least.

After a time, she straightened and mopped her eyes with the already damp tissue. She began to apologize for her display, but he cut her off, saying, "The Stations of the Cross," and she turned to look. "I rather think we're in for something here," he said.

Because of the rain there were no people walking about on the grassy hillside. The bronze statues streamed with water; they had an abandoned, lonely look to them.

"Have you a religion?" he asked, withdrawing his arm.

"My parents were Episcopalian, but I don't think I'm anything. What about you?"

"My grandmother, who raised me—and I'm being most liberal in that description—was so high an Anglican it wouldn't have surprised me in the least, as a boy, to see people worshipping *her* of a Sunday. In direct relation to her devotion, I became more of an agnostic almost daily. I do believe in something. I have certain theories I espouse, but I haven't belonged to any ordained religious group since childhood."

As the bus made its way into the town, he watched her attempt to tidy herself up. All his skullduggery and foolishness had been entirely worthwhile. She was just as bright, and bitter, and charmingly direct as he'd expected she'd be.

They separated at the entrance to the Basilica. Caley stood looking up at the columns immediately inside the front doors, made queasy by the sight of the countless prostheses appended to them. False limbs of every size, trusses, and braces hung from the roof all the way down to ground level. Mouth open, she stared, appalled by what had to be the most disgusting display she'd ever seen. Did they consider these abandoned contraptions proof of something? Did they hope others would be inspired to cast off their false limbs and proclaim themselves cured simply in order to partake of the ration of miracles? It was in such bad taste, she thought, going on to make a quick tour of the church's interior. There was a larger-than-life-sized statue of Sainte Anne, and in every available crevice were folded pieces of paper: written supplications tucked between her arms, into the creases of her clothes. Everywhere were abandoned crutches, mountains of them, and cast-off hands, arms, feet, entire legs. She had the impression of a lot of gilt glittering on the walls, and overall, the deathly scent of dying flowers. She all but ran back to the doors, pausing briefly for one last viewing of the grotesquely decorated columns.

Martin was already waiting on the sidewalk, and she hurried to join him.

"Quite something, isn't it?" he said with a smile.

"It's just sickening! It makes me want to throw down my

Kleenex and swear my runny nose has been cured. Did you see those *columns*? My God! I can't believe people would think God or anybody would see all that as anything but mass suggestion.''

"Better still," he said. "See that place over the road?"

She looked across at what appeared to be a small-sized replica of the church.

"I doubt you'll believe it," he said, "but that's a bloody cafeteria."

"You're *kidding*!"

"Truly, I'm not. I say, would you care to cross over and partake of a religi-burger?''

"That's terrible!" She exploded into laughter and he joined her, both of them bending double with it as several other passengers from the mini-bus went past casting disapproving glances at them. "People are going to think we're poking fun!" she cried, unable to stop laughing.

"God knows better! All those notes!" he guffawed. " 'Dear Sainte Anne, Frightfully sorry but I'm afraid I'm going to need my truss after all.' Bloody obscene!" he declared. "Why do they wish so to believe in such horrifying nonsense? Where are you staying?''

"Where? You mean which hotel? The Chateau Frontenac. Why?''

"What luck! Have dinner with me tonight!"

"We'd better get back to the bus. Or do you want to see the cyclorama?''

"Will you have dinner with me?" he asked again, trotting along at her side.

She came to a stop, and so did he. "What're you after?" she asked him. "I don't know why you're doing all this."

"But I haven't done anything. I mean, yes, I was following you. But we've met properly now. Come to dinner. Eating alone's dreadful.''

"Oh, all right. Sure. Why not?"

Having struggled free of his damp clothes, he stretched out on the hotel bed to rest for an hour before he was to meet Caley for dinner. His good arm folded under his head, disregarding the consistent throb of his broken hand, he let his eyes close, and reviewed the day.

He projected Caley's image and refashioned it in order to know what she'd looked like at another time. It didn't matter, he thought, smiling to himself as the original slide replaced the amended one. He felt extraordinarily lucky to have met her, and was moved once more, recalling her spontaneous, bursting sympathy when he'd told her of the airplane crash. He'd always envied people with the capacity for pure, unvarnished reactions; he admired anyone who could weep openly. It was such a blessing, that ability to respond unreservedly, withholding no part of oneself.

He'd been absolutely right in pursuing her. He liked her ready sense of humor, and even her defensiveness. The two of them were moving toward friendship, and he could easily imagine all sorts of things they might see and do together. The prospect of once more being able to share his thoughts and feelings was totally enticing.

As he descended into sleep, he could feel fragments of his shattered being fusing themselves to the whole. He considered Marian, and Harry, and Ian—caring cameos carved indelibly on the background of his life. I've found a smashing new friend, he told them. You'd be glad of that, I know.

While she showered, ridding herself of the chill she'd felt all afternoon, she wondered if she shouldn't throw her things into the car and get the hell out of there. For all she knew, she was tap-dancing her way into perilous territory with this Englishman. He actually seemed to think there was nothing wrong with her, and treated her accordingly. In itself that was suspect. Combined with what she knew of his history, it was nothing less than sensible of her to exercise caution in her dealings with him. Yet when she thought of the effect he seemed to have on just about everyone, the curiosity he claimed to have about her was paralleled by hers about him. Stan would undoubtedly have been able to sum up the situation instantly, with all kinds of nifty insights.

She recalled the unseemly emotional displays Martin had prompted from her: bursting into tears, laughing hysterically. Then there were all the philosophical issues he'd raised, stuff about God and human intercourse. All the while they'd talked, she'd been able, almost physically, to feel her mind stretching to embrace concepts no one had ever before suggested to her. He was very intelligent, and seemed not to take any topic lightly. She had no frames of reference for a man like this.

He had also renewed her awareness of her body. She had, for so long, been dominated by the damage done to her face, that she'd scarcely thought of any other part of herself. Now she could survey her flesh and see that here, at least, she was relatively whole; scarred areas, yes, but nothing remotely as hideous as the porcine features she had to carry out into the world like the artwork of a madman. God! She didn't want to think about her body, or have to view any part of herself. She had a trip to make to the end of the world, and maybe it would be a good thing, after all, to forgo this dinner and get on with the journey. Contemplation of the flesh container in which she lived was an itchy process, one that bred new fears and had her returning again and again to the question of why this man wished to be seen in public with her. Was it possible he was somehow seeking to punish himself with her presence? Or was he, in reality, one of those people she'd read about in Ron's copies of *Playboy*, the type who got off on making love to amputees?

If he laid a hand on her, she'd deck him, she decided. Yet she knew intuitively Martin wasn't going to touch her in any but the most innocent fashion. The seamy thoughts, the sexual ones, were all hers. The truth was he honestly saw more than her surface. He was an artist, and artists did see differently. He talked about her eyes, her dignity and bearing, and she wanted to believe him. Dangerous as it might be, she hadn't anything to lose in seeing this situation through to its conclusion. What could happen? He might harm her physically, but she didn't believe him capable of it. Psychologically, emotionally, there was no question that he was leading her into tricky areas. What the hell! He wasn't about to overpower her, with one hand in a cast.

He was waiting outside the Champlain dining room, and she had to pause for a moment in order to deal with the effervescence the sight of him produced in her suddenly too-small lungs. He'd dressed for the occasion in a cream-colored linen suit, under which he wore a beige silk shirt, open at the neck. His cheeks reddened from a recent shave, he smiled widely upon catching sight of her, and she went forward as if being reeled in on an invisible line.

"Ah, here you are!" He took hold of her hand and led her into the dim interior of the dining room where the maître d' stood at attention, menus in hand. "I was on the verge of doing battle to secure a table," he confided to Caley, "but our good host allowed himself to be financially persuaded." He smiled at the stocky maître d' and stood aside so that Caley might precede him as they followed the man to a banquette table directly opposite where a harpist plucked accompaniment to a tiny young woman playing flute.

"This is great," Caley said, seated on Martin's right and looking at the musicians.

"Will you have something to drink?"

"Does it make you uncomfortable . . . ?"

"What's your house red?" she asked the waiter who stood at Martin's elbow.

"Cuvée Speciale, madam. Very nice, dry, French."

"Why did I ask?" She laughed. "I don't know a thing about French wines."

"Have a glass," Martin encouraged. "You'll like it. It's a good wine."

"All right."

"A glass of the red wine and Perrier with a twist," he told the waiter, then turned back to her. "That's a very pretty frock. Did you wear it in my honor?"

"As a matter of fact, I did. That's a pretty sharp suit. Is that in my honor?"

"As a matter of fact, it is. Aren't we terribly twee, the two of us!" He smiled approvingly. "This is fun, isn't it? The flautist plays rather sharp, unfortunately. But never mind. I had a marvelous idea while shaving. I'll confess straight off the idea was inspired by the latest weather forecast. They're predicting more rain for the next several days. It's going to be terribly dreary, being shut in. So why don't you drive me back to Toronto—you did say you had a car, didn't you?—and have a proper visit? We could take our time, pooping along at a steady, legal sixty, and then, if you'd allow it, I'll show you around the city, even take you to the zoo, if you fancy that."

"But I was . . . It's going to keep on raining?"

"Afraid so."

"I was planning to go on to Nova Scotia," she said lamely, knowing she was going to accept his invitation. She couldn't have refused if her life had depended upon it. Just to be able to look at him and talk with him for a time, it would be worth it.

"You can always do that another time," he said. "I'm really not fond of flying, and I'd be more than happy to pay your expenses, and of course the petrol—gasoline." Afraid she'd not consent, he stepped up his offer. "I'll take you to Ontario Place, and to the Science Centre. We've got quite a decent art gallery, and the renovation's nearly complete on the museum. There's a good number of theaters, and masses of super restaurants. Aside from all that, think of the enormous favor you'd be doing someone temporarily handicapped. You've no idea what I went through getting into this gear tonight. Can you imagine the difficulties, getting the top off the bottle of after-shave?"

"I don't know. . . ."

"I'll even," he threw in, in a rush, "put you up in a suite at Grotty Groves."

"*Where*?"

"My house," he explained. "An enormous Victorian relic right downtown. You could have an entire floor to yourself."

"Listen," she said. "You're not into weird stuff or anything, are you? I mean . . ."

His laughter cut short her words. "I'll admit," he gasped, "that there have been occasions in my thirty-seven years when I was sorely tempted to dabble in the somewhat medieval practices of my friends. However, I am as straight as the proverbial arrow. Rest assured. You are perfectly safe. You're talking, my dear, to a man who spends the best part of ten minutes simply trying to take down his trousers. In the event of an attempted rape, you'll have ample time to ring for the police and then stroll casually back to your room.''

"Oh, what the hell!'' She laughed. "All right. When do you want to leave?''

"In the morning? Say nine o'clock?''

"Okay. Fine. You're on.''

Chapter 23

HE WENT WILD OVER the car, and had to inspect it thoroughly before climbing into the front seat and turning at once to admire the interior, and the leather upholstery.

"What a splendid motor!" he declared several times as Caley headed toward the highway. "And you drive so well! Why is it you don't wear your seatbelt?"

"The car doesn't have any."

"We'll have to have some installed. It's illegal, you know, to drive here without them."

"I know," she said, navigating cautiously through the rain. "Do you suppose we're going to drive out of this?"

"We might." He leaned forward to peer out through the windshield at the sky.

"Let's keep going until we get past it."

"As you like. What fragrance is that?" he asked.

"What? My perfume? Mary Chess."

"Most pleasant. You drive like a man."

"Oh, really? What do men drive like?"

"The better ones seem to have no nerve. Women so often appear to be wrestling with the wheel as if they're hapless victims of something they rather fear."

"I've seen plenty of men who drive that way."

"Oh, dear. Am I revealing myself to be a chauvinist piggy?"

"Just a little." She smiled over at him. "Why did you pay

my hotel bill? I had kind of an embarrassing scene there when I went to check out."

"I do apologize. I simply wanted to do something for you."

"It wasn't necessary."

"Of course not. It's the unnecessary things one does that give the most pleasure. It pleased me. Do be gracious and accept that."

"I don't have much choice, since it's already done, but I can pay my own way, you know."

"You're sure you're not the daughter of a banker?"

"Why do you keep asking me that?"

"Sorry. Just a bit of foolishness I indulged in while dogging your heels through the streets. I enjoyed having someone to do something for. I'm certainly not trying to purchase your interest, or anything of that sort."

"Why would you say that?" she asked. "You don't look like a man who has to buy people."

"Precisely. So think of my gesture as a gift. Tell me, what did you do back in Connecticut? You know, I've never been there. I've spent time in New York, what with preparing shows, that sort of thing, but I've never seen New England."

"I was a secretary."

"A secretary? You mean you're able to take shorthand, do typing, that sort of thing?"

"Right. Why do you sound so amazed?"

"I've always been intrigued by anyone who was able to decipher those lines and squiggles and render them into something approximating good English. I'm most impressed."

"If that impresses you, I'd hate to be around when you came across something really outstanding."

"You think I'm a nutter, don't you? You think I'm right over the top."

"Well," she said with a laugh, "you're not exactly your average, everyday citizen."

"Good God, no! What a dreadful thought! I've never aspired to the 'average.' Is that the sort of person you prefer?"

"Maybe not prefer. It just happens that those're the kind of people I've known mostly. Except for Stan."

"And who is Stan?"

"My shrink. He was."

"Your *shrink*? What a marvelously bizarre euphemism! The implication is that one goes to visit this person and he performs the service of reducing the size of one's brain capacity. Why on earth would you want to do that?"

"I had a few problems adjusting, after the accident."

"What accident?"

"The one that turned me into the Creature from the Black Lagoon."

"Don't refer to yourself that way!" he said sharply. "It does both of us a disservice. I don't think of you as a 'creature' and you musn't either. Now, tell me about your accident. Please," he added.

"You sound like my grade-five teacher, Mr. Harrell. He was English, too. Boy, was he ever out of it! He used to tell us we were 'in disgrace' if we did something like talking in class or passing notes, used to send us to Coventry. It was years before I realized Coventry wasn't the actual name of the far corner of the room. He was forever talking about things like 'coals to Newcastle' and 'blotting our copybooks.' " She shook her head, and Martin laughed. "What happened was, Ron and I—he's the man I lived with—we were driving on the Connecticut Turnpike and some drunk crossed the median and hit us. I wasn't wearing my seatbelt, and I went right out through the windshield, bounced a few times, and landed about forty feet away."

He winced, visualizing it. "You're lucky you weren't killed. How dreadful for you!"

"I don't know about lucky. For most of last year I was pretty sure it would've been better if I *had* been killed. But I wasn't, and so here we are."

"And you had this chap, Stan, to help you deal with that experience?"

"That's right."

"*Was* he helpful?"

"A lot. He didn't try to hand me a load of bullshit about how everything was going to be just fine. You know, all that nice, clichéd crap people who know nothing about it like to hand you. He was really teed off with me for not having the rest of the surgery."

"And why didn't you?"

"Because I'd had enough. Please don't even think about discussing that. Okay?"

"I wouldn't dream of it. It's no one's right to make suggestions as to how anyone else might improve upon the quality of her life."

"Are you patronizing me?" She frowned skeptically.

"Not at all. I do believe that."

"What am I doing?" she wondered aloud. "This is crazy! I'm driving some guy I don't even know back to a city I didn't like much, and I don't have a clue why."

"I'll give you a job, if you'd care to have one."

"A job? Doing what?"

"Well, for starters, my correspondence has managed to get rather out of control. Then, with the condition my hand's in, I could certainly use some assistance in the darkroom."

"I don't know anything about darkrooms."

"I'll teach you," he said airily. "Then there's the matter of bills to be paid, and bookkeeping to be done. I could find quite a number of things to keep you busy. And, of course, I'd pay you."

"Look, I'll drive you back, right to your front door. I'll even help you carry your bags. But I don't need a job. I don't *want* one."

"Don't be frightened," he said softly. "I intend you no harm." He looked down at his aching hand and gazed at it with fond sadness.

"What's the matter?" she asked. "Your hand hurt?"

"It's such a bloody bore! They said they couldn't set it properly, but I'm afraid I insisted, even though they recommended I go directly to a plastic surgeon. It would appear they were right. It doesn't seem to be mending."

"I've got some aspirin, if that would help."

"You've a generous heart," he said warmly. "Please don't be mistrusting. I know I've rather thrown myself at your head, but it's only because I like you enormously."

"You don't know me. How can you like someone you don't know 'enormously'?"

"I trust my instincts, even if you don't trust your own."

For a few moments, looking ahead, the prospect of spending two or three days in the car with this man struck her as something approximating torture. Resentment of her own impulsiveness stirred in her belly. Then she allowed herself another brief look at him and the resentment subsided, replaced by a sense of helplessness. "I like you enormously, too," she admitted. "I think you're out of your fucking head. I probably am, too, but I like you."

There was one bad moment on the road. Martin had fiddled with the radio, searching for a strong signal. He found a good, clear station and sat back to listen to quite a pretty piece of music, sung by what sounded like a boy soprano. When he looked over, he saw that Caley had frozen, her eyes fixed unblinking on the unraveling road before them.

"What is it?" he asked, as she put on the turn indicator and pulled the car onto the shoulder. "Have I said or done something?" he asked as she bent her head onto her crossed arms. "I *am* sorry," he said, "if it's anything I've done."

The song ended and another one began. She straightened and sat, dry-eyed, breathing tiredly. "That song," she said at last. "It was playing when we crashed. I guess I've been lucky, but that's the first time I've heard it since then."

"The music revived it all for you," he said softly.

"It reminded me of a lot of things. I'm okay now." She wet her lips and turned to look at him. "Did you really think it was your fault that I went into orbit there?"

"I thought it might be."

"Why would you give a damn? I'm nothing to you."

"Don't be that way, Caley. Of course, you're something to me. We're friends."

She had to look away; he was going to make her cry.

By midafternoon they'd driven into clear weather.

"Let's find a place with a pool and stop for the day," Martin said. "I think we've done a good day's driving, don't you?"

"Sure," she said, resigned to accommodating him. "Sing out if you see anything."

They stopped several times and, at last, found a motel with a pool. Martin went in to book the rooms, then returned, smiling, to direct her around to the rear of the building.

"Side by side, we are," he said, juggling the two keys in his right hand. "With a connecting door," he added, causing her to wonder if it was his intention to travel to her bed in the dead of night.

"I don't like sleeping with my door open," she said.

"Nor I," he agreed. "But I thought we might watch a bit of telly together. I'll light the old pipe, you'll fetch your knitting —a scene of terrifying domesticity." He laughed as she got the trunk open.

"Which bag do you want?" she asked him.

"Oh, I should think just the little one, thank you." He reached past her and lifted it out. "What extraordinary things you have in here!" He peered into the rear of the trunk, then stood aside as she lifted out her pillow, tucked it under her arm, and reached in again for the box with the coffee-making supplies.

"I like fresh coffee. In fact, I could use a cup. Want some?"

"Yes, please." He got the doors to both rooms open, swung his overnight bag on the bed, then returned to ask if she needed any help.

"I thought you were incapacitated," she said, moving quickly past him to deposit one load in her room, then returning for the rest of her things. He followed her every move, taking care not to obstruct her passage.

"Fancy a dip in the pool?" he asked as she slammed closed the trunk.

"I'll get changed, make the coffee, and meet you over there. I hope black's okay, because I don't have any cream."

"Black's smashing. Later on, we'll fetch in some cream."

While she got the coffee going, she listened to his movements in the adjoining room. She felt the need to move quietly and, keeping her eyes on the door as if expecting him to come bursting through it at any moment, stripped quickly and pulled on her bathing suit. As the coffee dripped through the filter directly into the thermos bottle, she heard his door close. He'd managed to change fairly quickly, she thought, lifting the filter to see how much more water was needed. She smiled at his remark about the pipe and the knitting. He really was funny.

The pool was deserted. Martin had seated himself on one of the chaises. A sketch pad and several pencils were positioned close to hand on a small table to his right.

"Ah, here you are!" he said brightly as she entered the pool enclosure carrying the thermos and her canvas bag. He jumped up and insisted on relieving her of the thermos. "Allow me to pour," he said in headwaiter tones. "Do have a seat."

"How're you going to get the top off?" she asked, amused.

"I hadn't thought of that." He sat on the side of his chaise and reluctantly surrendered the thermos.

"This is very nice," he said, both of the coffee and the afternoon. "My initial instinct was to plunge into the pool." He waved his broken hand. "Brought me up rather short. I've no idea how one might navigate effectively with one hand held aloft."

"Isn't that funny? Your saying that reminds me of all the trouble I had taking a bath, once I came home from the hospital."

"How so?"

"I had a few broken bones, and the cast was still on my leg the first time they let me go home, so I kind of had to slide into the tub and keep one leg propped on the side. The thing that was tricky was that I couldn't get out again by myself. Ron always had to come help me. I'd forgotten all about it."

"Was he not injured in the accident?" he asked.

She shook her head. "Just a few scratches and a sprained shoulder. You could always sit on the side and dangle. That's hospital talk, you know. They let you dangle as the first step after coming out of the anesthetic. Wipes you right out, just sitting on the side of the bed with your legs hanging over the side."

"It must be frightful."

"It's amazing what you can get used to."

"Shocking, isn't it? So many things one would never have thought. . . ." He trailed off and looked over at the rippling surface of the pool. He wished he weren't so completely impaired by the cast on his hand. The idea of splashing about in the pool appealed to him. "Please don't let me keep you out of the water. Do go ahead and have a swim, if you'd care to."

Ron would've dived right in, she thought. It wouldn't have occurred to him to curtail any activity simply because she mightn't have been able to participate. This man wouldn't consider anything of the sort. It seemed very clear that unless anyone or everyone involved in a given situation could join in, the activity would be abandoned.

"Is that British etiquette?" she asked.

"What?"

"Hanging back unless everybody can be involved."

"I don't know that it's British especially. I simply know it's always seemed to me most unfair to go larking about, having a splendid time at whatever, if someone else isn't able to join in your fun. It's kinder to find something else to do."

"Are all your friends that way, too?"

"All my friends?" He smiled. "I really couldn't say. It's how I am." He heard himself saying those same words to Grace as they walked in the garden, and had to pause for a moment now to question the truth of the statement. "It is how I am," he said again. "I remember as a small boy being allowed to attend a birthday party for the grandson of one of Lady Bee's chums."

"Who's Lady Bee?"

"My grandmother. In any case, what I most remember about the occasion is the little chap with the frightful cold who had to sit on the sidelines. A more miserably unhappy lad you've never seen. Entirely spoiled the outing for me. I went to sit with him—he wasn't an especially sociable chap—and the two of us watched the goings-on. I didn't feel right about joining in if all of us couldn't."

"That's a sad little picture," she said, shaking out the last drops of coffee from the thermos cup before setting it down on the table.

"It is, isn't it? I can see it very clearly, the two of us all rigged out in the mandatory velvet suits with the short pants and flowing collars. Precocious little sods, the lot of us. As a point of interest, the one with the drippy nose is presently a member of parliament. He's undoubtedly no less dour now than he was then.''

"But there's no one keeping him company on the side-lines.''

"Probably not,'' he agreed. "Were you a nice little girl?''

"Quiet. I don't know about nice, but quiet definitely. My adoptive parents were in their mid-forties when they got me. I guess I just fell into line with them. They were quiet people. She did her knitting and he smoked his pipe.''

"You're taking the mickey out of me!'' he accused with a laugh.

"Yup. My dad smoked Pall Malls and my mom did cross-word puzzles while they listened to the radio.''

"Did you always know you'd been adopted?''

"Not until I was sixteen. That's when they told me. I've got this file folder of clippings. There was quite a fuss about the whole business.''

"I'd like to see that,'' he said, "if you'd care to show it to me.''

"Why?''

"Well, because it's about you, isn't it?''

"You know,'' she said, "Ron used to get these magazines, *Penthouse* and *Hustler*, stuff like that. And this one time, I don't remember which magazine it was in, but there was this article all about these guys who got off on making out with amputees. You know. Women with a leg or an arm missing. I've never forgotten it. It made me so mad. Like it wasn't bad enough that they had all this power over women, but they wanted women who weren't even in one piece, so maybe it gave them more power or something.''

"That's appalling!'' he declared. "This was in an American magazine, you say?''

"Right.''

"Do you suppose these men they wrote about were actual people and not simply journalists creating sensationalism?''

"What difference would it make?'' she asked. "Either way, it was pretty sick.''

He made a face and again looked at the pool. Any doubts she'd had about the authenticity of his interest were greatly diminished by his obvious distaste. She could safely rule him out as being one of the men who might conceivably fall into the category of amputee fetishist. That left her with the alternative consideration that he was genuinely interested in her. She looked at his back and shoulders, thinking he was thinner than she'd thought. At once the idea of fattening him up occurred to her and, angrily, she dismissed it. He wasn't her responsibility; she'd committed herself only to return him home, nothing more. Yet for a few seconds she thought of the pleasure she'd always taken in cooking, in presenting meals to Ron, and suspected she was responding to Martin the way the mother of a newborn might upon first sight of the infant.

She got up, walked to the near, deep end of the pool, and dived in. The water was far colder than expected and her lungs fluttered protestingly. Staying underwater, her eyes open, she propelled herself toward the shallow end. She was furious with herself, mortified by the instinct within her toward caretaking. What did it take to turn off that instinct, stifle it permanently?

Surfacing, she tipped her head backward into the water to clear the hair away from her face, and stood looking at him. He was still seated on the end of the chaise, the cup of coffee in his hand, and he was beaming at her, as if the sight of her in the water gladdened him beyond telling.

"What're you smiling at?" she asked, her voice carrying easily over the disturbed water.

"I am smiling at you," he said, lifting the coffee to his mouth. "You make superb coffee and you swim ferociously, like an angry naiad. Were I sound of limb, I'd come cavort with you. I'd play sea lion. What would you be?"

"Wet," she said, and laughed.

"This is your house?" Incredulous, she pulled into the driveway and turned off the engine. "I halfway thought you were kidding, but I should've known you wouldn't be. This place is enormous."

"Leave the bags for the moment," he said. "Come along in and I'll give you a tour, let you choose which room you'd like to have."

"Now, you listen! I'm going to a hotel. I told you that."

"Piffle!" He dismissed her argument. "Let me get the keys organized here and then we'll have a look round."

He got the front door open and she stepped inside, stunned by the brilliant white-painted expanse of the ground floor.

"This is what you did?" she asked, hearing the echo of her voice and footsteps as she walked into the center of the room. "It's just fantastic! Did you only just finish it? I mean, where's the furniture?"

"Haven't any," he said baldly. "Tried a few times to shop for some, but . . ." He lifted his shoulders, then let them fall in a graphic illustration of his inability to proceed. "Kitchen's just there." He pointed.

"I can see that," she said, going to the threshold. "It sure is bright. You don't even have a table. Where d'you eat?"

"I go out, or I order in."

"That's ridiculous, with a kitchen like this. My God, you've got everything you'd ever need, even a microwave."

"Afraid I allowed the salesman to talk me into that," he apologized. "Personally, I'm rather afraid of radiation poisoning."

She opened one of the cabinets then, as if challenged, went on to open every single one. "No dishes, no pots and pans, not even knives and forks. Are you sure you live here?"

"Let me show you upstairs." He held out his good hand, and she followed him back to the stairs. On the second floor, he pointed out his bedroom, and she looked despairingly at the disordered bedclothes, which were exactly as he'd left them, and at articles of clothing scattered about on the floor.

"For a classy guy, you've been living like a pig," she said.

"True. I have no talent for organizing. Come, I'll show you the rest, although I think you might like the third floor."

He went along the landing, opening doors. "This was Harry's room," he said in an altered voice, "and this was Ian's. This was their playroom. These, as you can see, are bathrooms."

They climbed the stairs and he waited in the hall as she looked into each of the bedrooms and bathrooms. "See anything you like?" he asked when she came back onto the landing.

"You could put up half the Russian army in this house," she said with a bemused laugh.

"Never been overly fond of foot soldiers," he said. "Pick a

room, and then we'll find you some fresh linens."

"God!" she said. "I know what's going to happen. I can already feel it starting. I'm going to want to clean up around here, do the windows, and vacuum up the fuzzballs. I spent months being a cleaning lady, and now I'm going to do it again. I don't *want* to clean up this place!"

"I wouldn't dream of suggesting it. We'll hire people to come in and clean."

"You don't *understand*!" she argued. "I'm going to *want* to do it, just like I'm going to want to put food in your refrigerator, and get a table and chairs and stuff to eat with. I'll want to buy furniture for all those empty rooms, and do something about the windows. I'll want to cook in that goddamned kitchen, and pick up all your stupid clothes. I'll *wallow* in it!"

"If it would make you happy, then by all means, I think you should do it."

She started quickly down the stairs and he followed, hoping she wasn't going to leave. When they arrived at the front door, she was jingling the car keys nervously.

"You're not going to leave, are you? I'd so like you to stay."

"I'm going to get your stuff out of the car!" she snapped angrily, throwing open the door.

"But will you be staying?" he asked, a plaintive note in his voice.

She stopped halfway down the front steps and whirled around. "*I don't know!*" she half-shouted, then turned and continued on her way to the car. She dragged his two bags out of the trunk, then carried them up the stairs, past Martin, and on to his bedroom, where she deposited them just inside the door, letting them drop with a thud. She cast a disgusted look at the room, then stormed back down the stairs, quivering now with anger, and from the strain in her arms.

"Why're you so bloody angry?" he demanded. "I invite you to stay, offer you every bloody thing I can think of, and your response to that is anger. If you're so dead keen on leaving, then by all means, leave!"

Stopped short by his unexpected outburst, she gulped down

a mouthful of air, then let fly. "*You piss me off*!" she shouted. "I'm not some goddamned charity case or something. Paying for everything before I even have a chance to get my wallet out. I don't need anybody paying for me. And this place is *ridiculous*! No furniture. Two stupid mugs and one spoon. Your bedroom's a shit heap, and I don't want to clean it up!"

"No one's asking you to!"

"It's spooky! You know what I mean? *Look* at this! Down here, it's all brand-new and white as snow, and up there" —she pointed up the stairway—"it's like the House of Usher, for chrissake! Boy, oh boy! Would Stan ever have a field day in here!"

"Your 'shrink's' got nothing to do with this!"

"He does to me! I stick around here and he'd tell me I was nurturing some fucking frustrated mother instinct or somesuch crap. I don't want to be your goddamned *mother*!"

"Oh, dear!" Martin's previously angry volume vanished and he began to laugh. "I *see*! You think I've been soliciting you to play nanny. Oh, dear! It's too good." Laughter weakened him and he sagged against the wall, gasping out his words. "Caley, you're simply too funny! I don't want a nanny. I've no earthly use for one. I want your company. You make me laugh, my dear. It's been so bloody long since I actually enjoyed myself." Blotting his eyes on his sleeve, he put his hand on her arm. "If you like, you may stay forever."

"Don't *say* things like that!" She jerked her arm away. "Don't fuck with me!"

"But I mean it most sincerely. Fetch in your things and find a room you like. I'll ring up for some food, and in the morning we'll see to a cleaning service and shop for whatever's needed here."

"You've got to go to the goddamned *doctor*!" she ranted. "Go 'ring' about *that* while I get my stuff out of the car. Asshole!" she raged, stomping down the front steps again. "The man's a complete asshole! What am I *doing*?"

She wanted to, but she couldn't stop making comparisons. Everything Martin did or said seemed to contravene all the realities, as she'd known them, about men. Men were vain, short of temper and of patience; they were interested only in things or people who'd provide gratification in some way; they were games-players, inept in practical matters, and depended upon women only for services. She had believed all of this for quite some time and had entered into the relationship with Ron believing she had a fair comprehension of the ground rules.

Martin defied her expectations at every turn. He displayed a keen interest in everything that pertained to her, including her past; he appeared unafraid of revealing himself, yet at the very moment when she decided she had him taped and knew precisely what to expect, he surprised her either with a show of anger or with more from his seemingly limitless fund of sympathy.

Her inability to define the situation satisfactorily had her constantly on edge. It wasn't unpleasant, though, but rather like reading a novel with a story line so complex that it required tremendous concentration in order to keep track of all the tangential themes. The story was a good one; it kept her hooked, and this peeved her. She didn't want to be subject to anyone else's moods or wishes, but she couldn't find a way to make a break. Part of it had to do with her curiosity about him, which grew almost hourly. Never had she been so completely or so regularly thrown off guard.

Ron had quite quickly become predictable. She'd learned early on to anticipate his needs and had attended to them with a kind of indulgent fondness she'd interpreted as love. Perhaps she had loved him. Compared to Martin, though, Ron was a tuneful little melody played against the full-scale orchestration of a symphonic composition. Martin was cellos and bassoons and violins played pizzicato, and his effect upon her was to make her wish she'd studied ballet or the piano for a dozen years. She might have danced a pas de deux with an imaginary partner, or placed her hands upon a keyboard to produce the most perfect music ever heard.

That Martin could elicit such preposterous notions from her simply compounded her irritation. She was someone who, at most, had hummed to the radio while slicing carrots for a bastardized version of boeuf bourguignonne; someone who, once upon a time, had known how to play "Chopsticks." Now, for chrissake, she was being tempted to fantasize about her nonexistent terpsichorean skills. It drove her wild; it affronted her basic pragmatism. She had to keep reminding herself who she was: the newsprint foundling who'd never entertained more than minimal ambitions.

She'd affix the knowledge of her identity firmly at the front line of her attention, then Martin would laugh, or frown, or express some further proof of his continuing interest, and she'd be floundering again, trapped between her longing to believe in all things impossible and a lifetime's experience that insisted nothing was probable. She rode up and down, within the tidy walls of her dilemma, berating herself for finding Martin so worthy of her time and fascination. She dreaded, most of all, the thought that she'd end up having made a total fool of herself.

"Evidently he doesn't have a nurse here because he's only at this office one day a week," Martin was explaining to her in the empty waiting room. "His nurse at the hospital was almost as angry with me as you are," he said, with mild sarcasm. "It seems they've been waiting for me to ring up and I've been naughty."

"You're an asshole!" she muttered, rattling the pages of a months-old copy of *Newsweek*. "Once this is out of the way, I'm gone. And don't try to talk me out of it!"

"You've a veritable fever when it comes to escaping," he observed, keeping his tone light. "You're welcome to stay or go as you please. But do please stop referring to me as an asshole. I find it somewhat offensive. I am an artist, after all, and I'm not overly fond of round, brown images."

She was about to fire back a retort when the inner office door opened and the doctor appeared. His eyes went at once to Caley and remained on her for several unbearably long moments.

"Mr. Maddox," he said finally, with obvious reluctance ending his inspection of her. "Do please come in. We've been wondering when you'd finally get around to calling. My secretary's been phoning you every day for weeks."

"I've been out of town," Martin replied, going after the doctor into the inner office.

Almost the instant the door closed, the doctor, in a hushed voice, asked, "Who's your friend?"

Seating himself in one of the chairs facing the desk, Martin answered, "What do you mean, 'Who's my friend?'?"

"What happened to her?"

"Motor accident, went through the windscreen. Why?"

"Do you think she'd be willing to let me have a look at her?"

"I've no idea. What about my hand?"

"I promise you we'll get to it. I really would like to talk to her, have a closer look at her."

"Look, Dr. Horner. Caley's terribly sensitive about her injuries, but I'm really in no position to speak for her. Why don't you open the door and ask her to step inside?"

"If she's as sensitive as you say, she won't go for it. *You* ask her in. Say we need some help removing the cast. Which happens to be the truth. Why the hell didn't you come in sooner? You're in a lot of pain, aren't you?"

"I'll fetch her." Martin stood up, opened the door, and said, "Caley, would you come in here for a moment? It appears we're going to require a third set of hands getting this muck off." He held up his left hand, and smiled.

Abandoning the magazine, she got to her feet and entered the inner office.

"Actually," Martin said, "Dr. Horner wanted to have a look at you. Would you consent to that?"

"Why?"

"I expect," Martin smiled first at her and then at the doctor, "he simply wants to study another surgeon's work. Isn't that correct, Doctor?"

Horner nodded. Through suspicious eyes, Caley regarded the man. He seemed all right, but still. "Aren't you supposed to be taking care of his hand?" she asked Horner.

"I'm going to. May I?" He came around from behind the desk and, to her consternation, dropped to his knees in front of her and put both his hands on her face, tilting it this way and that. His hands, like those of the doctor in Minneapolis in the emergency room, had a profound impact on her. Large and strong and scrupulously clean, they were respectfully gentle. He looked at her nose from every possible angle, examined its interior with a light, stroked her facial skin, then sat back on his haunches, took a deep breath and said, "I can probably give you a play-by-play rundown. First, they wired the bones and used a split-skin graft. That got infected and they had to do a debridement. Then they did a temporary hip graft over the granulation tissue. After that, they did the first forehead flap. It didn't take and they had to remove it. Finally, they did a second forehead flap, and replaced some of the split-skin grafts with full-thickness grafts. And at that point, you called it quits." He paused, took a breath, then said, "I can fix that!"

"Oh, no!" she protested, shaking her head vigorously. "No! I'm not ready for any more surgery. Please, just take care of him, and don't tell me about the miracles you can do for me."

Martin, astonished by the doctor's recitation, followed their exchange with great interest.

In his seat again behind the desk, the doctor studied Caley thoughtfully. "It would be relatively simple," he said. "We'd insert bone taken from the iliac crest to create a strut for the dorsum and nasal strut. And there's enough good skin behind your left ear to replace that last split-skin graft on your forehead. Think about it. Here's my card. If you change your mind, call me at any time."

She refused to accept the card. Martin slipped it into his pocket and touched her reassuringly on the arm before propping his injured hand on the edge of the desk, saying, "Shall we get on with it?"

"I'm not going to attempt to influence you, but could you answer me two things? One, was that astonishing recitation of surgical wonders accurate? And two, why are you so adamant?"

"Why am I still here? I promised myself I'd leave once I'd taken you to get your hand looked after."

"Explain it to me," he insisted. "I only wish to understand. Tell me why, and I'll never raise the subject again."

"Oh, Jesus!" she sighed. "Haven't you had enough pain for one day? How's your hand? D'you need one of your painkillers?"

"It feels far better than it did. He did a jolly good job."

"Don't you try to sell him to me!" she warned.

"Not at all. He *did* do a fine job. There's nothing like the pain there was before. Is it that you're frightened? Is that it?"

"You're damned right I am! So would you be if you'd already been on that table five or six times."

"Fair enough. That's a perfectly reasonable explanation. We'll consider the subject closed. What sort of food shall I ring for?"

"I'm not hungry. What's that?" She pointed at a carton by the window.

"My post."

"Your what?"

"Letters, bills, correspondence."

"You're joking!" She got up from the floor and walked over to lift the carton's flaps. "Jesus Christ! You're not joking. These haven't even been opened. How come they haven't cut off your electricity and your phone?"

"The bank pays the utility bills."

"Boy! I don't believe this!" She sat down on the floor and began pulling things out of the box. "What's this? It looks like a check."

"It probably is. Among other things, I have a trust income."

"You don't need a nanny," she said, sifting through letters. "You need a keeper."

"The job's open."

"Shit!" She looked over at him and began to smile. "Now you've really got me hooked." At once absorbed in the task, she began sorting the envelopes. "Look at this stuff! Here's another check, and this looks like one, too."

He stretched out on the floor, and watched her work. "The light's very good on your hair," he said. "Very good." He made himself comfortable and studied her, mentally sketching the appealing bow of spine and the commendable curve of buttocks.

All that work waiting to be done was only half the hook. The other half was when, after they'd eaten and had climbed the stairs together, she continued on her way to the third floor, and heard him call up the stairwell, "Have a good sleep. And God bless." She just knew he'd said those same words, nightly, to his little boys. And now the mantle of his blessing had come to rest upon her.

Chapter 24

"PLEASE DON'T ASK me to do this," she begged. "If I start helping you pick out furniture, deciding on what kind of dishes you'd like, and cutlery and the rest of it, I'll feel involved. I'll feel that part of me's invested in this and then, when it's time for me to go, it'll be terrible."

"But there's no need for you to go anywhere. How's your taste? Think you've got an eye for furnishings?"

"Look, your paperwork's in order. I've answered all the letters, so you can call the rental place and get them to pick up the typewriter. The bank's happy; your agent's happy; your books are up to date. You don't need me hanging around. I mean, what'm I supposed to do, sit here every day and watch your hand mend?"

"We've done none of the things I promised you. The only worthwhile thing I've done is show you how to run film through the developing process. I haven't shown you the city, but for two or three local restaurants. And where, might I ask, are you in such an all-fired fucking hurry to get to?"

"Wh— Well . . . I don't know." She spluttered to a stop. "I've just stayed too long. It's already been over a month. If I don't go soon, I'll miss the best time of the year for traveling, and I've got to be settled before the winter comes."

"Settle *here* and stop being such a twit! Now fetch your handbag and keys and we'll go buy furniture. It's time."

She refused to budge, and stood groping for words that would free her.

"What now?" he asked, turning from the door.

"You defeat me."

"It isn't a bloody battle. At least not in *my* mind. *Your* mind is something else altogether." He opened the front door. "It's a blissful day. Come, we'll walk." He started down the steps, positive she'd follow. He heard the front door close and then the sound of her footsteps, and he waited for her to catch up. "We'll go over to Yonge and down to College Park. I haven't yet looked in De Boer's. You'll like the shops there."

"Who was the guy on the telephone this morning?" she asked, taking in the opulent houses lining the street.

"Oh, Mick. He's a writer friend. You'll like him. He's coming round tonight; the three of us are going out to dinner."

"What's he going to make of all this?"

"Make of what? I've explained to him I've a friend visiting from America. That didn't appear to strike him as surpassingly strange. People visit one another all the time, so I'm given to understand."

"Are all these private homes?" she asked, admiring a gray-stone, low-slung house on the corner of Cluny Drive.

"I honestly don't know. I expect the majority are, but quite a number are rooming houses. If you like, we'll go a walk this afternoon and I'll show you round Rosedale. It's quite lovely, if you don't mind rather tatty renovations here and there."

"Do you usually drive that thing in the garage?"

"That 'thing' is a perfectly good Jaguar. And yes, I usually drive it."

"And what's in all those crates in your studio?"

"Paintings I did last year in England."

"Oh! How come they're still in their boxes?"

"I haven't the heart to look at them."

"Sorry."

"You needn't be. You see, I have my prickly aspects too."

"Listen! We're driving each other up the wall. What's the sense of this?"

"I'm going to give you an answer you won't like."

"I have trouble with most of your answers anyway," she said.

"Right! Well, the sense of this is precisely what it was to begin with: I like you very much. You seem to have enormous difficulty accepting that. It's as if because you've had an unfortunate accident you think it's rendered you unlikable. You suspect me of having ulterior motives, which I categorically do not have, and you suspect me of possibly, just possibly, being a secret ax murderer, which, again, I am not. Answer me a question, will you? Do you think of yourself as being what you look like, or is the sum of your many parts the person you believe yourself to be?"

"You're sounding a lot like Stan now," she said warily.

"Be that as it may. Which is correct?"

"Of course I'm not what I look like."

"You say that, yet you behave as if the reverse were true. During the past four weeks, you've been busy as a little bee, working your trusty heart out, setting my affairs in order. Now, the minute the work's ended, you no longer have any reason to believe you should stay. Well, my dear, whether you choose to accept it or not, I am in no way bothered by any aspect of you. I also think I've a fairly good grip on why you're so accursedly angry." He took hold of her arm and pulled her to a stop. "Could you do something for me? Could you go back to being the way you were in Quebec, when we had such fun? You're testing me, and have been since we arrived back. I was very lonely before you came to stay. I'm not lonely with you. Give us a hug, and let's be friends again." He put his arms around her, then freed one hand to cup her chin. Smiling, he coaxed, "Let's have a smile now."

"God! You make me nervous."

"Why?"

"Because I don't know what you want." It was true. All the time she'd spent closeted with him in the darkroom, she'd been expecting something to happen. Even his slightest move caused her to tense in mixed apprehension and desire. She kept telling herself she was grateful he made no move toward her, yet it didn't seem entirely right. "I really don't know what you want," she told him.

"Well, good. Neither do I. Come on." He tugged at her hand to get her walking again. "Premeditation's not all it's cracked up to be. Wouldn't you agree?"

"It depends," she said, still in shock from his having dared to embrace her in the street.

"What on?"

"On whether you're one of the average, everyday type of people."

"Which neither of us is. So, therefore, you agree with my thinking on the matter."

"I suppose so." She wet her lips, then said, "I do agree with you . . . on practically everything. But, Martin, if I just give in, if I quietly go along with everything you propose, it makes me something. I don't know what. I have a hunch there's a name for people like that."

"What it makes you is trusting, and for any number of reasons, to trust me just now is something you find almost impossible."

"That's right."

"So for the present, we'll leave it be, shall we, and see to first things first."

"Wait a minute!" she said, hesitating. "I mean, how . . . Damn it!"

"You do like shopping, don't you?"

"Are you going to make one of your little piggy remarks?"

"Heaven forfend! Do you?"

"Well, yes."

"Then, come along." His hand applied a brief pressure to hers.

He held her hand as they walked in silence and noted again, as he did each time, the differing identities of hands he'd held in his lifetime. There hadn't been all that many: the girl he'd dated briefly before meeting Marian, Marian herself, his sons, and Caley. He might have been a blind man for all the significance each hand had. Caley's now was slim and anxious, tentative. Marian had disliked public hand-holding and only rarely, almost absentmindedly, had she allowed him to make this particular contact. Her hand had been long-bodied and exceedingly soft, the fingers lacking suppleness. The boys had had round, moist little hands, usually grimy; they'd clung to him reliantly and he'd always wrapped his own, far larger hand around those of his sons with a kind of investigative wonder, constantly pressing with his thumb and fingers the yielding, almost primal trust of their grip.

He had noticed Caley's dexterity, the flexible sturdiness of her pointed fingers, the strength of her thumbs, the sinewy tension in her wrists and forearms. She was a strong, capable woman: it showed in her hands. She was rather shy, yet refreshingly forthright, and that, too, was revealed by the cautious way she entrusted her hand into his. Had it been possible for hands to communicate, he'd have had no difficulty whatsoever in convincing her of his honorable intentions. But hands were insufficient. More was required. People needed words, endlessly, and shows of approval. He wished life were less complex, that less were required to prove oneself. Yet when, ever, had any of it been simple? He'd pursued Marian for months, hounding her with his telephone calls and witty greeting cards and florists' deliveries. He'd opened his features and put on display all that he believed was the best of himself. He'd had to track Marian with all the dedication of an archeologist in search of a lost civilization. This was not so very different. Perhaps one could never be exempt from the need of others to have their faith rewarded. There were times when all need felt too demanding, even one's own. But he couldn't stop. Perhaps leaving off, losing interest, represented some sort of ultimate surrender. It might have been why the elderly so often seemed content to sit on park benches and do nothing more than observe the world as it whirled past them. How frightful, he thought, to grow old, to become detached, to lose one's curiosity. The very notion of finding himself nothing more than a sidelines observer of life reinforced his determination to remain involved. He gave Caley's hand a gentle squeeze and was pleased by her brief, startled glance at him.

"I'm not sure about meeting your friend," she confided to him in the furniture showroom while the salesman was writing up the order for two midnight-blue velvet, eight-foot-long parsons sofas and a square, slab-glass coffee table, as well as two brass standing lamps with right-angled necks, all of which she'd selected.

"Don't be nervous. Mick's a good man, a bit of a rough diamond. He likes his beer, and he's fond of telling the odd off-color joke, but he's not someone who judges people without taking the time to know them." Was that true? he wondered. Was it possible he was setting Caley up to be judged?

Perhaps he should've given Mick some advance warning, but that wouldn't have been fair either to Mick or to her. Seeking to bolster her confidence, he ran his hand over her hair and smiled. "Pick out something for the kitchen," he invited. "You've done brilliantly so far."

"I've never been allowed to go crazy with someone else's money. It could become addictive."

"You've got your work cut out for you. There's an entire kitchen to rig out, not to mention the dining area."

"We should go to the supermarket," she said, hearing in her voice the echo of these same words uttered a hundred times before to another man. Domesticity was creeping through her bloodstream like a cat stalking a field mouse. "This is nice," she said of a round white pedestal table.

"We'll have this kitchen set, too," Martin told the salesman.

"Are you humoring me, or do you actually like all this stuff?"

"Darling Caley, I might humor you to a point, but I promise you if your taste was appalling I certainly wouldn't indulge you to where I'd actually have to live with the stuff. No, no. The sofas are smashing, the table's perfect, the brass will add a bit of warmth, and white for the kitchen is precisely the right choice. We're in complete agreement. Even if you and Mick don't hit it off for some reason, that's the sort of thing that happens, isn't it? I mean, one can't expect to establish perfect harmony with everyone one meets."

"This is different."

"Why?"

"Because he's your close friend."

"Some sort of female logic there I fail to understand."

"Don't go piggy on me," she warned, having fallen into using a number of his euphemisms; this one was a particular favorite. "It has nothing to do with 'female logic.' You know damned well what it has to do with. Your friend's probably going to think something's going on between us. Otherwise, why would I be there, staying in your house?"

"Frankly, I don't very much care what he thinks. I don't know why you do. And what if something were going on? We're neither of us children."

"I'm middle-class. I care about appearances. And you don't *have* to care, Martin. The way I see it, you don't have a hell of a lot to lose."

"And you do?"

"Just a few more pieces of the dream, that's all."

He paused in writing out a check to look up at her. "I'm sorry," he said. "Shall I ring up and tell him not to come round? It was never my intention to compromise you in any fashion."

"No. You were looking forward to seeing him. I could tell."

"True. But we can't have you upset."

Oh, God! she thought. How your wife must have loved you! "No," she said more firmly. "I don't have the right to mess up your friendships."

He finished writing the check, distractedly linked arms with her to lead her out of the store, then stopped just outside to say, "What an extraordinary sense of priorities you have! Now and then, you make me sad, Caley, because you fail to see the importance of what's immediate, and tend to look only at the periphery. Yes, Mick's my friend. But so are you. And if I were forced to choose between you, I'm afraid I'd have to choose you, because I'm able to talk to you as I've never been able to talk to him—at least not without feeling hideously self-conscious. What distresses me is how much time you seem to require in order to determine whether or not someone's valuable to you."

"I don't happen to be as impulsive as you are," she defended herself.

"I'm not always so impulsive as you care to think. Actually, it's only rarely. In fact, *you* are the embodiment of one of my very rare impulses, and I don't know how to make you aware of that." He hailed a taxi, held open the door, and climbed in after her. He gave the driver the name of a restaurant, then sat back to look at her. "What is occurring now is an impulse. We're going out to lunch."

She stared blankly at him, and he gauged the depths of her hazel eyes, then studied her mouth, a current of guilt galvanizing his system as he realized that he wanted to make love to her. Dismayed, he turned to look out the window, trying to measure the concussive force of this realization. He'd gone along thinking of this woman solely in terms of friendship. He'd been unutterably stupid, first because he'd actively denied that he was still a relatively young man—his family's death had started him thinking of himself as elderly—and, second, because her misgivings had, all along, been based on something so obvious he couldn't believe he'd done so good a job in skirting it.

For more than a month the two of them had been living in the same house. At night, he lay in bed and listened to her movements overhead, soothed by the sounds. She had to have been anticipating all along that moment when he'd give some sexual signal. Now he felt not only stupid but even more guilty. He wanted to touch her, and was stricken by the implications of this betrayal of Marian. He had no idea what to do, none. He'd been thinking only of himself, and it was unforgivable.

"What's the matter?" she asked. "Are you all right? Is your hand hurting again?"

He looked again at her, and it was there; he could see it. She was gentle, and caring; she cared for him. He remembered Marian accusing him of being too damnably British. It was all true. He could talk; he could speak in platitudes, the language of clichés, but when it came to a truthful discussion of feelings, he continued to be the failure he'd always been. And not only a failure, but a guilt-ridden one, at that.

"I've changed my mind," he said abruptly. He gave the driver the Rosedale address. "I'm sorry," he told her. "Suddenly, I'm not in the mood for another restaurant."

"That's okay. I can drive up to the market and buy something for us to eat at home."

He couldn't stop staring at her, seeing patterns evolving. She'd grow furious with him, but the moment anything became a practical concern, she immediately offered help.

"I'm sorry," he apologized again, bewilderingly.

"It's all right," she said. "Really."

He went at once to the studio over the garage. Confused, she stood in the driveway until the door closed after him, then she connected Clarabelle's battery cables, checked to be sure she had enough cash, and drove to the market on Summerhill.

As usual, the street was crowded with cars, and she had to park almost at the bus stop and walk back. Also, as usual, one of the market staff insisted on carrying the groceries to the car. Her tip was refused; the young man smiled and went whistling on his way back to the store.

She fixed some sandwiches and waited for Martin to return from the studio. After an hour, deciding he must be working, she carried a sandwich and the coffeepot out the kitchen door to the studio.

He'd positioned a large sketching block on the easel and was agitatedly pacing the length of the studio.

"I brought you something to eat," she said, a little cowed by this new aspect of him. "I'll leave it on the table for you."

"Pose for me!" He halted seven or eight feet from her. "Would you?"

"Pose? What . . . ? I . . . What?"

"Pose for me," he repeated in a softer tone.

"Where? How?"

"There." He pointed at the window beyond the easel. "Just there, looking out."

"Not my face," she whispered.

"Just the hint of a profile. You can put your clothes on the hook so they won't get soiled."

"My clothes?" She looked down at herself, then began shaking her head. "I couldn't. No, I really couldn't."

He was already at the easel, picking up pencils one after another to examine their points. "It's all right, Caley. You really could, if you think about it."

The sun lay between them like a wall, behind which he was an indistinct figure in a white shirt and blue jeans. The heat of humiliation rose upward through her body as she again looked at herself, and then over at him. Something was at stake here, something monumental, and she felt stupefied, mentally frozen by her inability to decode the significance of the moment. She covered her mouth with her hand and tried to slow her breathing, her eyes searching through the light for a clearer view of his features. He'd told her he hadn't worked properly in more than a year, had told her the sketches he'd so far done were nothing more than physical exercises to reestablish his prior skills. He was proposing to work now, and choosing her as his model. How would he depict her? Would he show her, with his artist's eyes, as a flawed vision everyone might share? Or would he simply blur her definition so that what materialized on the page could be any woman? Would she, finally, be offered the ultimate, true view of herself? This might mean the end of her sojourn here. In the act of baring herself to his eyes the wall of light might spread to absorb her completely, leaving behind only a faint outline. Her hands all at once uncoordinated, she fumbled with the buttons of her cotton dress. There was, she thought, really very little substance to the armor people donned daily to cloak their nakedness: a few buttons holding closed a garment that weighed mere ounces, a skimpy fabrication of straps and bands, and a pair of pathetically chaste cotton underpants. She stepped away from the small heap of clothes and stood by the window with her back to the room, overcome by the feeling that this couldn't possibly be real; her life couldn't have come to this —naked and afraid in the terrible light.

"Turn slightly more toward me." His disembodied voice floated over the wall to her, and she obeyed unseeingly. "Lovely. That's lovely."

Above the noise of her colliding thoughts, she heard the sussurating strokes of his pencil on the paper, and pinioned herself to those sounds. They authenticated what was happening here. Gradually, all other sounds abated and she tracked his pencil's passage, aware only from afar of his breathing, and her own.

Golden in the window's glow, she was the personification of vulnerability. He located it in the self-protective incurve of her shoulders, the slight bend of one knee, the delicate uptilt of a profiled breast. The sun drew fire from her hair; she appeared encased in slow flames. Turned entirely inward, his eyes spanned the gap between them; everything was forgotten. She was his alone; even her scent was a part of the image and, therefore, his. There was a faint down on her arms, golden, too, and aflame. Trapped within the vacuum of his own creating, every particle of him strived toward the image. Hastily, he made color notes on the perimeters of the page before returning again and again to the amassing details.

"Lovely," he whispered, snatching up a fresh pencil.

"That's lovely." Leaf-patterned glass, a mosaic; and poised before the translucence, this fine-boned woman with such a sweetness and poignancy in the attitude of her barely tilted head; forehead, cheek, and chin burnished by the all-forgiving light; light with no memory, light with its own contingency of time, light renewable. "Jesus!" He spoke in automatic response to the gift of translation contained within him, awesome in its refusal to die or be deterred.

At last, his energy drained by the massive effort, he slowly put down the pencil and moved through the fire to stand gazing close-to at the flawless length of her spine. She turned, having sensed rather than heard his approach, her eyes downcast, and became dizzied by the noisy inrushing of thoughts. Don't pity me, she begged silently.

"It's all right," he crooned, his arms encircling her; clasping her to his chest, he drank down her fragrance. "It's all right." Much as he longed for it, he could do no more than revel mutely in her presence. He couldn't free himself, couldn't absorb her into his system as he'd have liked.

The volume within her skull diminished once more with the understanding of her sudden safety. He held her, his cheek resting against her hair, and she subsided, steadying as if, for a very long time, she'd been racing, beating her way past limitless obstacles, headlong into a gale that had blown past.

After a time, they simply disengaged. She collected her dress and, holding it closed with one hand, carrying her undergarments in the other, went quietly from the studio. Dazed, she entered the house, went through to the stairs and on up to her bedroom on the third floor. Allowing everything to fall from her hands, she shed the dress and slipped beneath the bedclothes, succumbing at once to sleep.

Martin stood and stared at the block on the easel, his body feeling dented, as if she'd left upon him an actual physical impression. There were hollows now where her warmth had been. The bare skin of his hands and forearms and throat felt faintly singed, stinging.

Chapter 25

CALEY KEPT WAITING for the overweight Irishman to slip up and display some overt reaction to her. He didn't. Throughout the evening both he and Martin made a polite point of including her in the conversation, and smiled often at her. Mick's warmth and friendliness were genuine. She found she could read the sensitivity in his features, just as she'd been able to know what Ron was thinking by keeping close watch on his face. Her vigilance unrewarded, she relaxed and sat back to enjoy the constant badinage between the two men.

"Working on a new sexual space epic?" Martin was asking.

"Mind how you go, Maddox! I'm about to replace Arthur C. Clarke as the star in the college underground. Even as we speak, my advances are climbing ever higher. One day soon, I'll arrive at six-figure heaven and then, by God, you'll regret having spoken so slightingly of my life's work. This man," he addressed Caley, "has no bloody judgmental skills when it comes to the written word. Like all paint-smearers, books are beyond him. Ask him what he's read lately, I dare you! He won't be able to answer because he hasn't read anything with binding and covers in years."

"That is an utterly false accusation!" Martin stated. "I happen to have read quite a good deal."

"Come on, now," Mick challenged. "Name us some titles, then."

"I prefer mysteries," Martin said, coolly unflappable. "In the course of my travels through the city, I happened, some time back, to come across a splendid little mystery shop up on Bayview. I've all but depleted the entire stock of the Sleuth of Baker Street.''

"I'm waiting for a title, my old darling." Mick drummed his fingers on the cloth-covered tabletop.

"I'll go you one better. I'll recite you authors."

"Oh, do!" Mick smiled eagerly at Caley, relishing the game.

"Very well. I've read the entire works of Simon Brett, Jonathan Valin, Peter Turnbull, Michael Lewin, Lawrence Block, Stephen Greenleaf, Jonathan Gash, P. D. James, Emma Page, and a local chap who's very good, Howard Engel. For the most part, I prefer the Americans. Their detectives are less airy-fairy than the frothy types who prance through English drawing rooms, taking the time to observe all the social amenities. There are many more, but I have no wish to bore you with this recitation. Of course, I've also read the collected works of one Michael McEllimore. A load of old rubbish, but one must support one's friends."

"Where's the proof?" Mick pressed. "What've you done with the books?"

"Don't be tiresome! When I've finished a batch, I bundle them up and take them down to the Salvation Army hostel."

"Hmmm." Mick sat back, temporarily bested. "What do you read?" he asked Caley.

Tactfully, she said, "I'd like to try some of yours."

"Ah! Well, I'll see to it you have a complete set."

"You won't like them," Martin advised. "They're the ravings of a middle-aged, jaded Irishman; filled with sordid sexual fantasies, awash in violence and gore. Every other page is besmirched with gobbets of bloodied entrails."

"You *have* read them!" Mick sang happily. "I shouldn't talk, though, if I were you. I don't see there's all that much difference between my words and the stifled eroticism in the paintings of one crazed Brit."

"Stifled eroticism," Martin repeated appreciatively. "You're getting better, Mick. That has quite a nice ring to it. Total nonsense, of course, but a nice ring nonetheless."

"How can you bear to stay in the same house with this

man?'' Mick asked Caley mournfully. "He'll corrupt your judgment."

"It was already corrupted, long before I got here."

"Ah! I like that. A woman with a shadowy past. Where do you come from, anyway?"

"Connecticut."

"And how, if I may be so bold as to ask, did you come to make the acquaintance of this anthropomorphic Englishman?"

"We met in Quebec City."

"So *that's* why you abandoned me!" Mick rounded on Martin.

"Absolutely! She's far more interesting than you are," Martin said easily. "She's tidier; she doesn't leave her empties flung about the place; and she doesn't snore. She also has superb taste. She's been helping me select furniture for the house."

"He's using you to decorate that bogus shrine?"

Martin shot him a cautionary glance, and Mick at once regretted his words. Caley, noting the interchange, decided to swing right past it. "It's fun," she said. "I'm going to clean out the conservatory this week and get some new plants. Martin's got people coming to wash all the windows."

"Are you a traveling interior designer?" Mick asked.

"My services were volunteered for me." She looked over to see Martin smiling.

"I'm mystified! I'm also awash in brew. Excuse me." Mick pushed away from the table to go to the men's room.

"There was no need to be nervous, was there?" Martin asked.

"The two of you put on quite a show. Do you always go at each other this way?"

"Always. Even when we're quite miserable, we have to have a go. How was your meal?"

"Terrific. How was yours?"

"Terrific," he mimicked her accent, then grinned as she made a disapproving face. "Are you having a good time?"

"Yes, I am. Did you really abandon him in Quebec?"

"Not actually. He was planning to leave that same afternoon. I'd thought I might spend another week, but then, as you know, the weather turned.'' He'd caught sight of her and hurried in pursuit, and now she lived in his house, subtly altering everything she saw and touched.

Women really were extraordinary, he thought, smiling at her. They had, the majority of them, a degree of artistry he, with all his training, might never attain. They were the artists of the domestic environment, forever twitching shades into place or repositioning pots of flowers; they busied themselves with the making of beds and the adorning of the walls that contained them. They placed a ceramic pot here, or an ashtray there; they worried over details only they would notice. Even the arranging of crockery and foodstuffs in kitchen cabinets captivated them. Unlike Marian, Caley had an intuitive feel for color and symmetry, and this delighted him. He refused to stand the two women side by side in his mind and tick off the points in their favor. Rather, he preferred to concentrate on this one woman, here in the present, who daily was revealing herself to be gifted with a fine sense of physical proportions. The items she had selected for the house were, in truth, those very ones he'd have chosen. He'd recognized from the outset that she had an instinctive flair for simplicity, both in form and color. She would, he knew, furnish the ground floor entirely to his liking, and watching her pause and deliberate in the furniture showroom had heightened his fondness for her. She wasn't one of those women incapable of making a decision without anguished deliberation and extensive comparison shopping. She knew what was right and chose accordingly. What struck him as both a little sad and also most optimistic was her willingness to rise to a given challenge rather than protesting straightaway that the challenge was beyond her capabilities. She was in the process of learning more of her capabilities, and he was in the privileged position of being able to witness her progress. He felt about her, at that moment, as if he'd unwittingly opened a door onto a new dimension, one heretofore only guessed at.

''Are you happy, now that you're starting to paint again?''

''It frightens more than pleases me.''

''What does?'' Mick asked, returning.

''Beginning to paint again.''

"Oh, right! I feel the same way every time I start a new book. All those threatening white pages to be filled. And what if it's gone, what if there's nothing left to say? It's frightening, all right. *Have* you started painting again, Martin?"

"On the verge," Martin replied. His eyes were on Caley again, and Mick watched, fascinated by the slightly sleepy exchange between these two. He knew all the signs, and felt suddenly too alone, and envious. People in love fed constantly upon the sight of one another, to the exclusion of all and everyone else. The moment he'd seen the two of them, he'd been able to feel the dynamics of their attraction, and he'd been glad for Martin, and sad for himself. He'd treasured those awkwardly intimate conversations they'd had over the winter; they'd been as much of a lifeline for him as for Martin.

"You'll be enchanted to know," Mick announced, unable to stop himself, "that the great May-December romance has come to a tragic end. No more telephone recitations of Esther's young man's exceptional staying power and inventiveness. From what I've been able to deduce, the little bastard's taken up with a wealthier patroness. It would appear that dear, deluded Esther's been doling my hard-earned lolly out to the beknighted little shit, and now that her account's all but depleted, he's gone off."

"Poor Esther," Martin sympathized, then explained to Caley, "Esther is Mick's erstwhile wife. She left him sometime back."

"That's too bad," Caley added her sympathy.

"That's not the lot," Mick went on, deriving comfort from their support. "It seems she's had ample opportunity to consider the error of her ways and she's willing—God give me strength!—to consider coming home."

"And?" Martin prompted.

"I don't want her. Nothing to do with her extracurricular activities, as it were. Hell! It takes the strain off me. No, I've come to enjoy having the house to myself. The minute she moves back there'll be all kinds of rules. Very contrite she is and all, but I don't want her. She was horribly offended when I told her that—nicely, mind. I did a proper amount of hemming and hawing, but I said no."

"How did she take that?" Martin asked, suspecting Mick

was happy at, at last, having the upper hand.

"Went totally fucking crazy! Excuse the language," he apologized to Caley. "Did her nut, called me every name in the book, and swore she'd see me with nothing more than me boxer shorts and briefcase. Even said she'd take my IBM. That did it, needless to say. I said I wasn't quite so stupid as I looked, and hadn't I been the clever one and put a private eye on her who had documented evidence of her fancy fornicating, not to mention the journal my lawyer's been keeping that records how and when she left and sundry other nuggets of pertinent information. Imagine her threatening to take away my machine! Silly cow! Well, she quieted down after that and agreed to let things proceed as they were. Bloody incredible it is to think I lived with that woman all those years!"

"Suited you well enough at the time," Martin said. "And why is it I have the feeling that once you've convinced her the rules in future are to be laid down by you, you'll allow her back?"

"I haven't said that." Mick looked startled.

"But you will, won't you?"

Mick gazed morosely into his beer. "Probably," he admitted. "The last conversation we had wasn't all that bad."

"Do you want her to come back?" Caley asked.

Mick's sad green eyes met hers. "The kids are grown and gone," he explained, "and the house is too big with just me in it. But it's a fine old place and I've no wish to sell it." He looked away. "I'm going round the bend, rattling around there on my own."

"Then why don't you tell her to come back?" she suggested.

Mick shrugged. "There's a point of principle here," he said.

"And what point might that be?" Martin wanted to know.

"The point having to do with coming home and staying home. I don't trust her not to go off again, and I can't spend the rest of me life keeping the door half-open on the off chance Esther might be changing her mind."

"Maybe you should tell her that," Caley said gently.

"I'm thinking on it."

"Come on," Martin said cheerily. "Finish your suds and run us home. It's been a long day."

As they were getting out of Mick's car, Caley said, "When the kitchen furniture's delivered, you'll have to come over for dinner."

"Actual home-cooked food," Mick said. "Wouldn't that be a treat! Ring me the very day."

"Mind how you go, mate," Martin cautioned.

The two of them stood on the sidewalk and watched Mick drive off.

"He's so unhappy," Caley said.

"Not for long. Esther will be back and then he'll be his old self again, complaining endlessly about her, but happy as can be." He checked the time. "It's early. Fancy a walk? We never did get around to it this afternoon."

"Sure."

The air was cooler now than it had been that afternoon. They strolled along South Drive, all sounds muffled beneath the crowded foliage of trees that had likely been there long before anyone thought to construct an enclave for the wealthy of the city. The streets here meandered like country lanes, seemingly directionless; a rabbit's warren of devious byways that came as an agreeable surprise in the heart of a city laid otherwise on a strict grid system. The houses, many of them with deep verandahs and plush expanses of lawn, sat like Victorian dowagers overseeing the foot traffic, their brows darkened and speculative. Between those that had been renovated and those that remained calmly intact were jarringly modern dwellings, upstart youngsters that self-consciously proclaimed their gaudy right to be there, with highly polished outsized brass numbers and coy carriage lamps that cast dim circles of low-wattage illumination on the paths. The front gardens were uniformly well tended, planted with precisely clipped shrubberies and a lavish profusion of flowers.

Looking into ground-floor windows it was possible to see walls of books and discreet lighting, huge houseplants positioned with care to receive the sun's full benefits. There were few people about. The closely flanked dwellings might have been a false-fronted stage set. They passed the odd couple or individual giving their dogs mandatory evening walks, and the Rosedale bus rumbled past them on its way to the Glen Road bridge. The air was rich with the scent of damp grass and night-blooming flowers. Caley breathed deeply, the effects of several glasses of wine combining with the thick fragrance of evening to create in her a powerful sense of well-being. It no longer seemed unusual that Martin should reach for and hold her hand.

"My final appointment with Dr. Horner's for tomorrow afternoon," he said as they were circling back toward the house.

"I really don't want to go with you."

"No. I hadn't expected you would. I'll go on my own."

"You don't need an escort." She felt the need to apologize for not wanting to go, as if she were failing to keep to her half of some tacit bargain.

"Of course not."

"I suppose you think I'm a coward."

"Not at all." He looked confounded. "Why should I think that? You've got ample reason to feel as you do."

"That's right, I do." Why, she wondered, did her defense of herself sound so feeble? "Maybe someday I'll feel differently, but right now, I can't go through any more of it."

"And so you shouldn't."

His ready agreement prompted her to delve even further into her need to justify. "Aside from your hand, which doesn't really count, have you ever had surgery?"

"I never have."

"Did you understand any of what Dr. Horner rattled off in his office that day?"

"I can't say that I did."

"Oh, God!" she sighed. "When I think about it sometimes, I can hardly believe I'm the one who actually went through it all. You know? I mean, there are times when it seems as if it happened to someone else.

"Right after it happened, that same night, it seemed absolutely reasonable that I'd be taken into an operating room and fixed up. I expected it; I wanted it. I thought they'd put me on the table, give me some anesthetic, and when I woke up, every-thing would be back to normal. I was so naive," she lamented. "We're so trusting. You see a doctor and get all respectful because he went to school for years and years and knows all kinds of things you don't, things about bodies and organs and how to repair them if they get smashed up. He knows all this stuff and you don't know dick, so you agree to whatever he suggests. It never occurs to you to ask to have a look at his track record or anything to find out what kind of skills the guy really has."

"We are terribly trusting, aren't we? I must confess I've never given it any thought." He could, too readily, visualize the scene she described, and was overcome anew by sadness for her.

"Well, you should!" she said heatedly.

"But don't you think there are occasions when one has no choice but to trust?"

"Not anymore I don't."

"I wasn't referring necessarily to medical situations."

"I can't ever again look at things the way I used to, because nobody looks at *me* the way they used to. It tends to affect your views, you know, Martin. It's not just a case of self-pity, or anything like that."

"I know that."

"I forget sometimes," she admitted. "I start having a good time, like tonight, and I forget that the sight of me makes people sick. I begin to enjoy myself, and then I look over, and someone across the room is sitting there with her mouth open, staring at me with this horrified expression. And then I re-member, and I'm ashamed because I forgot. I dared to enjoy myself, and I'm not supposed to."

"We're all flawed, my dear." His voice sat gently on the evening air. "I know of no one who's content, either with the way he or she looks or the quality of his or her life. We've all grown up on the same fairy-story fodder; all of us are led to expect to be beautiful and happy. Other people's standards, but we take them as our own. If we don't receive our fair share of beauty and happiness, we're outraged by the injustice. I've thought for a long time now that if we were fed as children a steady diet of the misery and disappointment lying in wait for us, perhaps we'd go off and be happy simply to prove it's possible. Perhaps we'd have a better grasp of what it means to be happy; we'd have the ability to recognize the good and valuable things, and we wouldn't waste so bloody much time fussing over what we don't have.''

"Are you trying to say I'm making too much of a fuss?''

"I'll give you an example, one I hope you'll find inoffensive. If,'' he said, "after the crash, Marian had managed to survive, regardless of her injuries, I'd still have loved her. The face only symbolizes what we love in others; it isn't the actual thing we love. Given the option, any one of us would prefer a living, albeit damaged, person to the loss of that person altogether.''

They had arrived back at the house, and she waited as he got the front door open.

He stood with his finger on the light switch, looking at her in the darkness. "What I said was not meant to imply that I was attempting to make comparisons. Please understand that.''

"I do.''

"The thing of it is,'' he went on, "I'm still grappling with ghosts.'' He placed his hand on her shoulder. Somehow, even knowing she was real, she became more real to him when he could actually touch her. He listened to the soft expulsion of her breath, and wished he could break past the barriers holding him locked to the past. He wanted desperately to push forward into the present, but he wasn't able.

"I'll tell you something,'' she said softly. "I've always felt kind of outside, not really connected. Maybe the accident just pushed me all the way outside.''

"Didn't you feel connected to this Ron?''

"After a while, we got used to each other. We seemed to want the same things. I think we thought we were following the rules, doing it the way it was supposed to be done.''

"And how was that?'' he asked, feeling her shoulder lift slightly under his hand, like a small animal wanting to be petted.

"You know how it is. You live together for a while, and

then, when you've saved up enough to put a down payment on a house, you get married. You both keep working, saving up more money, and when you've got enough for that, you start having kids. It's the same stuff you called fairy-story fodder, except I always thought it was real.''

"You're wrong," he said, low. "That's the part of it that is real.''

"Not anymore, it isn't.''

"You're wrong, Caley. You still want the same things. We all do, Mick included. None of us wants to struggle through life alone. We want someone to be there; we want the raucous kiddies, and the arguments, and the messes to clean up. We need them to give definition to our days and nights.''

"Maybe you do, but I don't.''

"Not true. Simply not true. You care, and you want those things. And for what it's worth, every day I spend with you, I care more for you. You've taken to referring to this fucking horror show of a house as 'home.' You spoke to Mick of having him round for a meal. Whether you admit it or not, you've started putting down roots here.''

"Then I'll pull them up and be gone first thing in the morning.''

"Hush!" He held a finger to her lips. "You'll do nothing of the sort. Tomorrow you'll come to the studio and help me uncrate the paintings.''

Before she could give voice to any argument, he kissed her lightly on the mouth. Her response to this chaste kiss was alarming. Her entire being, body and brain, seemed to have received a massive electric shock that, for a moment or two, deadened all her senses but that of touch. She was, for those few moments, entirely at his disposal. Her flesh, like something with a separate life, would willingly have offered itself to him. He might have fashioned anything of it—a rug with which to warm himself, or some novel decoration he'd keep in the conservatory, anything. It was with a sensation not unlike terror that she realized she was utterly vulnerable to him because the sound of his voice and the shape of his eyes, the edge to his laughter, and the look of his mouth and hands had all become charged with meaning for her. She felt like a fish, snagged by dozens of small hooks he'd cast effortlessly beneath the surface of her skin. She could only dangle, caught.

"When the time comes right," he whispered, "things will sort themselves out."

"Oh, hell!" she whispered, abandoning her defenses. He'd succeeded in returning her to that same dazed state she'd found herself in earlier that day. Drugged by the sound of his voice, cloaked in the protective empathy of darkness, she turned and began to make her way up the stairs.

"Sleep well, and God bless." His voice floated up the stairwell to her.

"You, too," she said thickly. Loss of control had left her with the will only to locate her bed. She craved sleep and, not bothering with the lights, set aside her clothes and lay upon the bed, for a moment watching the curtains lift, billowing on the night-scented air.

Chapter 26

EARLY THE NEXT morning, carrying a cup of coffee, he went out to the studio. He knew Caley wasn't yet awake; he hadn't heard any stirrings above as he'd left his bed and pulled on work clothes. The knowledge that she was still asleep lent a criminal feel to his quiet entry into the room above the garage. The air was stale, and he set the coffee on the work table before opening each of the windows. At once the morning air began to displace the staleness, and he retrieved his coffee and drank it while eyeing the crates leaning in uniform rows against the wall.

He was apprehensive, and thought perhaps he'd been rash inviting Caley to view these portraits, especially when he had no idea what his own reactions to them would be. Now that he thought about it, his apprehensions weren't at all sudden. They'd come upon him last night at the moment when he'd extended his impulsive offer to Caley. He hadn't known he was going to do that; he also hadn't, until now, taken the time to reason through what he had in mind for her. He'd acted all along on instinct, and it seemed now as if he was on the brink of doing them both harm. He felt all at once as if he might start prying open the crates, only to discover inside the fragmented remains of Marian and the boys. He was, for several moments, so violently repelled by this image that he very nearly closed the windows and absconded. He'd tell Caley he'd changed his mind. It was that simple. There were no preordained formalities to be observed here. Neither of them was obliged to do anything they wished not to.

But Marian, he thought, had been gone a long time now, and life in a house with few walls and no Caley nearby seemed as impossible as life without those he'd loved had seemed in the immediate aftermath of the air crash. Time kept on going, and one had to find a way to go with it, had to fashion some new manner of filling the empty hours. He could go on knocking down walls, reducing the house to a shell suitable only for housing devoted recollections. And then what? Were Caley to leave, he'd find himself back where he'd been after returning from Tenerife, with only the prospect of physical labor to keep his wits of a piece.

"Fuck it!" He put down the cup with such force that coffee splashed across the table.

"What's the matter?" Caley asked from the door, her soft voice a jolt to his violent intent.

"If I'm going to do it, I might as well get on with it," he said.

"You don't have to."

His head snapped around and he glowered at her.

"I have the feeling you're doing this because of me in a way, and you don't have to do anything because of me. Half the time now I think I know why I'm here, and the rest of the time I don't know *what* I'm doing here, or who you are. Then," she said, "sometimes, I have the feeling I've never known anyone, or ever will again, as well as I know you."

"It has to be done," he insisted, noticing her feet were bare. She had long, arching insteps and perfectly formed toes.

"No, it doesn't," she disagreed. "I don't think I could do it."

"Ah, but you're not me, are you?"

"Nobody's anybody but the people they are," she said patiently. "We all live on the outside and spend most of our time trying to figure out a way to get inside someone else. I don't think it's possible. I think the most we ever do is rub against the surface."

"This is your educated opinion, is it?"

"Yes, it is." She folded her arms across her chest and leaned against the door. "I don't give a good goddamn whether you agree or not. I happen to know I'm right."

"As it happens," he said, experimentally flexing his fingers around the crowbar, "I tend to agree with you."

"I'm going to make some breakfast. D'you want some?"

He looked over at the paintings, then back at her.

"You could just leave them forever, cover them with a tarpaulin or something, and someday, after you're dead, and they come to sell the house, these paintings will be found and they'll be considered a great discovery: lots more work by the famous Martin Andrew Maddox. After you're dead, it won't matter, will it? D'you want breakfast or not?"

"I'll be along directly." His eyes were again on the crates as he considered her words.

"Fifteen minutes," she said, then turned and went away down the stairs.

Slowly, his hands gave up their hold on the tools and he replaced them on the work table. He went to stand by the wall, as if proximity to the paintings might clarify his thoughts. After he was dead, it wouldn't matter. She was quite right. There was no point to torturing himself, or her, with images from the past. They would remain a thirty-five-year-old woman and two eleven-year-old boys; they would never age or alter, never grow. In his memory, and the paintings, they would live on, captured as they'd been when last he'd seen them. She *was* right. He couldn't possibly sell, or allow these paintings to be shown. The logical thing to do was to leave them as they were. That was indeed the logical thing, but having at last delved into the issue, he knew he would choose the illogical. It was time to study their faces, and to bid them goodbye. Until he did that, he would force them to remain alive within him. And they were dead. They were.

Thirty-five minutes later Caley returned to demand, "Why aren't you down in the kitchen eating? I told you fifteen min—" Her words trailed off as she watched him quickly and efficiently tugging one canvas after another from its protective casing. "I'll go make you a tray." She left quickly, frightened.

When she got back, he was more than halfway through the job. The canvases were stacked in rows, painted sides inward. She put down the tray and lit a cigarette, sitting on the edge of the ratty armchair to wait.

"That's hungry work!" he exclaimed, rising finally to approach the table and attack the now-cold food on the tray. "Delicious! I'm out of the habit of eating breakfast. Do you do this every morning?"

"Only when there's a kitchen with pots and pans and all the rest of it."

"You don't feel it's demeaning to do household chores, it's not in violation of your rights?"

"Demeaning?"

"You know, all that feminist chat having to do with rejecting the kitchen as a place of employment."

"Listen, what's demeaning to me doesn't have anything to do with the things I enjoy. I like cooking. I mean, Jesus, Martin. You've got a kitchen people would kill for, and since I'm the one responsible so far for making it usable, why should I feel demeaned because I want to get in there and cook?"

He wiped the plate clean with a crust of cold toast, drank the last of the coffee, then said, "I am glad you feel that way, because I do like to eat. Well! What do you think? Are you up to this?"

"Are *you*?"

"Who knows? I've found, in the course of my highly eventful life, that the only way to discover whether or not I'm up to something is to go ahead and do the bloody deed."

"What'll you do with them? Afterward, I mean."

"I've decided to cart the lot down to my agent and let him store them until I'm well and truly dead. We'll sign a number of papers I'll have my lawyers prepare, and that'll be the end of it."

"That makes sense."

"You think so?"

"I guess. It's kind of hard for me to give an opinion when I don't really know what we're talking about."

"Let's have a look, then, and we'll both be better informed."

Taking her hand, he led her over to the center of the room, then began, one at a time, to turn the canvases. Once they were all turned, he joined her and, side by side, they examined the works in sober silence. After a time, they separated, taking their time, forming reactions.

What most impressed her was the love with which each

stroke had been applied. Plainly, he had cherished the little boys and their mother. He was indisputably gifted, and very complex emotionally. Examining the many portraits of Marian, she could only wonder, yet again, what on earth she was doing here with this man. His wife had had such warmth and beauty, such an impressive aura of tranquillity, that Caley couldn't begin to imagine how he could ever desire her, Caley, when he'd lived for so long with someone so utterly unlike her. Even nude, Marian had had innate elegance. It showed in the line of her shoulders, in her bearing, in the set of her jaw and the directness of her gaze. And the boys—laughing, wrestling in a garden, climbing a flight of stairs—were so vivid, down to the dirt rimming their fingernails, she couldn't see how Martin could bear to look at them.

The images offered up his humor, his dedication, and painful insights into his hectic emotional life. To think these people lived now only in these portraits was unbearable. She was grief-stricken and intimidated, and stopped to study Martin as he paced the studio, pausing here and there to look more closely at this painting or that, his brows creased.

Once more, she let her eyes sweep the moods and seasons he'd put on display, and once more, she was confounded by the beauty he'd captured and enhanced.

"Well, what do you think?" he asked with abrupt directness. "Were we up to this?"

"They're incredible paintings," she said, hesitant to reveal the full scope of their impact upon her. "Really incredible." She shook her head, close to tears. If she said anything more, she'd begin to cry.

"I'd actually forgotten quite a number of them," he said. "I did that one of the boys in the garden soon after I arrived in England. She left me, you see, and took the boys. I followed after, and we began sorting it all out. We had a rental cottage, and the garden had been allowed to go wild. And that one" —he laughed softly—"I climbed fully dressed into the tub when I'd finished the preliminary sketch. It takes one back."

"I don't understand how you could want me to pose for you when—"

"Don't say a word of it! I know what you're thinking, and you're quite wrong. You shouldn't *think* it! Comparisons are most assuredly odious, and you're not to attempt to find parallels. I could never replace them. It would be madness to try. They belong to another time, and you have to do with the present. I saw you in Quebec, and I followed you, without stopping to question why. I had any number of reasons, but none of them had to do with Marian, or Harry and Ian. They had to do with me alone."

"We don't have one single thing in common."

"Rubbish! We have *everything* in common. I mean to say," he smiled enticingly, "we've both managed to keep on despite the things that have happened. There's merely the most obvious, of course. I like to think that even at my drunken worst, I never lost my dignity. Neither have you, I'll wager, not even working as a maid in some grotty motel. Common ground has to do with the end product, not the origins. I find it shocking that you were abandoned as an infant, but, my dear, that knowledge has quite likely shaped the woman you've grown to be. I doubt that had you led a cosseted life, you'd have been able to cope as well as you have. I admire your courage in facing the world, and, as I've already said a dozen or more times, your defiance. I *very* much admire your defiance. I, too, have been known to display a bit of it from time to time. It was important that you see these paintings, these people, perhaps to help both of us understand what we do have in common."

"That's such bullshit! If I bought that, next thing anybody knew I'd be buying swampland in Florida from some guy with dandruff wearing a white polyester leisure suit. Jesus, Martin! Maybe we have something in common, but all I feel seeing these paintings is sad. You had a beautiful wife and two darling little boys. Why shouldn't you want to look at them, if that's what you feel like doing? Sometimes you start pontificating and I'd like to put my fist through your face. And don't go admiring my 'courage' and 'defiance' because I was on my way to kill myself when I met you. For chrissake! Courage and defiance," she scoffed. "It's all in your head. I'm a fucking coward, not some kind of saint. I still can't figure out why a man with your looks and money and background and talent and all the rest of it would want to hang out with a freak. And don't give me that shit about not talking about myself that way, because that's exactly what I am. I don't have any illusions. I don't have all my marbles, either, else I wouldn't be here, going into goddamned trances every time you hold my hand, or talk me into taking my clothes off. Shit! What's so funny?'' He was laughing, and it defused her anger and her argument.

"I am," he chuckled. "You are. My looks and money, et cetera. That's bloody marvelous! What's outside only counts for all those feckless fuckers who like to gape at oddities. What all this means, as you so aptly put it, is nothing more than the fact that I did, indeed, want to see them again. And I wanted you to, as well. Perhaps I was seeking your sympathy. Who knows, and does it really matter?"

"Sure it matters. Don't be an asshole, Maddox. You'd really be whacko if you could write them off without a backward glance. Boy, you're starting to make me mad."

"We don't want to do that."

As often happened, she was momentarily so captivated by the sound of his voice and by his energy that she failed to hear what he was saying. It was dangerous, she reminded herself, being lulled yet again, being drawn onto that other plane by his magnetism. He had the ability to make her forget herself, and it was only when alone, out of his range, that she regained her objectivity. In his presence, within hearing and seeing and touching distance, all her practical considerations seemed like so much smoke, readily cleared from the air with the wave of an impatient hand. His voice thrummed in her ears, a contiguous lure, and she found herself gazing at the occupants of his former life, and felt inadequate. Even if she hadn't been involved in an accident, she'd have felt unequal to this situation. There had been nothing in her life to prepare her for someone like Martin.

"You're not listening to me!" he accused.

"I was just thinking."

"What of?"

"That I've never known anybody like you."

"A question?"

"Sure."

"Do you feel familiar to yourself?"

"Not right now, no."

"Neither do I. Do you suppose that we go into transition,

that different parts of ourselves take command when circumstances shift? What I mean to say is, I've altered tremendously in the last year or so. Have you, as well?"

"A lot."

"And do you feel you've altered since we met?"

"Yes."

"So do I. Well, since we're no longer, either of us, the same people we were, it would appear we're free to continue on being the people we've become."

"There are times," she said, "when some of the things you say are so convoluted, I get a headache trying to follow you."

"I'm simply saying there's no reason why we shouldn't keep on together. Eventually, we're bound to work something out."

"They phoned to say the kitchen stuff's going to be delivered this afternoon."

"Good. I take it you don't wish to pursue this conversation."

"They offered me a false nose to wear, you know, after operation number three. It was amazing: like a Groucho kit minus the mustache."

"What, you mean a pair of glasses with a fake nose attached?"

"Right."

"How grotesque! Naturally, you refused."

"Naturally. I'm glad you feel the same way about it." She picked up the tray and carried it to the door. "There *are* reasons for the things I do."

"Of course there are. Would you be agreeable to posing again this afternoon when I return from my visit to the doctor?"

"Sure. I guess so."

"If you're concerned, I'll be happy to show you the sketch before I start in oils."

"No, I trust you."

"I'm glad you do. I trust you, too."

"You should. I'm eminently trustworthy."

"Why? Because you're a woman?"

"That, and because what I haven't earned doesn't interest me."

She went off and he stood with his head to one side, thinking.

She was waiting for him in the studio, and he knew at once she'd arrived at a breakthrough point of trust. Without a word, she handed him the file, then walked to the far end of the studio to stand looking out the window.

He sat on the edge of the old armchair guessing that he felt now as she was bound to have felt when he'd uncrated the paintings. They were exchanging artifacts, and the significance wasn't lost on him. He lifted open the folder and the headline raged at him from the yellowed, plastic-enclosed page: "INFANT ABANDONED AT COLUMBIA."

He read each page, his anger and indignation mounting until, arriving at the end, he jumped up, declaring, "There's only one thing for it!"

"What?" she asked, backlit before the window.

"Let's burn the fucking thing!"

"Really?"

"Absolutely! I suggest we do it this very moment."

"All right. Where?"

"Come!" He extended his hand. "We'll go down to the garden and make a proper ceremony of consigning this lot" —he flapped the folder in the air—"to the rubbish."

He took the metal lid from one of the trashcans and set it down on the grass, then invited her to help remove all the clippings from their protective coverings. He dropped a match onto the small mound of crumpled, brittle pages, and both watched as the paper ignited with a whoosh of heat and flames. In seconds, only white ash and the plastic coverings remained.

"These," he said, snatching up the pieces of plastic, "go into the trash, and that's the end of it."

"I feel really strange," she said, seeing the wind scatter the ashes over the weedy garden, "as if . . . I don't know."

His hand closed on her arm. "Listen to me," he said urgently. "I deplore all that sort of thing, people who abuse or abandon their children. It incenses me, and not because I've lost the children I had, but because on the ultimate scale of importance, it's the children who matter most. We are going to create for you a suitably appropriate background. And while we're about it, we'll work up one for me, too. They were wrong to tell you, dead wrong. Perhaps it was an act of conscience, but God save me from all the well-meaning people who feel it so necessary to vent themselves on the innocent. You," he announced momentously, "can be *my* infant, and I, in turn, shall be yours. We, neither of us, are parentless little fuckers. I won't have it! Now," he brushed his hands clean, "we've got work to do."

She remained unmoving, thinking of how Ron had reacted to the clippings, of how he'd kept his distance from them as if fearful their contents might be corrupting.

"Would you burn me, too, if I displeased you?" she asked.

"No," he stated firmly. "I would enshroud you in plastic and keep you on file for future reference. You, unlike that scabrous prose, are worth keeping. Do you think you'd like upper-class origins? I have in mind quite a fabulous scenario having to do with a certain great beauty, much abused by her worthless husband, who mothered a fine, frail child, and instilled in her great gifts which would only be revealed every five years throughout the course of her life. That way, you see, she became more gifted with time."

"What about the father?" she asked as they climbed the stairs. "Did he reform?"

"Oh, quite so! Once he came to see how very special his child was, he gave up all his bad habits—except, perhaps, for his addiction to snuff—and evolved into a thoroughly devoted husband and father."

"That's not bad," she said consideringly. "I'll give it a five point nine with the Russian judge abstaining."

He laughed loudly and patted the top of her head approvingly.

"Now I'll have to think about your family portrait," she said, feeling her smile overfull and so heavy she wondered if it might just fall from her face and lie on the floor. She was so swollen with caring for him she felt as if her body were actually filling, like a balloon held under a faucet.

"You can consider that while we work."

"Yes," she said, and turned to look at the spot where she was expected to stand. "I'll do that."

"Another week or two and the old hand'll be right as rain," he told her as he sharpened several pencils.

"That's good," she said remotely. She hadn't expected, this time, to feel again that mounting humiliation, the dragging malaise that arose at the prospect of disrobing in front of him.

He interpreted the lines of tension in her body and felt a need to ease her, to make her see that he didn't share the vision she had of herself. He crossed the room saying, "Don't turn round. I have something for you." He pulled the gold chain from his pocket and fastened it around her neck, for a few seconds savoring the lustrous weight of her hair in his hand.

"Why did you do this?" she asked, looking down at the intricately woven links.

"I wanted to give you a gift. Do you like it?"

She nodded, feeling unexpectedly less naked. "Thank you." Her voice had a sudden atypical density, and she was slipping again into that somnolent state. She wanted to demonstrate her pleasure in the gift in a tangible way—a kiss, or a hug, one of the gestures he seemed so effortlessly able to give and which she had enormous difficulty duplicating. "I do like it," she murmured, turning blindly to offer him an uncertain embrace.

"You do trust me, don't you," he said lightly, "even though I'm of the male persuasion? Could it be because *I'm* so eminently trustworthy?"

She laughed, the embrace no longer awkward. "I trust you because you like my cooking, and because I've got no goddamned sense."

"Don't go too far. I'm not totally stupid."

"No, not totally." Her laughter bubbled. "Not at all, really. I think you might just be the smartest man I've ever met."

"I wouldn't have fancied you in a false nose," he said, "unless it had the mustache."

She pushed him gently away, saying, "Go work! My time's expensive, buster."

"Consider yourself told," he told himself, falling into the routine from the mini-bus.

"Quite right. You do waste ever such a lot of time. You'll lose the light, at this rate."

"You needn't keep on. Can't you see I'm going?"

In position before the easel, he selected a pencil. "Turn just a bit more toward me, would you, love?"

She did as directed, then allowed her eyes to fall on the sun-dappled leaves of the tree beyond the window.

Chapter 27

WHILE MARTIN WAS at work in the studio, she ventured into his bedroom—until this time privileged territory to which she had refused herself access. She contemplated the muddle of abandoned clothing and crumpled bedclothes, took note of the dust-covered surfaces and the wall-to-wall carpeting in dire need of vacuuming, and determined that the moment had come for her to return this place to order.

Before approaching his chaotic bed, she imagined him asleep, sprawled beneath the unfurling panorama of his dreams. With little effort, she could readily picture herself at his side, wakeful, vigilantly guarding the sanctity of his sleep. It shook her to acknowledge just how much appeal this picture held. She hadn't the right to such aspirations. She was his friend, his sometime secretary, his darkroom assistant with the mild chemical burns on her hands as proof. She was the person who made cautious acquisitions in an ongoing effort to furnish the downstairs rooms; the woman who cooked meals at no one's instigation but her own, and then summoned him to share them; it was she who had taken over the task of paying the monthly housekeeping bills and preparing the bank deposits of his trust income and sundry other funds; she tended the greenhouse and the thriving plants she'd purchased with her own money. There was sufficient work to occupy her days, and she oversaw the maintenance of both house and man with increasing satisfaction, no longer torturing herself with questions of why she was there and what possible plans Martin might have for her. He stated he was happy to have her there and, finally, that was enough. She had a home that far exceeded any small dream she'd ever had, and she'd found security in the knowledge that no matter how people might gape at her when she went out to shop for groceries, or for dining-room furniture, the existence of Martin—in the kitchen making himself a cup of coffee, or out in the studio, or dozing on the living-room floor—endowed her with invisible armor. Because of him she was able to disregard the puzzling stares, the hastily averted eyes, the hovering suspicions of strangers. There was someone nearby who frequently smiled approvingly at her, who took hold of her hand when they walked the streets of the city, who periodically embraced her, and who laughingly dismissed her fears and reservations as being unworthy and time-wasting.

She stripped the bed and wrestled with the mattress, turning it. While the washer chugged and chewed at the soiled sheets and mattress cover, she tackled his bathroom, relieved to find that, although he was sloppy, he was essentially clean. Pulling on rubber gloves, she scoured the sink and toilet bowl and tub; she polished the mirror and the chrome faucets, and scrubbed the tiled walls and floor. With clean towels folded trimly over the rails and the shower curtain tugged into place, she peeled off the gloves and returned the cleaning gear to the kitchen before dragging the Hoover up the stairs.

When at last she'd done as much as she possibly could, and the room no longer had a sadly abandoned appearance, she went down to the kitchen to fix herself a cup of tea and sat at the round white table in the glaringly bright room to drink the tea and smoke a cigarette, suffused with a sense of accomplishment. Now that she'd done it once, she'd see to it that Martin's bedroom had regular attention. She was annoyed with herself for having resisted taking this step for so long, as if she might have been contaminated by some unspeakable ailment had she dared set foot over his threshhold. Stupid! She could only equate it with her early reluctance to ask Ron for a key to the Strawberry Hill apartment. She'd kept expecting and hoping he'd offer the key without her having to ask for it. It had taken months for her to realize that Ron, and perhaps all men, didn't place the kind of significance on things like keys and clean bedrooms that women did. Women, herself included, seemed determined to find symbolism in the minor details of their dealings with men: keys offered or withheld, rooms to be entered supposedly only on invitation, smiles or frowns. Every word and gesture, no matter how inconsequential, had to have some special meaning. The truth was that men simply didn't have the time or energy to devote to such arcane subtleties, and women drove themselves half crazy struggling to interpet the meanings of what were nothing more than words and gestures with no subtext at all.

It was odd, but the several months she'd now spent with Martin had enhanced her comprehension of Ron. She was able to see him far more clearly, and more sympathetically, as a result of her exposure to a man almost diametrically his opposite. Where Ron had been uncertain, Martin was decisive; where Ron had simply adopted parental values as his birthright, Martin had forged his own. The accident had compelled Ron to grapple with emotions and insights that hadn't fallen within the realm of his established values, and in dealing with them, he had voluntarily expanded his concepts. Both she and Ron had been permanently transmuted by the experience, and it had been to both their good. The last thing she'd ever expected when she set out in what Louise had called her "audacious" car had been to find sanctuary. She'd secretly been seeking a means with which to put an end to the horrific creature she'd become. Instead, she'd been salvaged, and installed in an environment so well suited to her needs that her only remaining fear was that Martin might suddenly find fault with her and turn her out. Her trespassing into his bedroom might be the act that drove him to it. But if he elected to respond to her good intentions with anger, then she'd go. It wouldn't be all that difficult to backtrack and relocate her route to the edge of the world.

Her tea and the cigarette finished, she put the cup and saucer in the dishwasher and left the ashtray beside the sink, then wandered into the conservatory. The steamy, earth-laden air and dazzling sunlight saturated her senses and she drifted among the palms and dracaenas, the Swedish and English ivies, the flowering gloxinias and African violets, allowing her fingertips to trail over the alternatingly furry and sleekly smooth leaves in a state of enthralled contentment.

Eventually, she left the moist air of the glass enclosure to travel at a leisurely, appreciative pace through the downstairs rooms, admiring the black lacquered Italian oval table and matching chairs in the dining area, and the deep blue velvet of the paired sofas before the fireplace at the far end.

At last, she climbed the stairs to the top of the house, where she cast off her clothes before surrendering to the cool welcome of the bed. Each afternoon, for an hour or so, she plummeted into a comalike sleep, from which she awakened restored, eager to sequester herself in the kitchen with her new collections of cookbooks and crockery. The production of esoteric dinners was the primary focus of each day, and she rose to the challenge of Martin's gustatory applause with all the determination of an Olympic pole vaulter: no ingredient was too exotic or beyond her obtaining, no single recipe was capable of besting her skills. She was evolving into a gourmet cook and enjoying each moment of it.

As she stretched her limbs to the delicious extremities of sleep, she was thinking about the preparation of cold avocado soup, a grape and breast of chicken salad with curried mayonnaise, and homemade raspberry sorbet she'd serve in the exquisite crystal dessert cups she'd found only the day before.

His efforts at the easel approximated the learning of a new language. Perhaps it was reasonable that he should have to labor so diligently to reproduce Caley's image. Although he'd never before phrased the concept in actual terms, each painting was a fresh collaboration. Every time he confronted a recently primed canvas, he was attempting to state some declaration—of caring, or anger, or bewilderment. He could only discover the true condition of his feelings through an application of light and form and color on canvas. This study of Caley contained elements of earth and fire that entranced and defied him. Where in the past he might have hurried to press tinted oils to his vision in broader strokes, he was forced now to use finer brushes, more ethereal hues in order to do justice to the complexities of the subject. It was far more than merely a matter of illustrating a nude placed strategically before a window. The emotional quotient of this work was unlike any other he'd attempted in the past. The brush stroked lightly, lingeringly, feather-swipes of smoldering flesh tones blending indecipherably, synergetically in a tirade of emotional comment. He could scarcely believe what was happening. The brush and canvas made love before his bemused eyes. How had he failed to see the interdependence growing daily? Had he been so caught up in the challenge of the woman that he'd neglected to recognize what had inspired his pursuit of her?

Whatever he'd been doing, it was impossible to ignore what was presenting itself to him as a fait accompli before his eyes; from beneath the still-wet, mounting layers of near-melted flesh came the bones of his dilemma. I love her, he thought, electrified into sudden immobility. He gazed at the image of the woman, then looked ruefully into the space beyond the easel where she should have been standing.

While drawing her closer with an endless net of words, he'd failed to admit his intent. It was far more than just his need to have her dispel the mesmeric tensions of a house haunted by the ghosts of his homeless emotions, more than the need for footsteps overhead and savory repasts offered up with clockwork regularity. He'd taken for granted her presence, once secure in the knowledge that she'd stay. He'd asked her to live in the house in order to help him hold at bay the howling memories that assailed his consciousness, but he'd given no further consideration to the instinct that had driven him to fly after her. He'd fallen in love, on sight, with someone who'd made an appointment with death. She'd told him that. A month or two ago, when he'd sought to praise her, she'd informed him of her rendezvous with a black finality, and he'd chosen not to respond. He'd allowed her words to slip past without comment. She had decided to embrace death, to fling herself into that bottomless chasm, and had told him outright of it, yet he'd refused to hear.

Guilt, like a layer of dirt, suddenly adhered to his skin. Hastily, he cleaned his brushes, took a final look at the work in progress, then hurried from the studio.

The house slumbered in the grip of an autumn afternoon's silence, its clean serenity a further assault. He ascended the stairs and came to a dead stop in the doorway of his bedroom, his guilt now complete in the face of her efforts. The tidy tracks of the vacuum across the carpet, the subtle gleam of polished wood and glass, the taut array of freshly laundered sheets all confirmed his discovery. The spotless bathroom was his final undoing. Her acceptance of him shone from the immaculate basin and the shaving mirror. He climbed under the shower and stared at the scrubbed tiles, marveling at the totality of his failure to see that the signs of tolerance and understanding weren't the obvious, overt ones, but the time-consuming, hateful chores one undertook to perform for another out of love—the laundering of someone else's garments and bed linens, the preparation of another's food; the minutiae of daily life.

He hadn't been up to the third floor since Caley had come to live in the house, and he went up the stairs hesitantly, as if something far more menacing than a number of empty rooms and one slight woman awaited him.

Her door was open, and he peered inside to see her asleep in a slab of light that made her hair dance with gold and russet tones. He sat on the side of the bed, wishing he were able to meld into her sleep, joining her inside her dream. He had to smile, recalling how, years before, when the boys couldn't have been more than five or six, Ian had asked, "Where do we go when we dream, Dad?" and Martin had fudged, unable to offer a suitable reply. "Your mind travels," he'd said, "but the rest of you stays right here." It wasn't true. He knew that now. Hadn't he covered hundreds of miles while in a dreaming state? Of course he had. And he'd awakened, all too recently, to find that at the end of the dream one might actually have eroded the heels of his shoes in the course of the journey.

She awakened with a start, saw him, and blinked several times.

"You love me," he said, smiling, "don't you?"

She wet her lips and turned in order to see him more clearly. "Is this Twenty Questions? Do I get a prize if I give the right answer?"

His smile broadened and he leaned closer. "I was out there, in my squalid place of employment, toiling away at a most worthy enterprise, when it occurred to me that I'm not going to allow you to leave here. I thought I might claim you as my personal wetback, dryback, illegal alien."

"What are you talking about?"

"Doesn't matter," he said, drawing the sheet away from her body. She remained unmoving under his gaze.

His eyes had the same impact his hands or mouth might have. Her shameless, uncaring body willed him to lay claim to it, to place upon it the approving stamp of his caress. She no longer had any desire to do battle internally over the question of when, if ever, he'd seek to create miracles within her. Sometime in the course of the past months she'd begun conceding in the skirmishes and she'd arrived, finally, white flag in hand, to signal her acquiescence. Supine, motionless, determined not to make visible her signal, she thought nothing in her life would be more difficult or suspenseful than these moments.

Unable to bear the tension, she drifted for a moment, picturing them together on a beach. Between them on the sand sat a crowd of fat, laughing babies, their chubby limbs sun-golden; blond-haired, with green or gray or blue eyes, the babies chortled and waved their dimpled arms, scattering sand on the wind. She so loved the image it was difficult for her to relinquish it.

"What're you doing, Martin?"

"I believe I am about to perform acts of an erotic nature upon your person. Unless, of course, you have some objection."

"That depends on whether they're natural or unnatural acts."

"That is the correct answer! Give this woman her prize!" He laughed and gathered her into his arms like garlands of flowers headily scented, exquisitely fragile.

"I just hope you're not going to be disappointed," she said. "I've never been very good at this."

"Women who claim sexual proficiency are always highly suspect." He laid his cheek against her breast. "Men who do are, too, for that matter. I adore you. And you do love me, don't you?"

"Somebody should. You're too weird to be allowed out on your own."

"Irreverent, you are."

"You're hardly an icon."

"True, but perilously close." Grinning, he sat up. "Undoubtedly, we'll both be dismal, first go at it. I have every expectation, however, that, with practice, we'll improve tremendously."

She wanted to prepare dinner. He insisted they go out.

"Put on your blue frock," he told her. "The one you wore in Quebec. It's a good color for you."

"Where are you going?"

"I'll only be a few minutes. Go ahead and get dressed."

She fitted the blue dress to her torpid frame, then went into the bathroom to apply her small store of cosmetics. Dazedly, she brushed her hair, automatically avoiding the mirror.

Her sandals strapped into place, her feet out of contact with her weightless body, she descended the stairs and stood with her hand on the warm mahogany of the banister.

He came in through the kitchen door and presented her with the folder he'd carried with him from the darkroom.

"What's this?" she asked, her eyes on his mouth. She could dispense with food, she thought, and feast indefinitely on him, gorging herself in an ecstacy of appetite.

"We don't appear to be disappointed with our first go," he said, stroking her hair.

"I'd like to forget about dinner and go back upstairs."

"Indeed we shall," he promised. "But after dinner." He lifted her hair to kiss the side of her neck. "You make sweet sounds, and you flutter, like a small bird."

"What is this?" she asked, holding the folder.

"Something from my sleuthing days. Go on, have a look!"

She opened the folder and emitted a startled laugh. "Christ! You even took pictures."

"A Maddox never lies."

"I stopped in this place to have coffee."

"And a croissant. Rather good, isn't it? Has rather a Mata Hari flavor to it."

"It's the hat that does it."

"You like it?"

"You can't even tell . . ."

He put his finger to her lips, then returned the photograph to the folder and set it down on the stairs. "I've made a reservation for Stop 33. It has a smashing view of the city."

"Martin, if I did it . . . I mean . . ."

"It wouldn't make me care for you more, but I do think it would help you care more for yourself."

"Would you be there?"

"Well, of course I would. You don't think I'd allow you to endure it alone?" He opened the front door and stood waiting for her.

"No," she said. "You'll probably set up your easel right beside my goddamned bed."

"I just might."

"Christ! You would, too."

"If you do decide," he said, as they went toward the car, "I may ask old Horner if I can't get all rigged out in surgical garb and come right into the operating theater."

"I'm not saying I'm going to do it," she expostulated.

"Entirely up to you. I do like that frock. It's most becoming. How would you feel about a holiday excursion this winter? There's someone I'd very much like you to meet in Tenerife. I think the two of you would get on well. You're both dotty about gardens."

She wasn't listening. She was studying an image of herself ensconced in a hospital bed while, not many feet away, Martin stood at his easel. She laughed, then saw he was holding open the car door, and hurried to seat herself inside. He'd do it. He'd probably book himself into the next bed and follow every step of the procedure with the same pathological interest he displayed in almost everything. He'd do it, all right. And, by God, she'd let him.

Critically acclaimed works
from a bestselling author!

Charlotte Vale Allen

Few authors today have explored the emotional landscape of women's lives with the depth and precision of Charlotte Vale Allen. Her bestselling books, Promises, Daddy's Girl, and Destinies have touched millions. All are sensitive accounts that probe the very soul of today's woman—as only Charlotte Vale Allen can do!

More Bestsellers from Berkley
The books you've been hearing about and want to read